Across the aisle, Thomas Devlin smiled at her.

She frowned and mouthed, "Go away."

He pointed toward the stage as if to say, "I'm only watching the show."

"Keeping him a secret, huh?" Deidre said.

"I ran into him in the restaurant. That's all."

"Looks like he wants to run into you again."

"Enough," Cleo shot back. "Not interested."

Face burning, Cleo focused on the acrobats. Some protection her new friends were, with tongues hanging out.

No wonder. Thomas was just as sexy as ever.

More. Shoulders impossibly broad in his white dress shirt. Intense and very, very male. Same thick brown hair, its unruly nature controlled by an expert haircut. Same square jaw and sensual mouth. Same eagle-fierce eyes and slashing brows. Same arrogance that used to piss her off, but with edges smoothed into power and confidence. Confidence that tempted her to lean on him, rely on him. Like he wanted.

Not gonna happen. She was safe here.

She'd left her feelings for him behind, or so she'd thought. Hot? Yowza. She flashed chills and fever just sitting across the aisle. If his gaze penetrated her reaction to him, he would use it to get what he wanted.

Praise for Susan Vaughan

"From Venice to Vegas, Susan Vaughan builds edge of the seat suspense... Highly Recommended!" – Linda Style, Daphne du Maurier award-winning author

Previous releases: Go to www.susanvaughan.com

Cleopatra's Necklace

by

Susan Vaughan

Devlin Security Force, Protecting Priceless Treasures, Book 3

Cleopatra's Necklace

Cover Art by *Kim Mendoza*

The Wild Rose Press, Inc.
PO Box 708
Adams Basin, NY 14410-0708
Visit us at www.thewildrosepress.com

Publishing History
First Edition, 2023
Trade Paperback ISBN 978-1-5092-5074-5
Digital ISBN 978-1-5092-5075-2

Devlin Security Force, Protecting Priceless Treasures, Book 3
Published in the United States of America

Dedication

Cleopatra's Necklace is dedicated to my husband, my best friend. Rough duty joining me in my research in Venice and Las Vegas. Thanks, honey, for all your support and patience.

Chapter One

Crystal City, Virginia - August

THE ASSASSIN LUNGED at his chest with a long-bladed knife.

Thomas had to move faster, fight smarter, dirtier. If he timed his move right, the assassin would be off balance. If not, he was finished. The smell of sweat hung in the air. Droplets slid down his back and off his chin.

Focus, dammit.

His gaze flicked from the assassin's eyes to the blade and back again.

Now.

He exploded to the right. The blade pierced the air instead of his chest. Before the assassin could turn and refocus his attack, Thomas grasped the attacker's arm with both hands. Pinned it in the crook of one arm.

He was about to pivot and take down the attacker but the man swung a leg and tripped him. Both went down. They rolled together like a roast on a spit. He landed on his back, the assassin on top. *Shit.*

The assassin brought the knife to his throat.

"Not as fast as you used to be, Captain. If this wasn't a rubber knife, you'd be a fucking dead man."

Thomas Devlin smiled. "Not quite, Sergeant."

A similar rubber knife in Thomas's fist pricked Lucas Del Rio's T-shirt at navel level.

1

Eyes so dark they looked black gleamed with sudden humor. Lucas barked a laugh and rolled backward onto the gym mat. "You'd have gutted me before I could reach your throat. Not bad for an old man."

Thomas sat up, fought to keep his breathing even and not suck in much needed oxygen. No way would he acknowledge he was winded to his more powerfully built sparring partner. The owner of Devlin Security Force had to maintain mastery in more ways than one, not unlike in his old Delta Force team.

Drawing on the small reserve of energy he had left after their two-hour session, he vaulted to his feet and held out a hand for his former NCO. "Thirty-eight's old only on the basketball court. Just means I have to be smarter than my opponent."

"No argument here." Lucas peeled off his safety goggles. "I hate wearing these wussy things."

Thomas smiled. DSF enforced safety rules. "Right. A slip of a rubber blade can puncture an eyeball like stabbing a grape. And then I'd be out a good operative."

Lucas winced but offered no further argument.

They crossed the company gym to the towel rack outside the locker rooms. Thomas dumped his safety goggles and grabbed a towel. Time to level. He'd delayed bringing up the new assignment until his field operative was too tired to raise much objection. Which he would. Thomas preferred he take the job willingly rather than under orders.

Lucas sat down heavily, apparently as tuckered as his boss. Good. Thomas plucked water bottles from the mini-fridge before sinking onto the bench, taking care to sit on the right side. His former sergeant wouldn't have worn his hearing aid during a bout.

Lucas chugged most of his water, then scrubbed a towel over his head, shoving his dark hair into devilish spikes. He angled his head, expectation in his eyes. "Whatever my new gig is, it must be bad if you put off mentioning it until I'm whipped."

Thomas grinned. The perception and analytical intelligence that had made Lucas essential in war also made him a valuable operative. "Should've known I couldn't put one over on you. Exactly why I need you. A multi-agency task force is going after Centaur."

Lucas's black eyes widened at the mention of Centaur, a criminal syndicate involved in stealing and copying valuable art and artifacts. He shook his head. "I'm no desk jockey. Coat and tie? Forget it. Send Rivera."

"No can do. Max has a broken leg. I have yet to drag out of him how he did it."

Lucas's laugh had an evil tone. "Probably tripped over one of their wedding gifts."

"If that's the case, he's sworn Kate to secrecy or she doesn't know." He rose and tossed the damp towel into the laundry bin. "I'm going to grab a shower. Meet me in my office in twenty."

When Lucas joined him there, Thomas led the way to two club chairs overlooking the busy Crystal City street far below. He pulled his around to face his operative. Ice clinked in the strained silence as he poured tea into tall glasses. Maybe his personal blend of sweet tea would ease the wariness in the set of Lucas's shoulders.

Lucas said nothing as he downed his icy drink, so Thomas picked up the recruitment pitch where he'd left off.

"Centaur's theft of the Cleopatra necklace a month ago in Paris made us look like amateurs. I want that choker retrieved. I want Centaur stopped. Dismantled. Destroyed. And I want one of my people in on the kill. You."

"Centaur's been plaguing us for a few years. Why a task force now?"

Lucas would find out soon enough once he signed on. "Centaur's been gaining power and influence, gathering a network of thieves and brokers to handle their stolen loot. First it was selling originals to underground collectors. Next it was selling copies, like that Han Dynasty horse you've been chasing for two years."

"Copies of that and more are quadrupling their profit. I heard some of their art forgers never resurface after working for Centaur."

"Loose ends. Informants have told my Interpol contact the heist of Cleopatra artifacts was contracted by Ahmad Yousef."

Lucas's brows winged upward. "That fanatic?"

"Right. And no art collector. My sources say he's preparing major terrorist attacks in the West. I can't begin to guess what part the necklace plays in his plot, but you can see why the Brits and the U.S. have signed on to stop this escalation."

"I get why you want a Devlin Security Force operative on the task force but why do *they* want a DSF operative, a civilian? Why not a Feeb?" Lucas's broad brow crimped.

Oh yeah, Thomas had him hooked now. He contained a grin. "The Centaur Task Force consists of Interpol, the FBI, and Scotland Yard, among others.

Must be some interesting politics going on in Interpol because the CTF head isn't French, but a tough FBI agent. DSF has worked for Interpol before, some on, some off-the-books ops. You won't be an office wonk. They need an investigator who's not a Fed. An investigator who can operate without portfolio."

"Hell. I was going to shave the beard anyway. My landlady says I look so much like a bear I scare her poodle."

"I agree the beard would make you conspicuous," Thomas said mildly. Lucas's light, self-deprecating tone masked a softer inside. Shrapnel scars had coarsened his heavy features. Brutish looks that intimidated bad guys weren't generally an asset in other situations. "For now the Centaur Task Force operates out of an Interpol satellite office in Paris. The syndicate's headquarters moves around, but the CTF has narrowed the current location to London."

Lucas eyed him as if he knew there was more. No one read people better. "Rivera's out but why not one of the others? And no bull about me being the best man for the job."

Time for the trump card to seal the deal. "But you are, Del Rio. The others weren't in my team in Iraq."

Lucas merely waited, the granite planes of his face tight above the bush of beard.

Thomas finished the tea. Set down his glass. Held Lucas's gaze. "Centaur came on the art theft scene around 2006. The leader is former American military. He goes after high-end stuff. His moniker is one letter—Z."

Lucas blinked twice. His mouth thinned. "Marco Zervas. It fucking figures."

"Only a hunch. After his sentence and dishonorable

discharge, he vanished. No trace of him anywhere. Proving Z's identity is part of your job with the CTF. If it's Zervas, they need someone who knows him. And I expect you to keep me informed."

A wide, white smile split the black beard. "Be my pleasure to take down that bastard."

****

Venice, Italy – September

Had she finally broken her string of Mr. Wrongs?

Cleo Chandler shoved away her irritation. René was late, two hours late, but flights get delayed or canceled. Stuff happens.

Earbuds firmly implanted, she boogied from the kitchen with a chunky red candle as her dance partner. René was coming home tonight with news about a jewelry commission. Odd but it was his second mystery trip in two weeks. He'd promised to explain later. He was talented, sincere, and oh, so sexy. Maybe not Mr. Right Forever, but definitely Mr. Right Now.

No more users like Daniel who never had his wallet with him. No more cheats like Roger who used her bed as a launching pad for flights with other women. No more sketchy guys like Kurt who tried to involve her in a fake lottery scam. No control freaks like the males in her family. Her fortunes had changed for the better. Smiling, she set the candle between the plates on their napkin-sized table.

"Perfect." She gyrated back to the kitchen to the rhythm of the latest hit ballad.

The white wine and garlic sauce needed a stir. For the *branzin*, as Venetians called sea bass, chilling in the small fridge. After leaving work at Bijoux Murano Rialto, she bought the fish from her favorite vendor at the Municipal Fish Market. Giancarlo even filleted it for her. She had never cooked much but how could you not be into food in Italy?

The sauce was thick enough, so she turned off the gas under the pan. Would anything be worth eating after all this delay?

"So where *are* you, René Moreau?" She yanked out the earbuds and tossed her iPod next to his laptop. Nine o'clock. She'd finished the cheese and crackers hours ago. Now she was starving.

Late plane, missed plane, dead phone. Too many possibilities. She lifted the neck of her long-sleeved white tee between two fingers and nibbled on the knit. Jeez, was she down to eating her shirt? She went to the kitchen and poured a glass of water.

"Note to self: Never cook anything gourmet before the man actually arrives."

She was supposed to meet Mimi at eleven outside the store. Why did everything have to happen at the same time? She'd hoped to have a nice dinner with René, and then the two of them would go have drinks with her cousin.

Her cousin. Wow.

She hadn't known until six months ago she had a cousin. She'd kept it secret until they could actually meet. They'd spent hours Skyping and posting on Facebook so Cleo felt she'd known Mimi all her life. So much in common. Amazing. Wait until Mom heard about their reunion. Not really a reunion, but never mind. Tomorrow she'd call. Definitely.

Cleo'd persuaded Mimi to take a break from her Mediterranean cruise to visit here in person. Having lunch and the afternoon together didn't give them enough time. Mimi had to return to Rome early tomorrow, so no way could Cleo blow off the date. She should ask her cousin to come to the flat. Yeah, that would work.

As she reached for her cell phone, she heard thumping on the stairs. Then a moan. *What the hell?* She rushed to the door and listened. "René?"

Another moan. A strained mumble that sounded like her name.

Was it safe? Should she open the door? "René?"

A moan was her only answer. Her fingers fumbled the locks, but finally she cracked open the door.

René fell through the opening and staggered into her arms.

She gasped, reeling with his weight. "Oh my God!"

Lines bracketed his beautiful dark eyes, his long lashes spiky and wet. He was pale and bent like an old man, smelling of sweat and something metallic. One hand clutched his jacket front and panted with the effort of climbing the three flights. Too strange for a fit, agile man who often took those same stairs two and three at a time.

"What's wrong? What happened?" Her ire over his tardiness gone, she helped him to the sofa.

"Lock… door," he muttered, sucking a breath between each word. His handsome face contorted in pain and shiny with sweat, he closed his eyes.

Oh, God, blood soaked the front of his jacket and shirt. The same blood smeared the front of her shirt where she'd held him. Her throat closed, and her breath came in short gasps. She recoiled, then forced herself to speak. "What happened to you?"

"Shot… me." He gestured with one hand. Drops of

blood clung to his fingertips. "The... door."

Snapped to action by his insistence, Cleo flew to click all the locks. She snatched up the dishtowel. Kneeling at his side, she pressed the towel against the blood flow. All too quickly, the stain soaked the cloth and seeped between her fingers.

Nausea threatened at the sight and coppery smell of so much blood. No time for panic. She reached for her phone. "I'm calling the ambulance."

His hand clamped her arm and the phone fell to the floor. "*Non, je t'en prie!* No ambulance. No police." His grip weakened and his arm dropped to his side.

He made no sense. No ambulance? She pressed more firmly on his wound. Not enough. He needed medical treatment and fast. "What do you mean? I have to get you help."

When he opened his eyes again, he seemed to breathe easier. But his face was gray, pale as ash, his cheeks tight against the bone. This couldn't be happening.

Her head reeled with the word *no*. She made herself breathe.

"No, it is too late. I failed. Listen." His voice a mere whisper, he seemed calm, determined. "The necklace... you wore... picture."

She frowned. "Like Cleopatra's. Yeah, but what—"

He squeezed her hand but with no more strength than a child. "Listen. *Real.* Beyond price. Was going to kill me. Hid it. Killed me anyway. Will not find it." He tried to rise, to get in her face, but fell back.

Her stomach clenched. Impossible. René couldn't die. He couldn't. "But you need an ambulance—"

"No time. Said they'd kill *you*... if I didn't give

necklace…" He stopped, struggling for breath. Blood trickled from the corner of his mouth. "You must leave Venice. Now."

"The necklace. I could give it to them. Tell me where it is and we'll be safe." Her voice broke, but she forged ahead. "I'll take care of everything. It'll be all right, René, you'll see."

"Pas possible." His voice faltered, grew fainter. He brushed the locket she always wore with a shaking hand. "Necklace gone. Close behind me… will kill you… like did me. Promise me… no police. *They* are everywhere. Leave Venice. *Hurry.*"

"Where is the necklace?" She bent closer to his lips.

His whisper was barely intelligible. *"Melon,"* then *"Pomp"* or *"Pope."* Maybe. *"Ladder."* Then he fell silent.

Was that all? What did it mean? She raised her head. "René?"

His eyes stared upward, unseeing, unblinking. Blank.

"No, no, René, wake up!" Her hand shook so hard she had to steady it with the other before she could press fingers against his neck. No sign of a pulse. None in his wrist. And the blood, the blood… no longer flowing.

She wailed and clutched at his shoulders, then fled to the bathroom where she lost what little was in her stomach. Huddling on the tile floor with a cool cloth on her forehead relieved the shakes and nausea.

Dead. René was dead. Killed by ruthless gangsters over that fancy necklace. Those bastards. Was it possible the elaborate choker really came from Cleopatra's tomb? No, how would René have such a thing? Or maybe…

"Said they'd kill you… leave Venice. Hurry."

The warning tolling in her ears pushed her to her feet. After throwing some clothing and toiletries in her wheeled suitcase, she tucked her passport into her handbag. Her breath hitched at the sight of his lifeless body on the sofa—his face so waxen, so wan. So still.

She picked up her mobile. She had to call the police. Her gaze flicked to the door. If the killers came, she'd have no escape. They could be here any minute. "*Hurry.*" She tucked the mobile away.

But she couldn't leave him like that.

"Oh, God, René. I can't face this. Why—" she choked out. She tossed a clean sheet over him and hit the door.

****

"The bastard's dead." Ricci fingered his mustache as he stared at the body on the sofa. "Keep your gloves on. The *polizia* will undoubtedly show up soon."

He let the sheet drop over the waxen face, then whacked his shorter partner on the head.

"What'd you do that for?" Panaro stumbled back a step, holding up both hands as if to shield his bald pate from further attack.

"You need target practice. Now how's he going to tell us where the necklaces are?"

"They're sure as hell not in his studio." They'd tracked Moreau from the Piazzale Roma to his atelier on an obscure *calle* in Santa Croce. Panaro's shot was supposed to stop him, not kill him. The bastard had gone down, but while they were searching for the real necklace and the copy Moreau had made, he'd somehow escaped.

Panaro waved a hand toward the body. "At least he didn't stink up the place. And somebody covered him.

The girl?"

Ricci peered around the flat. Couple of tiny rooms, closet-sized kitchen. Shabby but neat and clean. Laptop on a worn desk. Table set for two. "Split. Search the bedroom."

He checked out the kitchen. Lifted the saucepan lid and dipped in a finger, tasted. "Not bad." And still warm.

She left in a hurry. Moreau had time to warn her. Maybe she was going for the necklaces. She had to know where her lover stashed them.

Returning to the other room, he sat on the straight chair at the laptop. "Password protected?" His computer skills were good but didn't rise to the level of hacker. Awkward with gloves but he would manage.

"Bloody shirt on the floor. Easel and paint stuff in one corner," Panaro called. "Big suitcase still in the closet but racks pushed to the side, drawers left open. Don't see makeup or a toothbrush. She could've packed a small bag."

"Mobile phone?"

"No. Nothing." Panaro came around to look over Ricci's shoulder. The stocky man's breath reeked of garlic and fried sardines. "Anything?"

Ricci stifled a snarky reply. Panaro owned the pistol with the suppressor. And, loosely speaking, he was the local talent. He knew the city's crazy maze of canals and islands and streets. *Porca vacca*, he needed the idiot. "Just booting up."

There were two user icons, one for each of the lovers. He clicked on *Cleo* and her desktop appeared. No security whatsoever. People were so naïve, so trusting. So stupid.

He opened the browser to her home page. Facebook.

Of course. With a picture of her wearing the necklace. *Bella*, this Cleo Chandler, with her dark red hair pulled up to display the gold choker and jeweled collar that draped from her throat across her elegant pale shoulders.

Did she have anything on but the necklace? If Ricci had been in charge of the camera, she'd have been naked and there would be more pictures. "Moreau must have gotten a kick out of his girlfriend having the same name."

"Is that the original necklace or the copy?"

"As soon as I get my jeweler's certificate, I'll tell you." Ricci hated that Panaro habitually stood too close. If he was nearsighted, that explained a lot. But not all. Today the Venetian seemed to have eaten a big bowl of stupid.

Panaro made no reply to the sarcasm, but moved aside, thank the Madonna. Ricci clicked through to the woman's personal information. The airhead had listed everything, including what they needed—mobile number and place of work.

"Let's see where she ran off to." Ricci navigated to an illegal website for tracking mobile phones. He keyed in her number. A detailed street map appeared. A flashing icon pinpointed the mobile's location, stopped in one place. In case she'd called the *polizia*, they had to get out fast. "You know this street?"

"Between here and the Rialto Bridge in San Polo."

Ricci sighed. More walking through these impossible alleys. He'd be lucky not to fall in one of the filthy canals. "I don't know why, but she could be headed to the jewelry shop where she works. You'd better be able to find the address."

"*Si, si*, on a side street near the bridge. My cousin owns a bakery nearby."

The icon was moving again.

Ricci flipped over the laptop and pried open the bottom panel. The hard drive popped out easily. Now the *polizia* could not follow his search, and he might find useful information in the memory. He slipped the metal device into his pocket. "Let's go."

Chapter Two

CLEO WHEELED HER carry-on bag down the bridge's wide steps. The still waters of the Rio di San Cassiano gleamed beneath the streetlight. Light from windows spilled misshapen shadows onto the paving stones. For company, she had the occasional dog walker and the ever-present briny smell that permeated the city's ancient stones and mortar. The aromas of sautéing fish and spicy sauces drifted by.

She hustled along beneath the streetlights, turning one familiar corner after another, the route she followed every day to and from work, on automatic. It had to be because she could barely see through the tears that kept welling up. She kept picturing René's body, his staring eyes, the blood. He'd been so charming, such fun, so... alive.

She stuffed her mobile back into her jeans pocket. Once she'd put at least two canals behind her away from the flat, she called the *polizia*, but didn't dare give her name. Eventually they'd trace the call, but she'd be far away by then. Where she had no idea. She'd face that issue once she reached the mainland.

The second call had gone unanswered. Drat her brother. But maybe leaving a message on his voicemail saved time. And anguish. He'd have asked more questions than she could answer, more than she could bear to answer. Calling Mom would be disastrous; no way did she want her dad to know. She sniffed back tears. Where would she go? The image of René dead on the sofa played in her brain in an endless loop and she couldn't focus.

Now thirty minutes later, she was almost to the Rialto shop. Her key would let her in and she'd leave a note for her boss. Yes, think about the future, not the grief and panic clawing at her throat. Fewer *vaporetti* ran this late, but she could take the number one to the taxi square, then catch transportation to the mainland.

"Oh, Cleo, there you are! I was afraid I was lost."

Her heart took off like a Grand Prix racer, and she gasped and swung around. *Mimi. Thank heavens. Only Mimi.* Oh, no, she'd forgotten their date. Seeing her cousin hurrying toward her on the narrow side street, Cleo took a deep breath.

When Mimi had first contacted her, she thought their being related was a scam. Until she learned about the other woman's family and saw photos of Mimi on Facebook. Not just cousins, they were within two years of the same age and were mirror images of each other—down to the hair length and eye color.

We could be twins. Maybe not identical twins, but fraternal for sure.

Now that Cleo had changed from her work attire, they were dressed similarly, except Mimi's jeans were designer and pressed with a knife-sharp crease and she'd bound her auburn hair into a sleek tail. A black quilted backpack hung off one shoulder.

Mimi rushed toward her and enveloped her in a warm lilac-scented embrace. Her cousin's touch was just what she needed, a living human being to reassure her she was still alive, only numb from shock.

Mimi stepped back and cocked her head. "You've been crying. Here, damage repair." She fished a hand mirror from her pack and offered a tissue.

Cleo dabbed at the dark smudges beneath her eyes. Eyes that looked shell-shocked. She forced herself to focus on removing the mascara smears.

Mimi said, "René didn't come with you. What's wrong?"

René had warned Cleo that *"they"* were everywhere and would be after her. Telling Mimi might involve her, put her in danger. She could say nothing.

She waved an airy dismissal. "No biggie. Tears of happiness at seeing René. He was too exhausted from his trip to join us. You have to make do with me." She stretched her mouth into the semblance of a cheerful smile.

"That's so like a man, eh?" Mimi chuckled. She slipped her arm through Cleo's. "Make you wait and then bug out on you. Where shall we go?"

The *"they"* who'd shot René wouldn't look for her at the Mattio Bar. Too out of the way. Maybe a Campari and soda was what she needed to calm her stomach. If she could manage to choke it down. She couldn't take long or the killers might think of watching the *vaporetti*. "I know just the place."

"A suitcase, Cleo?" Mimi grinned, indicating the orange-flowered carry-on. "It's a little small if you're joining me on the cruise."

"Oh, that. Just some new beads to deliver to a craftsman tomorrow." Amazing how the lie tripped off her tongue. "But I need funds from the ATM before we hit the bar. Would you stay here a minute and watch my case?"

"Sure, but don't be long. I have to make it to the Piazzale Roma to catch a taxi tonight or I turn into a pumpkin."

"No word for pumpkin in Italian," Cleo replied as she whisked around the corner. "Maybe a zucchini."

Her cousin's light laugh echoed in the empty street as she fished out her debit card. She swallowed past the lump in her throat. She could do this. They would have a drink before saying farewell. She only hoped this night wasn't the last time she ever saw Mimi. They hoped to get the families together and figure out why the split so many years ago.

She inserted and withdrew her card, slipping it into her wallet before punching buttons. She slid out the euros as a commotion broke out nearby. A scuffle. Then low-pitched, angry words.

Male voices grunted threats in Italian.

"*No! No!* Leave me alone. Go away."

Mimi? She stuffed the euros in her pocket, then raced back. Nearing the corner, she heard an odd *phumph* followed by more Italian curses and the slap of leather-soled shoes on the street.

Cleo turned the corner as two men ran down the *calle* with her bag. The echoes of their steps disappeared in the maze of intersecting streets.

On the paving stones in front of Bijoux Murano Rialto, Mimi sprawled on her side, facing away from Cleo. Her legs and arms splayed like a discarded doll's, unmoving. The street light glistened on the crimson spreading down her face and beneath her head.

Cleo's heart stopped. She jerked forward, her limbs stiff as if frozen. She willed her feet to carry her forward. "Oh God oh God."

She fell to her knees beside her fallen cousin. "No," she breathed, a low moan welling up from the depths. "It can't be, Mimi. Not you." Her throat stung as if she'd swallowed acid. *Please, God, let her be all right. I'll do anything.*

She punched the phone buttons. Once. Twice. Damn her clumsy fingers. How could this be happening? First René and now... Finally the emergency dispatcher answered and Cleo stammered a report. "*P-per pi-piacere*, hurry! She could die."

After she disconnected, she reached out. Stopped. Reached out again, her hand trembling. She drew a deep breath and pressed a finger to the still-warm neck. Laid a hand on Mimi's back.

Nothing. No breath. No pulse.

She knelt there, white noise roaring in her ears, as the poisonous miasma of reality sank in. The now familiar metallic smell of blood assaulted her senses. Her hand went to her throat.

Mimi was dead.

Cleo could barely think for the sludge clogging her brain. Mimi must've been shot by the thugs who shot René. They thought she was Cleo. They thought the bag contained the necklace. She brushed her cousin's ponytail from her shoulder. Beautiful, innocent, sweet Mimi. Lightheaded, Cleo fought for air. Fought back the useless sobs crowding her throat.

Think, Cleo, think.

The killers wouldn't find what they wanted in her bag. They might return. If they knew she was alive, her life would still be in danger. She had no idea where René had hidden the necklace. His last words had made no sense.

But she knew what did make sense.

Mimi's death was her fault. Calling the emergency number did nothing to change that. But she couldn't stay, couldn't be seen here, couldn't answer questions by police or emergency techs or anyone.

"God forgive me. Mimi, I couldn't save you but maybe you can save me."

She pushed to her feet. She dropped her handbag onto the street beside her cousin and grabbed Mimi's backpack. She stared at her mobile. Was that how the killers had found her? The GPS chip? If so, they could track her again. She opened her hand and the black object clattered to the stones. She glanced around. No one.

Familiar two-tone sirens penetrated her panic. Rescue. Too late for Mimi.

Approaching footsteps echoed from the direction the killers had gone.

"Oh, Mimi, I'm so sorry." Slinging Mimi's pack onto her back, she turned and ran toward the Rialto Bridge.

****

Marco Zervas paced the spacious office of his London townhouse. He looked at the set of world clocks on the wall opposite his desk. Six A.M. in Tehran. Yousef would expect his call in no more than five hours. Where the hell was Ricci?

"Two in the morning. What about *'Keep me posted'* did Ricci not understand?"

"Big mistake, Z, crossing you." Nedik adjusted his bulky frame to a more comfortable position on the sofa. He scraped a wide finger down the scar bisecting his right cheekbone. Carbon-black eyes beneath thick black brows gleamed with anticipation. "I can take care of the fucker anytime."

Zervas waved away the offer. "Perhaps later. Moreau should've been easy to track. Talented at jewelry design but pitifully ignorant in the ways of business." Or so he'd thought. Until the Frenchie emailed him two weeks ago demanding a renegotiation of their deal. Renegotiation? A fucking insult. Zervas shot back his own ultimatum. Then Moreau had disappeared.

He could afford no time for screw-ups. Three other deals needed his attention. This one promised the highest return but he couldn't neglect other contracts. Staying on top meant completing deals, expanding his network, searching out new acquisitions. And recovering all his father had lost.

He smoothed a hand down the tail of hair at his nape. He wanted to pour himself a calming glass of single-malt except he needed to remain sharp. The plan had been for Moreau to turn over the necklaces, then to eliminate the man quickly, but plans change.

The ancient Centaurs were man-horse hybrids. Warriors, unforgiving and powerful, the reason he'd chosen their name. For double-crossing Centaur, Moreau would die slowly and painfully.

The intercom on his desk buzzed and he pressed the button. "What is it?"

"Bloke name of Ricci's on the line. Says it's important."

Zervas hoped like hell it was more than important. Ricci better have found the damn necklaces, both of them. With the chip intact. "Put him on, Hawkins. Then you can go." He gestured toward the door. "Call it a night too, Nedik."

The bodyguard sketched a salute and silently let

himself out of the study.

Nedik and the tech whiz Hawkins were the only men Zervas could rely on. If not trust, their instant obedience and total loyalty were ensured by generous compensation. They knew what would happen to them if they ever failed him.

When he was certain he had privacy, he punched the speaker button. "You'd fucking better have good news for me."

"*Signore*, I regret I do not," Ricci said in heavily accented English. "The *Veneziano* and me, we follow Moreau to his studio, but—"

"Cut to the chase, Ricci." When there was a pause, he realized the Italian didn't understand the American idiom. He sighed. "The most important facts. Now."

"*Si, si.*" Zervas heard a deep breath, as if the other man sucked in courage. "Moreau is dead. His lover is probably also dead. We cannot find the necklaces. Either of them."

Son of a bitch. These fools could not find their asses with a GPS. Guns were a clumsy way to make people talk. Dead, Moreau and the girl could reveal nothing. Bumbling idiots.

"Details." Zervas ground his teeth so hard his jaw popped while he listened to Ricci's stuttered account of his fucked-up mission. "The girl was running. We got her bag. Then she got shot. An accident. Her fault. We went back to the flat and searched again. Nothing there or in her bag," Ricci concluded.

"You shot the girl?" An accident? An obvious lie. "How so?"

Away from the phone, another voice spoke rapidly in Italian to Ricci. "Not me. *Mi dispiace*. Sorry. My local guy held the gun on the Chandler girl. She cried out, waved her arms. Tried to push away the gun and it went off. The bullet hit her in the head."

Head wound, Zervas mused. Lots of blood. Deceptive. "Where exactly did the bullet strike her? You're sure she's dead?"

From Ricci's reply, he could tell the two lunkheads had fled the scene without checking to making certain. If the girl lived, he had a chance to find out what she knew.

He dragged in a breath, then forced a calm tone. "Find out if she's dead. If she was taken to whatever they call the morgue or to a hospital. Next, eliminate your local muscle. Quiet and clean. No more shooting *accidents*, you got that? Just say yes and shut up."

"Yes, *signore*." Ricci's words came out labored, as if rocks weighted his tongue.

"Good. Call my secure mobile when you have carried out both orders. Then I'll tell you what to do next." He recited the number before ending the call.

The prestige of the deal and the exorbitant amount he was charging Yousef would cement his position at the top of the art-theft world. And allow him to add to his own collections. The Picasso lost for years and recently discovered in Rouen would be his next acquisition. He knew just the space for it in his villa.

Zervas poured scotch and drained the glass. Worthless, his old man had called him. Told him he'd never make anything of himself. "You were wrong, old man. Fuck you." Too bad his voice didn't carry to the depths of hell.

He could not allow Interpol or Devlin Security Force to get their hands on the Cleopatra necklace. Or its copy. If that happened, he would find safe haven nowhere. He would lose everything.

****

Arlington, Virginia

Why the hell hadn't he heard from Lucas? Was the Centaur Task Force tracking Z's syndicate or were they in a cozy office suite sitting on their asses?

Thomas longed to punch something, except air made an unsatisfactory target and the paved surface of the jogging trail a painful one. Absorbing the green coolness of the trees and the lazy flow of the Potomac, he strived for calm. Running two miles beyond his usual five had relieved none of his frustration.

Sweat dripped from his chin and soaked his favorite old Go Army T-shirt. He slowed to a walk and entered the Arlington National Cemetery.

"How was your run, Captain?" The guard at the Memorial Drive gate saluted him.

"Not bad, Winston."

He returned the salute before hanging a left to Visitor Parking. Other than guards, only the groundskeepers were here this early. The scent of freshly cut grass and the hum of a mower drifted across the rows of white crosses. Breathing in the peace and solemnity, he set off down a path to pay his respects. A walk through the grounds would cool his body and maybe his mind. A few turns took him past the graves of five men he'd known. He paused to salute each one. They'd all served with honor.

One who still lived had not.

Lucas had been with the task force for nearly a month and they'd turned up damn little. Was the Centaur leader Marco Zervas? Not that it mattered in the grand scheme of stopping them, but it made a hell of a difference to him. What was Lucas doing?

Dammit, tension still knotted his shoulders and he puffed like a steam engine. He turned back toward the parking lot and his SUV. No escape for him from the source of his frustration. Running his company meant hunkering down in Crystal City instead of seeing action.

His cell jangled. He noted the caller's ID and returned the phone to his pocket. Without breaking his cool-down stride, he activated the tiny headset. "Good morning, Del Rio. Or is it afternoon there?"

Lucas Del Rio's rich chuckle vibrated in his ear. "Early afternoon, and I'm in Paris now. Nice view of the Arc de Triomphe from this café."

"Swilling wine and sightseeing?" He dug out his key fob as he reached his vehicle. "That all you're doing over there?"

"Mostly I've been hanging out in places tourists don't dare go. But you're winded. I can catch you later."

He bent over, hands on his knees, and dragged in a deep breath. "Winded, hell. When you return to the States, we'll see who's winded on this run. Talk to me."

"Yes, sir." Lucas's tone flipped into serious briefing mode. "Word in the *quartiers* here is that until recently Centaur sent guys chasing all over Europe. Seems they had the necklace, and then it vanished."

Thomas snatched a small towel from the backseat and mopped his face as he surveyed the parking lot. A few other vehicles were parked now, families visiting a parent's or grandparent's gravesite, tourists paying homage to the fallen. Solemn voices mingled above the heating pavement. No one paying attention to his conversation. "One of their thieves stole from them?"

"One possibility. All I hear on the street is

speculation."

"Right. And what changed?"

"Yesterday everything shut down. A guy I know in Montmartre told me the only activity now is in Italy."

"Your source think the Mafia's involved?"

"That would make them the ones who filched the necklace from Centaur. Doubtful. Not the Mafia's gig. More likely Centaur has located the necklace."

"Nothing on Z?" Thomas tossed the towel inside his vehicle.

"Intel says he might be headquartered in a London townhouse. Hard to get anything. None of the creeps who've been arrested know much."

Thomas slammed his palm on the metal roof. "Insulation isn't just what you put in the walls." He thanked Lucas and ended the call.

Two different directions. London to nail Z or Italy to recover Cleopatra's necklace. Both based only on untrustworthy sources. Lucas was the best. He was doing exactly what Thomas would if he were there. Damn, if only he could get in the game.

When his cell rang again, it was his admin.

"Mr. Devlin, I apologize for bothering you so early," Francine began, "but I have a call you may want to take."

"I trust your judgment. Who is it?"

"A Rear Admiral Horace Chandler. He says he's an old family friend and he needs your help. It's an emergency."

Chapter Three

THOMAS SQUARED HIS shoulders and leaned away from the SUV. No lie that Horace Chandler was an old family friend. Thomas knew every harrowing detail about the Mekong Delta river-patrol operation when "Hoot" Chandler had saved his dad's life. And he remembered the emotional warm blanket Hoot and Irene wrapped around Andie and him when their mother died. Yeah, Chandler was a friend.

He adjusted the headset. "Put the admiral through, Francine."

A moment later the patch connected and he heard the familiar commanding tone. "Thomas, it's been a long time."

"Yes, sir. It's good to hear your voice. My dad tells me you're at the academy now."

"Couldn't just retire and do nothing. Whipping those youngsters into officers suits me just fine. I'd love to get caught up with you. Another time though. I need your help."

Curiosity piqued, Thomas ducked into the car to grab a pen and notepad. "I'll do whatever I can, sir."

"It's Cleo." Chandler's voice cracked on his daughter's name.

Cleo Chandler. Years since he'd last seen her—he knew to the day—just before his deployment to Iraq, but he could never erase her pixie features and free-spirit sass from his mind. A cookout at the Chandlers'. The last time the two families had been together. His gut clenched at the idea anything bad could happen to the youngest Chandler.

A jet screaming overhead jerked him from his memories before the pause became awkward. "What is it, Admiral?"

Thomas heard throat clearing sounds as the older man gathered himself. "She's been shot. Is unconscious, maybe in a coma."

Shot. Coma. Jesus.

He sucked in a breath against the anvil thrown against his chest. "Where? How?"

"Venice."

His mind raced. He knew she'd gone to Europe. But *Italy*? Had to be a coincidence. "What happened?"

"She's been bumming around over there for the last few years. You know Cleo. Can't tie her down, never had any self-discipline. She—" A long pause as the other man seemed to draw inward. After a shaky breath, he continued. "Here's what I have. The Venice police telephoned me late last night. They found Cleo just after twenty-three hundred their time. Bleeding from a gunshot wound to the head." The admiral recited the details in a matter-of-fact manner as if reading. Maybe he was, to keep his emotions in check.

"How did they find her?" Thomas clenched his jaw against a curse.

"An unidentified woman called it in. Gone when the emergency crew arrived. My girl was bleeding on the street, or whatever they call a street in that damn floating city."

"You have any more?"

A sniff and brief throat clearing before Cleo's father continued, calmer. "Happened outside the jewelry shop where she worked. Her phone and purse lay beside her with her passport and wallet but no money. The ambulance took her to the largest hospital in the city. They have her in intensive care. But dammit, she's not responsive. My baby…"

"A terrible crime. Pickpockets are to be expected in tourist spots, but Venice is usually a safe city. Robbery at gunpoint even that time of night is highly unusual," Thomas said, giving the man—and himself—time to settle. "When do you leave? What can I do to help?"

"I'm anchored to a hospital bed," Chandler said. "Fell down the rotunda steps to Memorial Hall the other day and broke bones in my left leg and hip. I'm asking you to go to Venice for me."

His gut tightened. See Cleo again? When she woke up, she wouldn't welcome his presence. Even under these circumstances. He could say none of that to Hoot. "Wouldn't family be better? What about your wife? Or the boys?"

More throat clearing. "Irene's in Florida. Keith's wife's in labor with their second baby. Irene doesn't even know about this yet. I want to get help nailed down first. And Greg's out. I trust you to do whatever's needed."

Out of the question. He had a company to run, and he couldn't leave Andie on her own. His sister needed him. "Sir, you know I'd do anything for you. For Cleo. One of my best men is in Europe. Lucas Del Rio speaks Italian. He can fly to Venice today."

"He can assist you when you get there. But Cleo doesn't know him. Your father said if I ever needed him, he'd be there for me. I don't need his help. I need yours."

Dirty pool. Chandler knew Thomas couldn't refuse now. "Sir, there's more to this. What aren't you telling me?"

"Good instincts. That's one reason I came to you."

"Thank you, but..."

"I'm afraid there's a great deal more to this matter. Another murder, in fact. Greg called me last night too, a little after eight."

"Before the police."

"That's right. The marines have sent Greg somewhere in the Far East. Location classified. Cleo hasn't spoken to me since she left the States but every so often she calls her mother and emails Greg. This time she left her brother a message. When he called back, he got her voicemail." The admiral's voice faltered and he swallowed hard.

Thomas's breathing rasped. He massaged his nape. "Take your time, sir."

"I'm okay. You need to know the rest. It's why you're the man for the job. I wrote down Cleo's message. *'René is dead. Shot by some gang. He said no police. Oh, Greg, I'm scared. I don't know what's going on, except it's about a necklace. I have to get away. I'll call when I'm somewhere safe. Love you.'*"

****

Venice, Italy

Lucas Del Rio tried to compose his features into a non-threatening smile but in his present mood, all he could manage was a grimace.

After Thomas's urgent call, he'd left Paris on the next plane. Arrived at the Ospedale Civile early in the evening. But they'd made him wait for two hours.

At the hospital quay, another debarking passenger

guided him to an imposing white-marble building that had been a monastery in the fifteenth century. Its façade struck him as more of a palace than a holy place for monks in brown robes. He had misgivings about the hospital as he entered between marble columns with carved scrollwork. But inside he found a modern facility.

He'd expected to have no trouble carrying out Admiral Chandler's request. But no, the stick-up-her-ass neurosurgeon didn't care if the father had sent his and Thomas's names as his agents. She didn't care if he had an e-mail to that effect. She wouldn't have cared if His Holiness had ordered her to let him see the injured woman. Her white-jacketed haughtiness looked as if she wanted to kick him into the adjacent canal.

"No information about *Signorina* Chandler's medical condition or care, no entrance to the room, *signore*, until I talk to *Commissario* Castelli of the Venice *polizia*."

Castelli. He brightened. Here was his in.

"Si, si, dottoressa." He used the respectful title to demonstrate his knowledge of Italian customs. "I will also phone the detective."

After his phone call, he'd parked his butt on a lumpy upholstered chair in the hospital's lobby. He endured whispers from the reception desk and, until the hour became too late for visiting, anxious looks from visiting families. Hell, a shave, dark pants and a collared shirt still didn't render him inconspicuous. They probably thought he was mafia.

The most he accomplished was surveillance, in case some suspicious-looking dude came looking to finish off the Chandler woman. The Centaur Task Force head honcho, an FBI agent nearly as tight-assed as the neurosurgeon, had snarled at his bugging out, so the sooner he returned, the sooner he'd help nail the Centaur leader.

When the reception desk clerk's bored expression morphed into sultry, he knew Bruno Castelli had arrived.

Damn, he'd missed the sound of the door opening. He'd removed the damned hearing aid in the noisy airport and forgot about it. He checked his breast pocket for the gadget. Still there but he'd put it in later.

"Old friend, you're the image of guard duty. All that is missing is the uniform and a weapon." Castelli strode from the double doors, hand outstretched.

Lucas levered out of the deep chair and took the other man's hand before pulling him into a bro hug. "Feels like guard duty, Castelli. I'm about to fall asleep. Good to see your ugly mug."

Castelli smiled. "A few years since Afghanistan and you haven't changed. I'm surprised you're not still in the Army."

"Yeah, me too," Lucas replied. "An IED booted me out on medical discharge, or I'd still be humping it. Private security's my gig now. I'm hoping you can work your charm on the *dottoressa*."

"Guaranteed, my friend. I'll persuade her to stop playing Cerberus and cooperate." He strolled across the marble floor as if on an awards red carpet.

Lucas had met Castelli when his Special Forces team coordinated with an Italian unit in an op outside Kabul. During long nights of patrol, he and the Venetian had traded insults, and Castelli had taught him Italian, including assorted rude phrases he'd avoided firing at the fanged doctor. After the army, he improved his language fluency during various security jobs in Europe. Until

Thomas had recruited him.

Castelli schmoozed the receptionist, who simpered like a fourteen-year-old at his white smile and pretty face. In moments the neurosurgeon appeared, as damned fluttery as the young clerk. She nodded her agreement, eyeing Lucas—the gorilla in the room—with suspicion.

Castelli beckoned and Lucas followed him through pastel-painted halls to the stairs.

"Did you find the lover dead like the admiral said?" he moved smoothly to the detective's left side.

"René Moreau. In the flat the two shared. He took a bullet to the chest. Found a trail of blood on the stairs. Someone, likely the *signorina*, covered him with a sheet. Probably shot elsewhere, maybe by the same gun as her. We recovered the other bullet from the jewelry shop wall. Nine millimeter. I will know more when I receive the ballistics report."

"Any leads?"

"Not yet. Once we discover what necklace she referred to, perhaps. Perhaps not." Castelli angled his head and twisted his mouth in a typical Italian dismissal.

Lucas made no reply. Thomas had advised him not to mention the Cleopatra necklace until they knew if that was the piece in question.

"I understand *Signorina* Chandler awoke briefly," Castelli said as they reached the correct floor, "but she was so distraught the surgeon feared she would further injure herself. There was also danger of a blood clot and brain swelling. They have her in a medical coma."

They stepped into the intensive care unit, hushed except for the hum of equipment and the squeak of soft soles. Lucas wrinkled his nose at the medicinal and antiseptic cleanser smells.

"And the damage? The bullet?" he asked.

"The bullet grazed the side of her head a few millimeters above her left ear." He pulled a small notebook from inside his jacket and flipped pages. "She has a depressed skull fracture. Bone fragments were removed. She is receiving antibiotics and steroids. The surgeon says she will not know the extent of damage until the swelling goes down and *Signorina* Chandler awakens."

If she awakens. Lucas had a bad feeling about her chances. War had taught him only a small percentage of victims survived gunshots to the head.

A middle-aged nurse beamed at the detective as she ushered them into Cleo Chandler's room. Castelli thanked her and she left, reluctantly, with a swoosh of the door.

Monitors surrounded the bed and tubes draped the slim, covered form. Thomas had said Cleo was twenty-eight. Lucas shook his head, struck by the tragic unfairness as he and the detective approached.

He left Castelli at the foot of the bed. He moved around to the side not snaked with tubes or hidden by bandages so he could get a better look. Castelli's details about the dead lover faded into the background. Everything faded away except the woman.

Dark red hair the color of autumn leaves. Heart-shaped face. Long eyelashes curling against sculpted cheekbones. Light freckles across her pale skin.

His pulse kicked into a hectic beat.

Protect Cleo Chandler? No shit. Lucas wasn't leaving her side.

Chapter Four

Arlington, Virginia

"I LEAVE LATER tonight, Andie." Thomas dispensed ice from the fridge into his tea and leaned against the center island. "Don't know exactly how long I'll be gone."

His sister rinsed her coffee mug and placed it in the dishwasher. She made no reply. The only evidence of emotion was a twitch of her shoulders.

These days, Andie hid her thoughts behind a wall or tossed them like grenades. He braced himself.

She pursed her lips. A light purple, probably to match the new streak in her spiky hair. "Let me get this straight. You're jetting off to Europe on some secret mission. Must be a special work of art."

Soft warmth curled in his chest. He smiled. Cleo was a work of art all right, but he couldn't tell his sister anything about protecting her former partner in crime. "Right. I'm sorry I can't tell you. It's confidential."

Andie's cell phone blasted the condo with a heavy metal riff. She dug in her voluminous purse. "My boss. I gotta take this."

"I'll be here," Thomas said.

"Something to think about, big brother. You can leave the country without me knowing where you are or when you'll return, but *I* have to schedule every minute of my day for *you*." Phone to her ear, she disappeared down the hall.

The bitter words hurt more than her ring tone. She was right, but his conditions weren't changing. And her major attitude didn't bode well for what he was about to ask of her during his absence.

Even after breast cancer took their mother when Andie was seven, she'd remained a cheerful, reasonable kid, bouncing back from the terrible loss. She and Thomas had coped together with the constant rotation of nannies and their dad's focus on his navy career and not on his kids' grief and problems. Thomas and Cleo's brothers had watched over the two little girls and sometimes let them tag along.

Until the teen years hit Andie. Boys, alcohol, drugs—mostly prescription pills—and total disregard for every rule the old man imposed. And God knew Thomas Devlin, Senior—then a mere rear admiral—expected everyone to live by his rules.

Anger spurted and Thomas squelched it. His bitterness didn't matter. He'd moved on. His objective was for Andie to be able to do the same.

At thirty, her lifestyle and attitude made her seem ten years younger, the fallout of a troubled youth. The shrink had concluded that depression was the original cause of her rebellion and drug abuse. Now Andie lived under Thomas's roof, Thomas's rules, and her therapist's guidance. Until she could make it on her own. What he did was for Andie's good, not arbitrary, as she obviously thought. He downed the last of his tea and set down the glass. He might pour a scotch after this conversation.

The click of heels on the hardwood announced her return to the kitchen. "One of the other bartenders called in sick. I have to go in now. Are we done?"

"Not quite. You'll be solo here while I'm gone."

"Hallelujah. Alone at last."

Ignore that. "I want you to phone me every day."

"To keep tabs on me, you mean. You don't trust me."

"I want to. But Dr. Olsen—"

"Fuck Doc Olsen. You just want to control my life like the old man."

His gut clenched but he schooled his temper. "I want *you* to control your life." Working in a bar wasn't the best way for a recovering addict to do it but he'd stow that subject for now. "Call me at this time every day. Like we usually share our days before you go to work, except it'll be on the phone."

"What you really mean is you're checking on if I'm staying clean." Cheeks flushed, she snatched up her purse and stalked out of the kitchen.

He followed her through the living room and into the foyer. "That's part of it. I care about you. Promise me, Andie."

Hell, he'd only made things worse between them. He would hug her but she'd probably construe it as force. He put his hands behind him and balled them into fists.

"Trust me or not. It's up to you. I'm making no promises. Have a *fabulous* trip."

The door slammed behind her hard enough to rattle the mirror on the wall.

****

Venice, Italy

Ricci grinned. Entering the *Ospedale Civile* during the shift change had been laughably easy.

In a staff laundry closet bin, he found white pants he

could pull on over his dark ones. He didn't look closely at the rusty stuff on them. *Dio* knew what it was. The white jackets had different colored stripes or no stripes. No time to figure out which were techs and which nurses.

He'd had little trouble discovering the Chandler woman had survived and tracing her to this hospital. At least he didn't have to deal with that dead weight Panaro. A smile curved his mouth at his own joke. *Si*, nobody would find the *Veneziano* for a long time, and Ricci now had the Beretta.

He racked the slide and chambered a round. After securing the pistol in his back waistband, he peered out. Nobody looking his way. He slipped into the hallway, dimly lit at the late hour. All the espresso he'd downed at the bar had his pulse pinging and nerves buzzing.

This floor—General Medicine, according to the sign—was quiet, patients tucked in. Nobody walking the hallway, making rounds, or whatever they called it. Two women at the nurses' station gabbed about another's cheating husband. He nicked a clipboard from the counter and strolled toward the stairs. No lift for him, where somebody might have time to look at him with suspicion.

He bounded up the stairs and opened the door, surveying the intensive-care unit before he stepped out. More active here. Monitors beeped and ticked and hummed. Nurses and techs looked more alert. No *polizia* guarding the floor. Lucky again.

He strode down the hall, clipboard front and center. On the fifth door down he saw a card with Chandler's name. He started to enter but heard a voice inside. The deep male voice was speaking English. He flipped through pages on the clipboard, trying to look official while straining to hear. His nerve endings crackled.

The man's tone was soothing—a doctor with a good bedside manner, but not all the words were clear. "… is on his way. He'll… sure they catch…"

What did it mean?

"You'll be fine. You just need to wake up."

Wake up? She was in a coma? No interrogation. Ricci would have to eliminate her, finish what Panaro had started. He glanced around for somewhere to hide until the doctor left. No obvious closets, no door labeled Laundry. Not as easy to pull this off during the day. His hand shook so much he nearly dropped the clipboard.

"You have to get better," the voice said, a little louder. Clearer.

The door swung wide open. A man stood there. Scarred jaw. Lumpy face like a boxer. Built like a boxer. Grim and hyper-vigilant like a soldier. Not a doctor.

Ricci shoved the clipboard at the man's face and sprinted for the stairs.

****

Lucas knocked aside the clipboard. Papers skated across the tile floor like wind-blown leaves. The wiry man in hospital white pelted down the hallway, knocking over a cart and barreling past a startled nurse. The bulge at his back waistband screamed weapon.

And Lucas had only his fists.

His whole body clenched with the need to chase down the fucker and find out who he worked for. But he gripped the door jamb and cemented his feet to the floor. *Protect the principal.* Never leave the client alone, vulnerable. There could be a second hit man waiting for the opportunity. Cleo needed him. For now.

"*Aiuto!*" Help, he yelled in Italian. "Call the

police!"

People sprang into action. An alarm buzzed through the hall like a hive of bees. The desk nurse reached for the phone. A man and a woman dashed for the intruder as he reached the stairwell door.

"No! Don't chase him. He has a gun." Again in Italian.

The creep slammed through. The white-jacketed staff raced after him. Thumps receded down the stairs. *Shit.*

Two nurses ran to his aid. Or that of their patient.

"She's fine," he told them. "The imposter didn't get inside." But he stepped aside to allow them to check their patient. Couldn't hurt. Cleo was sleeping, undisturbed, as usual.

The women's smiles were wobbly as they left, glancing furtively at him with a mixture of admiration and fear. Same effect he often had on women. They were happy to have his protection but that was all. He kept the clipboard and the papers he'd retrieved. The cops would want to see where they'd come from.

"The *polizia* are on their way," a nurse said.

He thanked her and she skittered away like a mouse.

A moment later the staff who'd pursued the hit man returned, out of breath but whole.

He beckoned to them. "Did you see which way he went?"

The two looked at each other. *"Si, signore,* but only partly,"* the man said, breathing heavily after his exertion. "He ran around the building toward the *piazza.* But there were too many people." He lifted a shoulder in apology.

Lucas had gotten a good look at the guy but he

should ask anyway. "Can you describe him?"

Both shook their heads. "Only his back," the woman said, edging away with her colleague. "I must return to my post."

"The *polizia* will ask the same questions," Lucas told them. "So try to think of details about his appearance." Satisfied he'd done what he could, he returned to his vigil beside Cleo's bed.

If the man had made furtive sounds outside the room, he'd heard nothing dammit. Thank God he'd seen the shadow of feet beneath the door. A nurse or technician would've entered right away without hesitation. He'd known as soon as he opened the door the man was an imposter. Deer-startled eyes. No ID on his jacket. But the kicker had been brown leather shoes.

He would alert Thomas when the doc came to examine Cleo. Hell, if only he'd been able to chase down the bastard. He laid his head against the padded chair back. Pounded a fist on the arm rest.

****

Thomas walked down the steps from the Venice taxi square to the Grand Canal. He checked his voicemail for the tenth time but found no message, no text from Andie. Six hours earlier in Arlington, so she'd still be asleep after her late shift tending bar. But what the hell. Might be the only time he'd catch her.

As he waited for the international call to connect to the condo's land line, he smiled despite the urgency knotting his shoulders. He inhaled the canal's briny smell, never forgotten. A water bus called a *vaporetto* pulled out of its station to the rumbling music of engines and water. Three gondoliers steadied their black boats in its wake. Tourists rolled suitcases toward bridges crossing the canal.

No answer. Voicemail. Andie wasn't in the condo? His right shoulder cramped. Dammit, where was she at this hour on a Saturday? Or else she saw his number on Caller ID and blew him off. He stowed the concern and irritation for later and gazed at the scene around him.

Venice. Years since he'd visited the city when he and two other lieutenants had leave from training in the Turkish mountains. The ancient buildings with the typical Venetian arched windows might have faded more. Scaffolding webbed different palazzos and hotels. A new boy at the kiosk hawked maps, carnival masks, and post cards in English and German. Still the same glorious, crumbling city. The only real differences were the clothing and the mobile phones at everyone's ear.

And on the other side of Venice, the flame-haired woman who lay unconscious.

Thomas felt the muscles around his mouth tighten. An intruder in the hospital—likely a Centaur hit man— had been stopped last night thanks to Lucas. Cleo would be all right. Dear God, she had to be.

No time for a leisurely *vaporetto* ride around the city's perimeter. He hiked his carry-on bag higher on his shoulder and strode to the nearest water taxi stand.

A half hour later he arrived at Cleo's hospital room door, slightly ajar. Over the hum of monitors and the whoosh of a respirator, he heard Lucas's low voice, mellow and soft rather than the usual growl.

"No wonder you stayed in Venice to work. Spent some time in Italy when I worked over here. The food. Friendly people. There was this one job—"

Thomas pushed through the doorway.

Lucas sat beside the bed, leaning forward, elbows

on knees, facing the doorway. He jackknifed upright, suddenly no longer a bedside comforter but a soldier on alert.

Broad face flushing as recognition sank in, he lurched away from the bed. "Thomas."

Thomas had expected Lucas to occupy a guard position outside the room. He felt his brows snap together and dismissed the rush of anger. Lucas's attention focused on Cleo as much as on a possible threat.

He nodded, the odd tableau forgotten as he walked to the foot of the bed. He couldn't take his eyes from Cleo. Covers to her chin, smooth except for the rise and fall of her breasts. A still and pale Sleeping Beauty. Perfect except for the respirator tubes in her nostrils and the bandages on the left side of her head, where the bullet had struck. He shuddered in a breath.

He flexed his fingers, cramped from being clenched. "Hey, excellent reaction time. I tried to be quiet." Lucas would accept the compliment better with only an oblique reference to his hearing issue.

"Thanks." Lucas edged away from the bed, deferring to his boss.

"The admiral was pleased someone was here so fast. But I couldn't reach you on the phone. How is she?" From the moment Hoot Chandler had told him about Cleo's injury, fear had tied knots in his shoulders. Rotating them to loosen the tightness, he kept his gaze on her while he listened.

"Can't use mobile phones in here. Something about all the electronics. I left the voicemail as soon as I could." Lucas cleared his throat and brought Thomas up to speed.

Swelling on the brain. Medical coma. The words sank into him like wet cement. But he told himself she was getting the best care. And protection. "And the intruder? Did you get a look at him?"

"Affirmative. A good look. Dark hair, thirties, deep-set eyes under a heavy brow. Brown leather shoes. About my height but scrawny. Might've looked thinner than he was because the scrubs he stole hung on him. Cops found them in a trash bin two streets over."

"ID?"

"Negative. So far. *Commissario* Castelli had his men ask around and check the closed-circuit tapes. Yesterday several of the nurses here saw a man who fit the description at the local bar. They admitted he probably overheard their gossip about Cleo."

"Explains how he found the right room. Could be one of Centaur's men. You said he had a gun under his jacket. Maybe the same one used to shoot her?" And her lover, but Thomas couldn't bring himself to say the word.

"Wouldn't surprise me. Don't have confirmation from Castelli, but the bullets recovered from both crime scenes were nine mil. The man, one René Moreau, an alias. Castelli said they found three other false passports hidden in the bedroom. Real name is Farris Pandareos."

"Greek?"

"Affirmative. Small-time thief and talented jewelry designer. Arrested in France for making paste copies of Marie Antoinette's necklace. Didn't stick. Clean ever since."

"Or more careful. Looks like Centaur contracted with him to make a copy of the Cleopatra necklace. Then everything went to hell." Studying Cleo's face, he angled his head to the right. Peered at her. Something was off.

"You sure, Thomas? That's a leap."

He moved around to her right side. "Not so much. Her Facebook page has a picture of her wearing the necklace. Or the copy."

Lucas punched a fist into his other palm. "Shit. The reason they were after her."

Thomas made no reply. He was barely aware of his operative backing farther away. He trailed a finger along the soft cheek, the fall of auburn hair on the pillow. Moved aside the sheet and blanket. Lifted the cotton sleeve so he could see her upper arm. At the sight of the smooth, unblemished skin, a wave of relief washed over him. His shoulders began to relax until the implications flooded him.

He turned. "This is not Cleo Chandler." Not the girl—correction, woman now—who'd heated his dreams for nearly a decade.

Lucas's watchful gaze morphed to shock. If he wasn't already leaning against the wall, he might've crashed to the floor. "How… how can you be sure?"

"I've known Cleo Chandler since she was a kid. Both our dads were stationed at the Charleston Naval Base then. When she was thirteen, she climbed a tree to rescue a kitten. In the process, she threatened a hornet's nest. They attacked with fury." He'd caught her—and the kitten—when she fell.

"Yeah, so?" Lucas said.

"One of the stings, here—" he pointed to a clear spot on the injured woman's upper right arm "—got infected, left a big scar. She covered it years later with an armband tattoo. Her hair is a sunnier auburn, and curly. The shape of her face is different. It's not Cleo."

Lucas's wide hands gripped the bed frame. "Then who *is* she?"

Thomas's shoulders cramped for the umpteenth time. "And where the hell is Cleo?"

Chapter Five

MARA MARTON GRABBED a bottle of green tea from the machine in the DSF employee lounge. Cort had gotten her hooked on the stuff. Better for you than all that high-test coffee, he insisted. She smiled, emotions welling up, suffusing her with the power of their connection.

Tea in hand, she took the elevator up to Thomas Devlin's office, where Max Rivera was helming the ship. Sort of.

When Max had called her early this morning with the assignment from Mr. Devlin, she chuckled at his gruff apology for waking her on a Saturday. Poor Max was having trouble issuing orders while he sat in the boss's executive chair.

Several of the field operatives in DSF were ex-Delta Force and it showed. Super competent in intel and security, intelligent and quick thinking under stress. Most didn't flinch at issuing orders or sounding like they were, but not Max. None of them liked being yanked out of their comfy aquarium. Max would flop around for a day or two until he learned to breathe the new, rarefied air. But then he'd be good to go. Better than good. He would excel. Her Cort was like that, but he'd honed his cool-under-pressure right-stuff in prison rather than in combat.

A ding and the elevator door opened to the top floor and the carpeted outer office. This case was so different from the usual. Yes, a valuable artifact had been stolen. Nothing new there. But *cherchez la femme*—a mysterious woman whose disappearance had the boss himself jetting off to Europe.

After Mr. Devlin had discovered the unconscious woman in the Venice hospital wasn't Cleo Chandler, he'd learned from Cleo's father about an estranged brother who might have a daughter. Fascinated by the convoluted puzzle, she'd dived into locating the other Chandler somewhere in Canada. Finding him was a little harder than usual, given the fifty years since his disappearance, but a cool challenge.

She wanted to know more about this woman and why she was so important to Devlin. No one in the office had heard of him ever having a serious relationship. Word was he hooked up with no one for more than a couple months. The women he usually escorted around D.C. were sleek society ladies-who-lunched or polished executives, not artsy rebels like the Cleo Chandler she found on Facebook.

Once she'd amassed all available intel about the uncle and family, she sent off the info to Devlin's cell phone. That was a couple hours ago. Time enough for him to phone Canada and devise a plan. Her boss was a decisive kind of guy, never one to dither. So she'd stuck around, expecting him to need more. Sure enough, he'd just called Max. She grinned as she entered the inner sanctum.

"Thanks for staying," Max said from their boss's massive desk. The big Texan lounged in the leather chair, one foot in a western boot and the cast-encased leg on an upholstered side chair. "Devlin said to send apologies to Cort."

"Not a problem. Cort went to Roanoke to deliver a desk." She sank onto a chair and sipped her tea.

"His custom furniture has really taken off since he moved out of the Maine woods."

"He's advertising now. Mr. Devlin ordering a new conference table and promoting the business hasn't hurt either." She smiled with pleasure at Cort's success. "You said Mr. Devlin needs more information. Research?"

"More than research," Max said. "A probe. Urgent and maybe dicey." He raised an eyebrow as if waiting for her reaction.

Here was her chance to find out more. "I've never known him to handle a case personally. This Cleo Chandler must be pretty important to him."

"I got nada on that." Max's expression was as carefully bland as Devlin's would've been if she'd had the temerity to ask him. Heaven forbid a guy would ever ask, not that the boss would give even Max a straight answer.

She sighed, resigned to ignorance. "Okay, what's this spy mission?"

"Apparently this Mimi Ingram took a day off from her Med cruise to pay a visit to Cleo. The Canadian cousin and Cleo look a lot alike."

Mara's eyes snapped wide. "The crooks shot the wrong woman."

"Give the woman a kewpie doll. We doubt the shooters know that yet. She has all Chandler's documents. Hers are missing. Devlin thinks Cleo's masquerading as her cousin on the cruise ship. First, verify whether Mimi Ingram returned to the *Norwegian Emerald.*"

"Meaning Cleo." Mara nodded as she tapped notes into her tablet.

"If that checks out, arrange for Devlin to board as a passenger when they dock in Palermo, Sicily, on Sunday. If they're full up, find a way to boot someone off the ship. I don't care how you manage this, just do it. Discreetly."

"*You* don't care how I do it?"

Max's brows beetled. "Those were Devlin's words."

"Orders from above. Thank goodness. Glad we don't have to worry about a coup." She jerked her head toward the leg cast. "How much longer you have to drag that around?"

"Another damn month. Kate may kick me to the curb before that."

"Growling at her, are you? How'd you say you broke the leg?"

"I didn't." He thumbed a shooing motion toward the door. "Devlin needs that A-sap."

She snapped a salute and clicked her heels together, not terribly effective with sneakers.

Max stretched out with his hands stacked behind his head and a master-of-the-universe smile on his face. "Hey, y'all, maybe this head-honcho job isn't so bad after all."

****

Munich, Germany

"Your computer program is not installed. Is this man playing you?" Marco Zervas bit out the words. He looked around the airport sports bar. Nobody was paying him or his men any attention. Saturday evening and travelers sagged in weariness.

"Don't think so, sir. Bloke's not much with computers. I 'ave to lead 'im by the nose. He'll do it though. The money's set 'im up." Hawkins hunched over his laptop, his wire-rim glasses propped on top his head. He murmured to himself as his fingers flew over the keys.

On Zervas's other side, Nedik rolled his eyes at the tech's absorption in his work. He picked up his beer stein and returned to watching the airport crowd.

Zervas caught the *Fraulein*'s eye and ordered another beer. A stopover at this airport without a few German brews was unthinkable. And allowed him a detour to throw the Interpol-led task force off his scent.

When the waitress brought his beer, he wiped the rim with a napkin, then slugged down a healthy swallow. They'd never find him now he'd changed his appearance and his passport. The impregnable security at the villa would protect him from intruders, real or digital. He could run his operations from there without concern for the fucking task *farce*.

They and Devlin Security had recovered more of his Cleopatra Tomb Exhibit haul. Their damned snoops intercepted his envoys en route to his buyers. He couldn't allow them to recover the necklace. Shit, he wished he'd never heard of the thing. Or of Ahmed Yousef. But no matter. He would prevail.

Hawkins looked up, settling his glasses on his long, thin nose. "Guv, are you certain about this hacking job?"

"What, having doubts about your abilities, your so-called Hawk Tool?"

The Brit straightened his Ichabod-Crane body. "None at all. It's the best utility for this job. Does it all.

Enumeration, scanning, root privileges—"

"Fucking spare me the geek jargon," Zervas said. He glared at Hawkins. "If not the technical issue, what?"

"Spying in this system is bloody risky. Their tech department people are no slouches. But if you insist on it, let me do this remotely without the bloody mole. The wanker might do something stupid afterward and get caught."

"Doesn't matter as long as it's afterward." That was his plan. They'd learn then who took down the company, destroyed its reputation. "You had your say. Now do what I pay you for. And while you're online with our mole, ask him where his boss is."

He returned to his beer and Hawkins to his computer.

DSF operatives had hounded Centaur all summer, getting closer and closer. They had to be stopped. He had to take down the company, screw Thomas Devlin himself, before they ruined his business. The hacking had to work.

The waitress delivered his pork schnitzel and roast potatoes. The sauce's rich aroma made his mouth water. He eyed Nedik's sausages with disdain. None of those Kraut stuffed cases for him. Who knew what was actually in those things? Germans were generally fastidious but he couldn't ignore that e-coli breakout a few years ago. He took no chances. He wiped his utensils with a sanitary wipe before testing his schnitzel. Cooked through. Good. Satisfied, he sliced off a piece.

Watching Hawkins click away on his keyboard, he drank beer, savored a bite of the tender pork. Glass clinked as the waitress delivered beers to a neighboring table.

The geek looked up. "Mole says Devlin won't be in for a few days. Odd, he says, because the boss never takes vacations. Gossip is it's a hush-hush job about a woman."

Zervas's mouth tightened. He set down his stein. Could the task force have made the connection? Devlin would jump on any mention of Cleopatra's necklace.

His heart strummed an erratic beat. He'd lived with hate for so long, he'd learned to contain the rage bubbling like lava. Perhaps there would be a showdown over the necklace. Perfect. He couldn't fucking wait.

He prided himself on keeping his voice even, modulated. "Find out where Thomas Devlin went."

****

Venice, Italy

When Thomas stepped from the hotel elevator into the lobby, Bruno Castelli was waiting. Lucas's description was on the mark. *GQ* looks and dressed for the part in a hand-tailored suit. Lucas had vouched for his credentials and ability. But how much would the detective cooperate on Cleo's safety?

"*Commissario* Castelli." He shook the man's hand. "Thank you for meeting me. You must have better things to do on a Saturday evening."

Castelli dismissed the apology with a shrug and a smile. "A major case like this one commands my attention on weekends as well. I need to make headway before your government puts pressure on my director. As for better things, my fiancée dines with her grandmother this evening." He spoke English with little accent.

"Will you join me for a drink?" The hotel's bar probably wasn't the best place, but he didn't know this area near the hospital well enough to suggest another.

Castelli's gaze assessed what passed for a bar in the boutique hotel. Scarcely big enough for the four customers already seated in the gloom, it promised no privacy. "Perhaps later. Let us go for a walk."

They made their way through narrow streets via a series of doglegs. As they turned onto the *Fondamenta Nuove*, a wide paved embankment, a sailboat and a rowboat passed each other in the deep channel. The calm water gleamed silver in the lowering sun. Across the canal, cypress trees marked the Venice cemetery on the island of San Michele.

"I suspect you have discovered by now that the injured woman isn't Cleo Chandler," Thomas said, hoping his up-front approach would earn him points. And trust.

Castelli's glance was sharp. "How do you know this?"

"I'm an old family friend. There are... small differences. I knew she wasn't Cleo." Before his brain, his body had known, not responding to her the way he'd reacted to Cleo from the day she stopped being a pesky kid and became all female. And too fascinating for his good. Or hers.

"You are right, *signore*." Castelli tucked his hands in his suit-jacket pockets. "Fingerprints on objects in the purse and on the mobile phone do not match those of the victim. Interpol has vouched for your reputation and that of your company. Before I share information from an on-going police investigation, what is it you want from me?"

Two twenty-somethings walking a German shepherd approached from the other direction. The women whispered together, hips swaying in their short skirts more noticeably the closer they came. Thomas's face warmed before he realized they were smiling at cover-boy Castelli, not at a man a decade their senior, the age difference between him and Cleo. He needed to remember that when he found her.

After the women passed, he said, "I know where Cleo has gone. I want assurance I can reach her and protect her before you reveal the identity confusion to the press. And to the bad guys."

"I can make no promises. *Signorina* Chandler is connected to two cases of murder. She is a suspect."

"Witness, yes, but no murderer. I believe she's the one who first called the police about Moreau's death, and then the emergency number about the second shooting. She's the reason that woman in the hospital bed is still alive." He had no proof, only supposition. He shouldn't have come across with such vehemence, dammit. "And Moreau? Do you think she shot him too?"

The detective's thin smile revealed nothing. "Too soon to say. We found blood at the foot of the stairs leading to his studio. Signs of a search inside. Clues in the flat where he expired indicate *Signorina* Chandler left in a hurry. Both victims were shot by the same nine millimeter. No witnesses to either shooting, except perhaps the *signorina*. No indication anyone else was there outside the jewelry shop. Perhaps the women argued. If I could question the *signorina*..." He let his words hang in the air, like Cleo's life.

Thomas forced calm into his voice. "Right. Once I've arranged for her safety, I'll make her available for questioning."

"But you will not tell me her location."

Thomas kept his expression neutral while he waited out the detective.

After a moment, Castelli spoke. "On her Facebook page, we found posts between her and Mimi Ingram, and her mobile showed recent calls to her. But whenever I ring the number, it is out of service." He raised an eyebrow.

Not unlike Thomas's attempts to reach his sister. But he was no longer worried. Much. Dr. Olsen had said she was working her regular shift, so she was just ignoring him. Sometimes space was good, the doc had suggested. Maybe.

He waited to respond to Castelli until they'd passed two men chatting at a gas station. Fumes feathered the salt air as a man filled the tank in his water taxi. Castelli had seen the necklace on the Facebook page. Every police officer in Europe knew about the theft.

Before he could speak, the detective stepped in. "The necklace. Is it the one stolen in July, the ancient piece unearthed in Cleopatra's tomb?"

"Or a copy made by René Moreau aka Farris Pandareos." He doubted Cleo had any idea she might've worn the real deal. She might be a little wild but never dishonest. Always open. Sometimes too open. If she was still the Cleo he used to know.

"Your security company was in charge of the transfer from the U.S. to the museum in Paris," Castelli said, sympathy, not accusation in his voice.

"To my great embarrassment. And the reason my company is cooperating with the Centaur Task Force. We believe Centaur is involved. You can understand the other reason I want this resolved." He didn't need to explain. Several thefts in Venice in the past few years had alerted Castelli's office to Centaur's dealings.

They reached the end of the *fondamenta* at a wide

opening between the banks.

"This is *la Sacca della Misericordia*," Castelli said, gesturing toward a line of moored boats. "It translates as Bag of Mercy. Not a descriptive or elegant name, merely a small basin separating islands and used for major transportation and a marina."

Dusk was falling in royal shades of purple and gold. The water flowed out toward Murano. In the distance along that cluster of isles housing Venice's glass factories, lights blinked on and details blurred to silhouettes.

After a moment enjoying the view, the two men turned and retraced their steps.

"And Mimi Ingram?" the detective asked.

Castelli would learn the truth as soon as Mimi's mother arrived. For now Thomas intended to withhold a key fact. "Mimi Ingram is Cleo Chandler's cousin. I learned from Cleo's father that he has a brother he hasn't seen for fifty years."

"A very long time. A family argument?"

Thomas nodded, pondering the history of that turbulent time. "Over the war in Viet Nam. Cleo's father Horace joined the navy. His brother Milton was a conscientious objector who left the U.S. for Canada. They haven't spoken since, and Horace didn't know where Milton lived."

"But you do?"

"My personnel are top notch, *Commissario*. My researcher discovered him, now Milton Ingram, in Toronto. He was an attorney with Amnesty International."

"Was?"

"Unfortunately he died a year ago in a helicopter

crash. His wife and teenage sons still live in the family home." As Thomas remembered telling the wife about Mimi being shot, his throat tightened. "This afternoon I spoke to his widow."

"I don't envy you that conversation. I dislike delivering bad news."

"She'll arrive here in a couple days. She needs time to make arrangements for the boys."

"And did she know how Mimi Ingram came to be in Venice?"

"When her father died, Mimi found information about the Chandlers in her father's papers. He'd kept track of them, although his American brother didn't. When she saw she had a cousin nearly the same age, she did her own search, found Cleo on Facebook. Mimi traveled to Venice so the cousins could meet. I have no idea how the shooting happened but I believe she was mistaken for Cleo."

"Because the man or men who shot Moreau think *Signorina* Chandler knows where the necklace is. She may or may not know, but she left behind her purse and she may have taken her cousin's, along with her identity."

"I don't want to endanger Mimi Ingram. Lucas Del Rio will remain here to guard her." Thomas had a feeling the only way to remove Lucas from her side was to blast him loose with an RPG. "But I need a day, two at the most, to secure Cleo."

Castelli's gaze dropped to the paving stones. He ran a thumbnail across his teeth. "I can give you a day or until *Signora* Ingram arrives, whichever is sooner. That is all."

Thomas could breathe again. "Thank you,

Commissario. It should be enough time. After that it won't matter whether Centaur knows where Cleo is hiding."

"They may already know, my friend."

The warning had his brows crunching. "What do you mean?"

"My crime scene people confiscated a laptop computer from the flat she and Moreau shared. The hard drive was missing."

Chapter Six

Shipboard

"THIS ROOM SAFE totally baffled me." Cleo batted her eyelashes, channeling the ditzy babe her dad thought she was. "Thank you so much, Erik."

His cheeks flushed. He looked tough and his bulk filled the doorway but, jeez, he had to be barely out of his teens. And naïve, thank you very much.

"Anytime, *madame*. Just call the security office and I'll be here." His color went from pink to crimson. He actually winked.

Great, she'd accomplished too much. He was hitting on her. From now on she'd have to avoid the guy.

In a move she suspected was an attempt at swagger, he nearly dropped the digital gizmo that had opened her safe. *Mimi's safe.*

Twin waves of grief and guilt rolled through her, wobbling her pulse and her smile. "Sure. Cool." For support, she yanked open the door, held onto the handle. "I think I have the hang of the thing now."

Grinning, he backed into the corridor.

She managed a smile as she pushed the door shut. She slipped Mimi's plastic ID from her pocket. Like the Canadian passport, the all-purpose shipboard card read Marie Ingram, not the nickname Mimi.

Marie. Their mutual grandmother, a wispy but

steadfast woman with a pouf of reddish-gray hair. Her hand clutched Grandma Marie's locket before she realized it. She had died when Cleo was twelve, leaving her the locket, but Mimi had never met her or known she had a grandmother with the same name. Or maybe she had known.

She was Cleopatra Marie Chandler, and Mimi was Marie—What? The driver's license in Mimi's backpack listed her as *Marie L. Ingram*. Louise? Linda? Lydia? Tears burned Cleo's eyes. She swallowed and leaned her forehead against the cool metal door and forced down the emotion.

She had to *be* Mimi, behave like Mimi—capable and organized, like Cleo should be. The dummy act had served its purpose with Security Eric, but she didn't like how natural the charade felt. Or was she just feeling sorry for herself?

A snippet of one conversation with her cousin came back to her.

"Can you believe it?" Mimi had said as they chatted. "We both carry sketchpads in our bags. How many other aspects of our lives are similar?"

"Similar, yes. But not the same," Cleo said. "Your sketches reflect your work as an interior designer. They're real. Mine are only reflections of dreams unfulfilled."

"What are those dreams, Cleo?" Mimi asked.

"Making it as an artist, but sometimes I'm not sure." But her cousin's question had forced her to think. For three years she'd been running from the restrictions and directions her father imposed. But what was she running *toward*? She'd gotten some of her tempera scenes into a small gallery, only baby steps. Was her dream only a mirage?

Arriving shipboard yesterday, she'd played the airhead, claiming to have forgotten the location and number of her stateroom. Like just now, Security helped her, and she'd hunkered down and used room service for what meals she could choke down. Solitary confinement. The decor's bright colors mocked her. The mini-suite boasted a sitting area with a sofa and a balcony from where she sketched the coastline.

She picked up Mimi's sketch pad from the counter. Everything reminded her of what happened to René and Mimi. And fearing what could happen to *her* seemed such a cowardly betrayal. What had René done? Why did he have that necklace? It couldn't be the real one from Cleopatra's tomb. She shook that thought out of her head. But somehow he'd gotten mixed up with criminals, and it had gotten him killed.

And Mimi. But that death was on Cleo. She'd pressured and wheedled until Mimi caved and left the ship to visit her all the way across Italy. And because Cleo ran like a coward, waiting too long to call the police, the killers…

On a sob, she sank onto the floor and hugged her knees. She could do nothing for René and Mimi now. All she could do was hide on this ship while she figured things out.

Dwelling on it all choked, a noose squeezing her throat. Unbearable. She so needed freedom, fun, forgetting—if only for a while. Working on a new project always spirited her away. But she'd lost her easel and paints, left in the flat with an unfinished watercolor. The sketchpad and a few pencils didn't cut it. Getting off the ship for a shore excursion would have to substitute.

When she hadn't found tickets for the shore excursions the ship's TV channel touted, she called Security about opening the safe.

Now she collected everything from the safe and spread them out on the queen bed. Tickets for guided tours at all the ports, including today's, for Naples. Just as well she missed that one and the city's major garbage problem. But she found tickets for the next ports, including tomorrow's Palermo tour. Also in the pile were printouts for Air France between Barcelona and Toronto. Canadian money.

After locking up everything but the excursion tickets, she showered and blow-dried her hair. In the closet, she selected mint-green linen capris and tunic that smelled of her cousin's lilac fragrance. More chic and expensive than the entire wardrobe she'd abandoned. Her vision shimmered.

Dammit, now she felt like a thief. She *was* a thief.

Oh, Mimi, I'm sorry, but you would want me to be safe. Wouldn't you, sweetie?

As she stood at the closed door, she summoned her grandmother's courage. Grandma Marie had defied her Quaker parents and married a soldier, Cleo and Mimi's grandfather. Not the same thing as pretending to be someone else but it was all she had.

Trying not to jump at every voice, every sound, she found her way to the elevators and down three levels, where savory aromas guided her to one of the main dining rooms. She would remain anonymous—yes, really—but at least she'd be among other people. Life.

"This way, *madame*," The young Asian hostess led her down a curving staircase.

Cleo had the impression of glittering chandeliers in

arched ceilings, potted palms dividing the cavernous space, and story-high posters of ocean liners from glamorous by-gone days. Families and couples laughed and chatted and clinked wine goblets. Waiters whisked by with loaded trays.

As she followed the hostess toward the back of the room, the two women at the table directly ahead looked up from their menus with smiles of recognition on their faces.

The tall, slim blonde in the hot-pink sequined tank top shot to her feet. "Mimi! Stacy and I were just talking about you."

Just her luck. Of course Mimi would've made friends on board. She stretched her lips into a smile and spoke to the short brunette in conservative black. "All good, I hope, eh?"

The hostess halted and spun on her heels, expectancy on her face.

Stacy's eyes widened in mild alarm. "Oh, totally. We were wondering about your side trip to Venice."

The blonde bobbed her head in agreement. "You can tell us all about it if you join us for dinner."

Cleo had no excuse now that she'd left her locked cell. Carrying off her impersonation had easy parts. Like the hair, the makeup, the clothes. But she could do little about other, more subtle differences.

Like her voice, huskier than Mimi's. And the accent. Though she'd lost her South Carolina honey-chile, the only Canadian she could manage was an occasional "eh." Mimi was friendly but more reserved than Cleo. People tended to see what they expected to see, hear what they expected to hear.

The two women gazed at her with welcome and, yes,

curiosity.

Cleopatra Marie, you can do this.

Definitely. Probably. Maybe.

"Fabulous!" She winced inwardly at her un-Mimi-like effusive tone. "I'd love to."

****

Munich, Germany

At the trill of his mobile phone, Marco Zervas stopped beside a concourse window on the way to his flight gate. Ricci. He barked a greeting and listened intently to the report.

Nedik and Hawkins waited nearby. The bodyguard shifted from foot to foot, watchful but nervous without a weapon under his shoulder. Hawkins clutched his laptop case and chewed his bottom lip.

"You *failed*? Chandler still lives?" Zervas spat into the mobile.

"Yes, and no, *signore*. It is a long story," Ricci said.

Another long story. He summoned patience. Ricci had failed twice. No, three times. The forger died without revealing the necklaces' hiding place, and Ricci's trigger-happy flunky had shot the girlfriend before she could be questioned. The idiot possessed the smoothness of day-old scotch. And no initiative. Finally, he'd needed detailed instructions before he could proceed to ensure she never woke up and spewed all she knew about the necklaces to the police.

Incredible. He'd failed at that simple task too?

"Be clear." He lowered his voice. "You were to take care of this matter Friday night. It is now twenty hours later. Did the cops detain you? Is Chandler dead or not?"

He heard Ricci drag in a deep breath. "The *polizia* did not find me. Chandler lives. But I did not fail. The

65

woman in the hospital is *not* Cleo Chandler."

Announcements about flights drowned out Ricci's next words. He cupped a hand over the mobile. "Details. Did you go to the hospital?"

"*Si*, I wore the white jacket and trousers of the staff. Nobody suspected. I went at the late shift change. A man was inside her room. He talked to her but she did not answer. Still unconscious, I think. I stood there too long and the man heard me. He opened the door and I ran. Some nurses chased me but I escaped."

Zervas pressed two fingers to his forehead to ease the headache taking root there. "But you say the woman in the hospital isn't Chandler. A police decoy then?"

"No, but I did not know the truth until later. I did not want to ring you until I had more information. This afternoon when things seemed safe, I returned to the *piazza* bar. Everyone was talking about the intruder. The man in the hospital room saw my face but he was not in the bar. He looked tough, ugly. Like a boxer."

"An inside guard? Venice police?" He pinched the bridge of his nose.

"No uniform. The nurses said he's an American. Private security."

Zervas gripped the mobile tightly. One of Devlin's Special Forces team now connected to DSF fit that description. But so did lots of security types. "Name?"

"No name but there is now a second man. Also American."

"Description."

Ricci paused, as if checking his notes. "I did not see him. This is from the nurses. They fanned themselves when they talked about him. Tall, handsome, in command. They thought he was the other man's employer or a family member."

Zervas's skin prickled. Thomas Devlin.

"What about the woman?"

"A nurse heard the second American say he knows Chandler and that woman is not her." Ricci's laugh was shaky, his voice choked with relief. "Do you see, Signore Z, I could have shot her and we would not have known it was the wrong woman?"

If the idiot wanted praise, he was shit out of luck. The news would have gotten out, but too late to do Zervas any good. The police, Interpol, and Devlin Security would've been days ahead of him. "Then who is she? And where is Cleo Chandler?"

"I have discovered both." Excitement pumped Ricci's voice like an over-inflated tire about to blow. "On the hard drive from her computer."

****

Shipboard

"Nothing. Shit." Thomas had only one more try before the light went permanently red, locking him out. Cleo would return anytime now from her shore excursion.

He had made it onto the *Emerald* easily enough. Mara had arranged for another passenger to receive word of an emergency at home. And like magic, a suite opened up for him, the only person on the cruise waiting list who could actually board in Palermo. Mara's miracle was like sausage—better not to know the ingredients. When this was over, he'd have to give her a raise or a promotion. And confirm reimbursement for the booted passenger.

He glanced up and down the stateroom passageway while he reset the electronic lock decoder. A housekeeping cart sat at the stern end, but he saw no white-coated steward. An elderly couple shouting at each other in German came toward him.

He slipped the decoder in his pocket, and turning away, faked a sneeze. For good measure, he blew his nose on a handkerchief as they passed him.

When the couple turned into the central section housing the elevators, he checked again. Still no sign of the steward. Only the cart. All clear. A silent whistle escaped him. Running his company from his office had made him soft, slow, too jumpy. Cleo needed him to be sharper.

She was probably safe in the shore-excursion group. Home of the Mafia, Sicilian towns were safe. As long as Centaur didn't hire some mobster to snatch her from her tour. His pulse thumped. Nah, no reason for concern. They couldn't have had the time to organize such a grab, even if they traced her to the ship.

He withdrew the lock decoder. When his tech department supplied Lucas with the device a month ago, they'd insisted it would open any door that required a key card. Not strictly legal but one of the high-tech gadgets for the occasional Interpol gigs they did. Thomas had wanted Lucas to have every possible advantage pursuing Centaur.

And Marco Zervas. The former small-time thief had gone big time. Zervas escaped the CTF's raid on his London townhouse, but in his haste, he left behind a single print. The way Centaur operated, with total secrecy, now made sense. Thomas's former weapons NCO had trusted no one in their team. Being paranoid about his teammates didn't make for good morale. Even if the man hadn't crossed the line, Thomas would've had him transferred.

He tapped in another code from the list. Universal-code cards used by hotel staff and ship stewards were designed to override the unique door codes. The decoder used the same principle but with a pad for keying in the universal codes.

His last chance. It had to work. He pushed Enter.

The tiny light above the stateroom number changed from red to green.

He yanked down the handle and stepped inside the room. As soon as he closed the door, he smelled her. Light scents of lilac and lemon, but also Cleo herself. Feminine yet full of zest.

Or else it was his imagination. And just the ship's soap.

Cosmetics littered the counter beside the closet. Clothing draped chair backs and hung on the closet door. He'd seen the same disarray when he used to hang out with her brothers. Cleo Chandler had moved in.

No time to waste. He stared at the tracking button in his hand. Wafer thin and sheer, virtually invisible. He could track her using an app on his phone. But where to plant it so he could follow her tonight, figure out the best time to approach her? He dreaded her reaction. God, he'd hurt her so badly.

Since her sixteenth birthday, he'd tried to stay away from her. He was ten years older and a soldier, disciplined, hard and tough. Shit, hard was the truth. He'd stayed that way from the moment he came home on leave and saw her in a miniskirt. She was his buddies' little sister, for God's sake, the kid who used to follow them around with Andie. How could he lust for her like a stag in rut?

She was attracted too. That was the rub. When he'd

joined Special Forces, she used the banter from her favorite author as a joke. Whenever he called her *Babe*, she mocked him with *Ranger*. She knew damned well Delta Force wasn't the Army Rangers. When he protested, she only laughed. They teased and laughed but he'd kept his distance otherwise.

Until a few years later before he left for Iraq, when she'd come on to him strong. And hell, horny idiot that he was, he responded, laughing with her, flirting with her, looping his arm around her shoulders. They rode her brother's motorcycle. He could barely straddle the cycle's seat with her breasts snug against his back, her thighs tight against his, and her arms wrapped around his waist.

That night their two families—her parents and his dad—put together a send-off barbecue. Too many toasts and wishes for a safe deployment fogged his mind. But something must've happened between them that she interpreted as an invitation. He didn't remember returning to his room over his dad's garage. He didn't remember getting into the shower. But he sure as hell remembered stepping out buck naked and finding Cleo in his bed and wearing nothing but a sheet.

The shock sobered him in a nanosecond. But not enough. He should've been diplomatic. He could've let her down easy. Instead he told her she was like a kid sister and he wasn't interested. He ordered her out of his room. Her face flamed nearly as red as her hair but she didn't cry. She nearly ripped her blouse and jeans getting dressed so fast. Then she called him a jerk and punched him in the gut before stomping out. When he looked for her in the morning to apologize, her mom said she'd gone to visit a friend and wouldn't be home for a few days.

So for the last ten years, he'd alternated between kicking himself in the butt and wondering what crawling into that bed with her would've been like.

Well, hell, enough reminiscing. He'd attached a few tracking buttons to random bags and pockets but mostly he just spent five minutes reminding himself what an asshole he'd been. If Cleo showed up now, she could order him out of her room, like he did to her. But he preferred to have their first meeting in public so she would listen without slugging him.

His gaze hit on a sketch pad. No help there but he was curious. He leafed through a few pages. Some of furniture layouts and wall treatments. Mimi's, he guessed. The next ones were totally different in every way. Not Mimi's. Bold, sweeping strokes captured the drama of the Italian coast and the busy port of Naples.

He'd known for years Cleo had talent but not like this. Even in black and shades of gray, the sweep and passion of the sketches moved him.

No time to ponder that. He dropped the pad. How could he figure out what shoes, what clothes, what bag she'd choose tonight? Too many possibilities. He was about to give up and try to find her later when he spotted the white square of paper beside the hair dryer.

A seven-thirty reservation at the French restaurant.

Chapter Seven

CLEO TORE HER gaze from the stairway. She'd caught only a glimpse of him.

No, it can't be.

"Join us for the show tonight, Mimi," Deidre held the elevator door open.

"The acrobats are supposed to be amazing," Stacy said from behind her friend.

"Maybe." Cleo blinked away the image. "I'll see how I feel after dinner. I'm pretty tired." True enough. Her feet hurt and her head swirled with the mosaics and frescoes of Palermo's Royal Palace and the Archeological Museum. But mostly what had exhausted her was sustaining a cheerful yet reserved demeanor. She waggled her fingers in farewell.

As the elevator door closed, she looked at the stairs. Four people with DayGlo-yellow T-shirts reading "McCoy Family Reunion" and a woman wearing a swim cover-up and flip-flops were descending. No one going up. No rangy man charging up two steps at a time. Her heart still scrambled from the shock.

She'd glimpsed only the man's back. Khaki pants and green polo. Nothing unique there, but worn like a uniform? And the tilt of his head, the set of his broad shoulders, the aura of power. She'd thought she was over him, over the infatuation and the humiliation, but the sense of recognition had lashed her like a whip. The stinging blow still burned inside her.

Probably the stress of the last few days. Tommy Devlin on a cruise ship? No way.

****

That evening the Cuisine d'Argent hostess led Thomas to Cleo's table. The first sight of her stole his breath. His blood rushed harder and his heart found a new rhythm. Or the rhythm he'd missed since the last time he saw her.

He took the seat opposite her and waited for the explosion. But seeing him turned her to stone except for the myriad emotions flashing across her sea-green eyes—shock and anger, and maybe fear.

He stared right back, drawn to the flame that was Cleo Chandler. Her elfin features seemed more defined. A ruddy flush highlighted her vivid coloring. Strange to see her in something other than jeans and a T-shirt, but of course she wore Mimi's clothing. She'd tied her hair back. A tempting thought, reaching across the small table to free her fiery curls from their ribbon. He spread the snowy white napkin on his lap.

Recovering, she sputtered and looked around as if for rescue, but the hostess had skated away to greet another patron.

"Sorry, Cleo." He smiled. "Unless you can top the fifty I gave the hostess to seat me here, you have a dinner companion."

She sucked down a long swallow of her cocktail, a Campari and soda, if he wasn't mistaken. An Italian aperitif, a long way from her usual light beer.

He gave her a minute while he checked out the scene. White tablecloths, candlelight and flowers, brocade wallpaper. Could be an upscale place in D.C. or

New York, except the view out the window—moonlight carving diamonds in a shield of water.

Couples, a few families with older children. A single man in the corner engrossed in his mini tablet. No one watching Cleo.

Her chin lifted and her shoulders straightened, but high color stained her cheeks. "You wasted your money. My name is *not* Cleo."

Thomas raised a hand and ordered a scotch. When the server left with his cruise card, he raised an eyebrow, pointed to the right sleeve of her blue silk blouse. "You can prove you're not Cleo by rolling up your sleeve. If you have no band of butterflies there, I'll leave you alone."

"I have to prove nothing. You're the one here under false pretenses. I could call Security."

"Go ahead. But it will cause a scene, call attention to you. Raise questions about your identity. Do you want that, Cleo? Or should I call you Mimi?"

The server returned with the scotch. Thomas eyed her as he signed the drink chit and stowed his card. All color had drained from her face, leaving only the shock and a few ginger freckles. And highlighting the smudges beneath her eyes. Not sleeping. Probably not eating much.

They placed their dinner orders. He ordered Coquilles St. Jacques. Cleo chose Boeuf Bourguignon, the first entrée on the menu. She probably hadn't even read the list. He added a bottle of Pinot Gris to the order, and the waiter left.

Deciding to wait her out, Thomas sipped his drink. Good thing they were stuck on a ship or she would hit the road.

She heaved a sigh and moved her small beaded bag from her lap to the table. "Why are you here and how do you know about Mimi?"

"I know what happened in Venice. Your father sent me to protect you."

"My father? But how did he—? Oh, Greg called him." She huffed. "But of course *he* couldn't tear himself away to come in person."

He'd hoped to save this until a more private place. "The admiral's laid up with a broken leg. He's in the hospital." He recounted the rest of the conversation, ending with, "He hadn't told your mom yet when I spoke to him Friday."

She looked stricken, by turns guilty and afraid. Finally her gaze sharpened as if she'd set aside the emotion for the moment. "But why *you*?"

"I'm out of the army. I own a security company. The admiral thought you'd trust me more than one of my operatives. I didn't tell him why you wouldn't want to see me."

The color found her cheekbones again. "You got that right. Tell my father I'm just fine. I don't need your protection. I don't know how you smuggled yourself onto this cruise, but you can smuggle yourself off at the next port."

"That's my plan, but you're joining me."

"No way. As Mimi I'm safe on this ship."

"You're not safe anywhere. By now the bad guys have probably figured out where you are. Centaur will stop at nothing to obtain the missing necklace."

"Centaur, like the mythological man-horse combo?"

Her puzzled frown told him the boyfriend hadn't shared any of his dealings with Zervas's organization.

No involvement. One of the knots in his shoulders eased.

"This Centaur is a criminal organization that deals in contraband art and artifacts. The men who killed your boyfriend took the hard drive from his laptop. Only a matter of time before they trace you by messages between you and Mimi."

"You're making this up. I don't believe you." Her stricken expression belied her words.

Oh yeah, she believed him. After what had happened to the boyfriend and her cousin, she had no choice. She just didn't want the messenger to be Thomas. But there too she had no choice. He had to persuade her to accept his help.

"Cle—" Better if he didn't say her real name, even here. "Look, I know you. You want to believe you left behind all the danger and death, that you're safe. Why do you think they suspect you know where the necklace is?"

She gave a small shrug. "Because of René, I guess."

"Facebook."

Her face went blank. Her eyes shifted away as she realized the ramifications of what she'd done. "The necklace. René took pictures of me wearing it. I thought it was jewelry he made on commission. Was it a copy or the *real* Cleopatra's necklace?"

"So you know what the piece is?"

"I do now. I looked it up in the ship's internet café. Egyptian archeologists discovered her tomb a few years ago, near Alexandria. The find included the necklace."

He nodded. "After they catalogued everything, the government organized a traveling exhibit of jewelry and coins and busts. After all the turmoil and changes in government, they need money. The exhibit opened in London and then went to Washington, D.C."

"But the necklace was stolen before the exhibit could return to Europe and open in Paris." Her gaze sharpened. "This Centaur criminal gang... the art thieves?"

"The obvious suspects, yes. Moreau made at least one copy for them. The police found sketches and measurements in his studio. You could've been wearing either, but both the copy and the original necklace have vanished." He leaned forward, laid his right hand on her small purse, and grasped her left hand with his right. A flash of awareness jolted him. "Let me get you to safety... Mimi."

Tears welled in her pretty green eyes. She shook her head, pulled her hand free. "No, I'm safe on the ship. I'll work something out myself."

"These are dangerous men. You can't pretend everything will be rosy like you used to do when you were a kid. Running won't fix this. They'll find you."

She pushed her chair back, nearly tipping it over, and snatched up her purse. "Leave me alone. I need to think."

Sidestepping the server delivering their meals, she ran from the restaurant. Her wrap-around skirt gave him a tantalizing glimpse of endless legs.

"Will *madame* be returning?" the man asked, his demeanor carefully neutral, as if a tearful spat was a normal occurrence.

Hell no. "Possibly. Leave the plate."

On the back of her abandoned chair lay a black pashmina. Now that he'd planted his tracking button on her purse, he could deliver her shawl later. Her denial and suspicion were understandable. What she'd had to face would traumatize anyone.

But why didn't she ask about Mimi?

****

Why, why, why did Tommy have to show up here?

Cleo gripped the ship's rail with both hands and fought to suppress the sobs crowding her chest. She'd managed okay before *he* appeared. Playing the part of Mimi and laughing with Deidre and Stacy helped keep up the pretense for herself as well as for them, but Tommy had to come along and scrape the bloody scabs off, rub her face in Mimi's death. And remind her of the fool she'd made of herself over him.

And could again.

The rush of water against the hull far below and the cool breeze in her hair should soothe her frazzled nerves. But in the black water she pictured Tommy Devlin's compelling face. No, *Thomas.* Andie said everyone called him that now, even her. He was the reason she hooked up with so many losers, his opposites. She could keep a part of herself distant, so when they hurt her, the pain didn't cut as deep. Oh great, she could analyze her issues but not fix herself. Dammit.

Rubbing the goose bumps on her arms, she jerked away from the rail and hurried inside to the forward elevators. She didn't want to think about any of this tonight. If the damn man bribed the reservations clerk to locate her, he could also find her stateroom.

A few minutes later, she entered the darkened theater. Beyond the sloping rows of seats, the acrobats leaped about on the stage. Halfway down the aisle on the left, she spotted Deidre's bright blond head. Safety. Escape. Perfect.

When the two women saw her, they scooted over to give her the aisle seat.

"I thought you were too tired," Stacy said, leaning across Deidre.

"I felt better after I ate," Cleo whispered.

She crossed her legs and focused on the gyrating figures under the stage lights. The small troupe executed complicated dance-like formations and tumbling to music. Her heartbeat slowed, finally settling.

Deidre elbowed her. She winked and jerked a nod toward Cleo's right. "A hot somebody's watching you."

A charge kicked her heart rate into high. Across the aisle, Thomas Devlin smiled at her.

She frowned and mouthed, *"Go away."*

He pointed toward the stage as if to say, *"I'm only watching the show."*

"Keeping him a secret, huh?" Deidre said.

"I ran into him at Cuisine d'Argent. That's all."

"Looks like he wants to run into you again, hon."

Stacy giggled. "And again."

"Enough," Cleo shot back. "Not interested."

"Mm-mm, if I wasn't happily married, I'd sure as hell be interested," Deidre said.

Face burning, Cleo focused straight ahead on the acrobats. Not on Deidre or Stacy. Some protection they were, with tongues practically hanging out.

No wonder. Thomas was just as sexy as ever.

More. Shoulders impossibly broad in his crisp white dress shirt. Intense and very, very male. A few silver hairs gleamed in his thick brown hair, its unruly nature controlled by an expert haircut. Same square jaw and sensual mouth. Same eagle-fierce dark-amber eyes and slashing black brows. Same take-charge arrogance that used to piss her off, but with the edges smoothed into power and confidence. Confidence that tempted her to lean on him, rely on him. Like he wanted.

Not gonna happen. She was safe here, as Mimi.

She'd left her feelings for him behind her, or so she'd thought. Hot? Yowza. She flashed chills and fever just sitting across the aisle from him. And if his gaze penetrated her reaction to him, he would use his knowledge to get what he wanted.

He wasn't finished trying to drag her back to Dad. To safety, he said, but the admiral hired him, didn't he? Cut from the same cloth. The kind of man who would control you and steer you without you realizing until it was too late. If she gave in and let him take charge, she'd end up living under her dad's thumb again, smothered, stifled, and stuffed into a box of his making.

But Thomas was right. This criminal gang Centaur thought she knew the necklace's hiding place. Or did they want to kill her? Either way, her prospects were grim. The cruise would end, and she'd have to run for her life. And hide again, but how? She knew zip about being on the run, being anonymous. Maybe if she could get far enough away, somewhere else in Europe, she could go to the police.

No police. They're everywhere. René's words sent her reeling. Again.

But of all people why did her dad have to send *Thomas*?

Everyone applauded and the lights came up. The show was over and she hadn't seen any of the antics that wowed the audience. On stage the dozen or so brightly clad acrobats lined up taking their bows.

She stood when her seat companions rose to leave. And Thomas. Her nerves sparked and leaped like the tumblers.

His smile showed perfect white teeth. *The better to bite you with, my dear.* "After you, ladies."

"Aren't you going to introduce us, Mimi?" Stacy's grin was bigger than the ship's buffet.

Without missing a beat, he said, "I'm Thomas Devlin."

Thomas. The name sounded right delivered by his deep voice. And *Tommy* didn't suit the boss of a security company. One who spoke with authority and wore woodsy cologne. She could kick him for smelling sinfully delicious.

Cleo squeezed the introduction to Stacy and Deidre from between clenched teeth.

The two women declared how thrilled they were to meet him. He asked them what port they'd liked so far and seemed to focus on their answers with sincerity. With Deidre prodding her from behind, she had no choice but to walk up the stairs beside Tommy—*Thomas.* Deidre and Stacy fell in behind them.

He took her arm and draped her pashmina over it. "You left this in the restaurant."

"Thank you. How did you find me?"

"A lucky guess."

Oh, right. He'd probably bribed another one of the staff. She seethed, unable to blast him with her two all-ears pals on their heels. How could she shake him?

When they reached the exit, Stacy spoke up. "We're headed up to the nightclub for karaoke. Won't you join us?"

Cleo closed her eyes. *No, no, please say no.*

He laughed, that sexy rumble she'd never forgotten and felt deep inside her, dammit. "Thank you, but I need my sleep. I have an early morning tai chi class."

With a wave, he strode away.

She managed to keep her mouth from dropping open as she watched him go. The man did have a fine rear view. His tailored trousers cupped his firm buns. Muscular legs propelled him. He moved with an athlete's natural and steady grace. Or was it a soldier's erect march?

She should be relieved he was going. What was he up to?

Chapter Eight

THOMAS STOOD TO the side, away from the stateroom door's peephole. He mouthed, *"Now."*

The white-jacketed waiter grinned and tapped on the door. *"Madame?* I bring you clean towels."

A rustling noise beyond the door. Then, "Just a sec."

Thomas held his breath. If she noticed the tray with its covered plate—obviously not clean towels—would she open the door? She could call Security, but no, too risky after what he'd explained.

After an interminable moment, the door opened. Cleo, still dressed in the slinky green wrap dress, gaped at the waiter. One hand flew to her throat, shadows of emotion darkening her expression. Fear? When her wide gaze lit on Thomas, her brows drew together and her mouth thinned.

Before she had time to object, he elbowed his way inside and held the door open. "You left without dinner."

She held up a hand. "You can't come in."

"I'm already in... Mimi." Her hair was loose on her shoulders the way he liked it. Her citrus scent tempted him to soften his approach. But no, he had to make her understand her life was at stake. "No karaoke?"

"Maybe I have an early tai chi class too," she huffed.

"I'll be there if you will." He turned to the waiter, who stared, rapt, at their exchange.

The man's cheeks flushed the brick-red of the carpet

before he ducked his head. He slipped past Cleo and deposited the tray on the cocktail table. "*Buon appetito, signorina,*" he said as he slunk out.

"Thank you, Armando." Thomas closed the door firmly.

"How much did you bribe him?"

"Bribe is an ugly word. He accepted a tip for his services. Worth every penny." He set the goblets on the vanity counter beside the closet and poured wine into both. "I had a glass of this at dinner. Very nice."

"I don't want any."

"You shouldn't have opened the door so readily. The stewards already prepared the room." He gestured toward the bed and its towel frog with coffee-creamer eyes.

"I suppose it could've been an assassin." She rolled her eyes. "Oh, worse. It's you."

"Give me a chance to explain some things, and you'll change your mind."

He put a glass in her hand and closed her fingers around it.

Sipping his wine, Thomas watched her expressive face, emotions clear in her sexy eyes. Resentment. Indecision. Her shoulders lowered a fraction. And resignation.

He might win this round. He skirted the queen bed and sat on the loveseat. Uncovering the plate with a flourish, he inhaled elaborately. "Eat before it gets cold."

"Not hungry." Her nostrils flared as the aromas from the beef dish lured her a few steps closer.

"Right. I just heard your belly growl. Eat. Have some wine."

She sidled over and sat on the other end of the

loveseat. Spread her napkin on her lap, gripped her fork and knife, and glared at him. He could hardly blame her if she attacked. But instead she stabbed the beef.

She held herself rigid as if ready to bolt, color high on her cheekbones. It wasn't *fear* keeping that thick wall of tension between them. He gave her a few minutes to enjoy her meal. Pick at her food was more like it.

"Something we need to get out of the way, Cleo. I apologize for the shoddy way I treated you ten years ago. I deserved that punch in the gut. And more."

She dabbed at her mouth with her napkin and pushed away her plate. Drew a shuddering breath. Shit, he'd made her cry.

But she hiked up her chin and met his gaze with dry eyes. "No, I'm the one who should apologize. I was stupid. I had too much to drink that night."

"We all did, but that doesn't excuse my behavior." An apology? Last thing he expected. Did she regret the whole thing? The reason for her anger and the major attitude?

"Tommy, it was *your* room at *your* dad's house. I sneaked in and climbed into your bed. I thought— Hell, I don't know what I thought, but I was out of line."

"We were both in the wrong. But I should've apologized long before now."

Hurt flickered in her gaze and vanished. Her lips curved in a small smile that zinged around inside his chest. "Just forget it ever happened."

Forget it? How could he when the vision of her totally naked, pale body as she hurried to dress—rose-tipped breasts, curvy rear end, toned legs—was lasered permanently into his cortex. He had a lot to drink that night but not nearly enough to wipe out that memory.

He swallowed, tried to puzzle her out while she returned to her plate. She'd abandoned the beef in favor of stirring around the potatoes. They weren't back to being friends, but it was a step.

Friends? Like hell. Every word in that husky voice licked fire across his skin. Every sip of wine glistening on those lush lips made him want to stretch her out beneath him and bury himself in her.

Although he liked his freedom and didn't pursue serious relationships, he never lacked for female companionship and sex. So why was he so hot for *her*? Hell, he knew why, and the reason began and ended with Cleo. He let his gaze roam over her, still slender but her curves had more… hell, just more. No longer a girl. All grown up, still ten years younger than him, but no longer taboo.

She'd made a life for herself in Europe and had remarkable artistic talent. She'd acted quickly to escape paid killers. More depth in her than he'd realized. Intriguing.

But now this impetuous run would send her into the killers' hands. Protecting her had his priority. With an inward groan, he reined in his libido.

He downed the rest of his wine and divided the last of the bottle between them. "Okay, we won't mention it again. We have more pressing matters. Like your safety."

She shook her head, delectable lips pursed. "Even if the bad guys know where I am, like you said, and I really doubt that. They can't get to me on the cruise. Security checks cruise cards and bags. When the trip ends, the cruise staff will drive me directly to the airport. I'll fly to Canada on Mimi's ticket. I'll be safe there."

She wasn't grasping the practical reality. Or she still objected to *him*. "Not possible. Mimi has been identified. The Venice cops are looking for you. At best, as a material witness. At worst, a murder suspect. You'll never get past customs or airport security."

She recoiled as if he'd hit her with the wine bottle. Until now she'd believed that her ruse fooled everyone. "Okay, that much makes sense. But why are *you* doing this? Why you?"

Hell, they'd been through it. Why was she being so stubborn? Couldn't she see reason? Air conditioning cooled the room, but not him. He felt sweat pop on his forehead. "The admiral knows I run a security company, and he knows I... care about you. Two reasons he sent me."

Her expression hardened. "That's my objection. *He* sent you. I'm twenty-eight years old. I won't let Dad run my life."

Whoa. Where did that come from? Echoes of his sister's complaints. For the first time he had an inkling of the reason Cleo'd stayed in Europe so long. Hoot Chandler was as much a hard-ass as his old man. She'd been running from him longer than from Centaur's thugs.

"No problem. All I'm commissioned to do is protect you until this is all over."

She sipped her wine and seemed to weigh his words. Her eyes narrowed with suspicion. "By *this*, you mean Cleopatra's necklace. I want nothing to do with that necklace or a possible copy. René and Mimi are dead. Finding it won't bring them back."

He stared, his wine glass in mid-air.

A quiver seized Cleo's stomach. Why was he

watching her like that—so intent and grim? She clutched her locket. "What?"

He set down his glass and jabbed fingers through his dark hair. "Mimi isn't dead."

She couldn't have heard him right. She brought her hands up to shield herself. "Whatever you're trying to do, just... don't."

He grasped her flailing hands. In spite of herself, the sensation of his touch rippled through her. "I wouldn't be so cruel. Mimi *is* alive. In critical condition, in a medically induced coma."

"It was my fault. Her getting shot, I mean." *Alive?* Oh thank God! But still her fault. Poor Mimi. Her chest ached and tears muddled her vision. "Those men must've tracked my mobile. The GPS signal."

"More than one? You saw them?"

"Yes, two men." She sniffed, mopped her eyes with the napkin he thrust at her. "They ran off with my suitcase. Mimi was holding it for me while I went around the corner to the ATM."

"Who else knows what happened that night?"

"No one. I haven't told a soul. I try not to think about it." She took her lower lip between her teeth to prevent trembling. "But I... I keep seeing Mimi bleeding on the paving stones."

"I need to know what happened that night. Telling me about it might help."

She steeled herself with deep breaths and latched onto his steadying gaze. She told him everything, beginning with René's lateness and ending with her run for the Rialto Bridge. "I wanted to wait for help to arrive but when I heard footsteps, I was afraid it was those awful men. I ran."

"Probably the ambulance crew. The police found no one in the streets."

"Oh, God, I shouldn't have left her. But I thought she was dead. She had no pulse. No sign of breathing."

"Babe, you just watched Moreau die. You were panicked, shaken. And loss of blood lowers blood pressure. Makes it harder to find a pulse." He lifted her hand and kissed her knuckles. "You saved Mimi's life by calling for help."

She couldn't speak for the tightness in her throat. He pulled her into his arms, and she wept against his hard chest, tears wetting the rich fabric of his shirt. Dammit, she'd promised herself she wouldn't cry. But he smelled so good and his arms felt solid and secure around her.

When she calmed, she forced herself to scoot away, hating the loss of his touch as his arms fell away. He squeezed her fingers before picking up his wine.

She wiped her eyes. Other women looked gorgeous when they cried. But not her. Red nose and puffy eyes every time. She must look like the baby he thought she was. The baby she'd acted like when he sat down at her table.

He regarded her with that penetrating gaze that heated every inch of her, inside and out. "Did you see the men's faces?"

"Just their backs. They were twenty, thirty meters away, in the dark shadows. The man carrying my bag was thin. The other looked shorter and chunky."

His straight dark brows crimped together over a turbulent gaze. His lips pursed as if holding back bad news.

"What aren't you telling me?" she asked.

"The next day an intruder tried to get into Mimi's

hospital room."

She couldn't stop a horrified squeak. "No! God, they're still trying to kill her. *Me.*"

"The attempt failed. My operative was in the room. Lucas Del Rio confronted the man, but he got away. The man Del Rio described could've been the thin one. The head of Centaur doesn't care who he hurts—or kills—to get the necklace."

If only she'd phoned that night to break their date, her cousin would be fine. If only—Nothing. To her shame. She blew her nose. She would *not* cry again. "And Mimi? Will she be safe in the hospital? Is your man still there?"

"For now. Her mother's arriving from Toronto today or tomorrow. The police will release the information that the victim is not you but Canadian citizen Marie Ingram."

"Thank God." Her pulse jacked up a notch. "But that means—"

"Exactly. Like I said, Centaur has the hard drive. They *will* find you and soon. The Centaur head—name of Marco Zervas—thinks you have the necklace or know where Moreau stashed it and the copy. The authorities don't yet know why, but this mess also involves terrorists." He leaned forward, his expression avid. "Do you know the location of the necklaces?"

"I have no idea." She did have René's last words but no idea what they meant. "And I don't care. I never want to see that necklace again. Or the copy. Whatever. Let the police or Interpol deal with it and the bad guys, this Centaur."

The corners of his mouth turned down. Damn, why did he care about finding the necklace? She was too tired to ask. And her head hurt.

"Cleo, come with me on Tuesday. You can't be certain you'll be safe on the ship or the shore excursions. You can't fly on Mimi's ticket or passport. I can protect you."

She pressed her fingers to her aching temples. "I need time to think."

He stood. "I'll go. For now. But whenever you leave this stateroom, I'm your shadow."

"I'm safe on the ship. How many times do I have to say it?" She leaped up from the loveseat and followed him to the door.

"As many as it takes to make it true." He stared at her, determination in the set of his chin. "Do you remember what happened to Fluffy?"

"My turtle?" When they were kids, Thomas had found the small creature and given it to her. "Greg ran over Fluffy with the mower. What does that have to do with anything?"

"Think about it. Your shell of denial won't protect you from real danger." He stopped in the tiny foyer and turned, less than an arm's length away. "Lock up, Cleo. Including the balcony door. And don't—"

"Open the door for anyone, not even stewards. I know. Good night, Thomas." She ought to back away, far enough away not to feel his body heat and inhale his scent. Salt air, evergreens… testosterone. But she stayed, absorbed, mesmerized.

She felt his gaze as a palpable touch, as if he reached inside her, completing that connection she'd once believed existed.

Hot awareness flashed in his eyes before he closed the gap and kissed her. She went utterly still as the blood leaped to her skin. His mouth captured hers, molded, and clung. He threaded his fingers into her hair and pulled her closer, tangling his tongue with hers, tasting her deeper.

Her muscles turned lax and her insides trembled. She wanted the kiss to go on and on, and she wanted much, much more. When he ended the embrace, she couldn't suppress a whimper.

"Good night, Cleo." His gaze held hers for a long moment before he left.

She hurried to push the door shut with a firm click and set the deadbolt. Her breath hitched. So he did he want her after all. She huffed disgust at herself and walked out onto the balcony. Fresh air would clear the crazy notions from her brain. More likely that kiss was another way to get what he wanted— her cooperation.

She'd been an idiot years ago. Apparently she still was. How had she found the guts to fake her way through that apology? Simple. Pretending she'd been drunk humiliated her less than admitting she'd been trying to seduce him all weekend. And failed. Miserably.

Damn. If she left with him, hiding her feelings and avoiding more bone-melting kisses would be impossible.

He was right about hiding in her shell. Running and pretending to be Mimi didn't make her feel any better, any happier, any safer—despite what she'd said to him.

No escape from guilt and grief. No escape from herself. And no idea what to do.

Chapter Nine

Venice

LUCAS STOOD WATCH at the end of Mimi's hospital bed.

"It's Monday, Mimi. Your mom's here. She's in the doc's office getting the lowdown on your injury. Nice lady. She's really scared for you. Told me your real name's Marie. Better. Classier. Like you." He wouldn't say so, but *Mimi* struck him as a stripper name. He tilted his head, examining her. Peaceful, the sleeping princess in that old fairy tale but with auburn hair.

Yellow flowers brought by Trudy Ingram brightened the bedside table. He bent to their light smell before taking his usual seat beside the bed. Medicine trays clattered as a nurse passed by the half-open door.

He tilted his head and linked his fingers with her slack ones, gave a gentle squeeze. The doc had said this human connection might help. Once or twice he thought she returned the clasp. His imagination. Or wishful thinking. The cool touch of her small hand, so delicate, in his big paw sent a shiver over his skin. Damn, she was beautiful. Just looking at her took his breath away.

He cleared his throat. Worked up an upbeat speech. "Hey, Marie, I'm no expert but even I can tell the swelling's down and your color is up. The chart says no fever, so no infection. Docs say you're responsive whenever they lighten your meds. Soon they'll bring you out of it but I'll be gone. Now the bad guys aren't after you, you don't need me."

He didn't need her either. He needed to get back to work.

"Besides, I don't want to scare you back into a coma with this mug of mine. Don't know why I'm telling you all this. You'll never know I was here watching over you." That was the way he wanted it. The way it had to be.

His phone bleeped, startling him. Then he remembered the hospital's tech people had given his phone the green light. On the screen, *Devlin.*

He slipped his hand away, leaving her fingers limp on the green coverlet.

"Hey, Thomas, how's it going? You make it onto the ship okay?"

"Right. Mara should work her magic on Cleo."

His boss's frustrated tone had Lucas's eyes widening. He grinned. The boss wasn't in control? He'd have to meet this lady from Devlin's past. "She's on the ship, right?"

"As Mimi, like we thought. But she insists on staying on board and continuing her masquerade. She's afraid but doesn't grasp the situation."

"You gonna kidnap her on Santorini?"

During the pause, Lucas could almost hear his boss shudder. "It won't come to that. What've you got?"

Lucas knew better than to press the Cleo issue further. He updated Devlin on Mimi, aka Marie, and her mother's arrival. "And I talked to *Commissario* Castelli. Workers renovating a building in Santa Croce found a man's body along with Cleo's suitcase. Suitcase had her passport inside."

"Dead man a short, stocky guy?"

"How'd you know?"

"Cleo saw two men the night of the shootings. Zervas must've ordered the other guy to eliminate this one."

"Castelli said as much. Shot in the head with a nine mil. Could be the same weapon as the other shootings. He suspected the killer counted on the building being abandoned. The construction crew wasn't slated to start for another month so the find was lucky. Glad it wasn't me who stumbled over the fragrant corpse." Lucas wrinkled his nose.

"ID?"

"Not officially. But Castelli recognized the guy. Local hitter named Panaro. The hospital's closed-circuit system caught his partner, once coming in the employee entrance and a second time lurking in the ICU hallway. From Rome, about five-nine, wiry like the second-story man he is. Two convictions. Name's Ricci."

"The thin guy Cleo described."

"Good bet. Castelli's on top of it. But I'm betting Ricci's long gone. I checked with the task force. They connected the name to Centaur."

"You've accomplished a hell of a lot in a short time, Lucas. You had time to arrange my transport too?"

"No sweat. Easy enough while I sit here with Ma— my principal." He had contacts and what he couldn't work out, the CTF did. "I set you up on Santorini."

The two men spent a few minutes discussing security and travel arrangements.

"Now that the news is out about Mimi's identity," Devlin said when they finished, "you can return to duty with the task force. Slight chance the hit men will try again, but more likely their boss cares more about the necklace. Castelli promised a uniform would watch the hallway. About the CTF, you'd better get there A-sap. I've had two calls from Special Agent Hunt."

Lucas groaned. "Don't get me wrong. I'm ready to get back to work. Beats sitting around, for damn sure." Except for one thing. As if Marie had touched his shoulder, he turned toward her. "But there's no pleasing SA Jessica Hunt."

"Ball buster, I've heard, but a crack agent. She's moving forward on finding Zervas." Devlin's tone carried a grin. "I need you back there too. We need new leads on him now he's skipped London. We have to know what Ahmed Yousef plans for the Cleopatra necklace and its copy." He paused. "Mimi'll be safe now. She'll be all right."

Did the captain read his mind? Wouldn't be the first time. Would she be all right? The doc wasn't saying. His gut clenched.

"Yeah. She doesn't need me... my protection... anymore." And it was better Lucas leave before she woke up. "I'll fly to Paris this afternoon."

****

Shipboard

Thomas clicked off his phone. Not good if Lucas was hung up on Mimi Ingram. Not professional and a potential conflict of interest. Deal with it later. Like he'd deal with his involvement with Cleo. No conflict of interest but damned unprofessional.

Why the hell did he kiss her? The darkening of her eyes and the flush on her cheeks had torpedoed his restraint. What began as a little taste became much more, kindling a hunger he couldn't remember feeling for any other woman. Through sheer force of will he ended the kiss before he could take her back to the bed and finish what he'd begun.

She insisted her naked seduction in his bed was a result of too much alcohol. Thinking back, he didn't buy it. Halfway through the evening she'd switched from light beer to Diet Coke. She'd wanted him then and she wanted him now.

Hell, once again she had him hot and aroused. He raised his face to the cooling breeze, hoping it would take the edge off the heat inside him. The weather in Italy had been warm but the farther south the *Emerald* sailed the hotter the temperature. Good thing he'd packed shorts. Baggy shorts.

The locator in his phone app showed him Cleo's quilted backpack at the pool. He left the ship's railing and followed the jogging track past the deck checker game and golf cage. Halting at the corner, he hung back in the shadows.

She lounged in the sun with her two friends, a prime spot on the far side of the Olympic-size pool. No missing her. She shone like the sun in that yellow tank suit. Charming the two women she'd made friends with. An open shirt kept her tattoo hidden but not her body. Her heat rays reached him all the way across the deck. The suit's neckline dived too damned low. Now why did that bug him?

She sat up, a big smile on her face, and slid her glorious legs off to the side.

He followed her gaze to a nearly naked guy carrying a plate piled with food. He crossed the end of the pool and stopped at the end of Cleo's lounge chair.

Thomas's mouth tightened. Abandoning his surveillance cover, he strode to the pool-side buffet and filled a plate before taking a seat facing Cleo. She'd spot him soon enough. He was here to protect her. Seeing him nearby should remind her of that fact.

Who was this long-haired dude? Mediterranean coloring. Twenties, slender but ripped. Wore a fucking Euro thong. He and Cleo shared the plate of food he'd brought from the lunch buffet. She laughed at something the guy said. The sight twisted inside Thomas. Not his business as long as the flirtation was harmless.

But he'd take no chances. If he could get on the ship, so could a killer.

Something about Centaur sending a hit man to eliminate Cleo didn't jibe with their search for the necklaces. He shook his head. His brain would work on it while she simpered at Mr. Thong. And while Thomas enjoyed his lunch.

He stared at his plate. Calamari salad? What the hell? He hated calamari.

****

Behind her sunglasses, Cleo watched Thomas take a seat in the lunch area at the pool's end. His shorts and T-shirt emphasized the mouthwatering definition of his muscled chest and legs. Damn him, *he* was the reason for her restless night. And that devastating kiss that had made her tingle from head to toe.

His mouth formed a grim line and his eagle eyes were trained on her. And on Sergio. What? Did Thomas think Sergio carried a weapon? That thong bikini barely contained or concealed the man's very nice package, let alone a knife or gun.

She smiled as she smeared more sunscreen on her

arms. *Enjoy the show, Tommy.*

"Grazie," she said with an even wider smile when Sergio arrived with the plate he'd fetched for her. The aromas of grilled sausages and pasta salad ought to make her mouth water, but she'd lost her appetite.

He chattered away in Italian about seeing her from the stage last night and dedicating his performance to her. With Thomas across the aisle from her, she barely recalled the show, let alone a single acrobat's leaps and bounds.

Keeping a low profile was her goal. Unavoidable and easy enough to carry on the Mimi charade with Stacy and Deidre, and she liked them. But a guy? Too risky. Not worth the hassle. Especially not with this guy whose breath smelled of fried sardines. A Venice favorite she could never force herself to like.

Goggle-eyed, the two women shifted on their chairs. Waiting for her to translate. They considered Sergio prime cut. To her only a hot dog. If her friends hadn't accompanied her, she'd have avoided him. She'd learned the hard way how to spot a player.

She held up a chunk of sausage. "This is way too much food for me. I'll share. Open wide," she said in Italian. Was Thomas watching?

As his moist mouth closed over the sausage, he kissed her fingertips. Not Thomas's firm lips. Stifling the urge to wipe her hand on her towel, she continued to smile.

She peered around Sergio. Thomas was gone.

****

Thomas ate an early dinner while Cleo was still in her stateroom. Later he planted himself behind a potted palm on the dining room balcony where he could observe her at dinner. Not with the thong guy but with the blonde and brunette. He ordered club soda and tipped the waiter to leave him alone. As always, the first sight of Cleo punched him in the chest.

Why couldn't this just be a job? Why couldn't he stow his ache for her, his damned obsession with her? He signaled the waiter for another soda. After she was tucked in, he'd have something stronger.

By the pool earlier, he'd dumped his disgusting plate of boiled rubber and taken a burger from the grill back to his original surveillance post in the shadows. He hadn't been sure what was going on, but Cleo gathered up her bag and towel and stood. She pressed a hand to her stomach and made apologetic gestures before hustling toward the nearest door. The guy watched her go, his pretty face skewed in bewilderment.

Thomas followed the transponder to her stateroom. He wondered if the guy slipped poison into her food, but through the door he'd heard her turn on the shower.

She was sure okay tonight, cleaning her plate of seafood paella and laughing at something one of the other women said. Whether she'd run off to escape the thong guy or to escape *him*, either way was cool. She'd left the phony stud flatfooted, mouth open.

When Cleo left the dining room, he trailed along at a discreet distance while she and her friends checked out the music at two of the lounges. No karaoke tonight, thank God.

By midnight Cleo closed herself in her stateroom. No one in the passageway. If she left again, the transponder would alert him. He turned back toward the elevators.

****

"Odd," Cleo muttered as the door closed behind her. The stateroom was dark. The steward usually left on some lights after turning down the bed. She slapped the wall beside the door. Where was the light switch?

She heard movement a millisecond before a hard arm banded her waist. The attacker jerked her backward. The air burst from her lungs as she slammed against a muscled body. Another arm came around her shoulders. A sharp blade pricked her throat.

She stilled as if the adrenaline pumping through her system were cement.

"Do not make a sound or I will cut you," the voice whispered in Italian.

That voice. Sardine breath. *Sergio.*

Icy paralysis shifted to blazing heat.

She grabbed the knife-wielding hand with both of hers. Flattened it against her chest, down and away from her throat. She kicked backward. Heard a crack as her kitten-heeled pump connected with bone. He grunted in pain and loosened his grip on her body enough so she could breathe.

She screamed. And screamed again. And again.

The stateroom walls were thick but not the doors.

He stopped her cries with a hand over her mouth. With the other arm, he wrenched her left arm behind her back. Pain shafted through her shoulder. No knife but he shoved her forward. *Oh, God, someone help me!*

She landed face down on the bed. A knee jammed against her spine, pressed her into the mattress. He flattened himself on top of her.

His weight held her immobile. She couldn't kick. Couldn't reach him. Couldn't get enough breath to yell. Foolish of her to talk to him today. All to taunt Thomas.

She'd screwed up again. Her breath came in short gasps.

The son of a bitch fumbled one-handed with something. Ripped at her shirt. The hard ridge of his erection pressed against her butt.

Sick horror clawed at her throat. She knew what would happen next.

A bang. Light spilled into the room.

"Get away from her, you bastard!" a male voice roared.

Thomas!

The door swinging shut blanked the illumination. But the heavy weight lifted. She sucked in air and rolled onto her back as she registered the sounds of a struggle. The solid sound of fists on flesh. Grunts. Furniture crunching. A ringing thump. A moan.

Then silence. Only the rush of wind.

She crawled up the bed. Groped for the bedside lamp button.

Blinking in the flood of brightness, she scanned the room. The sheers blowing inward through the open slider, the broken table, the phone on the floor. Beside Thomas Devlin, on all fours.

Her heart jolted, then raced. She scrambled to him and grasped his shoulder. "Tommy! Are you hurt?"

"Dammit," he muttered as he stumbled to his feet. "Bastard whacked me with something." He held onto the desk and rubbed his nape.

Cleo shivered in the night air. Or maybe it was from fear her attacker could return. She closed the slider and jammed home the lock.

Apparently still groggy, he let her guide him to sit on the loveseat.

"He hit you with the phone." She set the receiver on

the cradle, cutting off its jarring beeping. Her knees gave way and she collapsed beside him as adrenaline fled her body. "He got away."

"I hope the fucker fell off the ship and drowned." His eyes pinched in pain, he ran his gaze over her. "You all right, Cleo?"

She swallowed against the tightness in her throat. "I'm okay. Just..." She had no words for how she felt. "It's not enough but thank you."

He shrugged off her gratitude as if he performed life-saving acts on a daily basis. Maybe he did. Like in Andie's stories about him. He rubbed his neck. She would bring him ice as soon as she could trust her legs.

"Lucky I was nearby," he said. "Did you see where the mugger went?"

"Too dark. I forgot to lock the slider. Maybe he climbed the balconies and left the same way. He's one of the acrobats. Sergio, the guy at lunch."

"Right," he said, as if he knew. "Tell me what happened."

"The lights were out. He jumped me. From the bathroom, I think. He held a knife to my throat. He didn't cut me, just told me to be quiet or he would. He held me so tight I couldn't breathe." She hugged herself to stop the shakes.

"But I heard you scream." He smiled. "Loud enough to summon the entire security force and the Italian navy."

"*Security.* I don't want them to know, do I? They'd arrest me and not my mugger."

"Whatever they'd do, you don't want the notoriety. Let me handle this. Go on."

She nodded. Not that she was agreeing to put herself in his hands. He saved her life, but she was agreeing to zip.

"I took a self-defense course. I didn't learn much but I knew to loosen his grip so I could yell bloody murder. Then he pushed me onto the bed and held me down." Revulsion at the memory vacuumed all the saliva from her mouth. She fingered her torn shirt. "He… he was going to rape me. My own stupid fault for leading him on."

Chapter Ten

THOMAS SHOOK AWAY the horrific image her fear conjured. The stricken look in her eyes almost cracked his chest. "Maybe rape. Maybe something else."

He drew her hand away from the ragged sleeve and held on. Her palm fit perfectly in his. After a moment, the feel of her soft hand in his calmed him, stilled the turmoil and dread. Focused him.

Holding onto her, he reached across the broken table and picked up an object from the floor. "Not your fault, babe. If you'd never spoken to him, it would've made no difference. He was ripping your shirt out of the way for this." He held out the object he'd found.

A syringe.

Her eyes widened and her hand flew to her throat. "Poison? Why? He had a knife."

A knife the slimeball didn't use except as a threat. He must have taken it with him. Another clue to Centaur's plot.

He held the syringe to his nose. Sniffed. Set it on the side table. "This is the kind of poison that subdues, numbs. This stuff has a sweetish smell. Maybe ketamine." He shuddered inwardly. Ketamine had some nasty side effects, probably worse if injected. But now he understood what was going on. "Not rape. Kidnapping was more his aim."

She collapsed back into the seat, her face ashen.

"Centaur?"

"That's my assumption. Marco Zervas keeps himself and his close aides isolated—paranoia about security, probably rightly so—but he has a wide network of contacts. Wouldn't surprise me if that included Sicily. My people will look into it." He took out his phone and texted Mara.

"The Mafia." She still looked shell shocked but more determined than frightened.

"Right. Zervas is desperate for the Cleopatra necklace and he wants you tractable, not dead." Yet. Once Zervas got what he wanted from her, he'd have her killed. Thomas wouldn't allow that to happen. "Mimi being shot probably wasn't his plan either. His thugs screwed up so she had to be eliminated. But now he knows where the real Cleo Chandler is."

She withdrew from his grasp and touched his nape where he'd been massaging it. "You have a nasty lump. You need ice."

He'd take ice but he *needed* a shot of something strong. From the way his body reacted as he watched the sway of her hips, he hadn't taken a bad hit. She dipped a washcloth into the ice bucket and wrung it out. As if reading his mind, she poured him a scotch from the mini fridge. Observing him with a shrewd expression, she handed him both.

"Thanks." The ice felt good on his neck. The liquor felt even better in his throat.

Returning to the other side of the room, she folded her arms. "I don't know where the necklace is but apparently that doesn't matter. They found me and the danger is real."

He nearly cheered. "So you believe me."

"After what just happened I'd be a fool not to."

"This Sergio knows your stateroom location. He could have partners. You'll stay in my suite. Pack up what you'll need for a couple days."

At his clipped words, she cocked her head and straightened her slim shoulders. Rebellion blazed in her green eyes before she banked her ire. Without a word, she turned toward the closet.

Shit, here he was ordering her around like she was one of his SF team. He was more tactful with his employees. But they didn't rile him or challenge him the way Cleo did. Or rock him with a surge of lust. He had use diplomacy with her. Not give her an opportunity to balk. Taking her to safety was the main thing.

Then the necklace. And Marco Zervas.

****

Arlington, Virginia

"You were pretty angry with your brother when he left." Maggie Olsen tucked a strand of brown hair into the loose bun at her nape. Another escapee trailed along one shoulder of her crisp green jacket.

"So what." Andie folded her arms. She knew what her shrink was up to, reflecting what she'd said. An old trick. But the doc had to agree Thomas deserted her.

She glanced around the office. Bookcases crammed to overflowing and mahogany desk empty of all but a laptop, fitting for the therapist's contradictory style. Sailboat prints hung on walls painted an earthy tan. Supposed to be soothing, but the décor didn't work on her. The tightness like a malignant ball in her chest constricted her breathing and made her heart work harder.

"Who wouldn't be pissed off? He sprang that trip

with no warning. He just left." She kicked off her sandals and tucked her feet beneath her, pressing deeper into the couch corner.

"Have you called him?"

"Fat chance of that. Mr. Control thinks he can jet off to God knows where and expects me to keep him posted on when I eat my cereal?" She snorted her disdain.

"Do you think he's worried about you?"

He calls several times a day. I listen to every message, to the anxiety in his voice. "Maybe. Let him worry. He doesn't trust me. I'm doing okay."

"Are you?"

"Sure. Why wouldn't I be? I'm clean. I have been ever since—"

Olsen lifted her pencil from her pad. "Ever since?"

Her shoulders sagged. She blew out a sigh. "Ever since Thomas dragged me off the streets and I kicked the pills and coke."

Dr. Olsen said nothing. Andie hated it when she just waited like this.

"But I've had enough of his ragging on me about where I've been and what I've done. It chaps me I have no freedom. He probably monitors my phone calls." Odd, but he'd never mentioned knowing she talked to Cleo almost daily.

"Ah, but with Thomas away, you do seem to have freedom to come and go, to do whatever you want. Even cancel appointments?" A sly smile played on the therapist's lips. "So how is it going without anyone monitoring you?"

Andie rolled the question around in her mouth as if testing a sore tooth. "Okay, I guess. Work sucks but I get there on time. I do my job. All the other daily stuff. You know." She'd even cleaned her room. Every day she pounded out miles along the Potomac. Like Thomas. Shit.

"Good. That's good. But you're still angry."

"Hell yes. He deserted me and I don't know where he is or what he's doing. Plus I can't reach my best friend. I get out-of-service messages. And she doesn't call."

"You rely on Cleo. Are you worried for her or for yourself?"

"The all-about-me thing. Maybe a little of both. She'll tell me what the deal is when she calls." She hugged her knees to her chest. "But Thomas doesn't tell me *any*thing."

Dr. Olsen scrawled some notes on her pad. "What did he say when he left?"

Andie shrugged. "Some bull about it being confidential."

"Remind me what sort of work your brother does."

"Get real. He pays your bills, doesn't he? Yes, security, so some of his work is confidential. We've been through this before."

"We talked last time about opening up to him more. Have you told him yet what you've been doing with your days for the last few years?"

Andie chewed on her lower lip. "You know I haven't. You're the one who helped me with all that."

"You'll have to make a decision soon. Unless you want to keep working at that bar, going on like this forever. Didn't you just mention freedom?"

"I'm just not ready. You know all that."

"But Thomas doesn't." Olsen put down her pencil. "Why do you think you haven't leveled with him? Is it the same reason you lashed out at him for leaving? Is it the same reason you carp at him for staying, for what you call controlling your life?"

Andie went still as the barrage exploded in her head. Her muscles ached from the way she sat curled into herself. Her heart rabbited so hard she couldn't breathe.

"Here, Andie." The therapist pressed a glass of water into her hand. "Drink."

She sipped the water and squeezed her eyelids shut, noticing only then her lashes were wet. She sucked in air past the raw sensation in her throat. "It's not anger, is it, Doc?"

"Only you know that. Can you describe what you feel? Can you name it?"

Fear. An awful dread that eats into my insides like battery acid. "I'm so afraid I can't hold it together. Afraid I won't make it."

Olsen leaned back in her chair. "Ah, now we have something to work with."

****

Crystal City, Virginia

Max Rivera swung his leg off the upholstered chair and reached for his crutches. Time to call it a day. Damn, he couldn't get this cast off soon enough. Even working his upper body in the company gym didn't take the edge off. Running DSF in Thomas's absence wasn't his thing. Still, he was doing all right. Most of the field operatives already had assignments and reported in per normal. No sweat with the office personnel either. Earlier in the day, some computer snafus had popped up, but like any boss, he'd delegated. He'd had Francine refer the problems to the IT department.

No major challenges, no big issues. Maybe that was

the reason for his frustration—no challenges. Boredom.

He stood and adjusted his crutches. Before he made it around the desk, Barbara Gaspar marched in the open door. The IT director's short afro stood out in tufts like she'd tried to pull it out. She clutched a tablet computer against her pregnant belly.

"Rough day, Gaspar?" Max screeched to a halt, backing up to lean against the desk.

"You could say that. We've been hacked." Gaspar's brown face crumpled. "We have to shut down."

"Hacked? What do you mean?" Unease snaked through Max's gut.

"We have top-notch security. I reinforce the system daily as hackers come up with new threats. We use firewalls and—"

"Take it easy, Barb." Max held up a hand. "I know we're tight. Just tell me what happened. In lay terms. I'm no geek."

The woman shifted from foot to foot. She bobbed her head as if searching for words. "Some hacker installed a program that's taking over our systems. The loser's operating from a remote computer. Accessed our personnel files and deleted some people from the payroll. They eliminated *Mr. Devlin* altogether. They copied our list of clients, and you know how confidential—" She paused, her breathing rough. "And they're attacking our financial records. I've blocked that takeover so far, but I don't know how long that will last. This guy is no cretin." Eyes full of frustration and fury looked to Max for answers.

Gaspar's words hummed in Max's head and his heart jacked into sixth gear. "Tell me what we have to do. Tell me what you need and I'll see you get it."

No challenges? Boredom? Be careful what you wish for.

****

Shipboard

Thomas slugged his pillow hard enough for his fist to punch through to the floor. The damnable sofa was too short and the cushions too soft or hard or some damn thing. Whatever. He'd had no sleep since he brought Cleo to his suite.

Gritting his teeth to remain the gentleman, he shooed her into his bedroom. To *his* king-size bed. Then she stayed an eon in the bathroom, probably cleansing the attack's taint under the shower spray. Picturing the soapy water sluicing over her breasts and ass kept him up—in more ways than one.

He yawned. Finally.

A soft click shot him to his feet, his right hand reaching for the gun he didn't have.

Son of a bitch.

"Oh, sorry."

He turned on the table lamp and squinted in the sudden glare. The soft glow reached Cleo standing in the bedroom doorway.

Her eyes flared as her gaze dropped to his chest, then to his boxers, tented at the sight of her in a white silky thing that fell only to mid thigh.

Her chin shot up. "Um, I couldn't sleep. Every time I close my eyes, I see that dripping syringe and hear Sergio's cruel voice saying he'll cut me."

He crossed to face her. "I'm sorry, Cleo. I wish I'd been able to prevent that."

"Not your fault. I should've locked the balcony door." Her tongue peeked out to moisten her lips. Her hair in sexy disarray over her shoulders, she gestured toward the bathroom. "Thought I'd get a glass of water."

The blush coloring the high planes of her cheekbones told him there was more to her wakefulness than fallout from the attack. She was as hot as he was. He inhaled the scent of her skin, and of her arousal.

Hell. If he got this craving for her out of his system, he could step back. Be dispassionate. Concentrate on getting her out of this mess. Then he could move on.

"Mmm, in a minute." *Or an hour.* "When I apologized for kicking you out of my bed, I meant it. But I didn't explain."

He brushed the hair back from her left shoulder and bent to feather kisses along her ear and down her chin.

Her breathing hitched. "You don't have to explain."

"Oh, but I do. You drove me crazy all weekend, dialed my hormones to overload. I couldn't take you up on your offer. All my life you'd been the kid following us guys around." He was so hard he could barely breathe.

"I wasn't a kid then. I was eighteen."

"A kid. And I was ten years older." As he spoke, he fingered the neck of her nightgown, cruised the back of his hand over the upper swells of her breasts. "Plus, your brothers would've killed me."

Her lips curved in a wobbly smile. Through the thin fabric, he could see her tight nipples poke at the cloth. "Thomas," she whispered.

"Let me finish. I wanted you then and I want you now." He hauled her close, cupped her bottom through the silk and pressed her against his erection. "And you want me."

She trembled in his arms but held his gaze.

"We're both adults. I can't offer more than sex. I'm

still a decade older. You can say no and I'll take my hands off you and go back to the sofa."

Her eyes, molten with desire, searched his face. Without a word, she rose on tiptoes, cupped his face and pressed her soft lips to his.

Chapter Eleven

CLAIMING HER MOUTH, he slid his hands to her bottom, found the warm under curve, so smooth, so firm. So bare. No panties. Tingling heat spread through his chest. He wanted to touch her all over, imprint her softness, her scent, her very being into his skin. Lifting her higher against him, he backed her into the bedroom.

He stepped aside and ducked into the bathroom.

"Don't go away." She laughed, half gasp, half giggle.

Only two condoms in his kit, enough to cool his fixation. When he returned seconds later to the bedroom, he found the nightgown on the floor. Light filtering in from the bathroom revealed her reclining beneath the bed sheet, the halo of her fiery hair, the familiar shape of her face, the ring of color on her arm, the glitter of her eyes. It was as if the past years had vanished. He reeled at the sight.

"Somehow I get the feeling you won't kick me out this time." Her eyes sparkled. She flung back the sheet and patted the bed.

Jesus. His fantasy come true. He knelt on the bed, hands trembling, unable to speak, feasting his eyes on her slim legs, rosy skin sloping over the curves of her hips and stomach, up-tilted breasts with taut nipples begging for his touch.

"Thomas, come here to me."

When she reached for the waistband of his boxers, he stopped her. "If you touch me, this'll all be over too fast. I want you, but I want to give you what you need."

"Show me," she murmured.

"Right. My intent exactly." He stroked the fullness of one breast, then the other. His fingers found her nipples, and he smiled when she sucked in a breath. "Oh, yes."

His climax already clawed at him and he'd barely touched her. He'd always had enough control to give as much pleasure as he received. He intended to enjoy her completely, to make up for all the lost time—for both of them. When had he ever felt so charged, so alive, so aware? He dug for control. He'd have to start counting backward from a million.

Sliding onto the mattress by her side, he continued his exploration of her body, the textures of her skin, her hair, her lips. Licking her nipples evoked murmurs. Stroking and kissing her curves made her whimper. Gliding down her body to flick the sensitive cleft caused her to vibrate in his arms. If he'd known before she was so passionate, he'd never have been able to resist. His skin was hot, prickly, the cotton boxers too confining, so he kicked them off and away.

She kissed him with unabashed eagerness, ran her soft hands through his hair, over his shoulders and down his back, writhing against him, urging him to her. "Thomas!" Her breathing was ragged, her voice rough, and he caught her cry in his mouth.

"Not yet. There's no rush. Just lie back and enjoy." He suckled and laved, kissed one breast and then the other, until she was hot and trembling. He kissed her, memorizing her taste, licked his way down her body until he thrust a finger inside her, and a second, thrilling at the intoxicating scent of her arousal mingled with the sweet essence of her skin. As she lifted her hips to him, he thrummed with tension, feverish and aching.

When she stroked him, gripped him, the heavy pull deep in his body thundered the blood in his head. He covered himself and joined them, lodging himself in her tight body, gritting his teeth as she murmured his name.

He stroked and rocked her, his release licking molten flames up his spine. She shimmied her hips, clutching him, kissing him, moving with him, until he could barely breathe. When the ripples of her climax squeezed him, tugged at him, pleasure jolted him, streaming molten silver through his veins, and he let himself go, soaring with her, his whole body exploding.

****

At the small table by the balcony door, Cleo sipped her coffee and wished for something stronger.

Last night they'd made love a second time, more slowly, without the initial frenzy. Sex with him was electrifying, amazing and thorough, no slam-bam race to the finish that left a woman empty. Once he'd kissed her, she knew resisting what she wanted, what they both wanted, was futile.

Hearing the shower blast on, she knew she had little time to steel herself.

After he helped her to safety, he intended to stash her under guard somewhere. She couldn't allow that to happen. Part of this mess was her fault. What she intended to do scared the crap out of her. Physical danger, yes. The prospect terrified her. But so did remaining with Thomas. Another wrong man, though honorable and commanding and strong. Wrong because

117

he *was* controlling and stubborn.

The more time she spent with him, the more intimacy they shared, the deeper she would fall into something—she refused to name it—that could only end, and with a broken heart. Or maybe being under a male thumb. Diving in where the undertow could drag her to the bottom might be worth the risk of drowning. A second time. But now wasn't the time to test the waters. Not with danger pricking the waves around them.

A moment later he came out, sexy as hell in jeans and a black polo. He crossed to the desk where two covered plates and an insulated carafe crowded a tray.

"You shouldn't have opened the door." He poured coffee into the second white ceramic mug and lifted the cover from a plate. The aromas of hot croissants and scrambled eggs arrowed straight to Cleo's empty stomach. She should eat, but after their talk.

"Coffee would've gotten cold." She blessed him with a sweet smile. "I had him leave the tray by the door. I waited until he left."

"I see more holes in that tactic than in a block of Swiss cheese." Desire still gripped him, judging by the way he started to reach for her before he wrapped both hands around his coffee. "Couldn't sleep?"

After their second go-round, she'd heard *him* snoring. She hiked up her chin. "Speak for yourself. I slept like a baby in that comfy bed."

"Glad to hear it." He grinned. "No nightmares about what's-his-name, Sergio?"

"Maybe one." Cleo lifted one shoulder. In truth she hadn't slept soundly enough *to* dream. "But I imagined myself kicking him in the balls. After that, it was all good. I thought you were a tea drinker."

"Right, but always coffee in the morning. Stronger than this stuff." He lifted the pot and raised his eyebrows. When she shook her head, he poured more for himself.

Heat suffused her belly as memories of last night in his bed flashed through her head. *Note to self: Hang tough. Again.*

She couldn't bear to drink more of the tasteless coffee but kept the mug, needing something to hold. Her nerves sparked. Thomas just had to agree. If he didn't, could she carry out her threat?

She crossed the room, away from his laser gaze and the temptation to throw herself into the protection of his strong arms. She leaned against the desk, arms folded. "Yesterday afternoon I read my printout about the necklace theft more carefully. And guess whose company name I ran across. How did such a professional security organization as Devlin Security Force lose Cleopatra's necklace?"

She caught his wince. He hadn't expected her to uncover their involvement.

A sigh of resignation. "Wondered where you were going with this. You're right. We handled security for the entire Cleopatra collection on its move between D.C. and Paris. At the airport, my operatives turned over the crates to uniformed guards. They signed off. When the exhibit didn't arrive at the museum on schedule, we— and the French police—discovered the real guards stripped, tied up, and unconscious in an alley. Gendarmes found the truck later, crates open and searched, the most valuable pieces missing, including the high gold collar."

"Discriminating thieves."

He left the table and ambled toward her. He gripped

the desk edge, bracketing her between his arms, trapping her with his gaze. "Items they could haul away easily. Sell quickly. We've recovered some of the stolen pieces, but finding the necklace is urgent."

He was close enough for her to see the brown rim around his dark-gold irises. To catch his clean scent. To feel the heat of his focus. Every atom in her body stood to attention at his nearness. Every hair prickled. She swallowed, stared back, kept the mug between them, hoping he couldn't hear the deafening thump of her heart.

Last night made it damned tough to carry this off. "Recovering the necklace is personal. You're here not just to protect me. You want the necklace as badly as Centaur does."

He didn't flinch at her accusation. "I want it recovered, yes. Zervas wants it to complete a deal with an Iranian terrorist. Del Rio left Venice yesterday. He's back in Paris with the task force and should be working on that issue."

"And you think I know where the necklace is, like the bad guys."

He brushed her hair back from one shoulder and twined an index finger in one wayward curl. "Nice loose over your shoulders. Freestyle Cleo. You told me you don't know where Moreau hid his or the original. I believe you."

Her scalp prickled. She shivered, wishing she could step away, wishing she could step into his arms. "Thank you for that. I *don't* know. But I do have a clue to its location."

He jerked upright. "Cleo, don't joke."

She slipped away and dashed to the balcony, where

she could catch her breath. "Thomas, I'm not joking," she recited, mimicking his tone.

He herded her back into the room and closed the slider. "Too many ears out there."

She evaded his grasp and moved away but came up short against the sofa. With his pillow and rumpled blanket. Before he'd joined her in the king bed. She flashed on a vision of them tangled in the covers. Whoa. She skirted the sofa but the maneuver got her nowhere. He dogged every step.

She stopped at the table, set down the mug, and folded her arms. "I'm not joking. I'm negotiating. I don't have to go anywhere with you. The acrobats, Sergio included, leave the ship today. I'll be safe here for the rest of the cruise, as I said before. I can't use Mimi's airline reservation, but I have most of Europe to hide in. If you want my cooperation, you'll have to agree to my conditions."

His jaw clenched, likely so it wouldn't drop to the floor. "Babe."

"Ranger." She cocked a hip, scowled.

From his expression, she guessed he regretted falling back on their old banter.

"This is serious, Cleo."

"Then don't patronize me with *Babe*."

"You're right. A knee-jerk defense. My apologies." He heaved a sigh. "Conditions? Plural?"

"You won't shut me away in some safe house. I want to be in on the search."

"Out of the question. Too dangerous." She could see him struggling for calm, reason. "Why?"

"For Mimi." She expected him to consider her idea crazy. He would refuse. At first.

On a heavy sigh, he ran his big warm hands down her arms, held her hands, watched her as if fearing she would dash headlong into a Centaur ambush if he didn't restrain her. "You'll have to explain."

She raised her chin. "When René agreed to make a copy of the necklace for Centaur and then betrayed the crooks, he set his own course."

"They'd have killed him anyway. Like they silenced others of their forgers."

She suppressed a shudder. "That fits with something he said before he died."

"So he spoke? And told you where the necklace is?"

She huffed. "Let me finish. I was shocked to learn he was a forger and mixed up with a criminal gang. I should've seen, should've realized. Maybe I blinded myself to reality, maybe I was just naïve."

"This wasn't his first time crossing that line. Centaur hired him because he was a known jewelry forger. He knew how to hide what he was doing, even from you."

"Thank you for that." She managed a small smile. "I'm sad about his death, horrified at his murder, but I had nothing to do with it other than hooking up with the wrong guy." He didn't need to know René hadn't been her first wrong guy. "I didn't know any of that. But Mimi? What happened to my cousin is my fault. A vision of her lying in a hospital bed, connected to tubes and monitors makes me sick. *I'm sorry* doesn't cut it."

"Mimi will be all right." But the downward shift of his eyes belied his confidence.

"I hope and pray she will. But her recovery won't make up for talking her into leaving her cruise to visit me. And more, what I didn't do. Seeing René die and hearing his warning erased everything from my mind except escape. If I'd phoned Mimi to cancel our late date, she'd never have been hurt."

"No, Zervas's hired gun would've shot you instead."

His words struck her like bullets. This time she couldn't conceal a shudder. "I know."

"Finding the necklace won't change any of what has happened."

"Of course not. But I have to make amends. I *have* to. You said they were keeping Mimi sedated until the swelling went down. Can you swear she'll be whole again, that she'll recover?"

He looked grim. "The doctors won't know until she wakes up."

"She could still die. Or be permanently injured. And it would be on me." When he started to object, she pulled a hand free and pressed it against his chest. His muscles tensed beneath her fingers and his eyes darkened.

She steeled herself against his energy, against her own emotions. "Let me finish."

"Go ahead."

She was about to bare her soul, reveal her failings with his unrelenting gaze boring into her. She couldn't look away or move away, although he'd released her hands.

"During the past few years," she began, her voice reedy, "I've learned to rely on myself." Her voice grew firmer, as if absorbing his strength through her fingertips. "I made mistakes but they were *my* mistakes. If I caused pain, it was only my pain."

He jabbed his fingers through his hair. "Cleo, you're intelligent and imaginative. I've always known you to be genuine, to follow your instincts. But usually those instincts meant running *away* from pain and toward the next bright thing, not *toward* danger."

So much for admitting her failings. He already knew them. Well, most of them. "True. But not this time. I can't escape the pain and guilt of Mimi's suffering by running off to a new adventure or immersing myself in a new painting. The necklace really has nothing to do with Mimi, but the search for it caused her injury. I want to believe she'll be all right, so *when* she recovers and I see her again I can tell her I didn't just sit in a corner and wait for you to fix things. I *acted*."

She managed only shallow breaths as she waited for his next argument. In his gaze were the perception and decisiveness he'd honed to fierce perfection in the Army.

"Well, Thomas? Do we have a deal?"

He caressed her hair, trailed his hand down her neck, eliciting a tiny shiver. "You hold the cards, babe. We'll work out the details later."

Wonder of wonders, he wasn't arguing further. And this time *babe* had a different sound, an affectionate feel. She started to hug him but curbed the impulse, awarding herself a virtual high five for self-restraint. "I need your promise you won't back out of our agreement after I tell you René's clue."

"How do you know you can trust me?"

"I know you. When we were kids, you never broke a promise to me. My brothers did, all the time. But you, never."

"You don't know me, not anymore."

"We'll have to trust each other. Give me your promise we're partners in the search for Cleopatra's necklace."

"I promise." He smiled, a slow, breathtaking curve of lips that pooled sensation between her legs. "But a promise should be sealed with a kiss."

His mouth closed over hers.

His heat seared her senses. He slid his tongue along the edges of her trembling lips, then probed inside, sampling and savoring. She absorbed his coffee-flavored taste. Spiraling pleasure and yearning not stemmed by last night's loving flooded her veins, and her heart beat a tattoo in her chest. Barely aware she even had legs to support her, she wrapped her arms around his waist and answered the kiss with equal passion.

She wanted to yield to the seductive pull of his compelling masculinity. His compassion and caring tempted her to forget he was a man used to command, a man who could be ruthless to achieve what he wanted. Right now he wanted *her*.

Pushing gently against his hard chest, she ended the kiss. "Thomas, I can't."

She felt his arms slip away from her with reluctance.

He stepped back, eyes unfocused, breath coming in gasps. He jabbed fingers through his hair, shook himself to alertness. "Can't?"

She nodded, hoping she didn't appear as shaky and uncertain as she felt. "Last night was wonderful, but it was last night. If I'm to get through what's probably facing us, I need to put that aside. No kisses. No sex." She forced her lips into a smile.

"Right." He sidled toward the suite door. "I need to pick up some things. Um, from the shops before we reach port." He bolted out the door without reminding her to stay put.

Thomas Devlin, shaken, inarticulate. A first. She smiled, inordinately pleased.

Chapter Twelve

BEFORE NOON, THE *Emerald* tied up to mooring buoys in the deep waters of Santorini's volcanic caldera. Thomas made certain Stacy and Deidre had left for their shore excursion before he and Cleo boarded a beamy orange tender.

They squeezed between other passengers in the stern, packed as tightly as in a military transport, but with the benefit of a cooling Mediterranean breeze and a view of the crystalline Aegean basin. From that vantage point he could observe the other passengers as the craft sped to shore.

"Any sign of Sergio?" Cleo whispered.

He shook his head, savoring the puff of her breath against his ear and the familiar perfume of her skin. "There were earlier trips, so he could already be on shore. With other hired thugs."

"And on the lookout for me, the bastard."

Her bravado didn't fool him. He draped his arm around her shoulders, the only comfort he dared offer after his earlier loss of control. What the hell had he been thinking, kissing her? Easy answer. He hadn't thought. He'd simply acted. If she hadn't come to her senses, he'd have had her naked. Again.

Yielding to his need—correction, desire—for her now was nuts. After the danger passed, a few nights in his bed, a hot fling would satisfy his craving for her, only

126

sharpened last night. They were polar opposites. Cleo breezy and enthusiastic and fascinating. And he was, hell, a workaholic and boring.

And the age difference. He used to think of her as another little sister. Why was he so preoccupied with her? He had to control his impulses before he crushed the fragile friendship they'd begun to rebuild. More important, he had to regain objectivity before he endangered her further.

Right, now he had a mission strategy. So why didn't he feel better?

She'd extracted his promise but, dammit, had yet to share Moreau's clue.

After another check of their fellow passengers, he turned his gaze to the island's limestone cliffs, created millennia ago by a volcanic eruption and soaring skyscraper height above the harbor. Tourists on donkey back negotiated switchbacks, and chains of cable cars angled up the slope to Thira, its cube houses and domed chapels gleaming white beneath the clear sweep of sky.

Two boats rocked gently at the cement docks. A sign in English and Greek identified one as the inter-island ferry. The other was a speedboat with twin Mercury 350s. Beside it stood three burly men smoking. A good bet they were Sergio's cronies.

Cleo spotted them too, judging from her scowl.

As sailors tied up at the dock, all his senses energized into battle-ready mode. He hoped he'd thought of enough to fool the kidnappers. "All set, babe?"

"Roger, Ranger."

Her smile wobbled but if she could crack wise, she'd make it. He stood and hooked his arms into the pack he'd bought earlier. Their escape meant leaving behind belongings but he had some clothes and his phone. But damn, he felt naked without a sidearm.

On the dock, two uniformed police officers or harbor police with holstered sidearms chatted up the voluptuous blonde in the souvenir stand. The speedboat guys could snatch half a dozen women and take off before those cops ever noticed.

Cleo adjusted the broad-brimmed sunhat, his other purchase, keeping her features concealed as they stepped into the hot sun. "Two cops, not much protection against those big thugs." She hustled along with him to the cable-car line.

Thomas picked out Sergio but the acrobat appeared not to spot Cleo. A long line snaked ahead of them along the quay to the ticket booth. The longer they had to wait, the more chance for discovery.

"Might not need the cop." He hoped. The two officers looked too young to have experience with any bad guys more dangerous than pickpockets. "Sergio and company won't chance snatching you among all these other passengers." Plus, the goons were looking for a woman alone, not a couple.

"Junior here was a good idea." She patted her padded middle and switched the black quilted pack to her other shoulder.

Thomas heard loud commands in Greek erupt behind them. Angling his head, he saw a white-shirted cable-car company employee trying to shoo Sergio away from the queue. The acrobat had moved halfway along in a search for Cleo.

"Stand in front of me," Thomas ordered. He moved to block anyone behind them from getting a good look at her. "Turn slightly to look out at the water."

"Is it Sergio? Does he see me?" Her voice vibrated with fear. The creep's attack last night had done a number on her. And yet today she was ready to face the threat again.

Sergio must've said something convincing to the official because he once again advanced, surveying every female in the line. Thomas had fifty pounds and a few inches on him. While it would give him great satisfaction to deck the guy, a scuffle might draw in the other thugs. And the cops.

He clenched his jaw. "I've got you. We'll make it. Follow my lead."

Taking her hand, he pulled her up the line. "I'm sorry. My wife's not feeling well. We need to get up to the top, get her some cool water."

Already ashen with fear, she didn't need to do much acting. She flattened a hand against her protruding belly and offered a wan smile. Outraged countenances morphed immediately to sympathetic expressions.

Sergio yelled as they reached the ticket booth.

"He sees me." Her voice rose in pitch. She clutched Thomas's sleeve. "He's calling the others."

"Right. Keep moving." He shoved euros into the booth and plucked up the tickets.

Behind him, the same passengers who had allowed them to pass confronted Sergio and another goon with a solid wall of resistance. The cops joined the fray, Thomas pelted with Cleo up the stairway to where the cars waited, swaying on their cables.

They joined four others in the last car. As soon as the official secured the door, the chain of cars began gliding up the cliff.

He looked back but saw no sign of Sergio or the

others.

She sighed and laid her head on his shoulder.

"You'll feel better soon, dear." The matronly woman with gray curls sitting across from them smiled, indulgence in her soft gaze. "The first few months are the hardest."

"Thank you," Cleo replied. "I feel better already."

Thomas didn't. He wouldn't feel better until he got her off this island to Mykonos and aboard a plane to Athens. And picturing her slim form round with child—*his* child—didn't improve his objectivity.

Once disgorged from the cable car, they bought bottled water at a kiosk and asked directions to the taxi stand.

Cleo opened her bottle and savored the cold liquid. Her stomach was settling and her pulse finally normalizing. No wonder the woman in the cable car had been sympathetic. She must've looked positively grim from fear and heat. The only thing keeping her going had been Thomas's strong arm and his determination.

This might not be the last scare or the last narrow escape. If she didn't keep herself together, she'd never help him find the necklace, never hold up during the chase ahead, and never stand up for Mimi.

She dumped her belly pillow in a trash can and unwound the scarf that had held it in place. "Ah, better. I wonder if being pregnant is hot like that."

When Thomas made no reply, his rigid mask and long-distance stare told her he was on guard. She knew his military bearing, but not this wired, preternaturally alert aura. Scary protective. And lethally sexy. She'd love to sketch him. And more… *Note to self: Not going there. Stay focused.* She averted her gaze to the crowded lane of shops and restaurants.

They made their way through the maze of cobblestone pedestrian lanes lined with white-walled shops and houses. Olives in jars and cans, olive soaps, and T-shirts crowded shop displays. As they passed an outdoor café, aromas of lamb dishes and a sign for the local white wine reminded her she hadn't eaten much breakfast.

The brightly painted doors and the balconies and stoops splashed with bougainvillea and potted flowers charmed her. If they got out of this fix, she'd come back and paint these incredible scenes.

No, *when* they made it out. She pictured Cleopatra wearing the choker with its armor of jewels. The Queen of the Nile would be tough, bold, not quivering like a wet kitten.

When they reached the traffic-filled commercial street away from the souvenir shops, Thomas showed her his phone screen. "Del Rio said to look for this license number. He knows the driver. We can trust him."

"You keep looking for bad guys. Didn't we leave them at the bottom of the cliff?"

He regarded her with a soldier's cool vigilance. "That set of creeps, yes, but they could ride the next cable-car. We need to make it to the airport before they catch up. And others could be anywhere."

She swallowed as her pulse fired up again. She forced calm by searching the license tags. A European Ford waited third in the taxi line. "The tan Ford, that's the taxi."

She waited as Thomas scanned the area in a three-sixty sweep. A break in the two-way traffic allowed them to dash across the street, and he called to the driver.

The fortyish man named Andres smiled at the mention of Lucas Del Rio. "Ah, yes, Lucas said I should expect you this afternoon." A thick accent colored his English.

After handshakes all around, Andres ushered them into the taxi. In spite of the open windows, the interior smelled of the remnants of previous passengers—cigar smoke and perfume. Other drivers made vociferous objections to a driver taking passengers out of turn but Andres yelled something that quieted them.

"I told them you were my cousins from America." He chuckled as he pulled away from the curb into the bumper-to-bumper traffic on the narrow street. Voices, traffic noise, and exhaust blew in through the open cab windows.

"Del Rio did tell you there are men are after us?" Thomas leaned forward.

Andres bobbed his head. "I have a car for you, not far. You will blend in."

The transfer was meant to throw off any pursuers who saw them enter the taxi. Thomas had shared with her all the security steps he and Del Rio agreed upon. Knowing what they had to do gave her more confidence than being in the dark.

Note to self: The Queen of the Nile would deal.

A few turns onto a back street took them to an auto repair shop where mechanics toiled beneath a pickup on a lift. Andres led them to an older Fiat parked beside the garage. The go-cart-size vehicle was probably white beneath its layer of dust and dents. "The mechanic loans it to customers. I will return it to him later."

"It's not a long ride, right?" Thomas asked.

"Only twenty minutes. Very fast. A shame you

cannot stay longer and enjoy my beautiful island." He handed Thomas the keys and a map. "The airport is small. My brother Theodoros works for Avis. I wrote his number and mine on the map. Call him before you enter. He will spot any danger. Suspicious men will stand out."

"And the other thing Del Rio mentioned?" Thomas said, his voice and expression harsh as if he suspected a betrayal.

"A request more difficult to arrange." Andres gestured toward the car. "In the glove box. If not needed, I can return it."

"Andres, my friend Del Rio chose well in contacting you," Thomas said, reaching for his wallet. "What do I owe you?"

The cabby shook his head. "My youngest brother owes Lucas Del Rio his life. Marios borrowed money. He did not know his lenders were criminals until too late. He could not pay and they would have killed him. When Lucas rescued a kidnap victim, he also helped my brother escape. Those criminals went to prison, and Marios attends university in Athens. My family does not forget. Whatever Lucas asks of me, I do."

Hearing the emotion roughening the man's voice warmed Cleo. Mimi wasn't the first person Lucas Del Rio had rescued. She had to meet this man and thank him.

"He is an honorable man. And a good friend," Thomas said.

After handshakes all around and Andres's departure, Thomas held out the car keys. "Can you handle driving on these roads?"

She snatched the keys and slid inside the car. "I'll have you know I've negotiated Paris and Rome traffic.

Little island roads will be no problem."

Folding himself into the Fiat's passenger seat, he groaned at the tight quarters for his long legs.

"Good thing the car's owner isn't Procrustes."

He eyed her with a wry expression. "I'll keep the length of my legs, thank you. Been reading up on Greek mythology?"

"Nope. I remember that story from school. It gave me nightmares."

He reached into the glove box and extracted a cloth bundle. Unfolded, the padded cotton displayed a steel-gray pistol and two magazines.

She sucked in a breath. "Is that like the pistol that…" She couldn't say the words.

"Yes, like the nine-millimeter that shot Mimi. A common weapon in these parts." He examined the weapon. "In good condition." Apparently satisfied, he inserted one of the magazines and checked the safety before returning everything to its hiding place.

The reason he wanted her to drive. "I can handle a gun." Not that she wanted to. Channeling Cleopatra went only so far.

"I remember. We all used to do target practice together." His gaze softened, a slight crinkling around his eyes, before his expression reset in concrete. "But could you shoot a moving target? A *human* target?"

She forced a swallow down her tight throat. "I'll drive. I assume you can read a map. Or do you rely on GPS these days?"

"I use GPS but on this island, a map will be more reliable."

Plastic rattled as he set a plastic shopping bag in her lap. "What's this?"

"Something I picked up at a food stand when you were gawking at the local scene. You need to eat."

Damn, he was feeding her. Again. The first time had been a ploy to get into her stateroom but this time he was taking care of her. She could barely stop herself from pulling him closer for a kiss. The food would have to do. Her mouth watered. Inside the bag she found rolls, hunks of cheese, and grapes. The cheese was deliciously sharp, the roll thick and crusty.

Revived by the nourishment, to her body and her spirit, she started the small car's engine. She maneuvered around a small three-wheeled produce truck and returned to a main street. Pedestrians spilled from sidewalks. She inched the Fiat along, unnerved by the mopeds zipping among the taxis, tourist buses, and three-wheeled trucks.

Following his directions, she took the south road. At the edge of Thira, a sign for Monolithos displayed an airplane symbol. Traffic thinned and the road narrowed and twisted, one S-curve after another along the hills, permitting barely sixty-four kilometers an hour. Forty miles per if she remembered correctly how to convert. A tossup which scared her more, the bad guys or driving these crazy roads.

Thomas kept watch behind them while he wolfed down his lunch. At her questioning glance, he said, "Only taxis and a tour bus behind us."

Before long they turned inland, the narrow roads no less winding through the rugged terrain. Beside the car, vines straggled among a stand of pines and then the vista opened before them.

Clusters of the white cube houses, vineyards, and olive trees splashed the green ridges. She imagined smelling the ripe tang of olives on the breeze. The glorious scenery kept her from paying too much attention to Thomas's evident tension. Neither said much until they reached the airport.

"Find a place to park and I'll phone Andres's brother," he said.

The International Airport of Santorini was a low-slung white building. A covered stairway climbed up from the road but a parking sign sent her around to the side.

She pulled in between two cars. "Guess I should leave the motor running."

"You're catching on."

As he keyed in the number, she stared at the entrance's open doorway but could see little of the shadowed interior.

"Andres gave me this number," he said into the phone. "He said you'd know if the airport is safe." He listened, face impassive. "Right. Too warm for a jacket. We'll leave."

"What?" Her pulse raced.

He lifted the pistol from the glove box and laid it in his lap. "He says three men have been hanging around for an hour, watching the door. Theodoros doesn't see two of them just now, but he thinks one carries a gun under his jacket."

She gripped the wheel so hard a knuckle cracked. Her pulse kicked up a level but she refused to panic. Thomas would know what to do. *Cleopatra* Chandler would do her part.

He adjusted the passenger side mirror as they left the airport grounds. "Take the road south and double back."

"What? What is it?"

"Maybe nothing. An old Jeep Wrangler drove out

behind us." He palmed the nine-millimeter. His face turned to stone, his lips flat. "This Fiat Punto has less than a hundred horses but it should manage the curves better than the Jeep. Go as fast as the road allows."

As she turned south, she glanced in the mirror. Could the two men she saw in the Jeep be Centaur thugs? She prayed for more traffic. Witnesses. Vehicles had clogged the town of Thira but few other cars appeared out here in nowhere.

She accelerated but the bigger vehicle kept pace, about three car lengths behind. How could she stay ahead in this tiny car? She ripped the steering wheel to the right around the next hairpin. The Fiat hugged the curve, almost skimming the stone-wall guard rail. A horn blared as an approaching tour bus lumbered past.

When the Wrangler took the curve behind them, it rocked and fell back a little. But still too close. She could see the men's broad faces, focused and grim.

Her next glimpse behind stole her breath. One guy leaned out of the open window. He aimed a large gun at them. Her heart climbed into her throat.

"Floor it!"

She gripped the wheel with clammy hands and stomped on the accelerator. The little Fiat's engine whined in protest.

Gunshots cracked like small thunderbolts. Pops and thunks jolted the car's rear end.

Chapter Thirteen

"DUCK AS LOW as you can," Thomas yelled. "Weave back and forth. Give them less of a target."

"This is no snake," she gritted between her teeth. "I'm driving a roller skate."

The Jeep inched closer. Fuck, they had major firepower, not just a small semi-auto like his. Judging from the pistol's long barrel, maybe a bigger auto.

With the Fiat swerving on the winding road, his aim would be worse than a one-eyed dog's, but a few shots might force the other guys back farther.

The small engine screamed as they whipped around another switchback. The tires held traction.

He flicked off the safety and racked the slide. The fucking Wrangler was closer again. But the big, shiny grille made a prime target. He fired three shots and ducked back inside.

More gunshots rang out. Only one bullet drilled into the Fiat's rear. Aiming for the gas tank, he guessed. But his shots had backed them off, hindering the gunman's aim.

"You okay, Cleo?"

"Oh, sure." She hunched over the steering wheel, brows bunched, eyes wide, and her face as white as the few houses on the steep slopes around them. "I'm prepping for the Grand Prix next."

A sign announced a crossroads, forcing everyone to

slow. He glanced quickly at the map. "Don't stop," he said. "Hang a right. It'll take us north."

Cleo wrenched the wheel right at the intersection, barely missing a car at the crossroad. The screech of its tires faded in the din of the driver's curses.

The chase continued, the Fiat barely staying ahead of their pursuers. At the top of the next ridge, the gunman lobbed more shots. Another connected, shattering a taillight.

A box truck lumbered toward them, the uphill slope on his side. Cleo tackled the snaking course downward, the ridge's switchbacks too tight for bullet-dodging maneuvers. She slowed into the next hairy curve, narrowed by a stone wall blocking a sheer drop.

"How do we get rid of those guys?"

The plea in her voice plunged a spear into his chest.

"Working on it. Hang on, Kyle Busch." He turned and stitched a line of bullets across the SUV's grille in a Hail Mary effort. *Come on, come on, you bastard.*

He ducked inside and released the spent magazine, replaced it with the spare.

An explosion louder than gunshots swung him around.

"Thomas, look. Oh my God!" She pumped the brakes and they stopped.

The other vehicle's left front tire had blown. Shreds of black rubber scattered everywhere. Sparks fanned upward as the tire rim shrieked across the pavement. The disabled vehicle careened into the middle of the road.

The box truck took the inside curve wide. The driver swerved to avoid the Jeep. The two vehicles slammed into each other sideways. Metal crunched and brakes squealed as they skidded together toward the stone wall.

The truck driver steered out of the skid. The Jeep hit the wall. Rocked once, twice, hurtled over the wall and down the cliff. Metal exploded against rock like a bomb. Then silence.

"Those guys are done. Let's get out of here." He grabbed her arm as she started to open the door.

"But they…" Stark horror filled her eyes.

"Truck driver's okay. He's probably on his phone right now calling the cops. Nothing you can do. If they're alive, playing Samaritan could get *you* kidnapped and *me* killed." A sudden thought had him adding, "The truck driver too."

She urged the tired Fiat on downhill.

When they reached the next intersection, she stared ahead with dogged determination. "So are we headed north?" She enunciated each word carefully, her tone robotic.

He'd have to find a place to stop before she collapsed or went into shock. She'd had enough. "I wanted them to think we were. Take a left. We'll find an inn or hotel in one of the beach towns."

When a roadside bar appeared ahead, he didn't have to suggest twice she pull over. The Fiat rolled to a stop in the shade of a leafy tree, likely planted by the bar owner to lend class to his spare establishment.

Thomas raced around and opened Cleo's door. He hadn't expected she'd have to test the Fiat's mettle, if such a car had mettle. But Cleo did—out the wazoo. No cries or complaints, only sarcasm. He pulled her into his arms, her racing heartbeat reassuring against him. Trembling with the aftermath of horror, she wrapped her arms around his waist and laid her head on his chest.

"Hang on, babe. It's over."

"My adrenaline tank's empty and my knees are dizzy. You have to hold me up," she murmured.

"My pleasure. You were damn amazing back there."

"Dazed is more like it. Question. Who's Kyle Busch?"

"A NASCAR champ, like you."

"You did some fancy shooting yourself."

He sighed. "I was aiming to hit the radiator." When she chuckled, he knew she'd be okay. "We'll find a place to stay and leave the island tomorrow."

She leaned back and gazed up, fear stark in her green eyes. "If we don't show up today, won't they look for us at the airport tomorrow? This Zervas seems to have an unlimited number of cutthroats."

"Not if we go with Plan B."

She blinked. "There's a Plan B?"

"Babe, there's always a Plan B."

****

Paris

"You made me wait long enough," Lucas Del Rio said in street French to the man he knew only as Clodo, slang for *tramp*. One of his contacts in the Paris underground had suggested the man, who performed "errands" for anyone who could pay.

Clodo looked the part. Greasy, unkempt hair brushed the collar of his stained blue jacket. He hunched over the tiny table and eyed Lucas's beer bottle with small eyes, pale blue irises framed in a pink that matched the web of capillaries on his cheeks.

"I had to make sure nobody followed," Clodo said, licking his lips. "He has eyes everywhere."

Lucas didn't have to ask who or why the worry. Anyone who betrayed or failed Zervas got no second chance.

When the bartender delivered a second beer to this table in the back of the bar, Lucas cocked an eyebrow at his informant. His scruffy companion ordered wine and looked around at the other patrons.

This side street near the Gare du Nord boasted no trendy cafes, only dreary shops, porno houses and this dingy bar smelling of *frites* and unidentifiable wine. He sipped his brew and watched people trickle in, a ragout of immigrants from France's former colonies and non-Euro-Zone countries. Laborers, the unemployed, and some with the flat-eyed look of street toughs. None gave him or Clodo a second glance.

The other man fixed his watery gaze on Lucas. "Why do you want to know about the men working for this *salaud*?" A glass of dark red wine arrived and he downed half of it at a gulp.

"Not your affair. I'm not asking how you came by this information, *n'est-ce pas*?"

"*D'ac.*" Clodo lowered his raspy voice to a rough whisper. "There are two men he trusts, two who travel with him. One is his bodyguard, Otto Nedik. Ugly type like you. Big man with a scar down one cheek. Not sure which side."

Lucas drank while he filed the description in his memory. "And the other?"

"Gerry Hawkins, a Brit." Clodo's shoulders folded inward. A man trying to be invisible. "Tall, thin as a pole. Wears glasses. Always has his nose in a computer. That's all I know." He held up his empty wine glass.

Lucas motioned to the bartender. When the wine came, he paid the tab.

Lucas questioned Clodo for a few more minutes but

the snitch couldn't come up with more. Or wouldn't.

Lucas placed an envelope on the table. "The amount you asked for."

Clodo hurried to stuff the envelope in his inside jacket pocket. He downed the rest of his wine and gripped the table's edge as if ready to push away.

Lucas clamped down on his wrist. "I'm leaving now. Stay and order another wine. You have *le fric* to pay. If I see you on the street, you'll regret calling me ugly." He curved his mouth into what passed for a smile, twisting the scar tissue into more of a grimace.

The rubescent face lost all color. Clodo bobbed his head. *"Pas de problème."*

At the door, Lucas looked back. The informant rubbed his wrist as he called to the bartender for another glass.

Outside, Lucas drew a deep breath, glad to be out of the stifling miasma. If Clodo had friends waiting to jump him, they'd likely to be at one of the Metro stops but they'd give up after an hour or so. Instead he headed to the Brasserie Flo, a restaurant he remembered from his last time in the *dixième*.

Watching his back, he took a circuitous route. On the bridge over the canal he paused and took out his phone. He had a text reply from an earlier call to Marie's mother. As he started to read, anticipation mixed with dread.

M moving arms, head. May wake soon. Drs hopeful. Me too. TY.

He clutched the phone with both hands. Part of him wanted to be there when Marie opened her eyes. Part of him knew that was a bad idea. She wouldn't know who the hell he was and his gorilla mug would scare her.

Still, he'd just spent twenty-four hours in the swill of Paris sewers and deserved a break. After he reported in, maybe he'd make a quick trip. Before she woke up. Just to see her condition for himself.

No answer from Thomas, so he left a voicemail. While he waited for Special Agent Jessica Hunt at the Centaur Task Force headquarters to pick up, he checked out the scene around him. A pair of lovebirds kissing on the next bridge. People on the way home from work with baguettes and wine in their shopping bags. No sketchy guys with bulges in their pockets.

"Where've you been, Del Rio?" Hunt barked. "You were supposed to be tracking Marco Zervas."

He pictured the FBI special agent standing, not sitting, at her desk. In her fifties, with salt-and-pepper hair and skin the color of pecans, she'd be scowling and tapping her foot. Hunt was tough and smart and no nonsense. She had to be to rise to her stature in that man's world. Hard to believe but he'd heard she was a grandmother of five. Not that he knew anything about grandmothers. He'd never known his.

"Nice to hear your voice too, Special Agent." Grinning, he ambled in the direction of the restaurant. The fine woman walking ahead of him had red hair that reminded him of Marie. "I've been doing just that. Zervas may have changed his appearance and name, new passport. I have the names and descriptions of his fellow travelers." He relayed Clodo's information. "If they haven't changed their looks and passports, you might be able to find him by tracking them."

"Not me, Del Rio. You. The rest of us are working our butts off trying to find out what Ahmed Yousef is up to. I want you in here tonight to start checking flight and customs records. Got it?"

Shit. No time off for good behavior. "Roger that."

****

Santorini Island, Greece

Behind the small hotel sloped an expanse of gardens and vineyards, sprinkled with houses and outbuildings, barely visible against the mauve and coral dusk sliding into indigo. The breeze carried the scent of unidentifiable flowers and the Aegean. The landscape bore the evidence of the volcanic eruptions that had formed the island thousands of years in the past. In this hideaway, hard to imagine that violence, and the violence of the afternoon. Cleo wished for her watercolors. She'd sketch the scene if she could trust her hands not to shake.

She cocked her head. Through the open French doors came the splashes and thumps of a big man trying to wash in a shower stall too narrow even for her. She smiled, then closed her eyes, picturing Thomas's powerful body lathered with soapsuds—all that firm male flesh, all those muscles, smooth and slippery—

Stop it. She had to curb her fantasies. She wasn't Cleopatra of the Nile and he wasn't Mark Antony. Hanging onto that fantasy—or her teenage one about him—would only crumble her resolve to protect her heart. Her long shower had given her needed time alone to think. When Thomas joined her out here, she had questions for him.

Too antsy to sit in one of the cushioned chairs, she remained standing at the balcony half-wall, formed of the same white-painted stucco as the rest of the inn.

After the crash that had killed or seriously injured the second team of creeps Zervas sent after her, Thomas called Andres. Armed with a new plan he had yet to share with her, Thomas drove them to a beach resort town and this secluded boutique hotel, managed by the taxi driver's aunt and uncle.

Over a glass of the island's excellent white wine, she'd carried out her part of their bargain. René's last words provided little clue but Thomas seemed jazzed.

"Melon," then *"Pomp"* or *"Pope."* She couldn't be sure which. And *"Ladder."*

In spite of her fears and the trauma of the big chase, she'd eaten all of the dining room's simple dinner, a vegetable stew served with crusty bread and a dish of local olives. Now if she could only keep it all in her jittery stomach.

Thomas had told her she'd carried on like a soldier today. Maybe a raw recruit, not a battle-hardened soldier like him. She wouldn't tell him she used her Cleopatra mind escape to make it through. Or that she was out here trembling.

A bare foot slapped on the cement behind her. She jerked, turned, eyes wide.

"Whoa, Cleo, it's just me." Dressed in jeans, he stood there, arms outstretched. In the open placket of his green polo, dark hairs glistened, still damp from his shower.

Dammit, I knew that. "I'm an idiot. I don't want to be such a chicken." She spun back to the scenery so he wouldn't see the flush heating her cheeks.

When his arms came around her, she leaned against his solid chest. He smelled of the inn's soap and her shampoo. His strong embrace that promised protection and strength felt so good, she had to be careful not to be dependent. Vulnerable. Any man, but especially a man like Thomas would take control and never give it back.

"You're safe in the hotel." The warmth of his breath in her hair rippled down her spine. "Zervas and his minions don't know where we're staying."

"A criminal like that must know how to trace credit and debit cards."

"Not the ones I'm using. DSF keeps a European account under a separate corporate name so expenses don't involve transfer fees and currency exchange rate problems. The arrangement allows anonymity for clandestine work. Like Lucas with the CTF."

Some of her tension seeped out. "And like us."

Soon the brush of his hard body against hers, the synchronizing of their breathing replaced calm with the crackle of sexual awareness. She remembered the press of his heavy weight on her, the flex of his muscles as he moved inside her, and she wanted him again. Against her behind, she could feel the evidence of his desire.

"You look nice and smell even nicer," he said, kissing the top of her head.

"Nothing special. Hotel soap and Mimi's capris, but thanks." One last raid on Mimi's closet for the royal-blue pants and matching gauze top had supplied an alternative outfit to her own jeans and tee. Guilt cut through her enjoyment of being in his arms and she eased away from him. "Any word on Mimi? Have you talked to her mom?"

"Just had a voicemail from Del Rio. He spoke to her. Your cousin moved her arms, and her eyelids fluttered. The doctors are more hopeful. They'll wake her soon."

"Oh, thank God." She crossed to the small table where the waiter had placed a carafe of the island's white wine and two goblets. "You promised to tell me Plan B after your shower. Partners, remember?"

The shadows were deepening around him, but enough light remained to see his gaze, as hot and gold as the center of a flame. She left his wine goblet on the table so her fingers wouldn't brush his.

"Thanks." He picked up the wine. "I don't have all the details yet. Andres is arranging for a boat to take us to Mykonos, where we can get a flight to Athens. I expect to hear from him later."

She took a long, cooling swallow of wine as she watched the play of shadows on Thomas's strong features. He wasn't even touching her, and she felt the heat.

Turning to the dark countryside, dappled with house lights here and there, she expected him to pick up the conversation. But he seemed to be content to share the silence.

Here was her opportunity. "I've been thinking more about last night."

"So have I." His gaze gleamed hotter and he reached for her. "And about tonight."

Chapter Fourteen

AS SHE DANCED away from Thomas's touch, his hand closed on air and frustration.

"I didn't mean—"

"Sex?" He grinned. "No, but I did." But he wouldn't push. He held up his hands in surrender and blew out a huff of breath. "We're not done. We damn near combusted last night and the fire's not out. I can wait."

But not for long. The way she looked tonight in that wispy top that gave him glimpses of the skin beneath made control damn hard. The tiny pulse beating at the base of her throat said she didn't want to wait long either.

She cleared her throat. "I started to say, about last night, when you rescued me from Scrgio, I get that you were hanging around in the corridor. But how did you enter the room so fast to rescue me?" She slugged down some wine.

He opted for the minimum, only what she asked for. "Door wasn't shut."

She huffed. "I was careless about the slider but the door clicked shut. Try again."

He didn't like to disclose company secrets. But this was Cleo. He went inside to his pack and returned with the device. "This electronic lock decoder detects the key-card code to unlock the door. We have variations for other types of locks. I did what was necessary."

Her brows crimped together as she tried to parse his

admission. Probably deciding if she could trust him. "I'm grateful. I imagine you're not telling me everything. Maybe I don't want to know. A security company must have lots of surveillance devices."

"We do a variety of protection. With a variety of equipment." He kept his expression bland but saw skepticism in her eyes.

"High-tech equipment, no doubt. I see." She settled into one of the chairs, apparently leaving that topic, thank God. "You were in the army headed to Iraq the last time I saw you. How did Devlin Security Force come about?"

Why ask this now? He eyed her for a moment. When he saw her deliberately loosen her death grip on the goblet, he knew he had her off balance. He dragged the chair closer, angling so he could drape his arm over her chair back and breathe her in, touch her.

She twisted, swishing her soft hair just out of reach. "Problem? Did I ask too personal a question?"

Her anxious tone jerked him back to sanity. His delayed reaction must have ratcheted up her nerves.

He shook his head. "Surprised me you didn't ask before. No secret. Everyone in my company knows why I founded my company. Even after a new Iraqi government was installed, looting of archeological sites continued, in some places on an industrial scale. The Special Forces team I commanded rousted looters in the south at several sites. Some of my men were injured, but no one seriously. It was worse in Afghanistan. Much worse."

He looked away, memories of bloody losses a barrage behind his eyes. Cross, his engineer, blown to pink mist. If Lucas hadn't stopped to check his sidearm and Thomas hadn't gone wide to check the ditch... Comrades wounded. Comrades and friends—gone. A muscle in his jaw cramped. The scars on his ribs stung with fresh pain.

He saw the question in her eyes. Before she could ask, he returned to his story.

"Seeing the destruction of Baghdad, one of the world's historic cities, looting of the monuments and antiquities of ancient Babylonia, Sumeria, Ur—" He flung out an arm in a gesture of futility and disgust.

"You were a history major, art history. I can imagine your reaction."

"History suited the quirky part of my brain that retains odd facts. Helpful in my work now too." He leaned closer, wound his fingers in her curls. Her shoulders twitched but she didn't stop him. "You remember my college studies? I'm flattered."

"If you've forgotten my teenage crush, I'm *not* flattered." She smiled, easing the awkward moment, then poured them both more wine.

How had he forgotten this comforting ability she had, to be serious and gently humorous at the same time? She'd understood he didn't want to talk about Afghanistan and left it alone. She was sensitive and kind, brave and determined, not flaky and undirected like Andie.

"History, particularly ancient history. Art theft steals culture but robbing tombs and ancient sites and stealing artifacts from museums steals more—culture *and* history."

"I was horrified," she said, "just seeing it on the news."

"You're talking about the Baghdad museum, after

the invasion. But the real looting and destruction began afterward because the guards at the historical sites fled. First it was opportunistic thieves and later organized groups of terrorists funding their operations."

"Like al-Qaida in Iraq and ISIS?"

"Right. AQI when I was there. Damned frustrating witnessing it first hand and being able to do so little," he said, staring into the golden liquid. "But here's an example my Delta team handled. In the south, at a temple near Ishan, looters broke dozens of artifacts, hauled away lots more. Cuneiform tablets, metal and copper statuettes, some dating to 2600 BC. Many have never been recovered. Including some stolen by Marco Zervas."

"Ah, so your duel with him is personal," she said.

His mouth twisted. "Very. He was part of my team, my weapons sergeant." He gave her a thin smile. "I'd suspected him of petty thefts within the team but had no proof. When I saw him carting away statuettes, tiles, and medallions, I had him arrested. He blames me for his prison term and his dishonorable discharge." Then Zervas disappeared into the underground European scene, maybe building Centaur from looted treasure he'd spirited away before being nabbed.

"I've known guys like that. Nothing is ever their fault. Their screw-ups are someone else's fault or someone out to get them."

Bitter tone from personal experience? He let it go, for now. "Zervas to a T. Naming his criminal network for the mythological warrior tribe insults them and the U.S. military." He finished his wine and slid aside the glass.

"Did he come from the streets? How does a man go

from petty thievery to head a major crime syndicate?"

Thomas rubbed his nape. The last thing he wanted was to feel sympathy for Marco Zervas. "I received his file before he joined my team. His father was a wealthy New York stockbroker and art collector. When Marco was a teenager, his dad got caught bilking his clients and ended up in jail and dead broke."

"You mean like the Madoff scheme?"

"Not quite on the same scale, but yeah. After his own troubles with the law—minor stuff—Marco had a choice, the military or jail."

"So he chose the military, but followed in good ol' Dad's footsteps, sort of." She wagged her head, shook out her hair. "He could've gone either way, even straightened himself out."

"Taking the wrong road was his choice to make."

"And Devlin Security Force?" she prompted.

"When I came home from Afghanistan, I started DSF. I designed a narrower focus than most security companies. Our mission is to protect and retrieve art and artifacts."

"Totally makes sense to me, Thomas. They provide sort of art bodyguards?"

"Like for the Cleopatra exhibit. The term *bodyguard* makes me think of ex-boxers with more brawn than brains. My operatives are highly skilled and trained. I prefer the term security specialists. But yes, that's a big part of our operation. We also do consultations and security installations for museums, galleries, and private collections."

"Impressive. But not surprising. Your dad must be proud." Sorrow flickered in her green gaze. *Unlike mine.* Her unspoken words hovered in the air.

She placed a hand on his forearm, making a muscle leap beneath her warm, soft palm. When he withdrew from her touch, she flinched. Before she could think he'd rejected her, he linked his fingers with hers, circling his thumb on the soft skin of her inner wrist. When her breathing quickened, he smiled.

"Maybe he feels that way now but not at first. He has yet to say one way or the other. Not following the old man's lead into the Navy was a bitter pill. Then when I didn't make the Army a career, he nearly had a stroke. We butted heads over Andie some, but he got off both our backs now she's doing better. At least I think so."

They sat in silence for a few minutes, watching the stars.

Cleo covered a yawn, he stood, holding onto her hand and drawing her up with him. "You're falling asleep. No surprise you're exhausted."

She smiled, all sleepy eyed and sexy. Flushed and soft. "Tired, yes. Nothing like being shot at to make a girl burn up the pavement. And her energy supply."

They strolled inside. A table lamp diffused a golden glow across the whitewashed walls and the olivewood framed bed.

"A goodnight kiss, Cleo." He dragged her into his arms and dipped his head, nuzzling her neck, absorbing her scent, and tasting his way to her mouth. She clung to him, her lips demanding and yielding. Need pounded through him and his pulse hammered along with hers. "If after last night, you've changed your mind, I'll understand. We have nothing in common except our past. There's the age difference, the danger…"

He stepped back before hunger drove away the rest of his sense.

Cleo sucked in a breath, every cell in her body strumming. His grin raced her heart faster than that little car's engine today. She'd insisted that morning that sex would distract from dealing with the danger. But wasn't her awareness of him, the wanting beyond distracting too? She would have regrets later, legions of them, but what about regrets for what she missed?

She could see his arousal pressing against his jeans placket and still he stood there, hot awareness in his eyes saying he felt the same need. But he was leaving the choice to her. Honorable, true to his word.

Or something else? "You, Thomas Devlin, Junior, are full of crap. Nothing in common? An interest in art, for starters. And the age difference? Okay, when I was eighteen and you twenty-eight. Now it means about as much as the difference in our hair color. Zip. Plenty of men see no problem with hooking up with younger women. You're pulling excuses out of thin air. If you don't want me, just say so."

Heat but no humor lighted his eyes. He yanked her hard against him. Against her belly his hardness spoke for him. When you tease the eagle, be ready for him to swoop.

He made no other moves, simply watched and waited. Always in control, with that focus on whatever he did, he controlled his needs, his emotions, and everything else. Including her.

Okay, so he *did* want her. Last night he'd taken her beyond anything she'd experienced before. No man had ever left her completely satisfied, yet ready to make love again. Both times she'd been the one out of control, not him. Once, just once, she'd like to see him lose control.

Heart fluttering like the prom wallflower

approaching the star quarterback, she backed away a step. "I've heard race-car drivers need good sex before they go to sleep."

She pulled off her gauze top and lacy bra over her head. The capris came off next, leaving her in only bikini panties.

"This engine's already revved. But no racing to the finish." Heat burned in his gaze as he kissed her again and cupped a palm over one breast.

Her nerves melted away as his touch pulsated along her skin. "You have on too many clothes. Again."

"Easily taken care of." He pulled off the polo and kicked out of his jeans and boxers. He radiated heat and power, filling her senses with his male energy. He withdrew a packet from his jeans pocket and tossed it on the bed. "Picked up a supply in Thira when I bought the food."

"I should've known. Weren't you an Eagle Scout?"

Kissing her, he eased them onto the bed, turned down earlier by a maid. His hands and his lips were everywhere, on her breasts, on her belly, on her thighs, every caress lighting flames. When his tongue found her, she went boneless.

No. Not yet. She wanted him wild and aching the same way. She kissed him as she pushed him onto his back, sliding over him, licking his flat nipples until he moaned, kissing his taut belly, branding him with her tongue. When she found ropy scar tissue on his left flank, she kissed that. Her hand closed around him, big and heavy, and he jerked, engorged with need.

"Cleo." Scooping her up, he eased one of her legs over his hip. He slid inside, deeply, fiercely, hungrily, gritting his teeth, his head back, neck muscles straining.

Intense pleasure washed through her as he drove deeper and began to move. She abandoned all hope of control and gave herself up to the sensual journey, to the heat coursing through her to the rhythm of his thrusting. She tried to gather strength to reach for him, to drive him to the same peak but she had no power over her body. When she could take no more, incandescence flowed through her in a huge, pulsing wave, and she felt him move once, twice more before he came swift and hard on a deep groan.

Afterward, she let him tuck her close, and she lay there, dazed and dreamy after such arching pleasure. The man was tough, but his control slipped at the end. She awarded herself points for the groan.

She propped herself on one elbow and gazed down at him. Eyes unfocused and mouth relaxed, he looked as groggy and stunned as she. Whoa, another point. Next time, she'd have him begging.

He blinked. "What?"

"Nothing. Just wondering about those scars on your side. Afghanistan?"

"Not a story you want to hear."

Back to control. Not gonna happen. Control and keeping his distance. On his terms. Interesting. "Or one you don't want to tell? Or classified?"

"The location is, but not the disaster." He lay still for a moment as if deciding. Finally he turned to face her, scrunching the pillow beneath his head. "We'd left our transport and split up. A few of us headed into a village to talk to the head man. A regular Army squad had supposedly cleared the way but they missed an IED beside the dirt road. The explosion killed one man immediately." His breath hitched and his gaze seemed to turn inward. "The blast threw the rest of us into the next day. Made us a bloody mess."

"One man dead. The rest survived?"

He nodded. "Long road back for a couple with traumatic brain injury and lost limbs. Lucas Del Rio has facial scars. He lost much of the hearing in one ear."

Ah. The reason he left the Army before Thomas did. "And you?"

"Lost a lot of blood, concussion, but no internal damage. I was lucky. I finished my tour. My last tour."

More scarring internally, she guessed, after such horror and loss. He lost his mom when he was only a kid, maybe fourteen, fifteen, and had to grow up fast. Did he cry for her? Did his dad let him? And it looked like he blamed himself for the Army deaths, for not leading flawlessly, but he'd come out of it strong and with new goals. A man who cared, a man who acted with cool competence—and control—in difficult situations.

"You've done so much with your life. I wish I could say the same about mine." On a sigh, she flopped onto her back.

"You're doing it now, Cleo." He bent to brush his lips on hers, not a kiss of seduction, but tender and consoling. "And you've pursued your talent. On the ship, I saw the sketches you did. As a kid you were always drawing or painting."

"We sketched together once or twice summers when you were in college."

Color flagged his cheeks above his beard stubble. "Right. When I saw the drama and depth in those simple drawings of yours, I knew then I'd fooled myself into thinking I had talent. When I returned the next semester, I switched my minor from art to art history. Made my dad marginally happier with my choice of studies. Cleo, your work is even more compelling and powerful now. You have real talent."

His praise blipped her pulse. She smiled. "Thank you. You saying that means a lot."

"Let me guess. Hoot never said it." He brushed her hair back from her face, smoothed it across the pillow.

Her scalp shivered at the sensual touch. "Maybe when my paintings are hanging in the Met. Mom talked him into letting me do two years at the Savannah College of Art and Design. Only time I recall she really stood up to him. But he kept harping on me needing discipline, structure."

"In other words, the military."

"Specifically the U.S. Navy. Even dragged me to recruitment lectures. They gave me the hives." His smile, affectionate and sympathetic but not condescending, nearly undid her, but she swallowed the emotion.

"My dad did the same thing to Andie. She only rebelled more. She didn't have a mother to intercede. And by then I'd gone away to college."

Cleo had been very young when his mom died, but she remembered her as a lively and nurturing presence. The loss hit Andie and Thomas hard, cut adrift by Hoot's absence for his naval duties. Comforting and supporting each other, except she remembered his taking charge even then. It worked until Andie went off the rails. Thomas must feel guilty for leaving her now.

She soothed a hand down the ropy scars, up to trace a finger along the hard-hewn line of his jaw. "Andie's going to make it. She's doing all right."

His gaze sharpened and he grabbed her finger. "And you know this how?"

159

"Andie and I talk on the phone all the time. We have for years. Well, except for the past few days. I know she gives you a hard time. Striking out is a defense mechanism and you're the best target. That's what her shrink says."

"She's afraid and angry now that she's facing her problems. Dr. Olsen diagnosed depression as the cause of her rebellion and drug abuse. She felt deserted by both parents. The old man left her twice, once after Mom died and again when he couldn't—or wouldn't—handle Andie's problems."

No, he'd left them to his son. Thomas's expression, a mix of anger and misery, said it all. He resented his dad's desertion as much as Andie did. And mourned his mom's loss—even if he denied it to himself.

He straightened his shoulders as if shaking off the funk. "Andie's therapist says she's keeping her appointments while I'm gone so I shouldn't worry. I can't help it."

"You can't control everything, including other people. Especially your sister. How does she feel about you being away?"

"Blasted me with a verbal IED before I left. But won't answer my calls."

"She'll answer *my* call. I could use Mimi's phone."

He shook his head. "No calls. Zervas could track her phone like he did yours."

"Your phone is secure, you said, and encrypted. I could call on that. If I leave a message, maybe she'll pick up."

"She'd know you're with me. I can't allow it."

Ooh, that was a door slamming, a sound she knew only too well. She sat up, holding the sheet over her naked breasts. "I see."

He went still, his eyes searching hers. "You have to admit my decision is justified."

She threw back the sheet and hopped off the high mattress. "I don't know why, given your attitude. Andie's probably worried about why I haven't called since Thursday. And why she can't reach me. Instead of discussing it, you issue orders. Apparently I imagined you agreed we'd work together."

Turning her back and clenching her fists, she stalked to the bathroom. Inside, she leaned against the door, shaking. Her heart slammed around inside her chest. She drew in a shuddering breath and, after a moment, washed up.

She was an idiot. His display of control should remind her not to confuse sex with softer emotions. She was falling for him again. Per usual, falling for the wrong man. No sleazoid like some of her mistakes, he was honorable and protective, unfailingly loyal. But controlling, issuing orders, boxing her in to conform to his plans. The wrong man.

She stared at herself in the mirror. Lips still rosy from his kisses. Beard burn. The picture of a well-loved woman. But the wall he was keeping between them—the ten year gap in age—bugged her. She chewed on her toothbrush while she chewed on the idea some more. A weak excuse, easily refuted.

He'd told her from the beginning there could be only sex between them. Hadn't Andie told her he'd had no lasting relationships and romanced only sophisticated society types? A shop clerk slash starving artist wasn't anyone he'd want more than a few days, let alone long term.

And vice versa. So if all either of them wanted was a temporary hook-up, no other issues mattered. All she had to do was keep things simple. Sex, hot and uncomplicated.

Right, as he would say.

Chapter Fifteen

Venice

"THIS MOLDY OLD place was the best you could do?" Zervas cast the geek a scowl.

Hawkins looked up from organizing his equipment on a contemporary computer desk, incongruous in a parlor with discolored crown molding and cracked marble floors. He hiked a skinny shoulder as if unconcerned. "You wanted fast. You wanted convenient. You wanted untraceable. Building belongs to a friend of mine. Rents out the other floors, keeps this one for 'olidays."

The flat, in a residential section of Venice, was all three, Zervas had to admit, but only to himself. No hotel records and near the Grand Canal and transportation. Hundreds of years old—like everything in this water-logged city—and five stories of decay. He could feel mold spores clogging his nose, and damned if he'd eat fish that came out of that bay.

He wandered out onto the balcony, careful to stay near the French doors in case the fucking thing decided to give way. He had privacy all right. Shutters covered the neighbors' windows, and his view consisted only of a narrow canal and the adjacent buildings' walls lined with small open boats. How their owners got to them was a mystery.

How the Chandler bitch got away was another.

His Sicily contact said that Chandler and a man who fit Thomas Devlin's description had foiled their kidnap attempts. Gunshots sent the pursuing car over a cliff, killing one man and sending the other to the hospital. Then they vanished. Until a small boy on a beach told one of the Sicilians his dad had rowed a man and woman out to a fishing boat this morning.

Zervas smiled. No more hiding for Chandler. Devlin would persuade her to return to Venice for the necklaces, both necklaces. He would die, but not before Zervas made sure he knew his company lay in ashes.

He strode inside. "You have that computer running?"

"All set, boss," Hawkins said, his fingers flying over the keys.

"Report on the take-over of Devlin Security Force."

The hacker frowned. "Their IT guy is bloody good. Caught on fast my sniffers were in place. 'e's blocked some portals but their credit is shut down. Bound to be more portals. I'll find them."

"See that you do." Zervas crossed to a pair of contemporary sofas. They looked clean enough, but the oriental carpet under them might be as old as the fucking house. How much mold had slithered into the sofa cushions? He lowered himself gingerly. "What about Devlin? Got a trace on his movements?"

"Not yet. He doesn't seem to be using a company credit or debit card."

"Personal cards?"

"Got them. But no activity on either debit or credit since Friday in the States. Must have some other business cards I haven't found yet. Checked on the sister who lives with him. Not using her cards either."

Zervas's head shot up. *Sister?* Devlin had a sister? Why didn't he know that? He made a point of knowing everything about his enemies. "Tell me about the sister."

****

After their arrival on an afternoon flight from Athens, Thomas arranged a meeting at the Santa Croce *Questura*. The interior of the central police headquarters could've been government offices anywhere. Painted a generic cream, the conference room smelled of some officer's garlicky lunch.

Hoping for a detail he'd overlooked, he listened and watched intently as Cleo related the frightening events of last Thursday night. She gestured as she talked, as if reliving the jewelry forger's bloody death, then Mimi's shooting and the killers' escape. But he gleaned nothing new.

She was tense and pale by the time she finished replying to *Commissario* Castelli's questions. The detective didn't accuse her of any crimes. Finding the suitcase in a dead man's possession and identifying the hospital intruder had eliminated her as a suspect. Thank God.

Castelli arrayed photographs of six men on the rectangular table. "*Signorina* Chandler, do you recognize any of these men as the ones you saw in the street after *Signorina* Ingram was shot?"

The room's glass door blocked most of the bustle of detectives and uniforms in the outer office, so Thomas could hear her shaky breathing.

She wore jeans and a scoop-neck orange top that showed her too prominent collar bones. The pressures of the past week had taken a toll on her appetite and carved fine lines around her pretty green eyes and her mouth. Yet with her hair in a single braid she looked as young as the image of her he'd carried in his head for years. And still scrappy. He closed his left hand over her right one, fisted on her knee.

She didn't unclench her fingers but flashed him a small smile before bending her head to study the rogues' gallery.

God, he wanted to pull her into his arms and shield her against all this crap. Only two nights with her and already he was addicted. Last night had ratcheted up his desire for her by mega degrees. Since then he'd been kicking himself for ruining the night by playing commanding officer. Damn, he should've known better. But fear for her had overruled good sense.

She'd had enough of her father's iron-handed style. Thomas got that. The significance of her tattoo armband had escaped him but he got it now. Butterflies mean freedom. Getting back in her good graces might prove as difficult as their quest. If he wasn't careful, she'd bolt.

In the photos, the six men stared into the camera with sullen expressions. Shaking her head, she flapped a hand at the pictures. "*Commissario, per favore,* I told you I saw only the backs of the men as they ran away with my suitcase. They confronted Mimi. You'll have to ask—" She looked away.

"That's enough, Detective," Thomas said, curving an arm around her jittering shoulders. "She told you all she knows about that night. More than once."

"Of course." Castelli collected the photos. He punched the off button on the small digital recorder between them. "I wanted to be certain of the details."

Thomas clicked off the tiny recorder in his

windbreaker pocket. Having a backup of Cleo's interview wouldn't hurt. And it might help.

"What about my belongings, my passport?" Cleo asked.

The detective slid forward a large manila envelope. "I can return your passport, keys, and purse. I fear we must retain the suitcase and its contents as evidence."

She accepted that without a blink. "I understand."

Castelli beamed his pretty-boy smile. "You are free to go. I shall notify you when your statement is ready to sign. You will remain in *la Serenissima* for a few days?"

Thomas doubted Venice was still the *"Most Serene."* Too expensive to maintain. And much of the population had fled to the mainland. *He* sure as hell didn't expect to find serenity here. "We'll be at the same hotel where I stayed before, but only a day or two. You have my mobile number."

Castelli dipped a small bow and thanked Cleo. *"Molte grazie, Signorina* Chandler."

"Prego, Commissario."

Handshakes all around before an officer escorted them to the water-side exit. The *Questura* had none of the elegance of Venice's ancient buildings with their pastel paints and arched windows. The imposing façade with heavy brick and rectangular windows had all the ambiance of a jail. Thomas inhaled the briny air and noticed Cleo doing the same. Drawing a cleansing breath.

They walked along the dock past the blue-and-white police launches to the water taxi they'd taken from the mainland. The craft's white sides and faux wood trim gleamed with polish. Thomas had chosen this taxi for security reasons—the privacy of its enclosed cabin and a clear view out the stern.

The driver, a fifty-something man with an angular build and craggy features, ground out his cigarette. Remnants of smoke mingled with the salty air. He gestured a welcome. Earning extra for waiting, no wonder he smiled. Thomas expected to see euro signs in his eyes. The man held out his hand to assist Cleo onto the rocking craft.

Comfortable on boats her whole life, she stepped easily down the steps and onto the teak decking. *"Grazie."*

"Prego, signora." The driver barely nodded to Thomas as he boarded.

Remaining in the cockpit, she pointed to a picture of a woman and two children fastened beside the gauges and spoke to him further.

The man beamed and replied in rapid Italian.

Once the love fest ended, Thomas followed her down the short companionway into the cabin's interior. She charmed men everywhere. The hotel staff, this water taxi driver. Even Castelli, although he'd held his admiration in check for the interview. Their eyes were on her bright hair and brighter smile. Hell, she made the world brighter, happier. Including his world. He hoped to hell he could keep her safe.

Bench seats upholstered in a sea blue ringed the enclosure in a U, offering seating for eight. Cleo sat on the port side behind the driver's open cockpit.

Thomas deposited his pack beside her and took out his phone to call Max. Monday on shipboard and yesterday on Santorini, checking his email or even accessing the company website had been impossible. Perplexing. Should've brought his tablet, but he'd traveled light, expecting to collect Cleo and beat it back to the States. *Number not in service*, the screen said. Damn. Once he had Cleo settled in the hotel, he would try again.

He chose the opposite bench so he could angle himself there to watch their six. The twin engines whirred to life in the stern. Standing at the wheel in the open cockpit, the driver maneuvered them from the police dock. The required no-wake speed in the canals would make for a leisurely trip through the city.

"You did great in there, babe." He raised his voice to be heard over the engines' growl.

"I couldn't have taken much more," she shouted. "Worse than being grilled in the principal's office."

Buoyed by her earlier thaw, he leaned forward and tucked a finger beneath her lowered chin. "You're damn tough. I've lived rough and seen more violence than anyone should, but you're holding up better than a lot of soldiers."

Her eyes crinkled with pleasure. "Thanks. I wish I could've recognized one of those pictures."

She hadn't withdrawn from his touch. Good. "Don't know why he insisted on putting you through so much. The man who tried to enter Mimi's room was in the photo line-up. Name's Ricci. They have him on the hospital's CCTV. He's probably the taller man you saw. His rotund pal was found dead beside your suitcase. They wiped off the outside of your suitcase but not the inside. The cops have both their fingerprints. Career criminals. Probably Ricci offed the other man on orders from Zervas."

She gawped. "Why didn't Castelli tell me this?"

"He can't share case information with civilians, but

my Interpol connection gives me entry. I knew some of it but he filled in the rest while you were in the ladies' room."

"The one man, Ricci, he's still out there?"

"Not for long. Castelli has put out their equivalent of an APB on him. After his screw-up at the hospital, he probably left Venice."

"Probably." She stared straight ahead, not at all mollified.

And she shouldn't be. Zervas had connections everywhere. If Ricci left, plenty of other bottom-feeders would raise their hands to take his place.

As they'd left the mainland taxi dock, he'd noticed a dark green boat similar to the taxi but longer. He kept his gaze trained astern in case it popped back up.

Shortly they turned north into the Grand Canal. Barges, water taxis, and other work boats churning the waters around them into chop. Gondoliers steered their black gondolas among the motorized boats. The air smelled of salt and fumes. The mix of craft plying the canal made watching for a tail difficult.

He returned his gaze to her. "You've had a long day. We both have. Let's go check into the hotel and have dinner. I'd like to put off going through your flat until tomorrow but the sooner we go, the less chance Zervas's men have it staked out."

"The studio too." She nodded, shaking off her funk as she looked around. "Cruising the Grand Canal like this is great. Living here, mostly I walked the city. Couldn't afford the *vaporetti* too often, unless I sold a painting." A mischievous smile lit her eyes. "You can tell the admiral I'm starting to make money with my art."

"I'd say you could tell him yourself. My phone is

secure but I can't be sure Centaur isn't monitoring his calls."

She shook her head vigorously, flipping her braid. "My mom must be frantic with worry. I'd love to talk to her but no way do I want to talk to Dad until this is over."

Until she had success to show for the danger she'd placed herself in. "No surprise you're selling if your paintings are as good as the sketches I saw." Seeing the pleasure in her pink cheeks warmed him in another area of the body. He shifted on the padded bench.

One of the big yellow water buses, loaded with tourists, headed toward them.

"Our driver has to give that *vaporetto* a wide berth," Cleo observed. "It won't care about us. I've seen small boats swamped."

"Now who'd like to give orders?" He grinned, hoping she'd take his teasing remark as a peace offering. When she said nothing in reply, he tried another tack. "We can probably get your suitcase back from the police before too long."

"I don't want it. Or the clothing, not after—" Her shoulders trembled. She scooted closer, to the edge of her cushioned seat. "What I want to do is to see Mimi. Maybe she's awake by now, or I could talk to her mom." Her voice faltered and her throat worked.

Shit. Forbidding her visit would set the wedge between them in cement. They were approaching the train station on the left when an ululating siren saved him from a hasty reply. An ambulance boat zipped toward them. Steering to starboard, the driver throttled to a near stop beside the stairs to a domed church, its columned entrance draped with scaffolding and a canvas billboard.

When the taxi settled from its rocking and rolling

and set out again, the thin line of Cleo's mouth said she was waiting for his answer.

"I'm certain none of the Centaur thugs followed us from Santorini, but by now they know we've left the island. A good bet Zervas figures we've come to Venice searching for the necklace. He'll have his goons look for us here."

She folded her lips between her teeth while she thought about that, and then her shoulders sagged. "So he could have men staking out the *Ospedale Civile* as well as my flat and René's studio."

"Right. My take on it exactly." Maybe they weren't here yet but he wouldn't take the risk.

"We're in enough danger without me upping the threat level. Or endangering Mimi again." Her lips curved. "Did not issuing an order put a twist in your boxers?"

He lowered one eyelid in a slow wink. "I admit I had to stifle myself, but the boxers are tight for another reason." Her sputtered laugh made him grin. "So am I forgiven for last night's transgression?"

She tossed a saucy flip of her dark-copper braid. "I'll think about it."

"Tell you what. It may not be safe for you to call my sister, but doubtful Zervas has Mimi's mom's number. After we get settled in the hotel, you can phone her."

"Whoa, a compromise. I'll take it." She curled up on the seat sideways and peered out at the buildings lining the canal.

Off the port side rose a church square and the municipal casino but he'd rather admire the curve of her ass in the slim jeans. He dragged his gaze away and returned to his vigil.

Damn. The green boat. Hanging back, but following. Or was he paranoid? The Grand Canal *was* the main thoroughfare.

Chapter Sixteen

"CLEO, I DON'T want to scare you—"

She huffed. "What now? Is our driver the Centaur leader or something?"

Her bravado made him smile. He swung across the narrow aisle and sat beside her, wrapping his left arm around her shoulders and nudging her against him. "The dark green boat behind us has stayed with us since the mainland. I didn't see it when we left the *Questura*, but it caught up again."

She peered astern for a long minute. Color drained from her face. "Oh, God, not again."

He squeezed her shoulder. "Little chance of a high-speed chase in this traffic. And I doubt they'd risk gunfire. But yes, I think they're tailing us. Take a closer look. See if you recognize any of the guys from Santorini." When she began to move toward the back, he added, "Stay down. Don't let them see you."

She slid around the seats until she had a clear view out the stern. After a few minutes, she returned, staying low.

"Two men. A slender, gray-haired man. He could be the driver. And a big, tough-looking guy with dark hair. I think he had a scar down his cheek but they were pretty far away. I don't recognize either of them."

"Not Ricci then. The scar-faced guy fits the description Del Rio sent me of Zervas's bodyguard.

Name's Nedik."

"We have to lose them, don't we? So they don't find our hotel?" If she abandoned sarcasm, she was terrified.

"Right." Thomas chose his next words carefully. "I'd do this but our driver doesn't speak much English. We need him to lose them. If they're back there by coincidence, they won't follow and we're clear. If they stick with us..." He held out a palm, conveying the obvious conclusion. "You can tell him I'll double the fare."

She nodded and stepped up to the cockpit. Smiling, the driver moved aside to give her room.

While he listened to their rapid exchange of Italian, they approached the *Ca d'Oro*. Now the central post office, the landmark palace's blond façade and lacework balconies gleamed in the sun. Damn close to where they would enter a smaller canal to port and head to the hotel. The driver would have to power fast in the other direction.

A booming laugh jerked his attention back to the cockpit. The man grinned ear to ear and gestured broadly. He shook Cleo's hand and she stepped down the companionway.

As soon as she sat beside him, he felt the boat veer to starboard. They entered a side canal at a faster speed. "So he agreed."

"No prob. He said it was like an American movie. He'd always wanted to hear the words, 'Lose those guys.' He'll take us through a maze of tiny *rios* in San Polo, then back across the Grand Canal when he's sure no one is following."

The green boat turned in behind them. A muscle tightened in his jaw. "They're tailing us all right. Look."

The narrowness of the *rio* forced a leaden pace, a contest between a turtle and a snail.

Apparently the offer of a double fare had motivated their driver to ignore the speed limit and the danger of collision. When their wake rocked a gondola loaded with Japanese tourists, the passengers cried out and grabbed the gondola's sides to avoid being tossed into the murky green water. Thomas held onto the safety handle beside him and kept Cleo plastered against him with his other arm. The gondolier waved his fist and shouted.

The water taxi driver ignored the complaint and swung into the next, even narrower *rio*. The green boat had dropped back but stayed the course.

Thomas considered leaving the taxi and going it on foot. Being in the open and on foot could be riskier. Cleo was safer here. As long as their driver knew his stuff.

The *rio* made a sharp turn. The driver shot off into another side waterway. Straight ahead, a barge, its cargo of building stone already unloaded onto the adjacent dock, began to turn around. If it pulled out farther, it would block their way and the green boat would catch up. Then all bets were off on whether Nedik would use a gun.

Thomas had had to leave the borrowed pistol on Santorini. He had no weapon.

The driver pushed the throttle forward and the engines growled in response. He swerved to starboard.

Ahead loomed a narrowing gap between the barge's stern and a concrete retaining wall.

The taxi shot through the slot.

The barge reversed the rest of the way. It blocked the canal. And the green boat.

Furious shouts and the whine of a down-throttling

motor eddied across the water.

Slowing, the water taxi driver made three more zigs and zags. Insurance.

Thomas couldn't argue with that. He relaxed his grip on the safety handle but kept Cleo close.

The driver bent and called something down to them.

"He thinks they're gone," she translated, edging away to wave to the driver, "but he'll take some more detours before recrossing the Grand Canal toward our hotel."

Pink-cheeked after the chase, she looked excited and something else he couldn't put a finger on. "He said more than that."

"What makes you think so?" The color in her cheeks deepened to rose. She looked both vulnerable and sexy.

"You," he said.

She heaved a sigh. "Before, he asked if those guys were police. I said no, that we're newlyweds and the man following us is a rejected lover."

Cleo's ploy should've had him reaching for a hazmat suit but, hell, she wasn't serious. For long term she'd want a man closer to her age. The thought chafed like a blister on his heel. "Good call. And now?"

"He said a real man knows to accept no and move on."

"Our driver is a wise man."

Beside their taxi, laundry hung outside a blue house. Shirts and slips fluttered on a line from one window to another. A man strained to wheel a laden cart up the shallow steps of a bridge. Maps in hand, three women wheeled suitcases along a cobbled walk.

No sign of the green boat or their pursuers.

Cleo also kept watch. She drew her knees up and

wrapped her arms around them.

In this maze, their tail could find them again by chance. Leaving matters to chance all too often led to disaster. Chance and impulse. He had to curb his impulses where Cleo was concerned if he wanted any relationship with her beyond this mission. He surprised himself that he did.

He didn't want to be the rejected lover having to accept no before the affair ran its course. As they always did.

****

Seeing the joy on Cleo's face at whatever Trudy Ingram was saying on the phone told Thomas he'd done the right thing. He relaxed against a corner of the sofa. Instead of a single room, this time he'd booked a mini-suite with a king bed and a seating area.

The desk clerk had greeted Thomas by name but kept his gaze glued on Cleo. She'd chatted with him in fluent Italian, rendering him her slave. The bellboy hopped to, faster than he'd done for Thomas alone. Hell, he'd been glad to finally get her alone. Safe, behind locked doors.

She finished her call and handed him her phone. "Thanks *so* much. Mimi's mom says she's still about the same. Some movement of her hands. She mumbles words sometimes too." She blinked and swiped away a tear.

He pulled her into his arms and soothed circles on her back.

"Damn. Here I am weeping in your arms again. Soaking your shirt."

In his arms was the key part. *Hold her. That's all, Devlin. The next move is hers.* "But she hasn't awakened yet."

"Trudy's hopeful. More than before. I was afraid she'd hang up on me. Blame me for what happened to Mimi."

"Like you blame yourself."

"She was happy I called. Said she couldn't wait to meet her niece." She raised her head. He wanted to kiss away her remaining tears, but she backed away.

"One more thing," she said, her brow creased in thought. "Trudy said Mimi keeps muttering Lucas's name."

"Interesting," was all he could find to say. Lucas had a thing for Mimi, begun even before Thomas had arrived to point out she wasn't Cleo. Reactions to his intimidating appearance had made Lucas wary about women. But lonely.

Interesting, yes, to see how this might play out.

****

Early that evening, they left the hotel by a service door and grabbed a quick pasta meal at a *trattoria* two streets over. The sky, a black blanket draped over the city, allowed no stars to peek around the clouds to compete with city lights.

Cleo zipped up the lined jacket she'd bought earlier in anticipation of the cool night air. Well, Thomas had bought it, had insisted. Another way of protecting her. Or managing her. Aside from the search, she needed to pack her clothing and then she'd never return to that flat. Maybe to Venice. In spite of everything, she loved the city.

A water taxi motored them to the Santa Croce district. From there they traipsed a maze of *calli*, which were narrow side streets, and *rios*, Thomas always vigilant.

In René's studio, the overhead lights glinted off his tools and remnants of beads and silver. Cleo wrinkled her nose at the odd smell of the fingerprint powder left behind by the police. Overseen by the impatient landlord, they picked through the tools and a file box of design sheets and contracts. After an hour with nothing to show but specifications of the Cleopatra necklace, they thanked the landlord and left.

Another series of twists and turns took them to the flat, their last hope. She crossed her fingers they'd find more of a clue than whatever René had mumbled when he died. The building that contained her flat was one of a solid wall of dwellings, some with ground-floor shops. Hers housed a small stationery shop beside the entrance to the flats. Across from her building, Thomas backed them into a recess. The dark nook smelled of stale cigarettes and the fresh mortar binding the stones beneath their feet. He tucked her behind him while he observed. After a few minutes, he hustled her across the *calle*.

"Security?" he asked.

Seeing his skeptical glare at the wooden door, she bit back a smile. "No keypad or alarm. Only a passkey and nosy neighbors."

"Someone could've cleaned you out. Let's hope you find something left in the flat."

"Their guy followed our water taxi, so wouldn't they expect we'd come here?" she whispered as they entered the lobby. "Why are they hanging back?"

The outer door closed behind them. Familiar smells and sounds calmed her nerves—the aromas of buttery sauces and roasting chicken, the emotion-filled voices of a popular TV drama, and the hungry wail of the Fellinis' two-month-old son.

"Zervas may be a sociopath but he's a smart sociopath. His street muscle not necessarily. But to answer your question, I don't know. Maybe waiting to see what we come up with."

"Waiting for us to find the necklaces, you mean?"

"Right. Letting us do the work." He jerked a nod toward the hall. "What's back there?"

"Storage, the trash room, the furnace. And a rear exit."

He made no comment, only eyed the narrow, dimly lit stairway with suspicion. "I'll go up first."

She stayed close behind him, trying to ignore how sexy he looked in his jeans and body-hugging black polo and how the muscles in his butt and thighs flexed as he climbed. When they reached the fourth floor without incident, he stepped aside to let her join him on the landing.

When she'd obtained the key from her landlady, the impact of returning didn't hit her. The sight of the new lock, replacing the one the killers mangled, triggered roaring in her ears. As she inserted the key, her pulse jerked and her palms went damp.

He reached around her and opened the door. "Wait here, Cleo. I'll go in first, turn on lights."

She nodded, focusing on his clean scent rather than memories of blood and death.

All too soon, he returned. He opened the door wide, letting the living room light spill out. "All clear."

One step inside. Another. Queasiness swirled in her stomach and her gaze shot to the sofa. Gone. Only the square imprints of its feet remained on the carpet, a ghost of the death that soaked it in blood. She wouldn't have to see the ruined cushions. The flat smelled only of dust and her paints, and the fingerprint powder, thank God. Her pulse slowed.

"You okay, babe?" Thomas's hands, strong and warm, closed on her shoulders. "I've got you. You're safe. No one tailed us or came ahead of us. You left your phone off so they can't find you that way. No one knows we're here."

She forced herself to breathe. Realized she'd been swaying on her feet. "It's not that. It's just coming back to this place."

"Not surprising. Just take it slow." His eyes gentle as if he feared she might shatter, he gestured toward the window, its curtains pulled tight. "Stay back from the windows."

She ventured one step inside, then another and another, until the initial horror faded. Cupboard drawers left open, their contents strewn on tabletops. Books—her art books and René's collection of detective fiction—torn from the shelves and left on the floor. She shook her head at the disarray. "Why did the police tear the place apart? Were they looking for the necklaces?"

"Doubtful, but the two killers had time to search before the cops arrived," he said, probing the wood along the bookshelves. "Did René have any hiding places here?"

"None he told me about. Obviously he was keeping secrets, so maybe. If the police and the killers didn't find anything, how can we?"

"You never know." Coming from the bathroom, his voice was fainter.

She wandered into the kitchen. The smell of lemon

cleanser drifted in the air. The pot she'd left on the stove sat upside down in the sink drainer. Empty fridge, no food packages on the shelves. Not the cops, she thought, but her landlady, beginning to ready the flat for a new tenant as soon as Cleo cleared out her belongings.

"Nada in the bathroom. Anything?" Thomas's wide shoulders took up the doorway.

She couldn't get enough of looking at him, his straight black brows framing his dark-gold eyes, his hard, square jaw.

Amusement crinkled his gaze. Damn, he knew she'd been staring, that she wanted him still. She cleared her throat. Finishing their search, packing her things and getting back safely to the hotel meant moving quickly, not indulging in a round of hot sex. No way did she want to make love with Thomas in the bed where she'd lain with René.

She shrugged. "Nothing. But René hardly ever cooked. If he hid anything, it'll be in the bedroom."

She whisked past him, through the living room to the bedroom. No hot sex in here anytime soon. Mattress stuffing poked up from slices in the bedding, puffs of foam dribbling over the discarded covers. Clothing, her paints, and René's toiletries lay strewn beside the upside-down drawers. The scent of his cologne wafted up from the floor. She gaped at the mess, a sense of violation creeping over her.

"Feeling nostalgic?"

"Some. But mostly the thought of those creeps handling my stuff makes my skin crawl."

He squeezed her shoulders gently. "Don't blame you. Take only what you need for tonight. The rest can be replaced. I'll look through René's stuff for anything that might help us. Not a hard job. The searchers piled everything on the floor."

Nodding, she dragged her other small suitcase, a soft-sided shoulder bag, onto the ruined mattress and began sorting through her remaining clothing. In case René had stashed something in her belongings, she searched pockets and trinket boxes. "Nothing but wrinkles and lint."

"Same here," he said, sitting on the edge of the mattress. "Looks like René left *you* with the only clues."

"We might as well have nothing. That's what his mumblings are worth."

After packing underwear—which she absolutely would wash out by hand tonight—and a couple changes of clothing, she picked up a discarded sketchbook and eyed her easel.

"Don't think we can take that." He grinned. "But I like the scene you started."

She'd tried to capture the sun in a narrow courtyard as it spotlighted a carved door and a tabby cat sleeping among the flowers in a window box. "Thanks. I still have the preliminary sketches in this old sketchbook. Maybe I'll try again sometime."

"You said you were starting to sell. In a gallery?"

She dropped in the sketchbook and zipped up the bag. "The Calle della Vida Gallery, not far from the shop where I worked. I still have five paintings there." She snorted. "Unless the *signora* sold them. If she thinks I'm dead, she probably doubled the price. Dead artist, you know. She'll rake in all the profit."

He rose, regarding her with that steady look that seemed to see inside her. "If we drop in tomorrow, she might be persuaded to return them to you."

"If she hasn't sold them."

His offer soothed her prickly nerves and banished the remnants of her revulsion at the killers' search. More, his concern for her surpassed protection. In his demeanor and in his words, she found true affection. They'd become friends once again, after all. She'd ignored that in her zeal to guard her independence.

"Ready to go?" She tried to sound what her mom would call chipper.

"Almost." He straightened, again the alert soldier, and crossed to the bedroom window. "What's the view out here?"

"The street. We're above the entrance. Why?"

"Just because no one was hanging around out there when we arrived doesn't mean they haven't set up shop by now."

"Oh." Cleo said a little prayer of thanks for his security expertise, his almost eerie awareness of his surroundings, how he always knew to be vigilant.

He hustled her into the living room, turning off the bedroom light as they went. "Wait by the door while I check outside." He waited until she was in place before he doused the rest of the lights.

Clutching her bag to her, she huddled in the darkness.

He parted the curtain a slit and peered out. After a few moments, he said, "Shit. There's a man across the street in the doorway. Is there a fire escape?"

Chapter Seventeen

SHE STARED, THEN shook her head. "Only the rear door past the trash room." So much for chipper. She squeaked like a scared chipmunk. She drew a breath, willing calm and the strength of the ancient Cleopatra. These Centaur bastards would *not* beat her down.

Thomas crossed from the window and wrapped his arms around her. "I can't see the guy clearly but judging from his size it could be the big guy Nedik from the green boat." His lips moved against her hair, his warm breath infusing her with his confidence. "There could be another one staking out the rear."

"Many buildings don't have a rear exit or even a fire escape other than a rope ladder because of the canals. The rear door here opens onto a narrow *fondamenta*, um, a walkway, along the *rio*. A few of the tenants tie boats there. Maneuvering on foot would be tough, especially at night."

"Right. Then we watch for trouble *inside* the building." He tipped up her chin. In the dark she could see only the shape of his head. "Promise me you'll do what I say."

She started to object to his presumption she'd rebel, but thought better of it. "In this case, I'll follow orders. But don't assume anything from that, mister."

"With you, babe, I never assume anything."

"Good idea. Then let's roll."

"You've watched too many disaster movies." He brushed her lips with a kiss that blipped her pulse a couple of beats. "Move as quietly as possible. Staying on the balls of your feet helps. Tap my shoulder if you hear a sound that doesn't belong."

As he opened the door, she winced in the hallway lighting. They waited a moment while their eyes adjusted. Then he signaled her to follow. At nearly eleven o'clock, the building's tenants were settling for the night. Cooking aromas had dissipated, replaced by the spicy tobacco whiff of an after-dinner cigar.

Glad she'd worn soft-soled shoes, she descended each step as he had suggested. Her pulse clamored like a church bell and her palms went damp. If a thug waited downstairs, Thomas would—what? Jump him, fight him, yes, but his fists couldn't stop bullets. She inhaled and tried to block the image from her mind and concentrate.

No babies cried and no TV programs blared to mask alien sounds. She strained to listen, but heard only the familiar creaks and groans of the old structure and the ordinary shuffling and muted voices of her neighbors behind their doors.

As they neared the ground floor, the scrape of a leather sole on the entry tile scrambled her pulse. She tapped Thomas's shoulder and he nodded, clearly also alerted. They halted. She lowered her heels silently and pressed her bag to her side.

When he turned, she saw his mask of vigilance, the aura of power he always carried, but honed to diamond sharpness. He held up a hand, a tacit order to wait where she was, on the fourth step from the bottom, concealed by the stairwell wall. Only after she nodded did he continue downward.

A tenant would have walked on, to the trash room or out the door. If he'd gone back to a flat, he'd have passed them on the stairs. The footfall they'd heard had to be a bad guy. Thomas could be shot before he even saw the guy. She blinked against the image of him bleeding on the ochre tiles. Cold prickles scraped her spine. The muscles of her throat constricted, threatened to choke her. She'd agreed to do what he said. But dammit she couldn't simply wait here forever and do nothing.

At the bottom of the stairs, Thomas held his breath, listening as he slid his windbreaker off and to the floor for more freedom of movement. Assured Cleo was staying put, he dismissed worry for her from his mind. Necessary to optimal function. Anxiety and questions faded as he clicked into the focused intensity of combat mode—the zone.

A crapshoot whether or not the intruder had a gun. Nothing he could do about that. He felt the weight of the sheath on his belt. At a street market that afternoon, while Cleo tried on jackets, he'd found an Italian army combat knife, about five inches long. Shorter but similar to his Ka-Bar. A longer blade tended to get caught in clothing while a short blade penetrated. Good to go.

He pictured the hallway, more dimly lit than the small lobby. Two doors on the right. Another at the end, the rear exit. His man had to be waiting back there, in the shadows beneath the stairs.

From the hallway came a new sound. A faint clicking like a pencil on the tiles.

A trap? He slid the knife into his palm. Held his breath. Listened.

A small form streaked from the shadows. A gray tiger cat raced past him. Emitting a warning hiss, it flowed up the stairs and out of sight.

He exhaled a silent breath. He peered around to see Cleo, eyes wide and hands clapped over her mouth. She hadn't uttered a sound, thank God. He shook his head and pointed toward the building's rear. No cat had made the scraping noise they'd both heard.

She bobbed her head, seeming to understand.

From above came a woman's voice. He didn't understand the Italian words but recognized the affectionate tone that scolded the wayward pet. The door clicked shut. Other than his own rough breathing, he heard only muted gonging in the distance and the murmurs of competing shows upstairs.

The cat might have set the ambusher off balance. Thomas counted on that and on the element of surprise. A rush—some called it a prison-yard rush— didn't give the opponent time to get set. A better chance than waiting for an attack. He swung around the concealing wall and raced toward the back, his knife in a hammer grip.

A figure sprang from the dark corner. The overhead light glinted on a knife. Serrated edge. About two inches longer than Thomas's blade.

He jabbed at the man's side. The attacker thrust his knife at Thomas's upper arm.

Thomas sidestepped and pivoted.

His opponent was smaller and younger, wiry strong. Slicked-back hair and bulging eyes in a narrow face. His sly smile showed gaps in his teeth. Not the driver of the green boat. No one in the photo line-up. A local cutthroat.

The aim for the brachial artery meant the man had skill. One mistake and Thomas could be unconscious from blood loss in seconds. Dead in minutes.

And he'd have failed Cleo. *Focus, Devlin.*

The attacker stank of sweat and stress. He pivoted and came again.

Thomas turned to block the blow with his left arm. The attacker anticipated the move and struck the underside of his arm. A gash several inches long opened up. Blood welled. It would sting like hell later. Shallow but dangerous. Being jacked on adrenaline pumped the blood faster. He had to weaken the fucker, take him down.

He moved in fast, sliced across the man's forearm, just above his knife hand. Crimson welled in the long gash. Deeper than Thomas's wound. Blood dripped onto the tiles.

Blood would slick the knife handle.

The attacker's smile turned forced, tight, not as confident. They circled each other, blades glinting. The attacker slashed out but his reach fell short as Thomas darted out of range.

He feinted left, then slashed again. A second cut opened on the attacker's forearm, just above the first. The man struck but without the force of his earlier attempts.

Thomas blocked the blow. Moved in close, grasped the knife hand with his left and pinned it against his own body. A knee blow knocked the knife loose. It clattered to the tile. Before the guy could react, Thomas yanked him up and over his back. Slammed him to the floor. The guy's breath expelled on a loud groan.

Thomas lifted a foot to stomp his opponent but the guy moved fast. He grabbed Thomas's foot and the hard floor came up to meet him at warp speed. At impact, he rolled, protecting his head, and kicked at the same time.

His foot connected with the attacker's head.

The man grunted at the glancing blow but slithered out of reach of another kick. His lost weapon lay on the tile, its hilt only inches away. He stretched for the knife.

A sneaker-clad foot kicked it away. The blade skittered into a far corner.

Thomas dove for the man. Smashed a fist in his throat and sat on his chest, pinned his upper arms with his knees.

The downed attacker gasped a choking breath. He froze, his bulging eyes froglike, at the blade pricking the tender skin below his jawbone.

Thomas's chest heaved. Not perfect but he'd survived. And he had his man.

Cleo skirted him and his captive. Protecting her hand with tissues, she gathered up the knife from where she'd kicked it. He heard a gasp as her shocked gaze fell on his bleeding arm. "Oh, Thomas, he cut you."

He gritted his teeth, slanting a quick glance her way. "You agreed to stay on the stairs."

"Did I?" She held up the weapon and examined the blade. "Would you rather he'd reached this filleting knife so he could gut you?"

"Point taken. I'll thank you later." Maintaining his knife on his captive, he eased off the man's chest. "Tell this lowlife to lock his hands behind his head and roll onto his belly. Add if he makes a move or calls out to his leg-breaker pal on the street, I'll fillet *him*."

****

Paris

As Lucas entered the building where the temporary Interpol offices were located, his phone chirped. Agent Hunt looking for him already? Did the woman never sleep or eat? The pork tenderloin in mushroom cream sauce and the wine had deserved lingering over but he'd scarfed them down so he wouldn't be late. Checking the time on the wall clock, he considered letting the call go to voicemail.

But the chirping insisted. Maybe Thomas calling. He unhooked the mobile from his belt and checked the screen. *Trudy Ingram.* Mimi's mom. Was Mimi awake? Or was something wrong? He punched the elevator button and answered the call, hoping the connection would hold in the elevator.

"I'm so glad I caught you, Lucas," Trudy said, almost as chirpy as his phone.

Nothing bad then. "Do you have news?"

"Absolutely. My baby is beginning to wake up." Her voice broke on the last word. He heard her breath catch as she gathered herself. "She's going to be fine. Lucas, she squeezed my hand and smiled."

He closed his eyes briefly and let the tension drain from his shoulders. He was due in five minutes for a video-conference. But he wouldn't have skipped this call if his meeting had been with the U.S. president. When he opened his eyes, the elevator had arrived. Three people exited carrying briefcases and handbags, their workday done.

The lift reeked of someone's cloying aftershave. He wrinkled his nose as he pushed the button for the top floor. "Ma'am, that's wonderful news. I know seeing your face has to make her feel better." *Better her face than mine.*

When the doors whispered open at his floor, he saw no one in the foyer so he wandered to the window. A block away from the Avenue des Champs-Élysées, the modern office building sat at an angle offering a view of the fabled thoroughfare but too far east for a glimpse of the Arc de Triomphe.

"She's not completely awake. The doctors say she's still in pain. I can't imagine the headache from a bullet wound. They're still keeping her sedated, but she opens her eyes every now and then." Her voice was liquid. "She's asking for you, Lucas."

His throat felt tight. He no longer saw the spectacle below, only Mimi's beautiful pale face, her still form in the hospital bed. He loosened his tie and collar. "Asking for *me*?"

"She keeps murmuring your name. When she can have visitors, you *must* come."

How was it possible? She'd been unconscious. How could she have heard him, his meaningless ramblings? Seeing him would only disappoint her.

"Ma'am, I'm on assignment. I don't— I mean, as much as I'd like to, I can't get away."

"I'm not taking no for an answer, young man." Trudy Ingram's voice rang with the same steel as Hunt's. "Once my daughter is fully awake, the specialists will keep her busy with tests and therapy. We'll have weeks here before she's able to fly home. I expect you'll find the time to make the trip to Venice."

"Yes, ma'am, I'll do my best."

Apparently satisfied, Mimi's mother wished him a nice evening and ended the call.

He massaged the back of his neck as he sagged against the window sash. He was a damn coward. And a fool.

Marie—he still preferred that to Mimi— called his name. How could he deny her?

He wouldn't stay long, just long enough to assure himself she'd be okay. Long enough to see her smile, see her eyes bright with life, hear her voice. Keeping it brief would ease the awkwardness of the meeting. They were strangers.

As soon as he got the word from Trudy she was awake, he would go. His part in the Centaur Task Force was nearly done. They knew where Marco Zervas was, in Venice, searching for Thomas and Cleo. A cat and mouse game.

Once they had his location, the Interpol cat would pounce. Lucas would join the team sent to do the pouncing, and then he'd have his visit with Mimi/Marie.

As the last of his five minutes of grace expired, he grabbed his tablet from his desk and strode into the CTF director's office. Trace aromas of take-out meals hung in the air—wine sauce, beef, *frites*. He was still adjusting the noose around his neck. Damn, he hated ties and being an office wonk.

SA Jessica Hunt sat at the head of the conference table, her laptop open and ready for the meeting. Her reading glasses perched on top her head, anchored in her short salt-and-pepper hair. She waved him to the seat to her left.

Another FBI agent filed in behind him to sit farther down the long table. A few other seats were occupied by members of the CTF— another Feeb as well as intelligence agents of the French, British, and Italian governments.

He took his seat and noticed the screen opposite, where images of their remote conferees would be projected. He'd read the briefing. Security at a Palo Alto research facility with government contracts had contacted authorities with suspicions of one of their scientists and contacted authorities. The FBI obtained surveillance tapes of the man, a chemist and computer engineer, meeting with a courier of the Iranian terrorist Ahmed Yousef. Agents arrested the chemist, but Yousef's man escaped. The man in custody would be at the San Francisco office for the interview.

Because no actual sale had been witnessed, Lucas had his doubts about what a video conference could accomplish. How a geek selling secrets—if that's what he was doing— to Yousef had anything to do with his arranging the theft of Cleopatra's necklace, he couldn't speculate. He'd rather get back to locating Zervas's Venice hole in the wall.

The wall screen flickered and a man about fifty wearing black-framed glasses appeared. The suit and gray buzz cut pegged him as FBI.

"Good evening, Special Agent Hunt," he said in an official tone.

"Special Agent Parker," Hunt replied, nodding. "Nice to see you again."

"Likewise, Jessica. It's been awhile since that RICO takedown in Jersey."

"A few years." A smile might have crossed her lips but Lucas could've imagined it. "Several members of my task force have joined us. What do you have for me?"

Parker rubbed knuckles along his jaw. "I had hoped to know by now what exactly our alleged thief sold to Yousef's man. Unfortunately the lab where he worked had a small fire that destroyed some of their records. Suspicious origin, of course. We're looking into it. But the result means what might be missing is unclear."

"If your tapes don't show the chemist actually

passing something to Yousef's man," Hunt said, "what do you have on him?"

"This morning we discovered that two months ago Victor Chung opened an account in the Caymans with an initial deposit of three million U.S. dollars."

A murmur rippled around the table. What technology could Chung have passed to Ahmed Yousef worth that much? Spyware? A virus? A guidance component for missiles?

The door behind Parker opened. Two agents, one man and one woman, entered and took up posts on either side of the doorway. Another, a man as hefty as Lucas, escorted the prisoner, a slight man of medium height. In khakis and a blue dress shirt and wearing wire-rimmed glasses, Victor Chung looked like the geek he was, except for the handcuffs shackling his wrists and the bruise-purple bags beneath his eyes.

Bringing up the rear, another man strode in. Silver mane of hair set off by a golf-course tan. Tailored pinstripes. Red patterned tie that probably cost more than the threads of all the FBI agents in the room. The attorney. The look on his patrician face said stonewall. Now Lucas *knew* this was a waste of time. A charade.

Parker directed Chung to sit on his left. The attorney took the seat on Chung's other side. Parker made introductions, informing the chemist that SA Hunt would conduct the questioning.

Hunt began with general questions about the work of the research lab where Chung worked. The attorney permitted those, but when she asked specifically about the chemist's research, the attorney shut things down.

They were being too careful, too nice. Lucas keyed a question into his tablet, then angled it toward Hunt.

May I speak to the prisoner?

Hunt pursed her lips as she read. Her gaze searched his face before she nodded.

"Mr. Chung," he said, "The FBI seems to have enough evidence—or will soon— of your dealing with an international terrorist and enemy of the United States. You will go to prison for treason. Ahmed Yousef has financed and planned attacks and bombings on embassies and in public markets in countries in the Middle East and in Europe. If you sold him technology that results in more deaths—especially American deaths—forget prison. For that level of treason, the penalty is execution."

Chung's face paled and he mouthed the word *execution*. His shoulders hunched as if he were protecting his neck from the hangman's noose. He chewed over his words before he spoke again. "I swear I did not sell secret technology to Ahmed Yousef."

The attorney clamped a hand on his client's arm. "That's enough, Victor."

Hunt opened her mouth to interrupt but Lucas leaned closer to the camera. He'd known his brutish appearance to put the fear in hardened thugs. Up for grabs whether a close-up would work in a virtual interview.

When Chung recoiled, Lucas stifled a smile.

"Then consider telling us what you did sell him. Cooperation could save your life."

Chapter Eighteen

Venice

TWO HOURS CREPT by before Cleo could force
Thomas to rest. After helping him clean up, she sent his
blood-spattered clothing to the hotel laundry. Finally she
wrapped him in a terry hotel robe and propped him up on
the king bed with pillows.

She'd used his phone to call Castelli while she'd run
up to her flat for clothesline to tie up the thug and
toweling to staunch both men's bleeding. By the time the
cops and medical techs arrived, the trussed-up man's
backup was nowhere to be found. A tech bandaged the
captive before police hauled him off.

With the attacker gone, the impact of their ordeal hit
her hard. Thank God Thomas was so capable but even
warriors got seriously injured. And killed. Her knees and
hands trembled. She took a steadying breath as she
fought off the shakes.

The tightness of his jaw and the creases between his
eyes said his arm stung like a son of a bitch, but she knew
he'd refuse hospitalization. No way would he leave her
alone.

"No hospital," he said. "Sew me up."

The tech grumbled but closed his gash with butterfly
clamps and gauze. She injected him with antibiotics and
ordered him to see a doctor tomorrow.

After that, the two of them described the events of the evening to Castelli. The detective congratulated Thomas for capturing a Centaur hire. Before heading out, in a police launch, Thomas warned him of Zervas's pattern of eliminating compromised accomplices. The *commissario* saluted and nodded with a crisp air that relayed he would take care of the witness.

As soon as they returned, Thomas insisted on a shot from the bar.

Cleo opened her mouth to mention the emergency tech's orders to abstain, but relented. "After that experience, you need a drink and so do I. *One* drink."

When room service delivered the order within ten minutes, he gaped. "Record time. Faster than I got them to move when I stayed here before."

"Could be your appearance. Nothing like bloody clothing and a bandaged arm to get people's attention. The waiter probably hoped for the inside scoop."

"Babe, more likely it was the way you charmed the concierge. You had him and the bartender hopping like *you* were the bleeding victim."

Scoffing at that ridiculous statement, she had handed him his scotch.

Seated now in one of the suite's flowered armchairs, she sipped a flute of prosecco as she leafed through her retrieved sketchbook. Neither the drink nor loosening her hair from the braid relaxed her. She didn't see much of the drawings because she kept eyeing him, watching for signs of a fever or blood soaking the bandage.

Toward the end of the sketchbook, a page held her gaze. She froze, staring at the drawing. Not hers. Of some sort of building.

"Cleo? What is it?"

"I... I don't know." She went to sit on the bed beside him. "At the back of the sketchbook, among a few blank pages, I found this. Not my work."

Pleased for an excuse to have her beside him, Thomas accepted the pad, folded back to reveal the odd page. Not one of her pencil treatments, for damn sure. Thin, precise lines and metric measurements defined the floor plan in a large structure like a warehouse. The same precise hand had written in English on some of the rooms the words *offices, studios, workshops,* and *assembly.*

"René's doing?" He tilted the sheet toward her.

"Looks like his writing." Biting her lower lip, she pointed. "Is that an address?"

He read the smaller print, more of a scrawl as if hastily added. "Yes, and beneath it he wrote 'West Acton tube station.' "

"A section of London, sort of a suburb." Her forehead furrowed as she thought about it. Her hair tumbled free on her shoulders, tresses curling against her neck.

He resisted threading his fingers through the fiery mass. He wanted to reassure her he'd be all right. She'd been watching him as if she feared at any moment he'd geyser blood from all orifices.

When was the last time any woman had pampered him or worried about him? Not since his mom died. Odd, but every once in a while he saw something of her in Cleo. That made no sense. He hadn't lost enough blood or drunk enough scotch to be delirious.

Banishing the notion, he tapped a finger on the address. "Could René have gone to London last week?"

"Like I told the detective, he left Tuesday morning and returned Thursday night. He said something about a jewelry commission and catching a plane. I don't know what airline."

"He traveled with a false passport, which Castelli said was not found. Nor were any receipts or matchbooks or anything helpful. But the time frame fits a London destination. He'd have had time to find this building, whatever it is, when he arrived."

"And return to Venice the next day." She shook her head. "*Studios*, he wrote, and *assembly*. Could it be a jewelry manufacturer? Or maybe he sold the necklaces—the original and his copy— to someone in London."

"He already feared Centaur would kill him. Hiding the necklaces would give him leverage with Zervas. Selling them would sign his death warrant. If he sold the pieces, why didn't he use the money to disappear? Why return to Venice?"

She gathered up her hair and smoothed it back as if the action aided her thoughts. "None of this makes sense."

"Maybe it will once we identify this building."

"The killers must not have found this drawing and neither did the police."

"Panaro and Ricci were searching for the necklaces, not for clues to their location. And the police searched for clues to them. Nobody considered your sketchbook important."

"But we don't know if it *is* important."

"Not yet." He lifted his phone. "Still early enough in the States to catch someone in my research department. They can search for the address and for the phrases in René's last words." Time he tried Max again. Find out why he couldn't reach him earlier.

Max picked up after one ring. "Hey, boss, glad you called." His voice sounded strained, falsely jovial. "You'll never guess who was here—T. J. He dropped in to see you. Wants you to call right away."

Thomas's mouth went dry and a muscle cramped in his jaw. "T.J. I'll do that right now. Can I call you back?"

"I'm not going anywhere."

He ended the call, his mind racing with questions.

"What is it, Thomas?"

Her soft concern broke through his fury. He sought calm by taking her hands in his and forcing all the tension from his body. "Devlin Security's been hacked," he said in measured tones.

"What does it mean?"

"I'll call Rivera back on a secure number and find out the extent of the damage. For you and me, it means I have no backup or resources from my company. We're on our own."

****

Marco Zervas paced the living room of the Venice flat, his mobile phone held a good six inches from his ear.

"I transferred to you an exorbitant down payment," Ahmed Yousef bellowed. "And you have lost everything. It has been days. What are you doing about this disaster?"

The Iranian's guttural tones abraded Zervas's nerve endings. "Nothing is lost," he said in calm tones. "I'll have them in a few days."

Yousef muttered something in Arabic. "So you said before. I have a deadline. If you do not deliver within six days, I shall ruin you. Then I shall repossess my payment in blood. Do I make myself clear?"

"You will have the necklace on time." Before Zervas could say anything more, the connection went dead. As dead as he'd be if Yousef could follow through. Wouldn't fucking happen. Zervas protected his secrecy, his locations too well.

Six days. All he had was six days.

The silence of the moldy old building with its decayed elegance seemed to mock him. He tossed the phone onto a nearby chair as he continued pacing. He would figure it out, retrieve the necklaces and get the copy to Yousef by the damn deadline. He would earn the rest of the millions the Iranian was paying for this deal. Moreau's copy better be as good as he'd claimed, indistinguishable from the original.

Whatever cloak-and-dagger business Yousef planned, Zervas couldn't allow such a priceless artifact to disappear into a terrorist network that might pick out the stones and sell them. What the hell was the Iranian up to? Fuck, he was better off not knowing. Unless he could use it for his own ends.

First he had to recover the things. Forcing information from the bitch was the only way. If snatching her meant a confrontation with his old captain, Zervas would win.

Then Thomas Devlin would pay for his sins.

****

"Hacked? You mean a virus or spyware, Thomas?" Cleo asked.

Thomas had explained that T. J. meant Trojan Horse, the company code for a security breach. "I don't know yet. Probably worse. Although I said I'd call back, the reverse is our protocol. Rivera will need an hour to have IT ascertain if my call was detected by the hacker.

Then he'll call me—on a secure phone." The fire in his belly said this breach had Marco Zervas written all over it.

"You're thinking Zervas has something to do with it, the hacking."

"Seems too much of a coincidence not to be connected." He looked at the time on his phone. "I can use the hour to ask Lucas to look up our mystery building."

Nodding, Cleo yawned. "I'd like to take a shower. Unless there's something more I can do for you."

With her hair tousled and her cheeks lightly flushed by the prosecco, she looked soft and warm, and her innocent offer thickened his blood and sent it south. He raised a knee to hide his growing arousal.

His wound limited his range of movement. But it had other possibilities. "Babe, what you can do for me can wait until we're under these covers together."

She pursed her lips, making them plumper and more inviting. "Bite me. The EMT said no strenuous activity. Getting the blood… um, pumping—" her cheeks turned a beautiful rose "—could open your wound."

"I'm not so old I'll let a little scratch bother me."

She rolled her eyes. "The age thing again. The slick way you tripped up the knife guy didn't look like the actions of an old guy."

"A slip of the tongue. But the ten years between us is never going away." He waved away the topic. "What I meant to say was that except for my left forearm, all of my parts function just fine. I'll rest up while you take your shower. Then we'll see."

A grin twitched at her lips. "Really? After that knife fight, an *old* guy like you must be stiff and aching. I can at least offer a back massage."

"Back massage sounds good. I am a bit *stiff*." He waggled his eyebrows. "Growing stiffer by the minute. Aching too."

Laughter burst from her, the low, husky lilt diving straight to his groin. She grabbed the other terry robe from its hook and strolled into the bathroom humming "When I'm Sixty-Four."

Thomas relaxed against the mound of pillows. If he was any judge, the banter meant she was giving him another chance. Maybe she cared about him enough to allow him some leeway, some time to learn not to be a hard-ass like both their fathers. And maybe he could seduce her into some sweet, slow lovemaking.

He punched Lucas's number into his phone. Afterward, he'd try his sister again. Not once had she answered his daily attempts, but maybe she listened to his messages. God, he hoped her shrink had read her right.

"Yo, Thomas," Lucas said. In the background, voices overlapped with ringing phones and whirring printers. "Should've gotten back to you sooner. Lots going on here. But I got a surveillance capture of Zervas from Marco Polo Airport Security. He looks different—shiny dome and glasses—but it's him no question."

Thomas checked the jpg loading on his phone screen. Stills lifted from surveillance videos were often grainy and fuzzy. Not this one. Stark and detailed of the man's upper body and face. A beak of a nose, slightly crooked. Lean, ascetic build in an Italian cut suit and black T-shirt. Even behind the dark-framed glasses, an avid look in his eyes Julius Caesar would've mistrusted.

More fire flashed through him before he banked it.

He needed a cool head for the chase. "Marco Zervas. Yes. But that's not why I called."

"I'm pretty busy here, boss."

"This is important."

"I see. Just a sec." The force of Thomas's will must've transmitted through the connection because the extraneous noises were cut off. "What've you got?"

"Devlin Security has been hacked."

"No shit. When? Who?"

"That's all I know. I'm waiting for Rivera to call me back with the details. Don't call DSF or send any data until you receive the all clear."

"No problem. Wouldn't surprise me if Zervas's pet geek did the hacking."

"Right. My thoughts exactly." Thomas adjusted his sore arm on the pillow. He relayed the events of the evening, omitting his sliced arm. "Not having company resources leaves me hanging. I need your help. A search of Cleo's old flat unearthed a floor plan that might be connected to the forger, maybe where he hid one or both necklaces. I need you to find what the place is." He gave the London address.

Lucas cleared his throat as if temporizing. "Hunt has me on this other thing. A breakthrough on Yousef. If I can find your info fast, okay. Otherwise, it'll have to keep."

Keeping wouldn't work. "Look. I need to retrieve Cleopatra's necklace. The task force wants to nab Marco Zervas. Zervas is here trying to track us down because he thinks Cleo can find the necklace. We can set up a trap."

"Damn, sounds good to me, Thomas. So does Venice. But Hunt'll never go for it. Not now. What

Yousef is up to takes precedence. She has us all working on it."

A sharp right from the CTF's original mandate. But Thomas's gut said the necklaces were tied to Yousef. "Tell me about Yousef. Or do I need clearance?"

The light tap-tap-tap on a tablet came through the receiver. "I have authorization to share anything we have with you."

As Lucas described the interview with the chemist, Thomas sat up straighter. "So he sold a computer chip to Yousef's man?"

"Not just any old computer chip." The tapping stopped. "The chip contains explosive compounds. When this sucker is set off, anyone within six feet is blown to hell."

Chapter Nineteen

THE LUXURY OF the tiled shower—three nozzles, body wash and shampoo that smelled like lemons—relaxed Cleo at first. Until worry about Thomas's wound prickled her nerves like thistles.

Once again someone she lo—cared about had been injured. For her. Or because of her. The prickling moved, to the vicinity of her heart. She rubbed her sternum with her soapy washcloth. All she could do for now was tend her wounded hero.

By the time she dried off with one of the hotel's thick bath sheets, the steam and fragrant soap had eased her tension. After applying body lotion, she wrapped herself in the bathrobe and opened the door.

He sat higher in the bed, brow pleated with thought as he listened to his mobile. Spotting her, he patted the side of the bed.

No massage oil, but she snagged the small bottle of lotion before she joined him. As she joined him, he ended the call.

"The phone. Max Rivera about the hacking?"

He nodded. "Before I tell you, he said the admiral is home from the hospital and your mom's there. He'll be laid up for weeks but he'll mend."

She closed her eyes in a brief prayer of thanks. Now if she could only talk to her mom. "Thank you, Thomas. And thank Rivera when you talk to him next."

"Right. He says our head of IT has held off the cyber invasion. She protected most of our data stored off-site by closing down those ports."

"Great news." She tugged on his robe's sash. "Take that off and roll over. You're due for that back rub."

"Babe, you can rub whatever parts you want." Holding his injured arm gingerly against his body, he peeled off the robe with her help.

She poured the lemon-scented lotion into one hand and warmed it between her palms. Such a beautiful man. He was all firm muscle over strong bones, a man of honor made tough in battle and in life. His thoughtful expression belied his flirtatious words. "Does Rivera have any idea who's responsible?"

He turned onto his stomach. "Max agrees with me it's probably Zervas's man, Gerry Hawkins. Well known in underground cyber circles but never prosecuted or jailed. He seems to have created software specifically geared to take over a large computer system. He accessed ours with a DSF secure log-in device, a card an employee swipes for access to company computers. Then whoever did it uploaded the software using a USB drive."

"An inside job. One of your own people. That bites."

"With vampire fangs," he said on a groan. "DSF vets personnel thoroughly—background checks, financial checks, psychological, the works. Necessary because of the work we do. But we missed something or someone needs money in a bad way."

"Let it go for now and let me work out the outer soreness." She positioned herself on her knees and started with the taut muscles of his neck and shoulders with broad, gentle strokes. Often after long hours hunched over a workbench, René had asked her to massage him this way. Better not to mention that.

A low groan. "Damn, that feels good. I didn't know how much I needed this."

Rarely had the massages for René been sexual, only therapeutic. The circular motions of her lotion-slick hands over the firm flesh and tensile strength of Thomas's back both soothed and aroused her. She paused to drink water from the bottle beside the bed.

After a moment, she dug into his thick dorsals with the heels of her hands. "I don't know much about computers, obviously." Prime example, posting on Facebook her photo wearing the Cleopatra necklace. "So thank you for explaining in terms I understand. Can your company do business as usual?"

"Not completely. Most of our records are safe, but Rivera had to shut down credit and explain to all our clients. No new cases until this is solved. Then we'll notify everyone and put out a press release."

"I'm sorry. Embarrassing, big time."

"Zervas knew how to hit me where it hurt. Now more than ever I want his ass." The sharp vehemence tightened the muscles beneath her hands.

"You'll get him. I wish I had more of a clue to help find the necklaces." She moved farther down, straddling his hips for better access to his tight lower back. "What about Del Rio? Did he find the London address?"

"He's working on it. He found the company name but no information yet. Merlin Entertainment mean anything to you?"

"*Niente.*"

"*Nothing.* Even I know that much Italian. Del Rio had to hang up while he went ahead with his assignment. He'll call back when he has something more."

"Kind of late at night for him to be working," she observed.

"A California scientist under government contract was caught dealing with a man associated with Ahmed Yousef. He confessed to selling the highly classified computer chip."

"Military secrets?"

"Military applications for damn sure. This chip contains compounds that when triggered create an explosion. And nothing as small as you might think. Enough to kill anyone nearby."

Horrific images flashed in her mind. "I don't know much about Yousef except he's Iranian." She was breathing hard as she kneaded his back with her knuckles.

Small grunts of satisfaction rose from deep inside his chest. "A dissident, a fanatic on keeping Western influence out of the Middle East. He opposes his government's policies because reformers have eased toward rapprochement with the West. Trade agreements and such. The mullahs tolerate him because he also attacks their adversaries."

Thomas was relaxing, judging from the slurred sound of his voice. Pleased, she smoothed her palms down the muscles to ease out of the deep massage. In moments he should fall asleep. "An exploding chip like that could be used for an assassination."

"Mmm, no wonder finding it's a priority. Too bad it distracts from finding Zervas."

She conjured the image of a computer chip. Tiny, not just millimeters but smaller. Delicate but easy to hide. She went still. Her pulse pinged with excitement.

"What if the two are connected?" she said. "What if

Yousef paid Zervas to steal the Cleopatra necklace? Zervas paid René to make the copy. What if he hid the exploding chip inside one of the necklaces?"

Thomas turned over so fast he flipped her onto her back beside him. He kissed her, a hard, smacking smooch that stole what breath she had left. "Babe, you're a genius!"

He rolled away from her. He sat on the edge of the bed and stared at his phone, not calling. Once he took time to think about the idea, doubts? "There has to be a connection." Seconds later, he was explaining her theory to Del Rio.

Cleo leaned against the headboard while she listened. On speaker, Del Rio's initial reactions were only grunts and hums. Her cheeks burned. Thomas liked her idea, but exhaustion and pain had him half zonked. Lucas Del Rio and this official Interpol bunch would think her idea dumb.

"A damned handy solution." Del Rio didn't sound convinced. "But why such an expensive and elaborate method? Stealing Cleopatra's necklace and paying Chung three million for the exploding chip?"

Cleo listened intently as they kicked around ideas. Suggestions, challenges, and questions bounced back and forth as the men focused on the problem and examining all the possibilities.

"Suicide bombers are a hell of a lot cheaper," Del Rio said.

"Cheaper, yes, but ordinary," Thomas replied. "Maybe Yousef's target is a government official, one so secure a suicide bomber couldn't get close."

Cleo leaned closer to Thomas's phone. "And high-profile, someone who warrants a high-profile assassination, something public."

He squeezed her hand. "And witnessed by millions. Finding the chip means finding the stolen necklace. Zervas had a limited role in the scheme, only paid to get the chip implanted in the necklace. That's probably more millions. I figure the copy was our old friend's idea so he could keep the real necklace for himself. Still, he might know what assassination was planned. He followed Cleo and me to Venice. He'll follow us again. We have to work together."

Del Rio blew out a long whistle. "You may be on to something, Captain."

Cleo held her breath as Thomas stared at the ceiling. Finally, he said, "Yousef can't act on his plan without the chip. Let me talk to Agent Hunt."

****

An hour later in the darkened room, Cleo snuggled up to Thomas's uninjured side. He slept on his back, snoring lightly, his chest rising and falling in an even rhythm.

She smiled, warmed by his heat in more ways than one. After he'd ended the phone conversation, he'd drawn her into his arms and they'd made love, as he promised earlier.

"Don't worry about the arm," he'd said. "My blood will be pumping elsewhere."

Now she lay replete and sleepy beside him. And proud.

To the task-force boss, a hard-as-nails FBI agent, he had defended her deduction. Apparently Jessica Hunt couldn't say no to Thomas Devlin any more than she could. Tomorrow the two of them were headed to Paris for a strategy session with the Centaur Task Force. She'd be glad to leave Venice and Marco Zervas behind. Thomas had hinted Zervas would follow but she'd be safer in Paris, with more protection from the CTF.

Was he easing away from her already? He wasn't tired of sex with her. He seemed to like her company. When they weren't focused on the hunt for the necklace or evading Marco Zervas, they talked. They teased and laughed and shared. He told her more about his time in the Army and she shared stories of her European travels. Whatever they did, whatever they discussed, desire arced between them in a constant flow.

Tonight he could have died defending her. When she'd heard him grappling with the attacker, an oily cauldron of fear for him had churned her stomach. At that moment she'd accepted she was in love with him.

Desperately, deeply, irrevocably. Dangerously.

She sank into her pillow as feverish thoughts swirled in her tired brain. For the past several years, she'd closed her feelings for him in the dark shadows of her heart, but being with him again opened the door and out they burst in multicolor pyrotechnics. Joy and fear and tenderness and pain, mixed with her need to keep her hard-won independence.

She loved him and she didn't want to love him, didn't want to *need* him.

Earlier in the water taxi, he'd allowed her to realize the danger involved in visiting Mimi. Not heavy handed. Reasonable. Maybe he wasn't the arrogant alpha male wanting total control. Maybe…

Oh, great, less than twenty-four hours since her resolve to keep it simply sex and here she was totally denying reality, picturing a canvas daubed with bright yellows and blues. Instead the canvas was solid black.

No colors. No light. No future. Her stomach hollowed, eddying again with the toxic stew.

She needed a distraction. Like solving René's puzzle.

"Melon..."Pomp" or maybe *"Pope."* So *"Pope... Ladder."*

No better. Suddenly her eyelids felt weighted with bricks. She yawned. Somewhere she'd read that if you went to bed with a problem to solve, your brain would work on it while you slept.

Note to brain: You have your orders.

****

Paris

With Cleo at his side late the next afternoon, Thomas entered the task force headquarters' outer office. They brought with them the smell of the light rain that had begun as the limousine delivered them from Charles de Gaulle Airport.

The slice in Thomas's arm barely stung and hadn't swollen, so this morning he'd persuaded Cleo he didn't need to see a doctor. For now, she agreed. They intended to arrive by noon, but mechanical problems with their Al Italia flight and a French truckers' strike ruined that plan. He hoped to hell the delays hadn't given Zervas time to catch up to them.

He slid Cleo's soft carryon off his shoulder and handed it to her. He gave their names to the pretty young receptionist who sat at a sleek modern desk before an opaque glass wall.

"*Oui, monsieur, mademoiselle*, you are expected," she said. "Have a seat. I shall announce you." She tapped a button on her ear module and did just that.

"I admit we need the task force's help," Cleo

whispered as they wandered toward the chairs, "but letting them take over is out of the question."

She set her bag on a chair. Biting her lower lip, she brushed the raindrops from the jacket she wore over a hot-pink pullover and dark pants, her own clothing for a change. The reddish tone of the overhead lighting caught the fire in her auburn hair. And the determination in her eyes.

He dumped his backpack beside her bag on the chair. "On that we agree. We have different priorities." He captured her hand and rubbed the soft skin of her wrist with his thumb. "My highest priority is keeping you safe."

Her gaze softened. "That and retrieving the necklace. I'll hold you to your promise not to shut me out or hide me away."

Before he could reassure her, Lucas Del Rio burst through the inner door, his broad face granite-hard in an exasperated expression. When his gaze landed on Cleo, he stopped like a street mime colliding with an invisible wall. His eyes rounded and his face reddened.

Thomas laughed, looped his good arm around her shoulders. "Yes, Lucas, it's uncanny how similar they are. This is Cleo, not Mimi. Trust me on that."

Lucas blinked away his stupor, schooling his features in what Thomas recognized as an effort to mitigate his menacing appearance. "Glad to meet you, Ms. Chandler," he said in the same soothing tone he'd used at Mimi's bedside.

Cleo slipped from beneath Thomas's arm and rushed to the other man. Ignoring his outstretched hand, she wrapped both arms around his solid middle and hugged him.

Lucas looked even more stunned. The resemblance to Mimi had whacked him with the stupid stick. And having this beautiful woman give him the long-lost-brother greeting was clearly the last thing he expected. His arms hovered inches away from her as if this female mirage would vanish if he touched her.

Warmth suffused Thomas's chest as he watched the emotional tableau. He'd said nothing to Cleo of Lucas's rough appearance or of his insecurity. Respect meant letting his friend deal with people on his own terms. And knowing Cleo meant it wouldn't matter. Bless her for embracing Lucas without reservation.

She beamed up at the big man. "Lucas, I've been dying to meet you. To thank you."

"Ease up on the poor man, Cleo. Let him breathe." Thomas clamped his lips together against a grin.

"Oh, sorry." She released her grip and patted Del Rio's arm. "Thank you for saving my cousin's life. I..." She looked away briefly and swallowed. "You protected her. And make it Cleo."

"Yes, ma'am, uh, Cleo." Lucas's gaze still locked on her.

Thomas stepped forward and clapped him on the shoulder. "Agent Hunt said you were the one who got the scientist to talk."

"Shoved my ugly mug against the camera. Probably scared him into talking. Damned glad to see you." Two men shook hands. "If we're working together, maybe we can goose this investigation faster than slo-mo."

"Right." Exactly what Thomas had in mind. Keeping Cleo ahead of Zervas had become harder.

Lucas led them through an open-plan office space where about a dozen men and women worked in cluttered cubicles or hunched over banks of computers and other equipment. A few had already cleared desks in preparation for the end of the work day.

As Cleo passed, men glanced over with appreciation and women with speculation. Thomas leveled his gaze their way. They quickly returned to work.

Inside the conference room at the rear, Lucas introduced them to FBI Special Agent Jessica Hunt and three others of the team, a woman and two men.

Holding her gregarious nature in check, Cleo shook hands formally with each before they all took seats around the conference table with members of the CTF. The steady rain clattered on the skylight above. The aroma of dark-roast French coffee drifted from a tray with cups and a carafe in the center. Five cups, no extras for visitors.

Hunt, a pencil nestled in her salt-and-pepper hair, ruled from the head of the table. Judging from her take-no-prisoners manner, no matter where she sat, she ruled.

Her gaze flicked from Cleo to Thomas. "Unfortunate you've arrived so late. We've almost finished our meeting. You think stealing the necklace, copying it, all of that is connected to Ahmed Yousef and the stolen computer chip. Is that correct?"

Hunt's gaze, as hard and brittle as flint, probably meant she intended to blow them off. Lucas kept his expression carefully neutral. Poor guy was caught between two bosses. Thomas tried not to grind his teeth.

"Not just connected," he said. "The key to stopping both. If Zervas finds the necklaces, he'll turn them over to Yousef. Can you risk an assassination?"

She flipped through papers. "We have other means of dealing with that risk."

"Since Cleo left Venice, he or his thugs have trailed us. I've barely managed to elude him, although his hacker couldn't track me because I've paid with untraceable plastic. But this morning I bought our plane tickets with my personal credit card." He sensed Cleo vibrating with impatience. "I bought tickets for Amsterdam. Our travel delays may have given Zervas an edge to catch up to us but you might pick them up at the airport or spot them on CCTV."

"The head of Centaur is no fool," the gray-suited Scotland Yard man scoffed. "He'll smell a trap."

"Perhaps, but he won't be able to resist. Yousef must be pressuring him because of a deadline we don't know. Otherwise he'd delegate the search to minions. He's desperate."

"Zervas would not know Yousef's plans. Or reveal them to us." The French secret service agent's accent was light, her eyes shrewd.

The representative from the *carabinieri*, the Italian national police, nodded vigorously in agreement over his half glasses. He continued swiping his index finger across his tablet screen.

Across from Thomas, Lucas passed his right hand across his mouth, two fingers extended, the go-ahead signal from their Delta Force days.

Thomas respected the Italian and French push in this effort. Both nations, like Greece, invested heavily in protecting and recovering their stolen treasures. The U.S. didn't see art crime as a priority. Foolish and tragic, in his opinion. Jessica Hunt must've done some fast talking or politicking to get her plum position.

He hiked a shoulder in feigned nonchalance. "Zervas has woven a wide network. He probably knows some of Yousef's machinations. And the CTF's work. Left dangling out there on his spun thread, he could interfere." He leveled a gaze at Hunt. "How can we miss a chance to wrap up the head of Centaur in our own web?"

"Not *our* web, Mr. Devlin," Hunt said. "If I'm not mistaken, *you* are a civilian hired by Ms. Chandler's father to protect her, not to pursue the necklaces or Zervas or Yousef. If you want to protect your charge, I have a safe house ready."

Beside him, Cleo shifted in her chair. Leaning forward, she beamed the CTF leader her megawatt smile. "Special Agent Hunt, we're way beyond protecting me. Thomas wants to retrieve the stolen necklace—" she slid him a glance that thawed the ice block building inside since the conference room door closed behind them "— and his company's reputation. And I *have* to stop this evil man. He murdered a man I cared about and almost killed my cousin."

Caught by the emotion in her voice, Thomas closed his hand around hers.

SA Hunt steepled her hands over her papers. Her gaze softened and Thomas could almost believe Lucas's claim she was a grandmother. "Ms. Chandler—"

"Cleo."

"Cleo," Hunt amended, her sharp smile betraying her as the wolf in grandma guise, "you too are a civilian, an amateur and not a professional investigator. I appreciate you sharing your information. Our investigation will proceed. You may remain as our guest in a safe house until you can go home."

Cheeks pink and eyes blazing, Cleo pushed back her chair and stood. "No safe house. You have no jurisdiction over me. While you follow your *professional-investigator* path, I'll go find the necklaces." Chin high, she turned to walk away.

Thomas shot to his feet, ready to back her up. This meeting was going to hell anyway. Next he'd yank Lucas.

"I wish you luck," Hunt said to Cleo's back. "Moreau's clue is the raving of a dying man. Nonsense. Our search for *'Melon,' 'Pope'* and *'ladder'* or even *'Pope's ladder'* has yielded nothing."

Her fingers gripping the door handle, Cleo turned. "Not nonsense. I misunderstood him. Good luck to you with the wrong clue."

The door closed behind her with a soft click.

Chapter Twenty

WHEN ALL HEADS in the outer office turned Cleo's way like prairie dogs popping up from their dens, she slammed on the brakes. A flirty wave, a smile, and heads ducked down again. Spotting a familiar sign, she ducked inside the blue-and-yellow tiled and floral-scented ladies' room.

She stared into the white-framed mirror over the sink. *Dammit, what are you doing? Think, Cleo Marie. This is exactly what Thomas accused you of, running away when things go wrong.*

Which they had.

Hunt didn't buy the link between the chip and the necklaces. Yes, she had a job to do, and Cleo could be no part of bringing down Centaur. Except that for her, finding the necklace and bringing down Centaur were all bound up with René's murder and the attack on Mimi. Had her own impulsive exit—yes, dammit, impulsive— sent Thomas's strategy careening into a ditch? Now she'd left, she had nowhere to go. Nowhere safe. Not even a mind escape.

Her eyes burned and her breath caught. She couldn't give up.

After using the facilities, she wandered back toward the conference room. The brass nameplate on the open door of the adjacent office read *J. Hunt*. She dug in to wait, leaning against the wall between the two doors, her nerves sparking like live wires.

The door swung open. In two strides, Thomas joined her, his expression a mix of relief and surprise. He hustled her into Hunt's office.

She shrugged from his grip and crossed the burgundy rug to the window. New-carpet smell hung in the air with hints of perfume. Hunt's probably, but incongruous. On the Champs-Elysées, tiny lights draping the trees painted the scene in a romance of color. The way she'd paint it if— She pivoted away.

On the polished mahogany desk, piles of folders teetered beside a computer. So Ms. FBI did more than just preside.

She looked up at Thomas. "I won't be shut out. Hiding me in some dingy flat will accomplish nothing. Zervas is following *me*, not you. You promised." The sympathetic tilt to his straight black brows nearly had her caving.

"Right. These investigators are burning up their screens with nothing to show for it, both for the clues and for Ahmed Yousef's possible high-profile target. After you left, I argued that point, but got zip. So here I am, with you." He heaved a sigh, his gaze soft, and placed his hands on the desk, bracketing her between his outstretched arms. "You don't know how relieved I am you didn't leave."

The heat in her cheeks prompted a wan smile. "I almost did. Paris is a big city. I could hide for a while." And Zervas could've found her. She suppressed a shudder.

"What you said, about misunderstanding Moreau's clue, did you make that up?"

"Oh, please. I didn't say anything earlier because I

need more information before I'm sure. Lucas—"

"Somebody call my name?"

Cleo peered around Thomas to see Lucas's burly torso fill the door frame. A wide grin made his eyes twinkle as he took in their near embrace. His boxer's countenance complete with scars would be intimidating to some, but his smile and his quiet manner charmed her. Judging from his reaction to meeting her, he cared for Mimi, more than as a bodyguard.

"Sit rep, Sergeant." Thomas slid away from her.

"Yes, sir." Lucas executed a crisp salute. "I had to talk fast but Hunt agreed to give your way a chance." He shifted his gaze to Cleo. "She wants you to return to the meeting."

She whooped in victory and sailed past Lucas. "I'm in."

"I don't know how you did that, but when this is over remind me to give you a raise," Thomas said as a grinning Lucas stepped aside to let him pass.

All the agents glanced up as Cleo and the others entered the conference room. The French agent's mouth pursed before she averted her gaze. The Scotland Yard man focused on picking lint from his sleeve. The Italian, who'd barely looked up from his tablet earlier, studied her with an expression that might've been respect.

Taking her seat, Cleo waited to see what Hunt would do.

"I consider following your trail a slim possibility but it could narrow our search for Yousef's target. That is, *if* your supposed clue leads to the recovery of the Cleopatra necklace," Hunt said, her expression guarded, not too different from Thomas's warrior mask.

"I'll tell you what I believe the clue to be after—"

"*Believe?* You're still unsure?" Hunt demanded.

Beside Cleo, Thomas leaned forward as if to defend her. She gave him a small shake of her head. He subsided except for tightening around his mouth.

"I'll answer that question after Mr. Del Rio explains what's in that London building owned by Merlin Entertainment." She turned to Lucas.

Color rose to his broad cheeks. "Ah, um, I started a search until the exploding chip issue sent it to the back burner." His fingers flew over his tablet computer. "Give me a minute."

Hunt's mouth thinned but she said nothing.

Beneath the table, Thomas closed his hand around Cleo's, and she exhaled and deliberately relaxed her shoulders. Other than wanting her in bed, he kept his feelings for her guarded, except for rare moments like this. Whether or not he believed in René's clues, he was with her. Did he realize how much his support meant?

Lucas looked up from his screen, excitement on his countenance. He licked his lips. "Merlin Entertainment is a conglomerate running a wide range of international companies. The building in the West Acton section of London contains production facilities—design studios, workshops, offices and so on— for the chain of Madame Tussauds Wax Museums."

Cleo's heart sprinted like a greyhound. "Yes! That makes perfect sense."

"It does?" Thomas asked.

She shot him a grin, then addressed Hunt. "René once worked there, creating jewelry for the wax figures. He didn't say *'melon.'* He said *'Merlin.'* And the rest wasn't '*Pope'* and *'ladder,'* but *'Poe'* and *'letter.'* "

Consternation crinkled the agent's dark forehead.

"*Po* the river or *Poe* as in Edgar Allen Poe?"

"René was a big fan of Edgar Allen Poe's stories. The rest of what he said was *'Poe's letter.'* Remember "The Purloined Letter"? The stolen letter was hidden among others—"

"—in plain sight," Thomas finished.

****

Crystal City, Virginia

Mara Marton flopped onto the chair in front of the boss's desk, every cell in her body projecting frustration. "I can't access any of the databases I need for my research assignments, Max. I can't help Mr. Devlin. I can't do squat. I've resorted to playing Spider Solitaire. You have to stop this hacker. Now!"

As if Max's own frustration didn't already have his guilt meter zooming through the roof, her glare pierced him like a poison dart. He swung his leg with its two-ton cast to the floor and leaned forward. "Mara, I hear you. Everyone on this floor hears you. The security office downstairs hears you. Trust me. Gaspar is doing all she can to erect barriers and track the source of the malware."

"Sorry. Sorry." She fluttered her hands in apology. "Anything I can do?"

"Maybe. You're damned good at reading people. When you were working with Cort on the crown jewel thing, you picked up nuances on your suspects the police had missed. I could authorize you to dig into personnel records. Gaspar has them protected. You willing?"

"Just a different sort of research. And a whole lot more satisfying than Spider Solitaire." She grinned. "Count on me."

"Look for any motivation to betray the company.

226

Money, something in their background, a gripe against DSF. Anything, no matter how slight." *Dios*, they had to find something soon. With no new contracts and long-standing accounts leaving for other security companies, the company was losing big bucks on a daily basis.

Her gaze turned pensive, as if an idea had occurred to her. "Or something against Mr. Devlin personally. I'll get on it as soon as you clear me for access."

****

Paris

"It's Rivera." Thomas glanced up from his phone. "I have to take this."

Cleo raised a hand in acceptance as he strode away from the reception desk for more privacy. She fished inside her suitcase for a scrunchie. While he talked and while they waited for Lucas, also on the phone in his cubicle, she might as well braid her hair before they went out and the rain frizzed her mop.

Immediately following the assertion that René had probably hidden both necklaces in the Madame Tussauds building, Agent Hunt had adjourned the meeting. Afterward, the offices emptied like an ebbing tide. No wonder, it was after eight on a Thursday. A rumble in Cleo's stomach reminded her she'd eaten nothing but airline pretzels since breakfast.

She finished binding her braid as Thomas crossed to her, his call finished.

"The secure line, complete with encryption software, still holds against the hacker," he said, grim lines bracketing his mouth, "Small comfort."

"Any breakthrough?"

"Nothing has been lost, but that's all so far."

No data maybe, but DSF had other, serious losses—

some major accounts and new business— he clearly didn't want to mention. The fallout didn't compare to that day in Afghanistan, but she could see he felt just as helpless, not in control. "You wish you could be there to take care of the problem."

"Thank God for Rivera's cool head and Gaspar's expertise. The inside man didn't open a portal to our hacker. He fed the malware in using a USB drive."

"Why do it that way?" Cleo asked, zipping up her bag. "Doesn't he run the risk of being caught with the evidence?"

"Risky, yes. But the low tech aspect may help in nailing the guy." He fingered her braid. "Ready to brave the elements once Lucas is finished calling London?"

In spite of the success of her remembered clue, Cleo's stomach remained jittery. She didn't like where they were headed. "I thought you were on my side. No safe house."

"Only for the night. A flat in the Sixteenth, a quiet residential section of Paris. Much safer than a hotel. Temporary, but you could stay there and rest." He caressed her cheek. "Let Lucas and me go to London tomorrow."

"No, you need me. I've worn the necklace." She remembered the feel of the ancient collar on her shoulders and summoned Queen Cleopatra's confidence. "I know its weight, its jewels, its glitter."

"Could've been the copy." His wry expression told her he saw she had no rejoinder to that.

Except she did. "I handled the real one. Heavy as chain-mail. I'll know it. I won't stay here alone, Thomas. Zervas could still find me. Besides—"

"I promised," he finished. Cupping her shoulders

with his big warm hands, he fixed her with his steady amber gaze, the one that seemed to see inside her and never failed to heat her from the inside out. "We'll go together to London. But hear me. If I thought locking you in a safe house was the best way, the *only* way to keep you safe, I'd break that promise in a heartbeat."

Heat tugged low in her belly and she swayed toward him. Thomas in protector mode was irresistibly addictive, more powerful than any drug. She forced herself to remember protection was his job. She needed no reminder his other default mode was being in charge. Didn't he just warn her of that?

A throat-clearing cough announced Lucas's return, and Thomas released her.

The big man scrubbed a hand over his mouth, an obvious attempt to hide a grin. "Here's the deal. The Madame Tussauds director will tell me nothing over the phone. Apparently they've had trouble in the past."

"Stalkers? Wax figure perverts?" Cleo asked.

His laugh softened his scarred features. "Anything's possible. But he mentioned industrial spies. Anyway, the Brit agent here is having one of his Scotland Yard colleagues vouch for me. But he'll want to verify my ID in person."

Thomas nodded but a scowl crimped his forehead. "Hunt still has doubts. She's deliberate and by the book but too slow. We need to line up the tomb exhibit dates and places with locations of the wax museums. Tonight."

"We may already be too late." Cleo slung her bag over her shoulder and headed for the lifts. "The figures wearing the necklaces could still remain in the workshops or they could be in place in a Madame Tussauds anywhere from New York to Tokyo."

"Wait, Cleo." Lucas's hand covered the button before she could press it.

She whirled around. Lucas's tight expression told her something was very wrong. Thomas's face had that wary soldier look. "What?"

"No guards." Lucas pointed to the CCTV monitors mounted on the wall where the outer-office guard on duty during the day could see them. Two of the three screens showed the black-and-white marble floor, the potted plants camouflaging the exit door, and the half-circle security desk, but no uniformed guards. The third screen, which would have pictured the doors to all three lifts, showed a blank screen. Dead.

"Piss-poor security in this damn building. Cameras and a few rent-a-cop guards," Thomas said, disgust on his face. "The CTF is temporary but, hell, they ought to have automatic alarms, auto shut-down if the guards are compromised. Thomas pointed at the central monitor. "There, off to the side, a movement."

"How did Zervas get here so fast?" Her pulse zinged and she pictured shadowy figures brandishing automatic weapons invading the building like swarms of killer bees.

He wrapped one powerful arm around her shoulders and pulled her close. "He didn't. He probably called in a favor."

Her heart still rabbited. Her nerves felt wound, tight. Fear, yes, but more. Tuned in to her surroundings, even the normal sounds and smells—the hum of air conditioning, the distant blare of car horns, the spearmint sharpness of the receptionist's candies. Was this—every sense on alert—what hummed through warriors like these two men in the face of danger? In anticipation of adventure?

"Cleo?" Thomas began.

"I'm fine." She licked her dry lips, ready to do whatever was necessary. She trusted Thomas's expertise and instincts—and Lucas, loyal to his boss, just as vigilant and capable.

"No telling how many men are downstairs." Lucas reached behind him and withdrew a pistol that looked like the one Thomas had borrowed on Santorini. "Sooner or later they'll get tired of waiting for us to go down."

Thomas nodded. "Car's on fourth. They'll use the stairs. We have to get out of here." He now held an identical pistol. More of Lucas's doing.

He turned to her. "We'll need to move fast. Del Rio will take care of our bags later."

Her purse with her passport and money went into the zippered pocket of her jacket, a small attempt at protecting it from the rain she could hear peppering the skylight. A scarf wouldn't keep her dry but the Mondrian-print foulard would hide her bright hair. She tucked away her red flats in favor of black leather brogues. Ugly but practical in Venice. And here.

She observed intently as the men organized their escape in terse phrases and hand gestures, seeming to communicate almost by telepathy.

Their plans apparently in place, Thomas caught her to him. "Stick to me like paint, Cleo. Move when I say, stay put when I say." He demonstrated the corresponding hand signals. "Trust me. Can you do that?"

Like Santorini and Venice. Cleopatra could. *She* could. Think of the chase as an adventure.

Speaking might morph the mind-escape thrill coiled inside her into panic and paralysis. Rubbing her damp palms on her pants, she nodded.

Chapter Twenty-One

CATCHING THE FAINT gleam of what looked like mutiny still in Cleo's eyes, Thomas kicked himself mentally for coming on too strong. He would protect her however he saw necessary, but he needed her trust.

He prayed he had it, then shifted into the alert stillness of the zone. Ready, he brushed a kiss across her lips. "Then let's go."

He held her arm to keep her by his side as they approached the elevators. One on two, one on the ground floor, another on four. He punched the button. He noted her expression of alarm when Lucas slipped into the stairwell. "He's going to distract them while we beat it out a back door."

"Okay." Her voice was steadier than he'd expected, her gaze clear and alert.

A car started up from four, a floor Del Rio had said housed the offices of an insurance company. Probably empty, but he would take no chances. He motioned her to the side and plastered himself to the wall, out of range. They'd appear in the glass wall's reflection but so would anyone inside the lift.

Ding. The doors opened.

****

The Beretta comfortable in his palm, Lucas crept down the stairs, his sneakers silent on the concrete steps.

He had to give Thomas and Cleo time to slip out to

the Métro. Might have to take down the hired thugs, not just distract them. Problematic in the middle of Paris.

He paused on each landing, listened, processed. No indication of human movement above or below, only the faint hum of the building's ventilation, the dry smells of metal and concrete, and his own sweat.

On the last landing, he crouched and peered through the metal railing. Small window in the upper half of the steel door. The lobby light seemed dimmer. And not to save electricity during night hours, he bet. If he looked out, the brightness of the stairwell would provide Zervas's thugs a fat target—his head.

The hydraulic mechanism on this side of the steel door meant it opened inward. Fifty-fifty chance he'd have heard a man make that move. Recessed bulbs in the walls on either side of the door and the fluorescents overhead cast stark light in all corners. Nobody.

He let out a breath, slow and quiet. Checked the automatic. Safety off. His back to the green concrete wall, he edged down the last six steps. Tuned in with all his senses. Swung around to check below the stairs. Empty.

He crouched on the bottom step. Listened for sounds in the lobby.

The exit door swung open a few inches. A dark-jacketed figure hunched in the gap. The man's eyes narrowed as he spotted Lucas. Three shots blasted the stairwell. Bullets sliced chips off the step above Lucas. Another ricocheted off the metal railing an inch from his hand. He opened fire, put two rounds in the man's chest.

The man fell sideways through the opening, his free hand clutching his chest. The door swung shut.

Lucas's ears rang from the barrage in what

amounted to a vertical cement tunnel. Shit, now he couldn't hear with either ear.

He approached, low, dragged the assailant away from the exit. Blood pumped onto the floor then slowed to a trickle as the light faded from his eyes. The dead man stared at nothing with one blue eye and one brown. Average build, brown hair, soul patch. A neck tattoo pegged him as a local gang member.

A quick search of pockets located no ID, but he hadn't expected to find one. He pocketed the man's pistol and the extra clip stowed in the jacket. One less bad guy. One less weapon for the other dickwads to use.

He worked his jaw to loosen taut muscles, swallowed to clear his ears as he pictured the lobby. Double glass doors to the street, security desk to his right, seating area and bushy potted plants opposite. Whatever the plants were, their foliage would provide concealment. The shooters in the lobby would wait to see who came through the door—their man or somebody else.

He fired two shots into the stairwell's back corner. The blasts would confuse the issue, make them wonder. He gripped the door handle.

****

Thomas waited beside the open elevator car, listened, watched for any movement or shadow in the hidden corners.

Only the faint tang of sweat and a soft violin version of "Take Me Home, Country Roads" with a distinct French lilt exited the car. Before the doors could glide shut, he bent low and scanned the interior.

"Clear," he barked. "Cleo, with me."

Once she scooted inside with him, he punched the

button. "They might be watching the rear of this building. Third floor has a way into the next building. We'll leave from there." Del Rio would give them time. "Stand in the corner by the buttons. Just in case."

Cleo obeyed instantly, without a word, eyes as intent and focused as those of any soldier on a mission. He'd ask her about that later.

Offering a prayer they would have *later*, he steadied the Beretta with his left hand. This automatic model could fire controlled bursts of three rounds, close in operation to the bigger 9mm he preferred.

When the doors opened on three, he sidled into the opening, scanned the area, gun leveled. A closed door with three brass nameplates faced the elevator. A wide corridor stretched to the right and left. Empty. More doors with brass plates, also closed. Nearly eight o'clock, so those offices should be locked up and empty. He beckoned to Cleo.

Tapping the button for the ground floor, he sent the car down empty.

Toward the right, he spotted his goal. "Del Rio said to take that exit door to the next building." Their shoes swished in near silence on the dark green carpeting as they hurried toward the lighted *Sortie* sign.

"Is there any escape hatch or ambush spot Lucas hasn't checked out?"

"Doubt it. He's a worst-case-scenario kind of guy. A good man to have your back. He overlooks nothing."

They hustled along a dim corridor to the other building's exit sign.

He signaled her to stay to the side while he checked the stairwell. Silent and clear. "In case they've fanned out to look for us here, keep it fast and quiet."

They made it to the ground floor without incident. He groaned inwardly. No window in the door to see what was outside. Beretta ready, he inched open the door and caught the smells of wet pavement and car exhaust. No voices or scrape of shoes, only the rain's patter and the traffic's muffled roar. As he eased out farther, rain soaked his hair and splashed his leather shoes.

The scene before him explained the lack of near traffic. Shit.

He let the door close again. "Problem. Del Rio said to go right, then left up Franklin D. Roosevelt Avenue to the Métro stop. Outside's a U-shaped courtyard. Right end is closed. No public building entrances I can see. After eight everything's locked up tight."

She nodded, her eyes bright. The color of the freckles across her nose and high in her cheeks stood out against the pallor of her skin. "Maybe he meant to go right on the Rue Camille beyond the courtyard."

"You know the street?"

"Before I moved to Venice, I lived in Paris for a year and worked at an art supply store near here. Camille is lined with restaurants, hotels, and shops, busy even after offices close for the night. Turning right on Camille will take us to Roosevelt."

He should've known. She'd been knocking around Europe awhile. What artist wouldn't spend time in Paris? Kissing her would yank him right out of the zone but, man, he really wanted his mouth on hers. *Focus, Devlin.*

"Your route works, but it means going back the way we came," he said. "Maybe Del Rio has distracted Zervas's thugs. Maybe not. We don't know how many there are. Probably deployed outside as well as in the lobby. Definitely armed."

Concentration deepened the sea green of her eyes. "What can I do to help?"

"I need your eyes and ears. Watch for teams of two." He pulled her into his arms, absorbed her softness, the rapid thump of her heartbeat against him, the fragrance of her skin. She wrapped her arms around him, holding on as if her life depended on the connection. Damn, she was braver than he'd ever imagined.

Stepping away, he checked his weapon. "Cleo, my aim is to get us out of here without detection. I'm hoping these hired thugs won't risk a shootout in the middle of Paris. But if it comes down to it, I'll protect you with my life."

****

Lucas opened the stairwell door a crack and listened. His hearing hadn't recovered enough to distinguish subtle sounds. Hell, go for it. He scuttled low through the opening.

A staccato burst of bullets sprayed the door.

He answered with a burst of his own as he dived behind the plant pots. Shots cracked one washing-machine-size container, spraying ceramic shards and dirt. The shrub tilted at a precarious angle but didn't fall. He scooted closer to the other two, prayed their pots held together. Warm liquid trickled down his temple. Damn clay shards had dug a gash at his hairline.

The shots came from behind the security station. Curved desk rose about chest height, tall enough to conceal more than one man. But they wouldn't stay down long. He changed the Beretta's magazine and set it on the floor, then checked the other pistol he'd liberated. Nudged it through the green leaves, ready.

One man rolled out from the desk's right side, firing.

Lucas pulled the trigger. His bullets splintered marble and wood, sending the man diving for cover.

Shots erupted from the desk's other end. Two more men rushed out, bent low as one continued firing. The other spoke into an ear module.

Shit, double coverage. The entire block could hear this racket. How long before the *gendarmes* mounted up? And how long could he last even with two guns? What the hell, he'd offered to distract the bastards, hadn't he?

He returned fire, then took aim again at the first man. Heading for the glass doors beside the elevators. The corridor beyond led to a rear exit. Creep had to be stopped. Lucas's shots had to count. As he fired, more blasts from the other two shooters shattered the ceramics, his only cover. Dirt, shredded leaves, and clay bits showered him as the plants toppled to the floor.

He lay prone behind the wrecked pots. Gun firm in a two-handed grip, he lifted his head only to see the two men disappearing out the front doors and into the darkness.

Fuck, they'd played him. The first shooter had drawn his fire so the other team could escape. He turned toward the first man. Down just shy of his exit door. Not moving. One arm trapped beneath him, the right outstretched, hand still holding the automatic. No blood visible.

Lucas pocketed the liberated pistol and clambered to his feet, Beretta ready. He edged around the planter debris toward the still form. Dead eyes. Heaving a sigh, he kicked the man's pistol away into the corner.

He took out his phone and punched Thomas's number.

The faint wail of sirens penetrated his deadened

hearing. Shaking his head, he tried his hearing aid. Blown battery. He had bad enough news for Thomas, but what the hell was he going to tell the cops? And Special Ball-Breaker Agent Hunt?

****

With his life.

The declaration—delivered in a matter-of-fact tone—thundered in Cleo's ears. After the knife fight, she'd avoided thinking about the fact he was risking his life for her. Hearing him say the words again gave the possibility form and substance. Zervas's men wanted to grab her, not kill her, but that wasn't true about Thomas. If he were hurt or killed, she—

Icy shards scraped the back of her neck, but she kept her expression still. He held her gaze with his steady appraisal—always observing every detail, every nuance. She swallowed and nodded, calling on Cleopatra's boldness. "I'm ready."

She followed Thomas outside. No shots, no running footsteps, only the rainy tap dance on the paving stones. They dashed across the courtyard. Although the downpour had ebbed, the drizzle quickly soaked her face and hair, and the pounding of her shoes fountained cold water against her jeans. She ought to be shivering but maybe adrenaline insulated her from the discomfort.

When they reached the partial shelter of the opposite building, he backed them into a doorway and surveyed again. Always cool, always aware, always alert, he would see the bad guys before they saw him. Trusting him, believing in him helped her maintain her adventure mind escape. Deep inside, yeah, she did know it was a fantasy.

"The heavy rain kept people indoors," he said. "The

let-up is in our favor if more people come outside."

"Cover?"

"Right." He held up a hand as he pulled out his mobile phone, its vibrations humming. *"Del Rio,"* he mouthed.

His gaze scanned the courtyard, the street beyond. "Copy that. Don't see them yet." A pause. "Roger. ETA at least an hour to meet you."

He urged Cleo back into the drizzle. "I'll fill you in later. Two men got away, may come around the building after us. Could be others. Here we go."

They raced for the street. The Rue Camille teemed as usual.

As they joined the other pedestrians, he slowed their pace. "In this crush, they might not spot us. Don't act too careful. A dead giveaway you're trying not to be seen. Walk normally. Look in shop windows."

Slowing to the pace of the crowd didn't come too soon. Thank God. He was barely breathing hard, nothing like the frantic bellows pumping in her chest.

She angled her head. In the glare of car headlights, she saw two men in hooded black jackets striding toward them from the direction of the Champs-Élysées, about fifty yards back. Even though the team wasn't running after them, her heart somersaulted. She clutched Thomas's sleeve.

"I see them. And two more out the back door. Del Rio said there was another rear exit," he said, keeping her between him and the building. "I've got you, babe. They haven't spotted us yet."

Buoyed by the security of his arm around her shoulders, she forced herself to stroll.

Pedestrians scurried along, hunched beneath

colorless hooded raincoats and dark umbrellas. Street lights reflected the white sprays kicked up the passing cars and a bicycle slicing through the gutter. The scene could've been a shades-of-gray painting by Caillebotte. Little did people know they were actually in a black-and-white thriller film.

He steered her around a trio of tourists with maps and cameras and past a bakery, closed but still redolent of pastries and yeast. They edged by a gang of hoodie-clad teens studying an outside menu. In spite of her tension and the traffic fumes, her stomach growled at the aroma of herb-roasted chicken wafting from the restaurant's kitchen.

The Rue Camille was a long city block, a marathon distance to go before they reached Roosevelt. How much farther to the Métro entrance? She couldn't remember.

They nearly collided with a large woman toting a net shopping bag. She gasped and shrieked her complaint. Her umbrella dipped, dumping rain on them. One tip snagged on Cleo's scarf. She tried to pull it back over her hair but the soggy silk slipped away.

"Let it go." Thomas kept her hurtling onward as he replied to the shopper's irate French in English, "Sorry. Excuse us."

A shout behind them. Then another in answer.

"Don't look. They see us now," Thomas said, propelling her into a run.

Her damn hair. She might as well wear a neon sign on her head. She pumped her legs harder, ignored the protestations of her muscles. All that walking in Venice wasn't the same as running.

One pair of pursuers had to sidestep a family of four lugging multiple bags. Some passers-by turned to glare at the running men. The other pair darted across the busy street.

"Splitting up to flank us," Thomas said, tossing his head toward the team on the opposite sidewalk. "Too many people here blocking their way."

"Our way too." She panted as they wove through the gauntlet of hotel guests, diners, and late shoppers.

"We can't shake them. They'll stay with us all the way to the Métro. Cleo, you know the area. Is there a detour or short cut, some way to throw them off?"

She spotted the canopy entrance of a familiar hotel. "In here." She darted up the steps and tossed a smile to the doorman.

After a quick glance back at their bloodhound teams, Thomas took the steps up to the entry two at a time.

The doorman held open the door and they slammed through.

"They're not following?" she puffed. Their images reflected in the lobby's mirrored walls as they trotted across the burgundy carpet.

"The change in direction seems to have confused them. But don't count on them to wait for long. Where are we going?"

"Down here. The shop past the reception desk." She waggled fingers at the desk clerk. *"Robert! Bonsoir. Ça va?"*

The man blinked and nodded. Color rose to his cheeks as recognition clicked in. *"Oui, ah, Cleo, pourquoi—"*

She touched a finger to her lips. *"Tu ne me vois pas, d'accord?"* You don't see me, okay?

He bobbed his head, puzzlement on his face, but any further reply was lost as she hustled Thomas onward.

No time to explain. He'd take charge again soon enough but for now he trusted her knowledge of the city, trusted her enough to go along. She had to make her idea work.

"Here it is. I worked here for a short while too." She pulled him into the shop, its displays laden with miniature Eiffel Towers, posters, lingerie, and bottles of French fragrances, among other goods hotel guests might need.

Thomas remained watchful as always but also managed to look indulgent.

The clerk, a thirty-something woman draped in a fashionable scarf, looked up from the cash register and announced the shop would close in five minutes.

Cleo mollified her by saying they would make a quick purchase. She whisked Thomas into another section of the shop. Around them were racks and shelves of men's and women's clothing. The dyes of cotton and wool mingled with the oil of wood polish. The headlights of cars strobed the shop's exterior window and glass door.

"The shop door leads to a smaller street, around the corner from Camille. We can cut across to Roosevelt."

"Good call, finding this detour. Hope our guys are chasing their tails."

She plucked a hat off a shelf. A black felt fedora, perfect. So Thomas. "And while we're here, how would you like to buy a hat?"

His answering grin fanned crinkles around his eyes. "Babe, I love the way you think."

Chapter Twenty-Two

A few moments later, they slipped back into the drizzle.

While Thomas checked out the street for black-jacketed goons, she tightened the hood of the slate-gray raincoat over her bright hair. Not her color or style, but urgency meant buying the only rainwear her size. The large sum of euros he'd charged to his credit card switched the shop clerk's impatience into fawning gratitude.

Besides, now they could stay dry as well as incognito. All good.

Apparently satisfied, Thomas took the plastic shopping bag containing their wet jackets from her. Tucking her hand in the crook of his right arm, she set off at a brisk pace.

"Whoa, no racing," he said. "Cool and casual won't attract attention."

"As long as I keep this hood on. Casual, okay, if I can, dressed like a spy."

"What was that about with the desk clerk? He won't sell us out?"

"He owes me. When I worked in the shop, I let him buy an expensive gift for his girlfriend on the installment plan. Not a perk the hotel condones."

He worked his jaw as he nodded. "Girlfriend. I see."

She couldn't read the emotion in his voice. Jealous?

She watched him with fascination, the grim line of his mouth, the intensity belying his nonchalant stride. Why the predatory scowl if they'd ditched their pursuers?

When he turned his gaze on her, the heat glowing in his amber eyes scorched her. Whoa, more than jealousy. And he looked so 007 in his fedora and charcoal rain jacket—not unlike the ones their pursuers wore—she wanted to jump him. Nearly hyperventilating, she hustled along beside him. Unaccountably, he'd lengthened his stride.

At the end of the short block, he used the reflection in a shop window to check behind them. "Snuggle up to me. Smile and point like you want me to buy the display."

She clutched his arm, snuggling closer, and felt his muscles tense. "Ooh, Thomas, something I've always wanted—a dreadlocks wig."

They turned left on Roosevelt, a wide commercial street clogged with a steady stream of pedestrians headed to restaurants and clubs. As they neared a busy intersection, she spotted the orange *M* marking the Métro entrance and beyond it the white-columned front of Saint-Phillippe du Roule, the church lending its name to the subway stop.

Thomas slowed to scan the area. "There beyond the Métro railing, two men in dark jackets. Another team of thugs watching for us. The ones we lost must have guessed where we were headed and contacted them."

Definitely more bad guys. Who else would wear shades at night? Her stomach clenched. *Cleopatra, hang tough.* "Will our disguises be enough?"

"Insurance wouldn't hurt." He tightened his grip on her arm as he crossed the street toward the Métro. "I have an idea but your French is better than mine." He jerked a nod toward a woman struggling with a screaming baby and a stroller piled with bags. "She looks like she could use a couple of good Samaritans."

"D'accord."

The goons were surveying the cross street, at the moment toward the other direction.

Cleo hurried over to offer her "husband's" muscles to carry the stroller down the steps. The woman looked up, skeptical until she laid eyes on Thomas. No surprise, she melted and gushed her thanks. Quashing her own spurt of jealousy, Cleo cooed to the squirming baby, about nine months old, who smelled of a diaper that needed changing. Intrigued by his new conquest, he stopped sobbing and stared wide-eyed.

The foursome descended into the subway before the thugs could turn back their way. At least, she hoped so. The baby was now nodding off. At the bottom of the stairs, his mom settled him into the stroller, thanked her helpers, and headed for the turnstiles. Voices and the click of shoes echoed off the white tile walls. The smell of rain and wet clothing laced the air.

Cleo bought their fare cards while Thomas kept watch. "Where to?"

"Del Rio said to the Victor Hugo stop, where we're to wait at a café. We'll take the long way. No direct route."

She slid in her smart card at the automatic gate. "If we want indirect, then we go north to Saint Lazare."

A shout from behind froze her.

"Don't stop!" Thomas pushed her through the gate.

Her pulse rate shot up and she shot ahead as if from an automatic pistol. She searched the directional signs for the North Platform.

At last. *There!* She tugged Thomas with her. "This way! But those guys—"

"No buts. Let me worry about them. Just book it to the trains."

She didn't risk a glance behind as they raced through the tunnels for the platform. Fewer trains ran this late at night. What if— *No, just go, Cleopatra.*

They skidded onto the platform as people boarded a waiting train. Steam vents hissed and voices echoed off the curved tile walls. Her foot slipped on a wet patch, but Thomas held her up, kept her going.

He had never once let go. Since leaving the CTF offices, she'd felt his heat, his hard body beside her, his arm around her shoulders, his arm beneath her hand.

He pressed her on past the empty orange seats, past the slicker-clad commuters boarding the middle cars to a half-empty car. With him beside her, she leaped inside.

"Away from the doors." He pulled her along to a bench seat with two empty seats among other passengers.

The stubborn doors stood open. Waiting. A cotton ball replaced her tongue and needles pricked her nerves. She turned toward the dust-streaked window. Peered out.

The two black-jacketed men she'd seen above ground sprinted onto the platform.

****

"Give me a moment to check the flat."

Thomas jerked a sharp nod to the agent who'd met them with their bags and a take-out dinner.

Although they'd evaded Zervas's goons at the Métro station, he'd take no chances. Luck and irate passengers had forced their pursuers to stop and buy fare cards. He gritted his teeth and kept a hand on his gun until he saw the doors close in the fuckers' faces. A taxi and another Métro line took them to their destination. Del Rio was held up with the aftermath of the shootout, so the CTF agent met them at Café Victor Hugo. He'd driven them to the safe house, on the third-story of an ornate stone building a couple of centuries old.

While he mentally timed the guy's sweep, he curved an arm around Cleo's shoulders. Fought to keep the embrace supportive and tender. He ought to be bushed, but energy hummed in his whole body

On a sigh, she rested her head against his shoulder, ratcheting up his hunger to an ache. He'd known breath-stealing dread for her since the admiral had phoned him, but today's threat revved it up to the stratosphere. Not because Zervas's men were only seconds away from taking her. Not because she was more vulnerable. Not because she was terrified, but dammit because she terrified *him*, taking charge back there, her eyes bright with excitement and her face animated and trusting.

Part of keeping that trust meant not being at the mercy of his DNA, too much like his old man, domineering with those he cared about. Cleo'd suggested the loss of his mother handed him too much family responsibility. Is that when it started, his need to be in control? Didn't matter. Protecting Cleo was another thing entirely.

That need had evolved into a much larger one, all encompassing and inescapable. Every fiber of his being screamed his need to take her, to possess her, to have her. Not a good idea on a hallway landing. But damned soon.

The man returned with the all-clear. "Someone will contact you in the morning." He showed Thomas the security code. With a smart salute pegging him as former military, he stepped back into the ancient lift and folded the gate shut.

Inside, Thomas locked up and set the security system. "Stay here," he said. The Frenchman's once-over had been too quick. Safe house or no, he'd do a more thorough sweep.

The four rooms with the small closets typical of old buildings didn't take long. When he returned, Cleo let out a breath. "Satisfied?"

Not even close. But I will be. So will you.

"Hardly. Locks are okay. Flat's clean, but that security system couldn't keep out a poodle. No cameras, only sensors on the door and windows. Another reason to stay here only one night." He stalked toward her, ready to strip off her clothing.

Eyeing him as if he were a tiger on the prowl—hell, maybe he was— she tossed off her coat, then whisked past him with the bag containing their dinner to the small dining table. "Smells wonderful. Veal ragout, that agent said. Are you hungry?"

"Starving, but not for food." He pulled her to him. Drove his hands into the glorious mass of her hair and ground his mouth on hers, feeding, devouring her, aching for more.

She rose on her toes, gripped his shirt, meeting him with hunger of her own. "Dinner can wait," she mumbled against his lips, one leg hooking around him. Her body ground against him as if she couldn't get close enough.

"You were incredible out there." He backed her against the wall, slid his hands down to cup her butt. "Cleopatra."

A sly smile lifted one corner of her mouth.

"Cleopatra. Exactly."

He kept his mouth on hers while her hands made fast work of his jacket and shirt as well as her knit top. He groaned at the soft feel of her breasts against his skin, then filled his palms with their soft weight. His mouth watered, his breathing hitched, sanity rushed from his head.

When she slid away to step out of the rest of her clothing, the oddity of her reply surfaced in his blood-depleted brain. "How's that?"

"Nothing. You talk too much." Her hands went to work on his jeans.

"Then we won't talk."

He'd restrained himself with her so far. Didn't want to scare her with the force of his need. He'd always wanted her, had never forgotten. But now what he felt made those earlier desires pale. "Now. I need you *now*."

He lifted her and she wrapped her legs around his waist. He slicked a palm up her thigh, her smooth, bare thigh, to where she was open to his touch. On a moan, she jerked in his arms. He smelled her arousal, tasted her desire in her kisses. Her hands feathered down his back, rubbed his skin while her tongue danced with his and her slick heat beckoned. Air sawing in and out of his lungs, his heart banging in his chest, he backed her against the wall and ripped open the protection he'd taken from his jeans pocket.

"Thomas, yes, now!"

Her plea penetrated his craving. Hell, he couldn't treat her like a barbarian, taking her against a wall. "The bedroom," he gritted out between his teeth.

"No, no, here, hurry." She snatched the opened packet from him and reached down. The warmth and soft pressure of her strong artist's fingers wrapping around him snapped his control.

She filled his gaze with the bright light of her energy, the high voltage of her dark-centered gaze, the sweet scent of her arousal. Nothing could be more erotic. Light-headed, he plunged into her, groaning with the power of their joining. She gripped his shoulders, met him thrust for thrust, her legs locked around him, clenching him with her body. Her eyes went to smoke and her nails dug into his shoulders as her climax took her. Heat licked up his spine and he came in one long, shuddering spasm. He was lost in the shock waves, could think only of her, of how she found places in him he never before let anyone touch.

M*ine, you're mine.*

He rested his forehead against hers, both of them breathing hard. After a minute, he withdrew and helped her stand.

She closed her eyes, remaining in the circle of his arms but propping herself against the wall. "Whoa, do they have tornadoes in Paris?"

"Just this once." *Right. Hurricane Cleo.* "I was out of control. Did I hurt you?"

She pressed a finger to his lips. Something like triumph flared in her sea-green eyes. "I'm fine. You were perfect. *We* were perfect."

Too shaken to speak, he stood there holding her. For the past several years, she'd haunted his mind. And now in only days she slid into his head, into his bloodstream, into his heart. He wanted more than sex, a relationship lasting longer than this mission. A major change for him, sharing his life. The way things stood between them, would she go for risking her hard-won independence?

****

An hour later, Cleo watched Thomas from the doorway between the bedroom and sitting room while she pulled a comb through her wet hair. He sat on the tweed sofa working on the tablet computer Lucas had obtained for him. His dark hair, still wet from his shower, was finger-tousled, reminding her of the teenage boy she'd fallen for. But his sharp-edged intensity and the wide shoulders that tested the fine fabric of his clean white dress shirt were all man.

Out of control. Yes, he'd actually said it.

A smile spread from inside her chest to her lips. Thomas did care, more than he wanted to. His disorientation after their mind-blowing sex proved it wasn't just the danger painting them in hot hues. Could she risk a future? Would he? She couldn't yet visualize that picture.

What she did see was the fine lines around his eyes and the slump of his shoulders. "You look stressed. And no wonder," she said as she crossed to him.

"Just tired. The big chase today took its toll on these old bones."

She rolled her eyes. "Ah, yes, thirty-eight, such an advanced age. My bones, my muscles are tired too. All the walking I did in Venice wasn't the same as running. The difference in our ages was the Grand Canyon when I was a kid and you were a teenager, but now? Please."

He leaned against the sofa back. Eyed her, his mouth tight. "Cleo, that age gap is never going away."

"Of course not. And it's a weak excuse I don't buy. I wonder if you do, really." Heat rose to her cheeks as her temper sent rash words to her mouth and coiled into a knot in her stomach. "You said from the beginning it could be only sex. Is it that I'm not too young to fuck but too young for a real relationship?"

He jackknifed up straight, his brows beetled. "Ouch. Never what I meant."

"Sounded like it to me." She folded her arms. "Then don't bring up your age again. That race through the Paris streets had me huffing and puffing. You barely breathed hard."

"I run five miles or more almost daily. I'm used to it."

"My point exactly. Age shouldn't be an issue. Age has nothing to do with us."

"Cleo, you deserve a guy more your own age."

She leaned to one side, then walked to the end of the sofa and peered behind it.

"What the hell are you doing?" he said.

"Looking for who put *you* in charge of deciding what I deserve."

He tilted back his head and laughed, a rumble that rose from deep inside and crinkled his eyes with humor instead of stress or exhaustion. "Touché. You've made your point. I did it again, didn't I?"

"If you mean running things, making my decisions, yes."

He held up his hands. "I'll work on that and I won't bring up age again. Truce?"

The only likely concession. Her ire dissipated but the knot remained, as painful as the issues between them. She took a seat beside him. "Truce. So what are you finding?"

"Hard to say, but here's what we know or think we know so far. Iranian terrorist Ahmed Yousef arranged for the theft of the exploding chip and contracted with

Centaur for the Cleopatra necklace. Marco Zervas's goons stole the necklace and some other items en route to Paris. Then he hired René Moreau to make a copy of the necklace and embed the stolen exploding chip in either the real necklace or its copy. And I doubt Yousef told him the nature of the chip."

"You think he had René embed the chip in the copy so he could keep the real necklace. No honor among thieves and terrorists."

"Right. But then Moreau heard rumors of others Zervas had killed. Your theory—and mine—is that he hid both necklaces in the Madame Tussauds production building on wax figures of Cleopatra."

She nodded, pleased he believed the theory. "Maybe because he once worked creating jewelry for Madame Tussauds, he figured the necklaces would be safe on the wax figures until he could collect them."

"Very likely." He handed her a yellow legal tablet. "No printer so all I have are just paper-pencil spreadsheets. The Cleopatra's Tomb exhibit left Paris a couple of weeks ago for New York City. This is a list of all the upcoming exhibits with their dates. Madame Tussauds has fourteen museums around the world. According to the individual museum websites, the newest exhibit at ten of them is the Queen of the Nile. Looks like they've all shipped and are on exhibit."

She thought about it. "In the workshop, the figures might not have been labeled with their destination. And what would René have known about the chip?"

"Less than Zervas. Moreau probably assumed it held government or industrial secrets. He'd have been close." He peered at the screen image of the Cleopatra wax figure. "Odd so many Cleopatras at the same time. Her face looks familiar."

She bent closer, momentarily distracted by his scent. As soon as she saw the dark-haired figure wearing the now infamous jeweled collar, she smiled. "No wonder. The artist modeled her features from the star of the new movie, *Queen Cleopatra*. Way different from the old films. The screenplay's based on a new biography. That and the tomb tour are probably the reason for the multiple exhibits."

"Hard to escape the hype about a blockbuster movie. One more complication." He jammed fingers through his hair. "Cleo, judging from the Madame Tussauds' websites, I'd say by two weeks ago, all the wax Cleopatras had left West Acton. *Before* Moreau's trip."

She shook her head. "His mysterious trip last week wasn't the first. He made one two weeks before that."

"You didn't mention that in the meeting."

"Everything that happened afterward knocked it from my head. I just remembered."

"What did he say about it?"

"The same thing he said about the second trip. Something to do with an important commission." She slumped onto the cushions. "Assume both trips were to the Merlin studio. If he took the necklaces and hid them on the first trip, why did he go again?"

"Babe, we may never know. Let's hope for some answers tomorrow from the director."

"Thomas, no matter where the necklaces are now, more important is identifying Yousef's target. And stopping Zervas."

"But Zervas doesn't have an idea where the necklaces might be, so he can't deliver his commission to Yousef. Thwarting the terrorist plot and dismantling the Centaur syndicate are jobs for the CTF or one of their national law enforcement bodies. The Cleopatra necklace is *my* priority, whether or not finding it leads to Marco Zervas."

"Because stealing such an ancient treasure is stealing history."

"You remembered. Yes, its cultural value is infinitely greater than its gold and precious stones."

"If we find the necklaces, we find the stolen chip. Won't Agent Hunt want our cooperation for that search?"

"Makes sense to me. Del Rio's working that angle."

"If Yousef is pressuring Zervas to produce the necklaces, he must have an impending deadline." On a sigh, she blinked away the exhaustion hitting her hard. "Any ideas on that?"

When he looked up from the tablet, his expression was grim. He tapped the screen and text appeared. "One, yes. Here's a press release from the Metropolitan Museum of Modern Art about the Cleopatra's Tomb exhibit. They're announcing a gala reception to open the exhibit, with two honored guests."

"Two." she said. "Two high-profile targets for the price of one?"

"Right." He turned the screen toward her.

Cleo inhaled sharply when she saw the guests' names. "The U.S. Secretary of State and the President of Iran. The gala happens in five days."

"Ka-ching." He picked up his phone.

Chapter Twenty-Three

West Acton, London

THOMAS STOOD BY while Lucas Del Rio presented the Madame Tussauds production director their identification.

The middle-aged Brit looked up from the photo IDs and gave them each the once-over, his gaze lingering a bit longer on Cleo, at Thomas's side. And no wonder, in a knee-length black skirt and a tight tee and with her russet hair flowing across her shoulders, she was spectacular.

"All seems to be in order," Walter Percival said, returning the IDs. "Just as Scotland Yard said. Corporate has instructed me to assist you. What is it exactly you need?" His unctuous smile struck Thomas as false. The man clearly wanted them gone. He could just be a self-important prick or he had something to hide.

Thomas noticed the receptionist straining to listen to their conversation. "I'll explain further in your office."

Percival's eyes narrowed behind his blue-framed glasses. "Very well. Follow me."

Shoulders stiff with resentment, he led them from the nondescript reception area through a door labeled Workshops.

"He'll take some persuading," Lucas murmured.

They passed through a high-ceilinged, airy space

that resembled an aircraft hangar but with partitioned workspaces where artists were shaping the heads of new figures amid smells of warm wax and plaster.

Cleo's eyes lit up. She winked at Thomas, then scurried ahead to catch up with the director. "Mr. Percival, is this the famous Madame Tussauds design studio?" she gushed, slipping her arm through his.

Percival's pale cheeks flushed the color of cooked shrimp. "Oh, well, yes, this is where our artists and artisans create the figures, Miss, um…"

"Call me Cleo." Megawatt smile. "You must be a busy man, but if you're not too rushed, I'd love a tour."

The director's shoulders relaxed. He leaned closer to her and pointed out a sculpture in progress and described the process. The artist was working from photographs on the head of Churchill for a World War II exhibit, but he said, chest puffed out, that many living celebrities posed for the artists. At each studio cubicle, she softened up Percival with her enthusiasm and perceptive questions. His chest expanded even more.

Not hiding something. Pompous and self-important. Thomas chuckled. *Cleo Chandler, Secret Weapon.*

By the time the foursome reached the director's office, Percival couldn't wait to assist them. He ushered Cleo to the most comfortable seat by his expansive desk. Thomas took a straight chair nearby and Lucas pulled up a folding chair. Cleo crossed her legs and let her shoe dangle from her shapely foot. Her expectant smile held the director in thrall.

Percival propped his elbows beside his desktop computer and steepled his fingers. He smiled, warmly at her—too warmly, but Thomas let it go. "Cleo—and gentlemen—I'm not sure how I can help you about some stolen item. None of the Tussauds employees could be involved in nefarious business."

"We have no information any Tussauds employees are involved," Thomas said. "First, are any of the wax figures of Cleopatra still here, in West Acton?"

"None. All are either on exhibit or waiting on the museum site for their unveiling."

Del Rio's metal chair creaked as he leaned forward. "Scotland Yard tells me you reported a couple of break-ins. Tell us about that."

The dates coincided with René Moreau's clandestine visits. Thomas watched for the director's reaction.

Percival colored, flustered. He looked to Cleo, who nodded her encouragement. "Our security system serves us well but on two occasions someone overrode the alarms during the night. I alerted the police but nothing was missing so they didn't pursue the matter."

"But did you or anyone here notice anything odd, out of place or changed?"

Percival's eyes widened. He opened a desk drawer. "Curious you should mention it. A few days after the first break-in, a cleaner found these stowed behind a heating unit."

He laid on the desk two necklaces, high gold-toned collars bearing a cape studded with jewels. The overhead lights glinted off the dazzling stones.

Cleo sucked in a breath. Then her gaze sharpened as she peered more closely. She lifted each necklace in turn. Shook her head.

Thomas grimaced. *Glitter but not gold.* "Mr. Percival?"

"These were created here to replicate the original

found in Queen Cleopatra's tomb. Our jewelry designers had to work from photographs, you understand, because by then the real artifact had been stolen," the director said, as if excusing the lack of authenticity. "When none of the museums reported missing necklaces, I sent a memo to the jewelry designers about the matter, urging them to take more care discarding prototypes."

Probably fearing he'd be accused of theft if he was caught with them, Moreau had hidden the paste after replacing them with his copy and the real choker. "We'd like you to phone the museums with Cleopatra figures. Speak only to trusted employees." Thomas tapped the paste necklaces. "Ask them to check if the necklaces in their museums are heavier than these. *Much heavier.*"

Percival cocked his head, his mind obviously making the connection. "Heavier, like real gold. You mean, like the stolen, the real—"

"Right. This is all confidential, Mr. Percival. I hope you understand the sensitivity involved."

"Certainly, certainly. But that's ten museums. All those phone calls. I'm a busy man. I could e-mail them."

Thomas shook his head. "We don't have that kind of time."

Cleo cleared her throat. "Thomas, don't I remember a reward for aiding in the recovery of Cleopatra's necklace?"

"Reward, ah, yes." So far neither he nor the insurance company had offered a reward but why the hell not. He pulled a number out of the air.

The amount of cash scrolled across Percival's keen gaze. He swallowed, hard, twice, his Adam's apple nearly bounding out of his throat. He furiously tapped computer keys. "Ah, it appears possible to rearrange my schedule so I can make those calls."

****

Crystal City, Virginia

Max Rivera watched with satisfaction as Arlington police officers led away the man in the DSF green security uniform. Handcuffs bound his hands.

Several employees including other security officers stood by, relief obvious on their faces. The tension that had pervaded the company ever since the lockdown seemed to leave the building along with the guilty party. Did he fight this for only a few days? Seemed like a year.

"Show's over, y'all." Max pivoted on his crutches to head back to the office.

As the gawkers scattered, Mara Marton headed toward him.

"Epic, Max! You got the hacker." She bumped fists with him. "Wait. Was that Dinkins?" The recognition crimped her forehead into a frown.

"Ed Dinkins. Same guy who dissed your fiancé last May." He thought back to Devlin's cold wrath at the security guard's mistreatment of an invited guest.

"Mr. Devlin slashed his pay grade," she said. "The reason I put him on the list I gave you of possible turncoats. But I didn't think he had the skills."

"He doesn't. He's not the actual hacker. Just his mole. One of Gaspar's IT geeks figured out he inserted the malware with a USB drive. Too basic a tech level for most of the staff. Dumb sumbitch bragged to a couple guys about a big windfall, he's driving a new car, and he stowed the drive in his employee locker."

"Revenge and money. Big motivators."

"And tend to inflate arrogance over brains." He grinned as Mara accompanied him into the elevator.

"The state of Virginia, the Feds, and whatever European country is involved will wrestle each other for a piece of these crooks. Dinkins is looking at misdemeanor and felony charges that'll probably net him ten years in this country alone."

"Couldn't happen to a more deserving guy. And the malware?" She punched the button for their floor.

"Mostly cleaned up. Having the USB drive with the code sped up the process. I just notified the boss Gaspar has blocked and locked out Zervas's computer genius."

On the executive offices level, they passed through the reception area on the way to Devlin's office. Max nodded to the admin, who was on the phone.

"All this is good news." Mara took one of the upholstered chairs in front of the big desk. "I can return to business as usual. But I doubt it's why I'm here. Why did you summon me, my liege?" She performed a hand flourish.

"I do like the sound of that, but you're the only one who gives me my due respect." He sank onto the desk chair and propped his crutches against the wall. The aroma of fresh French Roast came from the tray at his elbow. He poured the fragrant brew from a carafe into two mugs. "Or are you off coffee altogether?"

"Not when it's the good stuff." She stirred in cream and sweetener. "I didn't know Francine stocked anything but Mr. Devlin's tea. Looks like she's joined your fan club."

"I must be doing something right." He inhaled the steam from his mug. "Here's the thing. Thomas needs the expert used for the Cleopatra necklace sent to the Big Apple. Sunday. For an authentication. Strict secrecy."

Mara leaned forward, her eyes bright with

excitement, to take the note he slid toward her. "The Met. Way too amazing. Oh, yeah, I can set that up. No problem. I'll get on it right away."

Max stood when she did but whacked his cast against the desk. "Damn. No business as usual for me until this damn leg is healed. But Thomas should return by Monday so I can turn over the reins. All this decision making gives me headaches."

Ringing announced he had a call. "If it's the boss, he might need you to do more." When he saw the phone screen, his shoulders fell. "Text message with more instructions, but for me. Shit, he meant he's coming back to the country, but not to this desk. He needs time to wrap up his case."

The corners of her exotic eyes crinkled. "Looks like you get to keep the corner office and Francine's French Roast for a while longer, *amigo*."

****

Andie Devlin checked her hair in the bathroom mirror, then hurried to the condo kitchen. Almost six p.m. For once in her life, she was ready on time.

She dropped her keys in the new red handbag she'd bought to celebrate. In the old days she'd have scored oxycodone or some worse shit. Hell, in the old days she'd have had nothing to celebrate.

The ringing of the house phone made her jump. Damn, was Frank canceling on her? Figured. But the number on the small screen was her brother's. Again.

Ring.

She gnawed on her lower lip. Doc Olsen kept ragging on her about talking to him. "*Have you talked to your brother yet?*" she'd say almost as often as Thomas called. And he'd called every day since he left, sometimes more than once.

Ring.

Now that she had news—good news—maybe she could answer. Her pulse pounded in her ears.

Ring.

She reached for the receiver. Yanked back her hand.

"Hey, Andie, sorry I missed you," Her brother's smooth, deep voice began as voicemail kicked in. *"I want to give you a heads-up. You might see Cleo and me on the news Monday—"*

Andie needed to hear no more. She snatched up the receiver and punched the button to cancel the message. "Thomas, I'm here."

"Andie, oh, kid," he said, his voice burlap rough, maybe with shock—and no wonder. "It's so good to hear your voice."

She swallowed, breathed. Clutched the receiver with both hands. "What's this about the news with Cleo? Cleo Chandler, *that* Cleo?"

"That Cleo. A complicated story. I'll tell you the long version later. The condensed version is this. Her father sent me to protect her. A gang of criminals think she has the necklace from Cleopatra's tomb."

Gang. Necklace. "What are you talking— Facebook. The picture she posted?"

"Right. We're on the trail of the necklace. There'll be a press conference in New York. I didn't want you to be blindsided."

Too late. "Good. That's good. Thanks. And Cleo's okay?"

"She's fine. I'll make sure she's safe. We're together."

Together? But— Before she could voice the

questions flying through her brain, he spoke again.

"Andie, I've been concerned about you, but I didn't want to crowd you. Is everything all right there?"

He didn't sound like the domineering brother she'd accused him of being. He sounded caring and warm. The tension inside her eased. *Now, tell him now.* "Better than all right. You mean you don't know?"

A pause. "Know what? What are you talking about? Was Dr. Olsen supposed to tell me something?"

He doesn't know. No tails, no phone taps? She'd been paranoid, and all this time he'd kept his promise. He'd offered his trust but she hadn't trusted him. She swallowed hard.

"Tommy, I— You wondered what I did all day before my shift at the bar, right?" She didn't wait for his response, needing to let it all out in a rush before a panic attack shut her down. "I've been going to school for two years. Yeah, I know, I *hate* school. But I made it through. In May I finished the degree in social work I started a long time ago. As of yesterday I have a job at the Arlington Family Services Clinic. With only a B.S., I have to work under supervision, but I'll be doing something important—working with families of kids who screwed up their lives with drugs. Kids like me. I start in two weeks."

"My God, Andie, I'm blown away. I can't tell you how proud I am, how proud Mom would be. And Dad. Why did you keep this from me?"

She shook her head, then smiled, knowing he couldn't see. "I was afraid I'd fail. I needed to see if I could keep it together, make it all work."

"I'd have helped."

"You did help, financially. The doc took care of that.

I made it this far, Tommy."

"Feels good to have you call me my old name again, sis. My hat's off to you. I'll be home in a few days and we'll celebrate."

He called her *sis*, not *kid*. The pride and affection in his voice made her breath catch. She brushed away the tears leaking down her cheeks. Confessing all to her brother would make talking to her dad easier. But not until Thomas came home for moral support. "I'll hold you to that promise."

"One more thing. Andie, these crooks are dangerous and clever. I had Max send in a team to check over the condo for bugs and phone taps. All was clear but they didn't find your cell phone. Until you can get that cleared, be careful what you say. Don't mention anything about this call, including Cleo. To anyone. Okay?"

She hadn't thought much about her brother's work in security but now *security* had a whole different meaning. A personal meaning. "I promise."

Now she could use some BFF support. "Tommy, is Cleo there? Can I talk to her?"

Chapter Twenty-Four

London

THOMAS LISTENED AS Cleo talked to his sister.
They supported each other, and being unable to connect
had chafed. Gratified, he relaxed against the headboard
of the St. James Hotel's king-size bed.

The hour had been late when they left the West
Acton building, too late to fly to New York. After days
on the move, exhaustion dimmed Cleo's eyes. And now
Big Ben would be chiming midnight.

The Madame Tussauds production director's search
had located the missing necklaces— one on the wax
Cleopatra in the Las Vegas museum, and the other in
New York, exactly where Yousef planned, but arriving
there by chance. Moreau couldn't have known the plan.
Once Thomas shared the information with the Centaur
Task Force, engines turned at a fast pace. They would
stop an assassination and have a good chance of snaring
Marco Zervas. The CTF would come out golden and the
original necklace could return to the Cleopatra's Tomb
exhibit.

If it all worked. He refused to let himself think it
wouldn't.

Other matters were working out. Max had identified
the mole who'd fed the spy software into the system.
Hell, Thomas should've fired Dinkins when he screwed

up in the spring. Luring lost clients back to the company would mean lots of schmoozing, but the necklace's return would help put DSF back on track.

He tuned back in to Cleo's conversation with Andie. Hearing his sister sound positive instead of angry amazed him. He hoped she could hold it together.

"Hey, Andie, you go have fun tonight. Talk to you soon." Cleo ended the call and handed him his secure phone. She walked fingers up his bare shoulder before laying her head there and snuggling closer beneath the silk coverlet. "Thanks for that. It means so much to me. Andie too. I knew about the social work degree but not about the new job."

He pulled her closer. "I hardly know the new Andie I just talked to. Thanks for being there for her. I've been too tough."

"You were scared for her. And she shut you out. I kept urging her to level with you, but she insisted on soloing. She didn't want you to know we talked either. She's leery of being managed."

Something he needed to keep in mind when dealing with *both* females. "What did you mean about having fun tonight?"

"Oh, she had to go because her date just rang the doorbell."

"Date." He nearly surged upright. "Did she say who?"

"Hoo boy, Mr. Overprotective Boss never left the building."

"Hard to break old habits." He slid farther down and kissed her deeply, drinking in her sweet energy. "And when I forget, I know you'll call me on it."

"You got that right." She smoothed back an unruly

strand from his forehead. "You're forgiven for your skepticism where Andie and men are concerned. In the past she hasn't been too discriminating."

"And don't forget the long reach of Centaur."

"No worries, Thomas. Her date's a guy she met on campus. A casual dinner, no big deal. She'll be fine."

She sounded much more confident than he felt. With Andie, he was never sure. Those kinks in his shoulders were tightening.

Rolling over her, he bracketed her slender body with his arms. He nuzzled her hair, absorbing her scent, her warmth and reveling in the press of her breasts against his chest, the friction of her body against him. "Not Andie I want to think about. Time for total focus on the woman in my arms."

"Total focus," she murmured against his mouth. "I do like how that sounds."

****

New York City

Cleo savored her third mug of coffee. Caffeine was the only thing keeping her awake and upright. They'd flown from London to the States two days ago and jet lag was a bitch. Putting more distance between her and Mimi twisted emotions—worry and guilt and fear— inside her. Not that she could do anything for the present.

Waiting to set the bait in their trap, she sat in a private lounge in the Metropolitan Museum of Art— a remarkably bland room for such a rich setting.

Her mobile phone—a new one, secure like Thomas's—buzzed in her lap. The screen displayed the code for the call she'd been expecting.

"Hello, sweetheart. Your father and I, we've been so worried."

Her spine went rigid. Of course the admiral had put her mom on first as a buffer. "Hi, Mom. I'm great. Tired, but this whole thing may be over tomorrow."

"Max Rivera has kept us posted but I doubt he told us everything."

Cleo smiled. *Definitely not everything.* "We'll have plenty of time to talk after this is all over. Do I have a new nephew?"

"Keith Horace Chandler, Junior." Pride filled Irene's voice. "Nine pounds, nine ounces. Everyone's fine."

"That's epic, Mom. I hope they don't call him Little Hoot." Her grin faded and she swallowed. "And Dad? How's Dad?"

From the amused *hmm*, she could picture her mom's eye roll. "Healing and it can't happen too fast. I may hire an ambulance driver to wheel him to his office during the day." She cleared her throat. "He's reaching for the phone but I want to have my say first. I've rarely gone against whenever your father insisted on something, even where you children were concerned. I'm sorry now I didn't, for your sake. I'm not like the rest of you, strong or tough."

"Mom, you didn't—"

"Let me finish, please, Cleopatra Marie. Hoot couldn't understand you had your grandmother's creative talents, but you have enough of his grit to stand up for yourself and pursue your own future. And I'm proud of you. From what Max has said, I have a whole lot more to be proud of. And so does your father."

"Oh, Mom, you're the one who's tough, for putting up with us kids." *And the admiral.* "I don't know what to say except thank you."

"Irene heard you, baby, but she's blowing her nose."

At the sound of her dad's gruff voice, Cleo uncrossed her legs and planted her feet on the floor. Would he demand she go home? Would he blame her for all this trouble? Hell, she *had* started it all with the Facebook picture.

"Dad. Sorry about your fall." Oh, God, how lame was that? What else could she say after four years?

"I'll live. And so will you, thanks to Thomas."

"Ah, Thomas, he… thanks for sending him, Dad. We've had a wild ride but he's protected me."

"We'll watch the press conference. You come see us when this is over, you hear?"

She mumbled a promise and other encouraging words before saying good-bye. Shaking her head in amazement, she ended the call. Not *come home* when this was over? Not *be sensible and get a real job? Like the U.S. Navy?* Admiral Hoot Chandler conciliatory? Compromising? Maybe on the phone with Mom at his elbow. Cleo would see what happened if she set foot under his roof. No, *when*. She'd promised.

But today's conversation was a start. And she was four years older. Four years wiser. She hoped.

A glance at her phone reminded her it was time to head to the Met's press room. She dropped the device in her small handbag and stood, smoothing her skirt. On the television screen across the room a noontime local news alert caught her attention.

"In a few minutes our reporter Ruth Nance will bring us a special announcement from the director of the Metropolitan Museum of Art about tomorrow's opening of the Cleopatra Tomb Exhibit," the blonde newscaster said in a perky tone. "While we wait, here's an interview she taped earlier with the U. S. Secretary of State."

The camera shot zoomed in on the two women seated opposite each other on upholstered armchairs, tiny mics clipped to their jackets.

"Secretary of State Vinton is in the city for final talks on a trade agreement with the president of Iran." Turning from the camera to the cabinet official, the reporter asked in a deferential tone, "How historic is this development, Madame Secretary?"

"Very important, Ruth," said Helen Vinton, elegant in an upswept blond 'do and a rose silk suit. "And it's more than a trade agreement. Our two countries have had our differences and confrontations during the past few decades. Because of dialogues with the Islamic Republic of Iran's new, progressive leaders, including President Farhadi, we enter a new era of trust and cooperation. Although the president is here primarily for a speech at the United Nations, I do have more than one meeting with him." Her blue eyes sparkled as she smiled. "Including tomorrow evening's reception. An opening at the Met is always a special occasion. I'm looking forward to seeing the new exhibit."

The reporter asked another question but Cleo had seen enough. Having Iran's leaders negotiate with the West for more than oil sales must infuriate such an extremist as Ahmed Yousef. An assassination would seem to him the only way to short-circuit the possibility of peace. He likely relished the idea of a reactionary outcome, even war.

Cleopatra's necklace was the centerpiece of an international success or an international calamity. What they planned for tomorrow's gala had to work.

She turned off the television as her phone buzzed

again. Mimi's mother.

"Oh, Cleo, my dear. I... it's Mimi, she—"

White noise filled Cleo's ears and she closed her eyes. "Oh, no, no."

"Wait, don't misunderstand. I'm just so upset. My daughter's taken a turn for the worse. She was waking up, starting to talk, responding. But now she's slipped back under."

The white noise receded a fraction. "Back into the coma?"

"That's what the doctors say. She seemed to be healing, getting better, but now—" She paused, her breath shaky and harsh. "The doctors here don't know what's going on. I've arranged for a medical transport home. To see a specialist in Toronto."

"Trudy, I'm so sorry. If there was any way I could take—"

"*No*, don't even say it. This was not your fault. Those men, it was them. Mimi will say the same thing when she's better."

When she's better. Hard to feel that way but Cleo had to cling to Trudy's belief.

"Please tell Lucas Del Rio about Mimi," Trudy said. "I don't think I can explain this again."

Cleo had no idea how she would either, but she agreed. They talked for a few more minutes about the flight schedule and ambulance transfer. She'd just ended the call when Thomas stepped into the room and beckoned. She whisked to him and threw her arms around his waist, taking strength from his solid presence.

"Hey, babe, what's the matter? Your dad come on strong?"

"No, he was fine. He didn't tell me to come home.

He said 'come see us' instead. And my mom said I was tough."

"Babe, you are tough. It's okay to lean on someone occasionally, even me." He chuckled. "Is there more?"

She couldn't bring herself yet to talk about Mimi. "I'll tell you later. Let's go. Showtime."

****

Marco Zervas stared in disbelief at the TV screen as the press conference drew to a close. The camera panned from the director of the Met to the two people standing to his right.

Thomas Devlin and Cleo Chandler.

Cursing, he threw the remote against the wall. Paced the sitting room of the Ritz-Carleton suite. The faint smell of Hawkins's efforts with antiseptic spray and air freshener hung in the air.

Hawkins ducked into his bedroom, laptop beneath his arm. The door closed behind him.

Nedik slid a glass across the mini-bar. A glass Zervas had personally washed. One couldn't be too careful, even in New York. He slugged down the whiskey, willing the smooth heat to soothe nerves shredded by the news.

How the fuck had Devlin recovered the necklace? Where the hell did Moreau stash it? Maybe he had only one. Could be either— the ancient one or the copy with the computer chip. Could be some kind of ruse. No trick, he decided. Not involving the museum director and the press. Too convoluted even for his old fucking captain.

What Yousef would do if he got wind of the recovery didn't bear contemplating.

His mobile phone shrilled. *Fuck, too late.*

"What have you done?" The Iranian's voice blasted

275

his eardrum.

"A temporary setback, I assure you, my friend." He sank onto a gold brocade chair.

"You have assured me time and again you would succeed. The FBI has my necklace. You have failed."

The FBI? Yousef must have gotten the news mixed up. A bad translation on Al Jazeera perhaps. Zervas scrambled for ideas.

"Not the FBI," he said, keeping his tone calm while his heart battered his sternum. "But the civilians I told you about. The necklace is being returned to the Cleopatra Tomb Collection. The exhibit opens Tuesday at the New York Metropolitan Museum of Art."

"The necklace will be part of the exhibit, you are certain?"

Fuck, yes, and with motion sensors, weight sensors, cameras, laser beams—all the technical crap. Except he knew a few thieves in Brooklyn who could steal anything regardless of the security set-up. "According to the news, the necklace is the centerpiece of the exhibit. After the excitement of the find ends, stealing—"

"No," Yousef interrupted. "Do not. The necklace is precisely where it needs to be. Watch for news of the opening gala reception and you will see."

"But—" Zervas spoke to dead air.

"Boss?" Nedik said, from behind the mini-bar. Perhaps he feared his boss would launch more missiles. "Whole deal in the toilet?"

His mind racing, Zervas meandered to the suite's telescope set up before the picture window. He stared down at the Central Park treetops, their leaves beginning to fade from summer green. Shriveling. Dying.

The leaves, yes, but not his scheme. He hadn't been

a fucking U.S. Special Forces sergeant for nothing. *When the enemy outflanks you, reposition your forces.*

Chapter Twenty-Five

THOMAS LIFTED TWO glasses of champagne from the waiter's tray and handed one to Cleo.

Stark white columns and ancient statues and busts lined the high-ceilinged central court that connected the Met's first-floor galleries. Concealed cameras monitored by federal agents panned the crowd touring the Cleopatra's Tomb Exhibit—on center stage in this gala.

The trap was set. Now for the prey to take the bait. His pulse rattled and he steadied his breathing. Focused on staying in the zone. A hell of a lot easier job if he'd persuaded Cleo to stay away, secure in the hotel. No chance.

Keeping her close by his side, he surveyed the crowd sipping bubbly. FBI and Secret Service agents in tuxes and gowns mingled with city officials, celebrities, and museum donors. Barely recognizable in a silver cocktail dress, Special Agent Jessica Hunt accompanied the agents guarding Secretary of State Vinton and President Farhadi. Thank God she'd persuaded the museum director to ban the media. Only the Met's crew was recording the gala.

He'd let the Feds and the task force nab the would-be assassin. Marco Zervas was his.

"Shiny dome with mustache at your three," Lucas said in Thomas's earbud. The DSF operative lounged beside a canopied bed with a golden headrest.

Thomas turned to face Cleo but looked over her head toward where the man in question stood chatting with a blonde. "Too short," he murmured into the mic concealed beneath his shirt collar.

He'd set out the first bait by using his personal credit card to reserve their hotel room. The Centaur task force had video footage of Nedik and Hawkins boarding a Paris-New York flight. Not their boss. No Marco Zervas in any of his known identities.

But he had come. Thomas knew it. The hairs on the back of his neck stood at attention. Yesterday's press conference had baited the second hook. The grinning museum director had thanked Cleo and him for returning the necklace in time for the Met opening.

A slap in the face. Zervas wouldn't be able to resist.

"Plenty of bald heads here," Cleo said as they approached the displays of jewel-encrusted boxes and jewelry. Velvet pedestals held gold and silver arm bands, bracelets, pendants, and rings beneath pinpoint spotlights. A plus-sized couple moved away, the woman's flowery perfume trailing behind her.

He nodded, working his jaw. Zervas could wear a rug. Or he could insert a man. Depended on his level of desperation.

The slide of Cleo's arm through his eased his tension and drew his gaze from the party to the one who mattered more each day. He slid an appreciative glance from her upswept curls to down the long black column that hugged her curves. The gown could be taken for skin except for its shimmering fabric. "You look amazing."

Her answering smile sparkled in her green eyes. "You look amazing yourself. You should always wear a tux."

"I will if you'll always wear that dress."

Her laugh drew his gaze to the cleavage displayed in the gown's low neckline. "Deal."

He forced himself back from the brink before he lost more vigilance. He returned to scanning the glitterati near Madame Secretary and her companion.

The dignitaries and their entourage of advisors and protectors, trailed at a discreet distance by security, glided in a small school toward the centerpiece of the Cleopatra Tomb Exhibit.

Cleopatra's necklace.

The other jewelry lay flat in cases, but the gold collar with its gem-encrusted cape draped the neck of a black velvet bust, as the Queen of the Nile might have worn it. Damned impressive. No wonder people wanted to steal the thing.

When a white-jacketed waiter walked by with a tray laden with empties, he stopped the man and passed him his glass. He needed both hands free.

Cleo felt the charge in the atmosphere when Thomas stepped to one side, his gaze eagle sharp, his stance battle ready. The honored guests stopped within a foot of the necklace. The Secretary, her blond hair perfectly coiffed, elegant in ice-blue satin. The Iranian president, a slight dark-haired man in a black suit. Thomas's gaze swept the gathering.

Cleo sucked in a breath.

Her hands were too clammy to hold a glass. She added her flute to the tray. "Thank you," she said to the waiter, who reeked of sweat.

Without a nod, he adjusted the tray and moved on.

Poor man. He must be new, to be so frazzled. Unlike the Secretary. "Vinton looks so cool and calm."

"Diplomacy requires ice in the veins," Thomas growled. "Like anticipating an attack."

Secretary Vinton bent her head to listen to what President Farhadi said. The entourage gave the two of them elbow room as they circled the stand, closing in only inches from the gleaming necklace.

Thomas turned away to watch whoever was watching the dignitaries, and so did Cleo. Security had scanned every attendee and the contents of their pockets and bags. Catching the assassin as he keyed the code left too much to chance, he'd complained, leaving them with no prey in the trap and their heads up their asses.

The clink of glassware drew her attention to the right. The sweating waiter had set his tray on a bench by a marble bust. He fumbled with something in his pocket.

"Thomas, over there, that waiter." She tossed a nod toward where the waiter hovered. "When he took my glass, I noticed he was sweaty and nervous. All the other waiters carried empties away. Why would he set his down?"

Already striding toward the waiter, he spoke an alert into his collar mic.

The man withdrew a phone from his pants pocket. He frowned as he tapped the screen.

Three men including Thomas circled him. Two agents seized his arms at the same time Thomas relieved him of his phone.

Thomas studied the screen, then jerked a sharp nod.

An agent handcuffed the waiter, who stood head lowered, mouth tight.

Conversation near the confrontation hushed, and formal-clad people backed away.

Hunt pushed through the spectators and relieved

Thomas of the phone with a gloved hand. She passed it to an agent who placed it in an evidence bag.

Agents gripped the waiter's arms. Others formed a front and rear guard. Hunt signaled toward a side door. As a body, they marched the man out.

Lightheaded, Cleo put her hand to her throat, forgetting tonight her neck was bare. She forced herself to breathe slowly. In. Out. In. Out. In. Out.

God, she'd known since yesterday when the authenticator examined the necklace Lucas brought from Berlin that it was René's copy but contained no embedded chip, explosive or otherwise. And still she'd nearly passed out from hyperventilation.

Around her, whispered questions crescendoed to excited speculation.

Thomas returned to her. He enfolded her and kissed her. "You're the best, babe. Could've used you in my team to spot the enemy."

"*You* took him down." She smoothed the front of his dress shirt, loving the thump of his heart against her palm. "He must've set down the tray so he could check the phone screen. Then he kept pressing the code, probably wondering why he couldn't set off the explosion. Thank God the trap worked and you're not hurt. Bummer you didn't get Zervas. He— I'm babbling. I'll stop now."

He smiled, kissed her again, soothing her vibrating nerve endings. "We'll have another shot at Marco Zervas."

"Ladies and gentlemen, may I have your attention, please." The museum director stood on the mezzanine steps with a hand microphone. The tall gray-haired man removed his glasses and slipped them into his tuxedo pocket. When the voices died to murmurs, he continued. "I apologize for the unfortunate interruption. For now I can say only that a disaster was averted and the man responsible is in custody. Please continue to enjoy this magnificent exhibit and the refreshments."

"Now what?" Cleo said.

"I'll answer that." Lucas Del Rio joined them.

She'd noticed the reactions to him earlier. Gala guests gave him a wide berth. He might as well have been carrying an AK-47 and wearing field gear instead of formal black.

His somber expression was belied by the twinkle in his eyes. Great the take-down had lightened his mood, as gloomy and ominous as a thundercloud when she'd told him about Mimi's downturn. When Mimi's condition improved—she *had* to get better— Cleo would ensure the two of them met.

"Special Agent Hunt sent me to deliver you to the director's office," Lucas said.

"Why? What else has happened?" Thomas asked.

"Didn't say. Just following orders."

With that cryptic reply, he set off with them in his wake. As if by magic, the crowd parted for them.

She whispered to Thomas, "Next time I go to Macy's after-Christmas sale, I'm taking Lucas for crowd control."

"He'd probably rather face all the Taliban in Afghanistan."

A few moments later, they entered the director's private quarters, a spacious office of royal blue and cream. European artwork and expensive books lining the walls infused the room with essences of old leather and older oils. A striking Baroque tapestry riveted her gaze.

Until the director turned from the knot of people by a massive mahogany desk.

He stepped aside, revealing Secretary of State Vinton and President Farhadi. Cleo hadn't even noticed they'd left the gala.

Smiling, hands outstretched, Helen Vinton crossed to them. She shook hands, first with Thomas, then with Cleo. "I'm told you two are responsible for finding the stolen necklace and uncovering this entire plot. I can't tell you how grateful we all are."

Thomas dipped his head. "My honor, ma'am. Felt good to be back in the field. I've sat at a desk for too long."

She turned her smile to Cleo. "You've had quite the adventure, from what Special Agent Hunt says."

"Yes, ma'am," Cleo began, at a loss. She couldn't say what she'd gone through was nothing. "If only I hadn't posted my picture wearing the necklace—"

The Secretary's rich laugh cut her off. "I never thought I'd be grateful for Facebook."

Grateful? "But—" Cleo snapped her mouth shut. Whoa, yeah, posting her picture online had set off the entire search. Not yet a total success but maybe she'd done a good thing after all. Except for Mimi's injury.

Secretary Vinton introduced them to President Farhadi, who bowed as he took Cleo's hand in both of his.

"My country is thankful to you both and to the fine agents of the American government and the Interpol task force. I recognized that so-called waiter when he was watching us. He is well known to my government. A minion of Ahmed Yousef. The Islamic Republic has tolerated this enemy of the state for too long. Five minutes after my phone call to the Council, his threat will be eliminated."

"Yousef will be arrested," Secretary Vinton added.

Farhadi's mouth creased in a scythe of a smile.

Cleo blinked away the scenario that leaped to her imagination.

The museum director stepped forward. "I agreed to this evening's charade to catch an assassin and because I was assured Cleopatra's necklace would be returned. The copy will fool most of the public, but the integrity of the Metropolitan Museum and of the Egyptian people is at stake. When will we have the original piece?"

****

Later that night, Marco Zervas sat in the backseat of his rental limousine, parked a block away from the Met. One of the bartenders at the gala had been open to extra money. As he listened to the man's report on his secure phone, every word twisted his gut.

"My man will deliver your payment as we agreed," he said, ending the call.

"Where to, boss?" Nedik said from the driver's seat.

"I don't fucking care. Just drive."

As the car rolled silently from the curb, he smoothed on his leather gloves. No telling what had gone on in this damn backseat.

The sequence of events the bartender had described led to only one conclusion. The waiter's phone was supposed to trigger an explosion in Cleopatra's necklace. The chip? Probably. Not stolen secrets exactly but military explosive. Damned ingenious.

The Feebs had removed the chip. Or that necklace wasn't the original. Even better and more likely. He smiled. The down side was that Yousef would need

285

someone to blame for the assassination's failure. *Him.*

Not his fault but the terrorist wouldn't care. With his accounts cut off and no payment forthcoming, Zervas needed funds. He could contact at least half a dozen investors who would pay big. Eliminating Nedik and Hawkins—dangerous liabilities— would come next. Then he would disappear. He'd done it before and come back.

First the antique necklace.

He would force Devlin to fucking hand it over. And he had the perfect leverage.

****

Thomas woke from a fitful sleep with Cleo tucked close to him. Her confidence and the knowledge she was safe were the only reasons he got any rest at all. Every time he woke, thrashing over all the dire outcomes, she was restless too. They each had their personal stakes in this mess. For him, Marco Zervas handcuffed and behind bars. And none too soon. For her, the guilt about her cousin's shooting and sudden turn for the worse was driving her to take risks he'd never imagined she'd consider.

A hell of a security expert he was. Nothing was secure.

Later after they'd showered and dressed, room service delivered fruit and rolls.

"Anxiety has you in knots," Cleo said over her mug of coffee. "You think Zervas won't be lured."

"I'll have him in my net soon. Interpol has cut off access to his Swiss and Cayman accounts. He won't know until too late Yousef can't go after him. He's cornered."

"Then what?"

"The explosive chip."

"It wasn't in the copy. We've known that since Monday." She leaned forward, her gaze narrowing with doubt. "Isn't it in the original?"

He set down his mug. "One of my operatives in Vegas called while you slept. Nothing is embedded in the original but gemstones. So where the hell did Moreau hide the damn chip?"

"Maybe he didn't hide it," she suggested. "Maybe Zervas just hired him to make the copy and never gave it to him."

He slammed a hand on the table, raising a tsunami in his coffee. "Shit! Double cross Yousef? A suicide move, even for Marco Zervas. His funds are cut off, so now he needs the original necklace. But even worse—"

She shuddered. "If he does have the chip, he could sell it to another terrorist."

Chapter Twenty-Six

Las Vegas, Nevada

CLEO PROPPED HER elbows on the fence outside the Bellagio and watched the casino-hotel's fountains. Multicolored lights sparkled on the towering sprays in time with the music wafting from hidden speakers. She'd left cool autumn breezes in New York for oven temperatures in the desert, even at midnight.

And she was wide awake. During the past few days she'd crossed so many time zones the batteries in her body clock had expired. She would allow herself to crash after the FBI locked Marco Zervas in the slammer.

Around the dancing fountains, dozens of people pointed and exclaimed at the light and water show, but Thomas and Lucas paid scant attention. During the trip she'd dozed, but they'd spent most of the time plotting strategy. Even now they were brainstorming and discarding scenarios for snaring the head of Centaur.

Operatives had spotted Zervas's man Nedik following them from the hotel to La Guardia. Thomas had used his personal credit card for the tickets, so Zervas knew where they went. And where they were staying. The Bellagio wasn't far from Madame Tussauds at the Venetian, but not near enough to be obvious.

"Any word if he's arrived in Vegas?" she'd asked after Thomas's last call to Hunt.

"Not yet," he'd said, his gaze stony. "Agents identified his thugs at the La Guardia private terminal. They took off in a charter jet with a gray-haired man— had to be Zervas— and an unidentified woman. First we've heard of a female in his entourage. The pilot filed a flight plan for Vegas but no word yet they've arrived. We're here. The necklace is here. *He'll* be here."

The only scenario that would work to trap Zervas was using his belief that Cleo knew the necklace's location. So far he didn't seem to connect to the wax museums. She could be the bait to lure him out of hiding to the museum. When she'd brought it up in the evening meeting with Special Agent Hunt and the other Interpol team members, she could see the realization in their eyes. And in Thomas's tight jaw before he exploded with *"Never."* Hunt too insisted on finding another way.

Cleo *had* to do something to help. Thomas kept assuring her she'd been invaluable. Thinking of poor Mimi, she knew whatever she'd done wasn't enough. Would never be enough if her cousin died.

As the water slowly subsided and the music ended, families with infants asleep in strollers and couples arm in arm meandered past them back to the gambling tables and slots. She yanked herself from her funk and turned to see Thomas's gaze on her.

The fierce concentration and anguish told him what she was thinking. "Forget about it, Cleo. You're not going to be the cheese in the rattrap."

"It's the only way," she said, lifting her hair off her neck. She twisted it up and secured it with a clip.

Elegant and still the girl next door, he never tired of the warmth of her bright spirit. She had to stay safe. No way would he put her in Zervas's crosshairs.

The jangle of his phone yanked him to attention. He frowned at the small screen before taking the call. "Yeah?"

"Been too fucking long, Captain."

A shot of adrenaline rushed through his bloodstream.

"Marco." He motioned to Lucas. "Wrong. Hasn't been long enough."

The color drained from Cleo's face. Her hands gripped the railing.

A rusty-gate laugh. "You won't *want* to wait. You have some*thing* I want— the necklace, the original," Zervas said. "In exchange, I'll give you some*one* you want. I expect you want proof." He spoke to someone in the room. "Bring her over here."

Her? Not Mimi. God help us all.

"Tommy? Oh, God, I'm so sorry. I screwed up bad this time."

Andie. The world stopped, his lungs seized up. He made himself breathe. "Andie, honey, are you all right? Did they hurt you?"

"I'm okay but dammit, Tommy, they fucking drugged me. That… that asshole I went out with, he delivered me to these three bastards and—"

"Ah, there," Zervas said, "that's all the assurance you need. Your sister's fine. I'll call again with instructions."

"You hurt her, you fucking piece of shit, and I'll kill you with my bare hands."

A man's deep bellow from somewhere in the background.

Then, "Take your hands off me, you fucking gorilla, or I'll bite you again."

The phone went to dead air.

He clicked to his tracking software to locate his sister's phone. No signal. Zervas's geek had found the tracker the DSF tech guy had installed. He'd ask Hunt to trace the phone's GPS signal but that was probably futile.

Images flashed across his mind's screen. Little Andie, mischief lighting her eyes, as she and Cleo sprayed him and Cleo's brothers with the garden hose. Teenage Andie, strung out on stolen prescription painkillers and tranquilizers. Angry Andie, the last time he'd seen her, reaming him out for abandoning her. Let that be the Andie who faced down Marco Zervas and his thugs.

He swallowed the acid taste in his mouth, summoned the calm and logic he would need, waited until he felt it cloak him in armor. "Lucas?"

The other man shook his head. "Prepaid phone. Untraceable number. I'll call Hunt." He stepped away with his phone.

"Thomas, they have Andie?" Cleo gripped his arm, her short nails digging into his skin.

He pulled her into his arms, steadying himself with the feel of her. "The guy she went out with was a plant. He drugged her, handed her over to Zervas and his thugs. She was the woman on the plane with them."

"No, oh God, drugs, no. Is she... is she all right?"

"So far." The phone call replayed in his head, the last part offering a glimmer of hope. "She bit one of Zervas's goons. She may give them more trouble than they counted on. And she managed to tell me there were three of them." No new players. Good.

"He wants the necklace and he'll free Andie?"

"He'll call back with instructions." He held on

tighter. "I should've suspected Zervas would know about Andie. I should've had her protected. They drugged her with who knows what, maybe the same chemicals she left behind. Anything could set her back, destroy the recovery, her future."

Cleo stepped from his embrace and took his hands, gripping them in a kind of solidarity. "She's tougher than that now. And you couldn't have known. It's not your fault. But there's one upside to this twist in his plans. His demand will set up a way to trap the son of a bitch."

"I hope you're right." Because Zervas wouldn't hesitate to hurt Andie. To make her suffer. To kill her. *The ultimate revenge.*

"What do we do now?" she asked.

Lucas strode toward them. "Hunt called everybody for a strategy session. Five minutes."

Thomas nodded, not taking his gaze from Cleo. "I have to focus on getting my sister out safely. Del Rio and I will handle this. You can't be part of it from now on. It's too dangerous."

****

"Hell, all those other times it wasn't dangerous?" Cleo said to the empty room.

She gave the suite door a shove but it glided shut with an unsatisfactory click. Just as immovable as Thomas Devlin, dammit. Her cheeks burned. A painful knot throbbed behind her sternum.

She stalked to the window, stared down at the pool. Far below, a mother soothed a sobbing toddler in pink while an older brother stood by. Okay, so Thomas was scared shitless for Andie. So was she. Andie was her BFF. They'd always been there for each other. How could Thomas block her out now? He'd accepted, even welcomed her ideas and her help before. So now he didn't need her?

Gradually her goal had broadened from atoning for Mimi's injury. She needed to prove to herself she wasn't the family airhead. And to help prevent more death because of the damn necklace. Shut up in the hotel, she'd go bonkers. She had to *do something*.

Her phone buzzed. She'd forgotten it was in her pocket. "Yeah?"

"Cleo Chandler, at last."

At the harsh voice, her breath caught. "Who's this?"

He barked a laugh. "The Easter Bunny, who else?"

Evil bastard. She bit her lip, remaining silent, forcing herself to wait.

A huff of disdain. "Marco Zervas at your service. Don't play with me, Cleo. I hold the cards. *All* the cards, especially the Queen."

Andie! She closed her eyes and mined strength from her anger. "What do you want?"

"You know the answer to that. Devlin won't find me. You're the only one I trust to bring me Cleopatra's necklace. The antique, not that copy at the Met."

He'd figured out that much, just as they'd hoped. "How do you expect me to do that? It's the middle of the night."

"This is Las Vegas. Up all night. Get the necklace. An hour."

She considered her options. "An hour's not enough time. I'll need longer. Two hours."

"Fuckin'-A. Two hours. Then send me a photo of yourself holding the piece. You can wear it again." He chuckled. "If I'm satisfied, I'll tell you where to meet."

"What about Andie? Is she okay? If you've hurt

her—"

But he'd disconnected.

She pressed the heels of her hands on her tired eyes. Now what? What Zervas demanded was impossible. Or was it?

Without knowing it, he'd handed her ammunition.

She headed for the door. *Tommy, here I come.*

****

"The alleged phone call isn't enough, Devlin," Special Agent Hunt declared.

"Not enough? That was Marco Zervas threatening my sister. I know his voice." Thomas fisted his hands at his sides. His jaw hurt from maintaining a calm façade.

"Judge Martinez is holding firm. If you'd recorded the call, we'd be ahead on getting a warrant to track his credit card usage. We have the names the party traveled under but we need the airport tapes to ID the gray-haired man as Zervas or the woman as your sister."

"How long will that take?" Three seconds was too fucking long.

"Agents are working on it. When we get Zervas, I want everything done right so we can put him away for good." Hunt's expression softened. "I know this is tough. Try to be patient."

Patient? Not with Andie's life at stake.

He scrubbed his hands through his hair and hauled in a deep breath. He signaled to Lucas. The two of them walked out of the conference suite.

The corridor was empty except for another operative, Lincoln Trask, who kept watch at the turn leading to the elevators. He acknowledged Trask then said to Lucas, "I can't wait for their red tape."

"Do what you have to," the other man replied,

remaining by the conference room's closed door. His relaxed posture belied his watchful attitude.

Thomas took comfort in the support of his friend, who clearly suspected what he was planning. He turned his back to put through a call to the DSF Research Department. He selected the direct line to the newly appointed director. "I know this is short notice but I need a search."

"Anything, Mr. Devlin," Mara Marton said. "Shoot."

"I can't wait for the Feebs to obtain a warrant. Zervas has my sister."

She gasped. "I'm so sorry. I'll get on it personally."

He'd hoped she'd say that. Mara was the best. "He could be traveling under more than one alias. So could his thugs. I need their credit card expenses traced. Off the books." He waited as she wrote down the names.

"I'll call you back A-sap."

Normally he'd have smiled at Mara's use of his military speak. "Thanks."

"Incoming," Lucas said sotto voce. "Hostile redhead at your six."

Thomas turned to see Cleo approaching from their suite farther down the hall. The fire in her eyes matched her hair, a wild halo, as if she'd scraped her fingers through it in frustration. Not unlike him.

"Thomas, it's Marco Zervas," she began.

"Cleo, I can't do this now. Not again." He held up a hand. "Rescuing Andie is a job for the FBI."

"But you don't understand." She held up her phone. "He called me. He—"

"*Called you?*" He jabbed fingers through his hair. He couldn't listen to any more. She'd talk him—and the

FBI— into letting her be the bait. "The bastard's trying to lure you in. I know you want to help, but I can't allow it. You need to stay in our suite where you're safe. Out of his reach."

Just what Zervas would want—two women his enemy loved.

He stepped back and motioned to the operative farther down the hall. "Trask, please escort Ms. Chandler back to our suite. Make sure she stays there."

****

A ragged wail erupted from deep inside Cleo.

Control freak finally showed his true colors. All that compromising and consideration was an act. He wouldn't hear her out.

She held up her phone, ready to lob it at the mirror over the mini bar. On a sigh, she pulled herself up short and sank onto the floor. She hugged her knees and lowered her head. What to do now was *her* problem. Zervas had called her. She had to do something.

"You're the only one I trust to bring me Cleopatra's necklace."

Yeah, right. The only one Zervas trusted to be gullible enough. He'd get her to take him the necklace and then he'd have two hostages. But she was no cat burglar who could bypass security and creep around a locked and darkened museum. No way could she get into Madame Tussauds and lift the necklace from the wax figure.

And not necessary if what she had in mind worked.

Less than the two hours now. Before reality—and panic—shattered what little courage she possessed, she pushed herself to her feet. *Cleopatra, guide me now.* And hadn't she learned a few things from Thomas?

Using the room phone, she called for room service, then headed to the bedroom to change clothes.

****

Seeing the fear and anguish, the desperation on Cleo's beautiful face was too much. Determined to block out emotion, Thomas closed his eyes. Didn't open them until he heard the door to their suite close behind her.

Lucas sucked in air between his teeth. "So now Cleo's your prisoner?"

"I'll make it up to her later. She'll understand." *Right.*

"I dunno. I'm no expert on women but you were kinda rough on her, Captain."

Shit in a soup can. I behaved like the fucking admiral, ordering her around. Make it up to her. Maybe. I could've lost her. He shoved the thought into a dark corner. He had to concentrate on Andie. Like he'd told Cleo. "At least she'll be safe. Butt out."

Lucas sketched a sloppy salute at the same time Thomas's phone rang.

He listened to the researcher's report, thanked her, and disconnected. "Motel off the Strip. Only two blocks away. Let's roll."

"We'll need backup. What about Hunt and the task force?" Lucas asked, nodding toward the door as he checked his weapon.

"Hunt would still wait for the warrant. No time." He headed for the elevator. "Cassidy's on duty at the wax museum. I'll have her and the others meet us at the motel."

Pulling the operatives from Madame Tussauds meant leaving Cleopatra's necklace unprotected except for the Venetian's rent-a-cops. No choice. In a short time, they'd have the Centaur leader and his men under wraps. Marco Zervas would be no threat.

Chapter Twenty-Seven

CLEO WAITED FOR her eyes to adjust to the only illumination, the half-moon. It was darker than she'd expected by the bridge from the Venetian to Madame Tussauds. Some lights must be burnt out. Fine with her. She'd worn skinny black jeans, a black tee and a dark scarf over her hair to hide from guards, not because she was afraid of running into Zervas.

He didn't know where she'd gone, had no idea where the necklace was. She was safe enough. *Yeah, tell yourself that, Cleopatra. No need to be afraid.* Except for Andie. She pressed a clammy palm to her stomach.

Oh, God, her ploy had to work.

Fifty bucks persuaded the room-service waiter to distract the DSF man at her door. While the two guys yakked about the new football season, she slipped through the connecting door into Lucas Del Rio's room and out.

Between Zervas's call to her and arriving at the Venetian—she'd had barely enough cash left to pay for the cab ride—she'd figured out a few things. Understanding had evaporated her anger at Thomas but didn't make any difference in what she had to do. In the cab, she texted him what she was doing.

So here she was, waiting. Cupping the lighted screen with her hand, she chanced a look at her phone. No reply from Thomas. But he ought to know where she was anyway. An hour had elapsed since Zervas's call. An hour until his deadline.

"Where are you, Thomas?" He—and some of his people—should be here by now. Unless... Of course. She was supposedly locked away so he wasn't checking on her. She needed another way to catch his attention. Or the attention of the operatives here.

She peered at the glass wall that formed the museum's façade, spotted protrusions at the roof's edges. Being seen on closed-circuit cameras ought to get things moving.

Leaving her dark corner, she hurried up the arched moving sidewalk. Waving at the cameras would be overkill. She removed her scarf and angled her face upward before edging into a dark corner beside the entrance to wait.

A hand covered her mouth, yanked her backward. Cold metal bit into her neck.

****

Andie Devlin yanked, twisted, heaved harder. Clamped her jaw against the burning pain in her wrist. Out of breath, she let her head fall back onto the pillow. Sweat drenched her scalp and plastered her clothing to her skin. She worked her stiff shoulders as much as possible with her hands bound to the bed frame.

Tommy would search, she knew it, God knew why. Dammit, he'd supported her, stood by her when all she'd done was push him away and snipe at him. But if she'd learned anything these past few years of struggle, it was that doing nothing got her nowhere. She had to rely on herself to save herself. He might not find her in time.

Her efforts had stretched the zip tie. A little. Maybe. She had to keep trying.

Darkness cloaked the motel bedroom. Only a sliver of white neon through the drapes illuminated the blood from her wrist staining the white sheet. She had no idea how much time had elapsed since Zervas left. How much time she had. He'd crowed about hating Tommy and anticipating her death at his hands.

Tears swarmed her eyes and her breathing trembled. She swallowed down the panic. She had to free herself before the asshole returned.

A little more stretch of the zip tie and she could slip through the bond. Maybe the damn blood would lubricate her wrist. Then she could free her other arm. She'd be out the room's first-floor window in a flash. Shit, escape *had* to be possible now that she actually wanted to live.

She shifted her hips, causing the bed frame to creak. She stilled, listened. Couldn't let the fuckers in the other rooms hear her. She hoped to hell they were asleep, especially Nedik. She didn't want him looking in on her. Touching her. The slimy gorilla felt her up more than once before Zervas warned him. Why the big boss cared, she had no clue. Unless he was saving her for himself.

Oh, fab, more gross out.

Another try. Inhale. One. Two. Three. She yanked. Through the sting of sharp plastic, she felt the tie give. *Yes!* Almost free.

The handle clicked and the door swung inward. The overhead light blinded her. She squinted and blinked at the massive form in the doorway. Her heart stumbled, then raced with painful thumps. *No, God, no, dammit. I need more time.*

The door closed behind Nedik.

She watched, mind racing, as he stalked toward the

bed. The bodyguard was strong and heavy-boned. He could overpower her—and had— with no trouble. His eyes, on the other hand, were flat black. Blank. His boss often talked in riddles and layers of meaning, but this man had all the subtlety of a chainsaw. The bulge against his zipper said it all. His lip curled into an ugly smile, contorting the scar on his cheek.

As he lowered his bulk to the edge of the bed, she suppressed a shudder.

His gaze went to her right hand. "Tsk, bitch, you hurt yourself. Don't bother. You can't get loose."

When he slid a thick finger along her arm, she jerked away. "Zervas warned you," she said. "Or has your tiny brain forgotten?"

His head wagged from side to side, his brow lowered, the smile gone. "You got a sharp tongue for a bitch fucking tied to a bed." He backhanded her across the face, snapping her head sideways.

Pain ripped through her. Colors burst behind her eyes. Working to control her breathing, she glared at him. Shit, angering the asshole wasn't the best tactic. Unless verbal attacks would distract him. "You touch me again and my brother will kill you. Unless Zervas beats him to it."

He eyed her nipples, pebbled by the air conditioning and outlined by her sweat-soaked bra and shirt. One meaty hand pawed her breasts. "Touching won't hurt. You'll like it. I'll like it. My boss won't care about what I got in mind."

Stomach pitching, she pressed her case. "Not what I meant. After Zervas gets the necklace, he doesn't intend to share. He plans to kill you and the nerd as well as me." A fabrication conjured from thin air and fear. But now she'd said it, the bits and pieces she had overheard meant exactly that.

The black eyes clouded. His fingers twisted her right nipple until the pain ripped a groan from her throat. His hand withdrew.

"You lie, bitch. Zervas needs me. Needs my protection."

She banked the fury vibrating every nerve. Pinned him with a steady gaze. "I heard him on the phone with someone about buying the necklace. No complications, he said, no witnesses. He'd take care of us all."

His broad forehead crimped with deep creases before confusion drained away, leaving only malevolence in his unblinking eyes. The hideous smile was back.

"Thanks for the warning, bitch. Plenty of time to be ready for his return. Plenty of time to enjoy your fucking charms."

****

Thomas and Lucas edged around the side of the Wagon Wheel Resort Motel toward the other operatives crouched behind a sprawling cactus.

They'd arrived within five minutes of the operatives he'd pulled from the wax museum. Creative hyperbole to call this place a resort. Three one-story stucco buildings with tiled roofs around a swimming pool. Painted the color of oatmeal, the motel was pimped out with Western nostalgia—wheels that had never seen a wagon, longhorn skulls, a burro—all plastic, a comedown for the head of Centaur. But the thick walls were ideal for concealing a kidnapped woman.

No one in the pool or on the chaises. Security lights too dim to be secure. Without a casino, all quiet at two a.m.

Satisfied he had the layout, Thomas hunkered down and adjusted his Kevlar vest. He nodded to the man and woman, experienced field operatives who'd flown with him from D.C. They and the one scoping out the motel room had proven their abilities and loyalty more than once. Not for the first time, he was thankful to have his own people to rely on. Especially now.

"Sit rep." Recalling Lucas's mention in the SUV of how intimidating it might be to work with the company owner in the field, he tried a smile and added, "Please."

The skin above Jo Cassidy's collar turned rosy. Chalk one up for Lucas. The boss's presence was a factor. Like the image of his sister bound and gagged he couldn't quite keep stuffed in its box.

Her gaze direct, the operative settled a black ball cap on her short blonde hair. "Targets are in the north building, last unit, a two-bedroom suite. Only one entrance, into the living room slash kitchenette. No patio door or easy window access. Sir."

Boyd Kirby touched the transceiver in his ear, scraped knuckles across the two-day growth of beard he always seemed to sport. "Pagano's back there with the laser scope. He reports three warm bodies in the suite. Two in the northeast bedroom, one in the living room."

Two in the bedroom. Thomas's nerves pinged. *Who?* Little more than an hour ago, Andie had been all right. He ground his teeth. Fucking Zervas. *If any of those assholes hurt my sister…*

"Should be four." Lucas Del Rio's gaze locked with Thomas's. "Zervas one of them?"

"Can't be sure," Cassidy replied. "The kid in the office gave up the license number of the rental SUV. Not in the lot, but no witnesses to say who drove away or when."

Zervas might get away. But the odds of rescuing Andie improved if they faced only the geek and the bodyguard. *Nedik. Don't think about it.* "We can't wait. You have a key?"

She nodded. "And more." She extracted transceivers for him and Lucas from the small backpack on the rocky ground.

Mike Pagano scooted into the group, handed Cassidy the laser scope. Large red-and-white dice on his T-shirt were the only splash of color to his usual all black. He nodded to Thomas. "Boss."

Thomas greeted the man and laid out the plan. All had been briefed on Zervas and his men, knew the risks. Nedik and Zervas were the dangerous ones but Hawkins could also be armed. "We go in hot. But remember, my sister's in there. Whatever happens, she's priority. We get her out safe."

They checked their weapons, DSF standard issue 9 mils driven to Vegas by a Los Angeles operative. Vests adjusted over their shirts, the five of them trooped silently to the suite door. They deployed on either side, Thomas, Kirby and Cassidy on the left, Del Rio and Pagano on the right.

Cassidy dipped the plastic card in and out of the slot. At the tiny green light, she grabbed the handle. She and Pagano rushed inside, low, guns in two-handed grips.

The others followed, fanned out once inside the room.

A tall, raw-boned man scrambled up from the sofa. Hawkins. Gasps like a choking chicken emitted from his flapping mouth.

Pagano's pistol in his face sat the computer hacker back down.

Kirby shut and locked the door, positioned himself at the draped window.

Lucas checked the other bedroom. "Clear," he mouthed.

Cassidy cuffed Hawkins with zip ties, slapped duct tape over his mouth. A quick search came up with no weapons, only a USB drive.

"Who's in there?" Thomas whispered, indicating the nearer bedroom. "Zervas?"

Gaze ping-ponging from the pistol jabbing his chest to each of his captors, Hawkins shook his head.

Nedik. In there with Andie.

"Armed?"

Hawkins's head bobbed as fast as his Adam's-apple.

A yelp came from inside the bedroom. *Jesus.* "Now," he mouthed to Lucas as he took up position to the left of the door.

Lucas stationed himself on the right, then lowered the handle and kicked the door inward. Bent low, pistol gripped in both hands, Thomas burst in, Lucas behind him.

Andie lay spread-eagled on the bed, one hand cuffed to the frame, her shirt and bra torn down the front.

Nedik, bending over her, turned his head toward the invaders.

Andie kicked out with her right leg, connecting with a solid blow between the bodyguard's legs.

The big man roared, dropped like a bag of wet sand, cradling his balls in both hands.

"Fucker was going to rape me." She tugged on the plastic cuffing her wrist. "Hurry. Get me out of this."

Lucas grinned at her weapon, a high-heeled sandal, as he relieved the still groaning bodyguard of two knives and a pistol.

Thomas held his weapon on the double-wide thug while Lucas cuffed wrists and ankles. Then he freed Andie of the zip tie and hustled her into the living room. He had Kirby take the hacker into the bedroom and stay there on guard. Pagano searched the other bedroom and found one of the skinny man's shirts for Andie.

Insides clenched, Thomas sat beside his sister on the sofa. "Did he... I mean Nedik..."

She shook her head, rested against his shoulder. "It was close. Tommy, what the hell took you so long?" On a sniff, she added, "I knew you'd come."

Mike Pagano stood watch at the window by the door.

Thomas breathed a sigh, taut nerves unknotting. Until he saw the blood on her wrist. "That bastard. We'll need first aid," he told Cassidy. "Asshole cut her."

Andie held still for the former U.S. Army Medic to treat her bloody wounds. "He didn't cut me. I worked at the zip tie to get loose. The plastic edges dug into me. Hurt like a son of a bitch. Pissed me off. I'd have gotten free, made it out the window if dick for brains hadn't come in when he did."

Thomas's jaw dropped. "But I heard you yell. We all did."

"That was Nedik," Andie said. "I got my right wrist free in time to slug him when he tore my shirt."

"Wondered why his nose was bleeding." Pagano winked at her. "Remind me not to rile you."

Andie sent him a shaky grin.

Jo Cassidy finished bandaging her arm. Closing the

kit, she stood and moved aside. "Don't do any sparring with her unless you wear a helmet."

"And a cup," Thomas said. "You got the best of him, sis. That kick was impressive."

"Self-defense classes. Doc Olsen insisted. Said they'd give me confidence."

"Dangerous move. He could've killed you." He brushed strands of her damp hair off her face.

"He was going to kill me anyway," she said, her voice rough. "Or Zervas would when he returned."

"Any idea where he went?"

"No, but—" Her gaze sharpened and she sat up straighter. "Where's Cleo? Is she all right? I think he phoned her cell. He got the number from mine."

He'd wondered how Zervas got the number. "Cleo's safe at the Bellagio." Ignoring the text-message alert, he opened the tracking software in his phone. Before he could decipher the location on the screen, the green blip that was Cleo's phone winked out.

Blood drained from his head.

Chapter Twenty-Eight

"YOU DO WHAT I say and I get the necklace. Then I'll take you to the Devlin bitch. One wrong move and I give the orders to kill her."

Chills skittered down Cleo's spine. Darkness kept her captor's features in shadows but the distinctive gravel-rough quality of his voice identified him. Marco Zervas.

"Okay." Her voice was reedy, strained.

Apparently satisfied she was under control, the Centaur boss stowed his pistol in a pocket but kept a tight grip on her upper arm. He ground the tracking button and then the battery from her mobile phone into the cement beneath his boot, and then hustled her through one of the glass doors into the wax museum.

She gawped as the door closed behind them. He'd arrived ahead of her. Way ahead. With time to cut outside lighting and unlock the entrance. He'd waited for her. The realization rocked her. She was a gullible fool, walking right into his trap.

He ran his hand across his bald dome. The growth of light hair looked as if he'd dipped his head in sand. Like her, he wore black. The museum's low security lighting lent a sallow cast to his features. Aquiline nose, a distinctive beak. Strong bones in a lean face. Beady eyes, a buzzard looking for carrion. About Thomas's height but nothing like him.

She tightened her shoulders, banking down a shudder of revulsion. "How did you know to come here?"

He barked that nasty laugh. "On the drive from the airport, I saw taxis toting *that* on their roofs."

The beam from his penlight illuminated his answer. An advertisement for the newest exhibit. The floor-to-ceiling banner displayed the waxen Cleopatra wearing the necklace.

She'd missed that piece of the puzzle, but Thomas and the task force probably hadn't. That's why Thomas had stationed operatives here.

Operatives. A balloon of hope. As Zervas dragged her deeper into the building, she glanced around. Cameras, motion detectors? DSF guys?

"Don't bother, Cleo. I've taken care of the guards and disabled the security devices."

Hope deflated and stole her breath. What had he done to Thomas's people? She hadn't the strength to protest as Zervas marched her up the dark and unmoving escalator.

****

Five minutes after the cell-phone blip vanished, Thomas and two of his people left the Wagon Wheel, Pagano driving their rental SUV. Cassidy and Kirby would remain until Hunt's team arrived.

His tracking program showed other signals. Three separate blips from buttons. She must've found them in Mimi's clothing. Wore them on purpose. She wanted him to find her. The tightness inside him eased a millimeter. "She's at the wax museum. GPS says a ten-minute ETA. Pagano, make it five."

In response, the driver muscled the big vehicle past

a green sedan and through a red light. He jumped lanes, hurtling by the late-night traffic on the Strip.

Thomas tuned out the complaints of brakes and horns. And Lucas, who was coordinating with SA Hunt to send reinforcements to the motel and the wax museum. Thomas would take any shit Hunt dished out about his unauthorized raid on Zervas's motel. Bottom line, his sister was safe.

But not Cleo. He was an idiot for pulling his people from the wax museum. Zervas must've seen the Cleopatra posters. If Zervas hurt her, was a dead man. Fuck.

If Thomas had only listened to her. Maybe... He checked the text message. *Cleo*.

Gone to Tussauds. Z xchange A for ncklce. Plz come

Dammit, if only he'd read this earlier. He sucked in a desert-dry breath and made himself work out tactics.

The SUV screeched to a stop at the Venetian entrance. Pagano tossed the keys to the valet and the three of them took off running. Stairs and a few turns took them to the darkened ramp.

"No lights," Lucas whispered. "Venetian security guards should've reported that."

"Zervas." Thomas withdrew his weapon, checked it as they approached the glass wall.

Del Rio shone a penlight on two small objects littering the concrete. "Looks like the asshole stomped out a phone battery and one of your trackers."

"But not the others. Cleo put more trackers in her clothing."

"Smart woman."

Lucas had no idea. Thomas nodded. He tried the glass door. "Unlocked. They're inside. You two use the employee entrance. I'm going in here."

"Roger that," Lucas said.

"Low lighting only at night," Pagano said. "Enough to find your way."

Thomas thanked him. Then Pagano and Del Rio disappeared around the building.

Inside the wax museum, Thomas tuned in to the building as he let his eyes adjust. Hum of air conditioning, electrical clicks, creaks of expansion and contraction. All normal. Odors of floor cleaner, warm wax. Life-size figures loomed on either side of the ticket entrance. Black Panther. Indiana Jones. Ahead of him an escalator.

Nowhere to go but up.

He climbed quickly on the balls of his feet, silent in rubber-soled shoes. A sign on the curving corridor pointed to the Hollywood stars exhibit. Random thumps from above, maybe plumbing. Or footfalls.

At Lucas's voice in his earpiece, he pressed against the wall. "Report."

"We're in the Operations Office. Two Venetian guards, dead. Looks like single bullets to the head."

His mouth tightened. More deaths to lay on Zervas. "What else?"

"Alarms and cameras shut off. Pagano's nearly got the cameras back online. Will have a visual A-sap."

"Hurry." They didn't need his urging but dammit to hell, Zervas had Cleo.

****

Zervas, forbidding and silent, marched Cleo through the maze of exhibit halls. The wax figures, posed as if about to speak or move, appeared like apparitions in the dim lighting. If she hadn't seen the artistry of their creation, their ghostly forms would freak her out. But somehow the lifelike presence of Whoopi and Johnny Depp buoyed her. She could use Captain Jack Sparrow's sword or his wits. He would know how to slow this grim march to give Thomas more time.

Slow, yes. When she stubbed her toe on an invisible protrusion in the floor, she stomped her feet to catch her balance. She gave Zervas a *clumsy me* grimace.

He caught her elbow and shoved her ahead of him.

As they passed Arnold Palmer and Tiger Woods scoping out a putt, she stumbled. But the soles of her sneakers clomped barely enough to be heard outside the room.

If anyone was listening.

She touched the tracker button inside her tee neckband. *Thomas, where are you?*

Finally they reached the gallery labeled World Icons. Past Gandhi, Churchill, Genghis Khan, Mother Teresa, and a few past American presidents, there she stood.

As if she'd stepped out of history or out of the new film, the Queen of the Nile held court beside a gold-painted chaise. Her hand cupped the cobra's head capping a golden staff. A gold crown banded her dark hair. She wore white silk, the perfect backdrop for the gold collar and its gem-studded capelet.

Cleopatra's necklace.

A gasp slipped from Cleo's throat. No more delay.

Zervas led her into the middle of the room. "Stand there. Don't fucking move."

Leaving her, he moved closer to Cleopatra. He set the pistol on the chaise and hefted the capelet's edge. "Heavy gold. Fucking real. Finally."

In the beam of his penlight, Cleopatra's eyes glittered and her smile seemed encouraging. "The necklace should bring you a good price," she said, relieved at the steadiness of her voice. Keeping him talking would take up time. "But you can probably get a whole lot more for the computer chip. You have a buyer for that too?"

His hand stilled on the clasp at the wax figure's nape. He cocked his head, his eyes boring into hers as if searching for deception. "The chip. Explain."

Either he didn't know the chip was explosive or he didn't have it. "You know, the chip you gave René to attach to the necklace. That chip."

His smile matched his carrion-feeder eyes. "So that assassination attempt was all a charade."

She shook her head. "Yousef's plot was real. Just thwarted."

"And used to make me think the Met had the original necklace. And make Yousef believe it contained the computer chip." He scratched his chin with the gun barrel. "But you think *I* have the chip. So the copy did *not* contain *anything*." He turned toward the Cleopatra figure. "Or it's here."

Thank God he didn't have it, but where *was* the damn chip?

He returned to working loose the clasp, a slow process with the ancient design. "Moreau screwed up. Fucker was supposed to put it in the copy. Funny how things work out. Now I'll have both."

Cleo waited for him to examine the necklace. *Take all the time you want.*

He lifted the heavy ornament loose and placed it on the chaise. He played the penlight's narrow beam over the underside. Straightening, mouth tight, he picked up the gun.

He stalked to her, prodded her chest with his weapon. "No chip. It's not there. Where the hell is it?"

She held out her arms, palms up. "I don't know."

"Fucking liar!" He backhanded her with his gun hand.

The blow knocked her to the floor. Pain spiked through her head like an electric charge. Her vision dimmed, and her breath came in short gasps.

"Tell me," he roared. "You must know. You were there. Where the fuck did Moreau hide it?"

Oh God, she had no idea. Her brain flashed René's last moments... last words... gesture.

But then, suddenly, she did know.

****

Cleo's outcry burned Thomas's ears. Clenching his jaw, he crept to the World Icons entrance.

She sat curled up on the floor, one arm raised in defense. Blood trickled down the left side of her face. Zervas stood over her, right fist clenched around his 9mm.

Thomas had been afraid before, but always for himself or his men. Or for his sister, first the drugs, now tonight. This was worse. Red haze singed the edges of his vision.

He tunneled his thoughts. Focused on the situation. He couldn't take a chance with Cleo's life. Couldn't wait for Lucas to get in place.

He stepped around the corner, pistol in his hands. "Put down your weapon and step away from the woman."

Without flinching, Zervas grabbed the thick mass of

Cleo's hair and yanked her backward against him. He jabbed the pistol against her head. "I've been expecting you. Fucking Galahad. Just like the old days. But I came out on top in Iraq and I will again."

Something flared in Cleo's eyes, whether relief and hope or fear Thomas couldn't tell. He needed her alert, able to react quickly.

"Hurt her again, Marco, and I'll kill you."

"You're in no position to threaten. You shoot me and I'll blow her away." Zervas's lips pulled taut around his teeth. No eyes involved. An enemy's smile. He stroked Cleo's jaw slowly, lovingly with the barrel of the pistol.

She shrank from the metal's obscene caress, with fury and contempt on her pale face.

"Nice weapon," Zervas said. "Better than army issue, right, *Captain?* Put it on the floor or she bleeds." He aimed the pistol at her bent left knee.

No choice. Thomas set the gun down. Straightened, hands fisted at his sides.

"Now kick it over there." Zervas indicated the wall to Thomas's left.

He complied. The pistol skittered across the floor and thunked against the baseboard. Twelve, fifteen feet away. A stretch to reach it if he had the chance.

"Now the one in your ankle holster."

A nice right cross would wipe off that damn smirk. Thomas's fingers cramped and he uncurled his fingers. He lifted his pants legs above his ankles to display only his socks.

"And now for the bulge in your pocket. With two fingers, remove the weapon."

"Only my phone," Thomas said, holding up the

device.

"No spare sidearm? You're slipping. Been behind a desk too long."

"Maybe. But you've been underground for too long. Your crimes have caught up to you. You can't escape. The FBI and their task force are on their way."

Zervas yanked Cleo's hair. Jammed the pistol against her head. "The bitch is my ticket out. Don't forget I have your sister. A call from me and she dies."

"I don't think so. Does the Wagon Wheel Motel and Resort ring a bell?"

White blotches appeared on Zervas's cheeks. His expression serrated. "You're guessing."

"Andie's safe. Hawkins and Nedik are under arrest. The FBI has blocked the funds you still had access to. You're done, Marco. Put your gun on the floor and give up."

The other man shook his head. "I won't go to prison again. The redhead goes out with me and this." He jerked a nod toward the necklace. "And there's one more thing."

"Thomas, he wants the computer chip," Cleo said, wincing. The purple swelling of a bruise bloomed at her temple. Her voice was thready, but her gaze was clear. In control. Determined. Trusting.

"The computer chip?"

"The bitch here says you think I kept it." Confident mask firmly in place, Zervas smiled. "News stories reported the chip was removed from the necklace at the Met. But there was no chip. So where is it?"

Cleo's right hand moved up from her stomach to her throat. She didn't hold her locket for comfort as he'd seen her do many times.

Instead she pointed to the locket with her index finger.

Because her back was against Zervas's legs, he couldn't see her pantomime.

When Zervas again focused on the necklace, Thomas chanced another look down.

Cleo tapped the locket, then spread her fingers wide in a burst.

If a grenade had exploded in front of his face, he couldn't have been more shocked.

Not Cleopatra's necklace, but Cleo's necklace.

"I'm in the gift shop," Lucas said quietly in Thomas's earpiece, "To your right. Got a clear shot. Give me the word."

Even if Lucas made a kill shot, Zervas could still pull the trigger. Could still kill Cleo. Maybe gunfire wouldn't explode the chip. Maybe it would. Neither was a chance he'd take.

He cleared his throat, the signal to wait. "The chip's in the original."

"Nice try, asshole. I already examined the fucking thing. No chip."

"You didn't look closely enough," Thomas said in a reasonable tone. "Moreau was an expert jeweler, a craftsman. He hid it well. Look between the gemstones."

Doubt crimped the other man's forehead. He stepped aside and scooped up the heavy collar. Holding it close to his face, he kept the gun on Cleo. Greed was making him sloppy. Instead of taking the necklace and his hostage, he wanted more.

Always wanting more, that was Marco Zervas. This time he would have nothing.

Thomas glanced from his enemy to Cleo. Put his

free hand to his throat and pantomimed ripping the locket's chain free.

The corners of her mouth lifted in brief acknowledgment. She gripped the necklace and yanked. The links bit into the tender flesh of her neck but held. Another tug.

A silent snap left the thin gold chain dangling on either side of her closed hand.

He shut his eyes for a second. Called up the numerals. Then keyed the explosion code into his phone. All he had to do was press Send. He cut his gaze toward the far corner to her right. Sweat poured down his back. Could she throw it far enough away? More than six feet?

Understanding shone in her eyes. Her hand started to move.

Eyes on Zervas, he shook his head. *Not yet.*

Zervas raised the pistol, aimed it at Thomas's chest. "There is no chip. You're a fucking liar. I'm getting out of here. As soon as I kill you, *Captain.*" Confusion and fury chased across his gaze. He might shoot them both.

"Now!"

The locket and chain flew across the room, bounced between two figures.

Thomas pushed Send.

The corner exploded in a fireworks burst of color and noise. The wax bodies splintered. Legs and arms leaped into the air, dark suits shredded and aflame. Shrapnel from the metal stands flew outward like molten daggers.

One of the molten pieces struck Zervas in the leg. He cried out and bent to his smoldering pants leg.

Thomas slid across the floor. Dived for the man's weapon.

Zervas turned back, saw Thomas.

Fired.

Thomas jackknifed up, weapon in both hands. Aimed.

Zervas's bullet struck his left side, a two-by-four that knocked him backward and drilled pain through his torso. Black dots swarmed before his eyes. He sucked in a hissing breath but maintained a grip on the gun.

The sprinklers whirred on, dousing everything in cold water and the smells of smoldering cloth, melting wax, and gunpowder.

Blood stained Zervas's ruined pants leg, but he stumbled closer, smiling. He held his pistol aimed squarely at Thomas's head.

"No!" Cleo surged up from the floor.

She grabbed Zervas's gun arm and swung him around.

The gun fired, the bullet zinging into the wall.

Zervas flung her down as if she were a pesky fly. Slammed the gun butt on her head, dropping her in a heap.

Thomas blinked away the daze and the water in his eyes. He pulled the trigger.

A hole opened in Zervas's black shirt. Blood spread and his gun arm faltered. But he stumbled forward a step. "Not dead yet, asshole."

"You will be." Thomas fired again. And again.

The gun fell from Zervas's hand. He clutched at his throat. Blood poured crimson between his fingers. He tumbled backward onto the floor. Still. Eyes vacant. Blood pooled, turned pink in the water beneath him, and then flowed no more.

Lucas rushed in. Picked up the gun. "He's done for.

Thomas?"

Thomas breathed against the white-hot pain in his side. Struggled onto his knees. Crawled toward Cleo's crumpled form.

"Never mind me. Cleo, check on Cleo. She's..." *Everything.*

Chapter Twenty-Nine

CLEO FLOATED UP from somewhere black. A dozen bass drums thundered in her head. A throbbing agony she'd never experienced before. Wet and chills. Shivering awareness lifted her up another layer to a foggy gray. She tried to open her eyes, but hadn't the strength.

Nausea crawled up her throat. Worse than the pain. She breathed in shallow pants. *Must wake up.*

Through a semi-consciousness muddled by the incessant drumming, she felt cool air and rain on her face. Big, gentle hands cradled her, moved her onto her back. She heard voices. Both deep, one anxious, speaking her name.

"Cleo, wake up. God, please."

Thomas.

She opened her eyes a crack. Fought through the swirling confusion and pain. Slowly the room came into focus. The wax museum. Not rain but sprinklers.

And Thomas, beside her, bent over her, scowling, the skin across his cheekbones stretched taut.

"Thomas." She grabbed his hand. Rough, warm flesh. Living flesh. "Thank God. But he *shot* you." It was all she could manage. She lay back, in the grip of the throbbing.

He gave her a crooked smile. "I'll be okay. Bullet-proof vest. Dented but not bleeding. A whole lot better off than Zervas."

"And the Bushes." Lucas Del Rio's voice came from somewhere across the room.

"Bushes?" Frowning cued another drummer to action and she gasped.

Thomas chuckled. A most welcome sound. "The chip explosion assassinated two presidents."

Lucas added, "Bush 41 and Bush 43 will need limb transplants."

"Andie?" she asked, her voice barely above a whisper. "Was it true, what you said? She's safe?"

"All true. She'll tell you all about it." Thomas lifted her hand to his lips. "God, Cleo, I thought—"

His words were lost as overhead lights flooded the room and the sprinkler's rain ceased. What seemed like dozens of men and women ran in with weapons and other equipment. In moments Cleo found herself borne off on a stretcher and away from Thomas. As the EMTs slid her into the ambulance, she let go and drifted into oblivion.

****

At University Medical Center, nurses replaced Cleo's sodden black spy garb with a blue-flowered gown. Amazing, it was long enough to cover her butt. Assorted physicians poked and prodded her, commented on her bloodshot eyes but even pupils. They finally declared she had a mild concussion. Duh. She could've told them that. Zervas clobbered her twice, didn't he?

After she answered a few of Agent Hunt's questions, a shouting match among the medicos and the FBI and Thomas threatened to add to the pounding in her head. The hospital wanted to keep her overnight. Hunt and a Las Vegas officer wanted to ask more questions. Thomas declared he would watch over her, and tomorrow the authorities could grill her. And him.

"You are injured too, Mr. Devlin, and have been prescribed pain medication," a dark-haired nurse in flowered scrubs said, "Let us do our job."

After a pause, he threw up his hands. "Fine. Just promise you'll keep these vultures away from her tonight." He punched the air toward Agent Hunt and the cop.

She had no love for hospital stays but Thomas needed rest. He insisted he had no broken or cracked ribs. Not likely. She could see pain digging lines in his forehead and tightening the corners of his mouth.

Once the agony in her skull eased to manageable levels, she'd have major thinking to do. Now was not the time, but soon Thomas and she needed to have a long conversation. He remained ever her protector, but he might not want anything more after how badly she'd messed up falling for Zervas's trick. Pain throbbed in her chest but not from any of his blows.

She closed her eyes as a nurse wheeled her to a desert-tan room and tucked her into bed.

"It's okay," Thomas said, sidling past the nurse. "We'll be just a minute."

Whatever he might've said to her was cut off as someone else rushed in behind him and skidded to a stop beside the bed.

Andie.

Her right cheek sported a purple bruise and a gauze bandage circled her right wrist. Thomas had told her the Andie saga. Except for her wounds, she looked wonderful. Stronger and more together than she'd been in years.

She wore a tight white tee with the Bellagio logo,

skinny jeans the same pink as a stripe in her spiky 'do, and a smile as wide as the Nevada desert—except for the wobble in her lower lip. "Shit, you didn't have to get yourself beat up to save me. You look like hell."

"Back atcha. Shut up and come here," Cleo said, opening her arms.

Andie bent into the hug.

Cleo held her best friend tight as if she might vanish if she let go. "I was scared I'd never see you again," she said through tears of joy. The demons in her head were pounding their drums with giant hammers. *Let 'em.*

"Seems I had to get myself kidnapped for us to have a reunion."

"I hear you almost took out one of the bad guys by yourself."

"Felt damn good after what they put me through." Andie touched the bandage on Cleo's cheek where Zervas had whacked her with his pistol. "Bastards."

Cleo grinned. "We have a lot of catching up to do."

"No shit." Andie eyed her brother sitting on the edge of the bedside visitor chair. "*A lot* of catching up."

"But not tonight." He pushed up off the chair. His breathing hitched, and he straightened with effort. "All of us need rest. Especially the one with the concussion. Sorry, babe, but they'll probably keep waking you up."

He called her *babe.* Before Cleo could speak, the nurse returned and evicted her visitors.

****

The next day at the museum, Thomas did a walk-through of the previous night's battle for Agent Hunt and the LVPD detective. It torqued him that they'd already questioned Cleo. Hunt assured him Cleo was feeling better, but he needed to see for himself when this charade

Susan Vaughan

was over. Numbered evidence tags marked the wax body parts in the explosion site, bullet holes, expelled casings, and bullet trajectories. Chalk outlined where Marco Zervas had died.

The damp clothing and disheveled hair of the remaining wax figures looked as if they'd been caught in a sudden downpour and stumbled inside to dry off.

When the walk-through and various agents' questions were mercifully finished, Hunt admitted the museum personnel, who'd been waiting in the gift shop. Some began carrying off the damaged figures.

A petite blonde in a pale blue business suit approached Thomas. She introduced herself as the manager. "Thanks for letting us begin the renovation."

Thomas shook the hand she extended. "Renovation's a polite way of saying it, ma'am. Sorry about all the mess, especially the Bushes."

"No problem. Insurance will cover it." She waggled pink manicured nails toward the damaged corner. "Don't worry about those two. They were due to be retired."

Behind her, Lucas ducked his head and his wide shoulders shook with mirth. He was as worried as Cleo— maybe more— about Mimi. Good to see him smiling.

The manager's beaming countenance made Thomas smile. "You seem cheerful about something that'll shut down this gallery for some time."

"Not long. Only today," she replied. "As soon as we're cleared, this room will be repaired and painted. Costumers and an artist should arrive from London tonight to fix Cleopatra, although minus her adornment. When we reopen, I expect the publicity will double our ticket sales. Every social media platform is all abuzz. I hear comedy shows at two casinos have added jokes

326

about Cleopatra and the Bushes. The PR department is writing a press release about how Madame Tussauds helped recover the Cleopatra necklace."

He bent in a slight bow over protest from his sore ribs. "Devlin Security Force needed this recovery. I'm happy to share the spotlight."

Her smile winked out. "Sadly, the necklace the London staff is bringing won't be nearly as stunning as the real thing. My people had wondered why the artist had made it so heavy."

Thomas looked over her head at Lucas, who gave him the all-clear sign. Both the FBI and the LVPD would immediately release the necklace to Devlin Security custody. Hunt had said although evidence, the piece was too valuable to remain in custody. The police photographs would suffice.

He grinned at the manager. "Once the original returns to the Cleopatra Tomb Exhibit in New York, I should be able to send you a nice replacement."

****

"I'm so glad, Thomas," Cleo said from the passenger seat of the SUV. "I can't think of a better use for René's copy." She smiled but her gaze was solemn as she donned shades.

He left the University Medical Center campus and headed east on West Charleston Boulevard. She was unusually quiet, her mouth soft but down turned. Probably pain from the concussion. He wanted to talk about *them*, but this wasn't the time.

He reached over to cup her nape. "You sure you're okay? I can turn around."

"God, no. I couldn't get any rest at the hospital. They kept me awake asking me question after question.

By now I can recite my answers by rote. *My name's Cleopatra Marie Chandler. I live in Venice. Well, I used to live in Venice but right now I guess I live at the Bellagio. My birthday is the ninth of April.*"

"You must feel better if you can joke."

"Truthfully I do feel better. Last night—oh, wait, it was this morning—I had a dozen drummers banging competing solos in my head. Today only the winner is performing. More ibuprofen will help."

He slanted a glance her way as he turned south on the freeway. The dashboard clock read five-fifteen. Almost time. "But there's something else. Mimi."

She sighed. "You read me too well. Yes, Mimi."

"Guilt, guilt, guilt."

"Yes, guilt. No shit, as Andie would say. She knows nothing about Zervas and the necklace, but that whole thing is the reason I needed to *do* something. Chasing after them was the only thing I *could* do for her. Maybe it doesn't make sense, but she's still in a coma and there's nothing left, no way to make it up to her. I feel so helpless." She twisted to face him, propping her left knee on the padded leather seat. "I can't even reach her mom on the phone. Lucas says he can't get through either."

He'd planned to surprise her but maybe that wasn't such a hot idea. "When I heard that, I tried the house number this afternoon. Trudy lost her mobile phone on the flight to Toronto. She has a new one now."

"And Mimi?"

He whipped his vibrating phone from his pocket. "Here. This call's for you. I'll let her tell you herself."

Mouth agape, Cleo took the phone and said hello. She pressed shaking fingers to her lips as she listened. "Mimi! I thought... I mean, oh, thank God."

Mimi's mother had told him the Toronto specialist could find no reason Mimi wasn't waking up. Then yesterday Mimi opened her eyes. Today she was sitting up and talking. He guessed Cleo and Mimi would talk until his phone battery died.

Cleo emitted a soggy laugh. "Thomas, Trudy told her about my concussion. She says I have a much harder head than she does." Tears spilled down her cheeks beneath her sunglasses.

"No argument here."

He handed her a tissue from the box in the console, then grabbed one for himself.

Chapter Thirty

Arlington, Virginia

CLEO'S HEAD STILL ached when the red-eye landed in D.C. but she'd slept in the cushy first-class seat. And her talk with Mimi had cheered her. She promised to visit as soon as the doctors okayed visitors. The specialist saw no reason that after therapy her cousin shouldn't make a full recovery. The good news slid away some of her guilt.

About Andie as well. She'd bounced back, her triumph over the bodyguard reviving the confidence dormant for such a long time. The drugs Zervas had administered seemed to have no lingering effects, and Andie'd already spoken twice with her therapist.

At Andie's insistence, Cleo would stay in his condo until they could visit Mimi in Toronto. It seemed to be her only option. Her carryon contained her only possessions including her last seventy-five dollars. With so little to show for her Grand Tour of Europe, she couldn't, *wouldn't* go to her parents in Annapolis.

But living with *him* was an option fraught with complications. Since leaving on the flight to D.C., she'd had no moment alone with him. Andie made it an inconvenient threesome. Now that the series of events that had thrown them together and kept them together had ended, what about Thomas and her?

The need she'd had to make him lose control had faded, replaced by a deeper understanding of the man. His innate mode was leading the way because he was usually the dominant one in the room. And heck, he was usually right.

She had no idea if his feelings went beyond desire and friendship. If he might not want her after their intense thirteen days together—not that she was counting. If returning to his office and his social life would change how he saw her. If he was feeling awkward about ending it between them. And worst of the worst, if he hated her because of what her impulsive actions had caused. She ached so much she might split apart.

Whatever, she would put on a brave face. Thomas had saved her life more than once, and either he or the admiral had paid for everything. If the affair ended, they would always have Paris. And Venice. And London. And New York. And Las Vegas.

Maybe not Vegas.

She shook off her funk as they walked into the condo.

"Having you here is *so* outrageous!" Andie tugged her through the foyer into the living room. "We can talk again later. I have to rush out."

As Cleo shed her jacket, she had only a vague impression of the room—deep-pile cinnamon carpeting and a chocolate sofa— very masculine and so Thomas.

He set down their bags and laid their jackets on top. Shoulders squared, he turned slowly toward his sister. His expression scared Cleo. Stone chin and thousand-yard stare.

When Andie's words sank in, she panicked. She'd

be alone with him. "*Out?* Already?"

"Got a text from Dr. Olsen. She's in her office doing paperwork, who the hell knows what. She wants a full report, not the Twitter version. I'll see you guys later." She grabbed car keys from a tray on the hall table. After a whirlwind of kisses and hugs, she slammed out the door, rattling the wall mirror.

"She hugged me. Kissed my cheek," Thomas said, breathless. "Who *was* that girl?"

Cleo barely registered his astonishment. She was staring at paintings leaning against either side of the kitchen arch.

A gondolier hawking rides beside the Rialto Bridge.

An accordion player serenading tourists in the trattoria beside the San Paolo bell tower.

And three more. *Her* paintings.

Her eyes burned and her throat constricted. Damn, tears had puffed up her eyes the past couple days more than in years. The doctor had said a concussion intensified emotion, but jeez if she could only dam the waterworks. "Thomas, my paintings. How did you do this?"

His hands were warm and steadying on her shoulders. He pressed a kiss on the back of her head. "The gallery owner was willing to part with them for a reasonable cost when my attorney persuaded her she couldn't claim ownership of a dead artist's works, especially one who still lived. One of my people uncrated them yesterday."

She turned into his arms and flattened her hands on his chest, taking care with his bruised ribs. "This is *outrageous*, like Andie said. Way beyond possible."

"Devlin Security Force specializes in the

*im*possible." He chuckled, a rumble against her palms. "Besides, I wanted an original Cleo Chandler. I know a gallery owner who'll be interested in the rest."

"Of course you know a gallery owner." Her head was reeling. She shook off the shock and drew a deep breath.

"Thomas, we haven't talked." When he opened his mouth, she held up a hand. "Let me do this, please. I'm proud of some of what I did. Secretary Vinson seemed to think that posting my picture wearing the necklace helped in the search. But Zervas suckered me into his trap, so I was the bait after all." Not the tracker buttons and not texting Thomas, nothing made up for her stupidity and the tragic outcome. The weight of it ached in her chest.

"Hush, Cleo. Yes, you did a lot to be proud of. You got us out of some tight situations in Venice and Paris. You did what you had to because I was so bullheaded, not listening to you and shutting you out. I owe you a big apology for my uncalled-for, shitty behavior."

"Shitty is close. Controlling and dictatorial. Overbearing and high-handed." She brushed a hand down his arm. "And terrified."

His eyes widened. "What?"

"I should've realized the truth when you went into commanding officer mode. You were scared for me, scared for Andie."

"Afraid? You have no idea. Fear for what Zervas might do to you nearly paralyzed me. All I could think to do was push you away."

"Lock me away, you mean. I was pissed off and called you every name I could think of. The taxi ride to the wax museum gave me time to think. To reflect on the man I know. You understood Marco Zervas, but that knowledge went both ways. He knew you'd do whatever it took to rescue your sister. And to keep *me* safe, you'd stash me somewhere. Then he could call me using Andie's phone."

"He would have two bargaining chips to help him get away with the necklace."

"You like to be in charge, but the only time you've ordered me around was when you were scared for me. At heart you're not a control freak. You're a protector. Zervas knew that and so do I. Now. You're sensitive and honorable." *Some of the reasons I love you.*

"If you hadn't gone to the museum, Zervas would've gotten away with the necklace." He brushed fingers across her throat. "And you'd still be carrying the explosive chip in your locket."

She shuddered, thinking about what would've happened if she hadn't removed the locket for the Met Gala because the simple piece didn't look right with her gown.

"Thank you for that. During this whole—" she held up a hand, frustrated at not finding the right word "—*thing*, I've learned a few things about myself, but apparently I haven't grown wiser." A sigh slipped from her throat.

How could he possibly want her after what she'd done? She steeled herself. "If I hadn't rushed out in the middle of the night... those men... would still be alive. Because of my stupidity and impulsive actions, those two security guards died."

"No wonder you've been so quiet. You're wrong. Their deaths were not your fault. It's all on Zervas. He phoned you from the museum. As soon as my operatives left, he killed the guards and disabled the alarms." Thomas pulled her into his arms.

Because it might be the last time, she didn't fight the embrace. "You're sure?"

"Right. Checking on phone records gave us his locations and times of calls."

That weight lifted, but what about Thomas and *her*? "How can I ever thank you?"

He clasped her hand and pulled her down the hall. "I have a few ideas. I'll show you."

An acre of bed sat in the middle of a five-acre room. Done in forest green and woodsy tan, it could only be the master bedroom. "U.S. Army colors. *Really?*"

"The decorator was so thrilled with the idea I didn't have the heart to tell her I'd prefer something else. Makes me feel like I'm always on maneuvers." Arms around her, he two-stepped her closer to the bedside.

"Maneuvers are what you're up to now, mister." He still wanted her. A good sign.

"You're on to my subtle stealth. He peeled away the plush quilted spread and turned back the sheets. "Want to test how comfy the bed is?"

"Tsk. No stealth at all." She kicked off her flats and shimmied out of the yoga pants she'd worn on the flight, then lay back on the stacked pillows.

The strain carved into his face shifted to relief. And a more potent emotion—hunger. He shed his khakis and pullover and stretched out beside her. Her head pillowed on his biceps, he tucked her against him.

She absorbed his achingly familiar scent, the warmth and strength of his hard body.

"On the plane you and Andie gabbed or slept. We haven't had a chance to talk."

"You were the one who insisted Andie and I sit together. Don't complain. I noticed you cutting Z's the whole flight."

"Yeah, okay." A sigh growled through him and his arms tightened around her. "That night in Vegas, I was afraid I'd lost you."

"Your little tracking buttons worked. You found me."

"Thanks to the extra ones you used. Damn clever how you got out of the suite. The man guarding the door may never live it down. The others are riding him hard."

"I'm sorry about that. But I had no choice. You reached me in time, Thomas. Then I was afraid you wouldn't catch on about the explosive chip."

"You blew me away." Muscles flexed beneath her head. "Sorry. Bad choice of words. But as soon as I realized what your gestures meant, it made sense. Moreau must've hidden the chip when he fixed the locket's clasp."

"If Gram's watching, I hope she forgives me for losing her locket."

"She's proud of you, babe. And so am I." He turned her so they were face to face, body to body. "Our choices form the patterns and courses of our lives. Things happen for a reason, not fate exactly, but something in each of us acting when we face crossroads and challenges. Disasters and death. You made the best decisions you knew how. Those bad guys are done for. My sister's fine and Mimi will be." He kissed her forehead.

"There's one thing we never sorted out—why René made two trips to the Tussauds workshops."

"I have a theory on that. Not one I like because it puts Moreau in a good light." She looked up to see a knowing look in his eyes. "After he hid the necklaces on the wax figures, Zervas threatened not just his wayward forger, but his girlfriend—*you.* Probably saw your picture on Facebook."

As she thought about it, relief washed through her that René might not have deliberately endangered her. She rubbed her aching temples. "He tried to retrieve the necklaces to protect me. When he was dying, he even reached for the locket, but I didn't understand until Zervas demanded to know where the chip was."

She lay quietly in his arms, her mind flipping through the good images of the past weeks and locking away the bad. Comforted by the incense of his hot skin, she let the rest of her guilt drift away on a tide of acceptance. "And now it's finally over."

"The danger's over." He tipped up her chin. "But *we're* not over. When I said I was afraid I'd lost you, I meant more than at the hands of my enemy."

His mouth rocked over hers, cutting off words and thought, leaving only the feeling they'd always been heading to. "What happened to telling me you're too old for me and all that crap?"

"You told me that was cover. It took me a while to look deeper, but you were right. When Mom died, I closed off my emotions. Dad retreated to his work, and I had to be strong for myself and for Andie. I held everyone at arm's length, even her." He brushed a finger down her cheek. "But not you. With your sass, you never once let me keep up my walls. You scared me, so I resorted to the age difference excuse.

"I'm done fooling myself. I need you, Cleo, more than I ever believed I could let myself need anyone. I want your light and laughter in my life. I've been too serious, not letting myself think beyond work and getting Andie straightened out."

"Not *too* serious. You went out with a lot of women."

"And you know that how? Ah, the BFF network. Andie must've also clued you in on more than my social life. You knew about Devlin Security Force before I sat down at your table on the cruise ship."

"You'd just invited yourself to dinner. I needed time to process, to adjust. But no side-tracking. All those women?"

His hand continued down her neck, then her shoulder, along the curve of her hip, and fanned her pulse with every caress through the thin cotton tunic. She felt him hard against her belly.

"Not that many. I haven't been celibate, if that's what you're asking, but they weren't important to me. *You are.* When you agreed to stay here, we said it was only until we could go see Mimi. But that's not good enough. Stay with me. Andie's moving out."

"She told me. She's going to share an apartment with a woman at the clinic where she'll be working."

"Her room could be your studio. Great morning light in there."

When he kissed her this time, his lips were tender, his tongue coaxing, persuasive. Irresistible.

He was asking her to live with him, a long-term relationship. Her whole body smiled, yet a painful bubble swelled in her throat. Commitment. Sort of. He hadn't said the L word.

"I can't say you don't know what you'd be getting," she said finally. "You know me better than anyone. I'll probably still make impulsive choices."

"One of the things I appreciate about you— as long as one of those choices is me."

She grinned. "Like I said, I've learned some things about myself. I've had relationships too, but ones I could walk away from. I was afraid to *need* someone, afraid of being hurt."

"Of being dependent."

"So you *do* know me. I needed those few years on my own and these days with you to learn that needing someone, loving someone doesn't make me dependent. So… my own studio and you in the bargain? How can I refuse?"

Thomas held her hard, the life-giving connection swelling his chest with a mix of emotions—softness, passion, need. And fear.

He didn't want her to feel trapped but she was *his*, the woman he wanted by his side and not as a roommate. He couldn't stop wanting her, wanting to make her happy, wanting to plan a future together. He reached in his jeans for the package he'd unwrapped when Cleo was staring at her paintings. He slipped the small box beneath his pillow.

Damn, he rarely had trouble knowing what to say, but how to begin had his tongue stuck to his teeth. "Babe, this deal, I need to make the commitment clearer, defined."

The light in her gaze dimmed. "Want to negotiate on terms, like a lease?"

Shit, she thought the C word had him running scared. "No negotiation. No compromise." He drew a fortifying breath, trusted his strategy. "When you were a hot teenager, all I could think about was getting you naked. I lost the friendship we'd had. And have found again."

"Oh, Thomas, I—"

He placed her hand over his heart. "No one else reached me *here*. Because this place was already taken. By you. I've loved you half my life but didn't let myself think about it. About *us*. No one else knew the real me or made me examine myself. And change some things, like not being so uncompromising and ceding some control to others."

"Even me?"

"Especially you."

Doubts clouded her gaze. "Thomas, are you sure? Aren't you afraid I'll run away if we have tough times?"

Her question washed over him like a balm, eradicating his fears. "Times couldn't get much tougher than we've just survived. No matter the risk, you were brave and resourceful and reliable. You ran away from nothing—except when you lost yourself in your art. Yes, I did notice. But no cage. I'm not worried you'll fly away."

Her acceptance of his trust shone in her eyes. "I've also learned something during our odyssey," she said. "Freedom is hollow without commitment to something or someone." She kissed him lightly. "My some*thing* is making a success of my painting. And my some*one* is you. So what do you want in our contract?"

"I want forever, a lifetime commitment."

She closed her eyes briefly. When she opened them, her answer was in their shining depths. "Forever? Can I get that in writing?"

"Absolutely. Signed and witnessed. And as soon as possible." He withdrew the velvet box and opened it. "I had my dad overnight this."

Cleo's hand flew to her throat. "Oh, Tommy, your mother's ring."

He swallowed. "I wanted to do this right. It was my great-grandmother's, big but an old mine-cut diamond. If you don't like it—"

She silenced him with a smack of a kiss. "Don't like it? It's perfect." She held out her hand for him to slip on the ring. "It fits. Like us."

He lifted her left hand and kissed the ring finger. "I made a contract offer. And gave a token of my pledge. I need an answer."

"The head of Devlin Security is *in*secure?" she teased. "The answer is a big *yes*. I love you. I've always loved you. I want that forever with you."

"Sealing this deal calls for more than a kiss."

He peeled her tee and her bra off over her head. His fingers moved aside her bikini panty, slid it out of his way.

"But your bruised ribs. And my concussion. Although my headache has backed off."

He hushed her with a kiss and stroked her, stirring her to writhe against his hand. His pulse rioted and he shuddered with need. "We'll take it easy." Between kisses he removed the rest of his clothing.

His breath hurried and shallow, he lifted her leg across his hip. When he joined them, they sighed in unison. Languid strokes in a gentle rhythm and lazy kisses shimmered through him, surging fire through his blood, reeling his senses until she spasmed around him. Gasping moans of pleasure parted her lips and her undulations pulled his release from him in a huge, pulsing wave.

Long moments later, they held each other and

kissed, slowly, gently, filling him with her scent and her softness and with the assurance she accepted his claim binding them together. She saw into his heart and understood him like no one else. With her, for the first time in years, maybe since he was a kid, he didn't feel alone.

Epilog

Toronto, Canada - Five days later

THOMAS EXPRESSED THANKS and ended the call and turned to Lucas Del Rio.

A woman in blue scrubs pushed along a cart laden with empty lunch trays past the half-open door to Mimi's room. Aromas of chicken and gravy mixed with that of disinfectant, squelching his hunger pangs in mid-growl.

"Good news for a change?" Lucas asked in a distracted manner. Beside Thomas in the corridor, he shifted from one foot to the other and scrubbed his palms down his jeans. He touched his hearing aid, so tiny it was nearly invisible.

Thomas wished a curse on all those women who'd sapped the confidence of this kind and generous man. Lucas and Mimi had yet to speak to each other. The Beast had come to care for his Beauty only by watching over her silent and sleeping form.

"French agents raided Zervas's villa in the south of France," he said in answer to the question. "They found originals of most of the copies he sold. Including the Han horse. Mara's authenticator in France declares it's the genuine horse. The Tate Museum director is ecstatic."

"Getting rid of Centaur should improve our PR," Lucas said. "You must be glad to be back."

"Back to stress level normal. No one shooting at

me."

The past weeks had made him see it was time to groom someone to be chief operating officer. He'd continue to be CEO but the fire in his belly to spend all his time and effort running the show had cooled. He couldn't wait to return home every day.

To Cleo.

On Monday, they'd driven to Annapolis. Her mother was thrilled to see her—and them *together* and engaged—and cried as she hugged them. Her father worked himself up to a gale of bluster about the danger his impulsive daughter had put herself in. Fear for his youngest and frustration with his injury made him testier than usual. But Cleo's announcement of her impending gallery showing and Thomas's obvious support dumped the winds of indignation from Hoot's sails.

Lucas's gaze slid to the room where Cleo and Mimi were visiting. A drop of sweat dripped from his forehead to his nose. The hospital was warm, but not that warm. "Maybe I'll go for a walk. Or something."

"Give them a few more minutes." Cleo had promised not to prepare Mimi either for her protector's appearance or for his ambivalence. But the two women had had enough time alone. More delay and Lucas was likely to bolt and not return.

Lucas shuffled his feet again. "Your sister okay?"

"Better than in years. Says her therapist thinks kicking Nedik in the nuts empowered her. She feels she has more control over her life."

Cleo appeared at Mimi's door. "Lucas, she wants to see you."

Panic skittered across his broad face. He pushed away from the wall, edging a step away from Thomas.

"You sure you two don't need more time alone?"

Thomas laid a steadying hand on his friend's shoulder. "An hour's long enough. You've come all this way. Do you want to hurt her feelings?"

Jaw clamped tighter than a vise, Lucas trudged through the open door.

Mimi sat upright in the bed. Short auburn growth covered where sutures had pinched the shaved place above one ear. The rest of her hair fanned across the nest of pillows and brushed her shoulders. Caramel freckles stood out in relief against the pallor of her cheeks. Her eyes, the same green as Cleo's, shimmered with emotion when they locked on Lucas Del Rio. No hint of fear or revulsion. Only relief and happiness.

Thomas slowly exhaled as he felt Cleo press closer to him. He slipped an arm around her shoulder.

Mimi's smile was summer sunshine warming the entire room as she extended both hands. "Lucas, oh, Lucas, come closer. I'd know you anywhere. You're just as I pictured you. Rugged and strong. You saved my life."

The magnet that she was pulled Lucas's steel to her side. She reached for him and he wrapped her small hands in his big ones. "Didn't do much. Just kept that thug out of your room."

"And I thank you for that, eh? But I meant something much larger, more personal. I kept floating away toward a distant light. But your voice, your gentle, warm voice brought me back every time."

The tops of his ears reddened. "I must've talked nonsense. But I wanted you to know you weren't alone." His normally gravel rough voice, was as she described, syrup smooth.

She lifted his hand and held it to her cheek. "You did that and more. You made me keep fighting to come out of it. To live. So we could have this moment."

Thomas was mesmerized.

Cleo's tug on his arm uprooted him and they crept from the room. He followed her to the elevator and down to the main floor café where they purchased hot cider. As if afraid to burst the magical bubble they'd witnessed, neither spoke until they were outside at an area with seats. The air smelled of autumn crispness and the apple fragrance wafting from their paper cups. Leaves of nearby shrubs were turning color.

"That was beautiful," Cleo said, turning her face to the blue sky. She pulled her wraparound sweater closer and tied its sash against the chilly breeze. Smiling, she accepted her cup from him.

Thomas sat beside her on the smooth granite bench, warmed by the sun. "Almost as beautiful as you."

She smiled over her cider, her eyes twinkling with mischief. "A poetic compliment from Thomas Devlin. Whoa."

Pulling her into his arms, he kissed her gently, with the love and gratitude in his heart and soul, then claimed her lips as need hardened him. Deep, wet kisses followed that took away his breath and left her clinging to him.

"You make me happy," he said against her mouth. "You make me want to be more than a workaholic. I'm thinking a house bigger than my condo, maybe a family?"

Her lips twitched. "Oh, I don't know. Lucas has suggested you should hire me for more cloak-and-dagger missions. I kinda got into the excitement of the chase."

A groan slipped between his clenched teeth.

"Heaven help me. I've created a monster."

"A life with you is all the excitement I need. I think we should start that family soon. You know, one of us is getting older."

"Babe," he warned. But he was grinning.

"*Ranger.*" She wrinkled her nose. "I meant *me*. In a couple of years I'll be *thirty*." She laughed, that husky, sexy sound he loved and wanted to hear for the next zillion years.

Printed in the USA
CPSIA information can be obtained
at www.ICGtesting.com
LVHW062231060823
754499LV00010B/188

9 781509 250745